OUTBOUND

Other Books by ISFiC Press

Relativity and Other Stories by Robert J. Sawyer
Every Inch A King by Harry Turtledove
The Cunning Blood by Jeff Duntemann
Worldcon Guest of Honor Speeches edited by Mike Resnick and Joe Siclari

Other Books by Jack McDevitt

NOVELS

The Hercules Text, 1986
A Talent for War, 1989
The Engines of God, 1994
Ancient Shores, 1996
Eternity Road, 1997
Moonfall, 1998
Infinity Beach, 2000
Deepsix, 2001
Chindi, 2002
Omega, 2003
Polaris, 2004
Seeker, 2005
Odyssey, 2006

COLLECTIONS

Standard Candles, 1996
Ships in the Night, 2005

OUTBOUND

by
Jack McDevitt

ISFIC PRESS
Deerfield, 2006

OUTBOUND

Copyright © 2006 Cryptic, Inc. All Rights Reserved.
"Lighthouse" Copyright © Cryptic, Inc. and Michael Shara
"Collaboration for 'Lighthouse' Copyright © Cryptic, Inc. and Michael Shara
Cover Art Copyright © 2006 Stephan Martinière
"Ways Of Considering An Absent Introduction" Copyright © 2006 Barry N. Malzberg
"Interview, conducted by Thomas Harbach" Copyright © 2005 Thomas Harbach, Originally appeared in *Phantastisch* 18, April 2005
"Celebrating Jack McDevitt" Copyright © 2003 Michael Bishop

Without limiting the rights under copyright reserved above, no part of this book may be reproduced in any form or by electronic or mechanical means, including information storage and retrieval systems, without written consent from both the authors and copyright holder, except by a reviewer who may want to quote brief passages in review.

ACKNOWLEDGMENTS

"These Foolish Things Remind Me of You," by Holt Marvell, Jack Strachey, and Harry Link. Copyright 1935 by Boosey & Co., Ltd., London, England. Copyright renewed. Publication rights for U.S., Canada, and Newfoundland controlled by Bourne & Co. Used with permission.

Published by ISFiC Press
707 Sapling Lane
Deerfield, Illinois 60015
www.isficpress.com

ISFiC Press Logo Design: Todd Cameron Hamilton

Book Design by Robert T. Garcia / Garcia Publishing Services
919 Tappan Street, Woodstock, Illinois 60098
www.gpsdesign.net

First Edition
10 9 8 7 6 5 4 3 2 1

ISBNs: 0-9759156-4-9
978-0-9759156-4-6

PRINTED IN THE UNITED STATES OF AMERICA
by Thomson-Shore, 7300 West Joy Road, Dexter, Michigan 48130-9701
www.tshore.com

Contents

Ways Of Considering An Absent Introduction   vii
    by Barry N. Malzberg

Local Aberrations

The Candidate	3
Henry James, This One's For You	7
Date with Destiny	17
Windows	39
Combinations	49
Nothing Ever Happens In Rock City	60

Deep Space

The Mission	67
Melville On Iapetus	76
The Far Shore	91
In The Tower	105

Cosmic Cocktails

Whistle	147
Valkyrie	155
Act of God	165
Ignition	175
Lighthouse (with Michael Shara)	185
Collaboration For "Lighthouse," with Michael Shara	203

The Big Downtown

The Big Downtown	213

Shots in the Dark

Where Do You Get Those Crazy Ideas?	281
Infinity Beach	289
Why We Should All Be Reading Science Fiction	293
Blundering Through	298
A Golden Dozen: Twelve Stories to Demonstrate to Reluctant Seniors What They're Missing	316
Science Fiction: An Eye On Tomorrow	318
Interview, conducted by Thomas Harbach for *Phantastisch*, 2004	323
Celebrating Jack McDevitt, by Michael Bishop	330

Bibliography

Bibliography	338

Seven Ways Of Considering An Absent Introduction
by Barry N. Malzberg

You are staring at blank pages in this otherwise excellent and teeming collection; where has the promised Barry N. Malzberg Introduction gone? What has happened? Surely its presence has been justly emblazoned. You have not of course bought or borrowed this book for a Malzberg Introduction; you are a sensible and literate reader, admirer of Jack McDevitt and science fiction itself, hardly to be swayed in purchase by a 1000 word essay. Still, you ask mildly, reasonably, what has happened? Why is Malzberg Missing In Action?

We hasten, ever helpfully, to explain. There are seven reasons why the promised Introduction is missing:

Reason The First: Michael Bishop's essay really covers all of the material usually associated with the Introduction requested of me. Discusses the stories individually, praises them, limns the career of the writer, etc. Makes clear what a good person Jack McDevitt is; a person so good as to be the crown upon his own works. There is nothing that can be said on the subject supplementary to the Bishop essay; only an endorsement and agreement which, we can agree, are hardly inspiring or original material; such endorsement only feeds the readers' sense of the predictable but science fiction readers, understanding their grand medium devoted to unpredictability, would hardly be the most receptive audience.

Reason The Second: My favorite McDevitt story, the novella "Time Travelers Never Die," is absent from this collection; I would like to have devoted hundreds of words to its various excellences but such praise would only frustrate since the story itself is lacking. It is available in another collection surely and many anthologies (including one of my own) but it isn't here and therefore in writing about it I would only frustrate the reader and cast a question over the collection at issue and this would hardly be fair.

Reason The Third: A long essay yearns to be written about the role of the consolidator in science fiction, the writer who comes in later but carries the intensity of earlier, the writer—sometimes unfairly called "decadent"—who reconstructs the aspects of the genre which caused us to love it rather than those later aspects of evolution which are the mark of our own distance from inception. McDevitt is a sound, a dedicated, a severe traditionalist; he is moved as am I (and probably Michael Bishop as well) by the science fiction of the 1940's and 1950's which framed his own first passionate encounter. McDevitt is trying to reconstruct that history within a modern context; he is a consolidator but sometimes such are misconstrued and instead called "decadent".

There it is, the essay which could lie atop this collection like Milhaud's *Bull On The Roof*, a torn and haunting discussion of the way in which "consolidation" and "decadent" are tangled and interwoven by critics of less discrimination, intelligence, superb insight than myself. This would be a mournful and elegiac essay with flashes of occasional, thunderous wit and would have almost nothing to do with McDevitt's self-perception, his mission or the value of his work. It would be foolishness to impose such an essay as Introduction and therefore I am not and therefore you are grateful.

Reason The Fourth: I have always perceived Introductions (by the author or others) as irrelevant even though I have perpetrated my share. The author is a nice guy, a good friend, a good writer, a convivial soul with many stories to tell? This may well be and there's that business of 5/12/87 to nod and wink about but what does it have to do with the collection or the reader and why would anyone want to sit and read such stuff or (worse yet) broad hints of such stuff which point out that of course it must be kept secret.

Reason The Fifth: Some Introductions are so concerned with the secret stuff—remember that wild business at Boskone in 1983? well we had better pass on—that they make the reader an intruder, if subject and introducer have such colorful common history which cannot be shared with the lesser ranks, well then why bother at all? Everyone in science fiction has a secret history; science fiction itself is a secret map of the world which conforms now and then, but only by indirection or accident, to the more real world and secrecy is the enemy of art. . . the work must be self-standing or not at all.

Reason The Sixth: I wrote Introductions to my first dozen collections with a collective callowness of voice which make me shudder at a distance. The thirteenth, the most recent collection, has no introduction at all. Just the stories ma'am. Those orphans, the stories, nestle whispering without benefit of a voice from the anteroom telling them to stay in line. All seem to have profited.

Reason The Seventh: If I had nonetheless prevailed against reason and circumstance to write the Introduction it would have been a wearying imposition upon the material. You are doing better than you know. Jack McDevitt, a good guy, a good writer, occasionally a great writer (you really should have included "Time Travelers Never Die") would probably endorse. "Read the stories. let the poor man gibber without witness," he would say. So do I. Read these stories. They are about as good as we can get in a difficult but continually provocative time.

New Jersey: May 2006

Dedication: Mike Resnick

PART ONE
LOCAL ABERRATIONS

The Candidate

This one was written for Nature's *Futures series, which was introduced to me by Greg Benford. The assignment was to do a short-short, approximately 900 words, depicting something that might happen during the next fifty years.*

Usually, you can tell how well a story will work by how much pleasure derives from the writing. If I'm struggling with it, it's an indication the reader won't be swept along either. This one was pure joy.

"The Candidate" was originally published in Nature, *March 23, 2006. Copyright Nature Publishing Group, 2006.*

*

The high and low points of my career came on the same night: When we beat George Washington, and Peter Pollock returned to the White House for a second term.

Well, okay. It wasn't really Washington; it was an artificial intelligence programmed to behave like Washington. But a lot of people got confused. When you've been in politics as long as I have, you know how easily people get confused.

President Pollock's numbers were down, but the Democratic candidate was a non-stop talker who put everybody to sleep. We knew it was going to be a close race.

Then Washington showed up. He was a software package developed at the University of Georgia to preside over seminars. But he was so believable that somebody put him on a radio show, and the next thing we knew he was on his way. People were desperate for a candidate they could believe in. The bloggers got in line almost immediately. The General gave an interview to the *Florida Times Union*, the wire services picked it up, and by God he did sound like George Washington.

Next thing we knew a Federalist Party had sprung into existence, donations started showing up, first in small amounts, and ultimately in a tidal wave.

I was running the president's campaign, and we all had a laugh when they tried to put him on the ballot in Georgia. The Democrats tried to block it. Candidates have to be born in the U. S. , they pointed out. And they have to be at least thirty-five years old.

We could have stopped it then. But if Washington got into the general election, he'd pull votes from the Democrats, not from us. So I called in some favors and the Supreme Court surprised the country: They examined the candidate and ruled they could find no reason to suppose he was not a Washington-equivalent—the first time that terminology was used. He was therefore clearly well past the minimum age limit. As to the requirement he be born in the United States, the software had been written in Georgia, and the meaning of "born," said the court, is not limited to biological events. It was a six-three decision.

I watched Washington on cable, and he *was* persuasive. He didn't like the frivolous spending. Didn't like the fact that people who'd worked their entire lives couldn't afford medications. Didn't like corruption. He came across as wooden, and maybe a trifle stern. Americans don't like being lectured.

They could have done the programs electronically, but somebody in his campaign was too smart for that. He was housed in a Coreolis 5000, and his campaign people set it on a table along with a display. So we got an animated image from the Gilbert Stuart portrait, except they'd cut the general's hair and put him in a dark business suit.

He made the rounds of the network talk shows. And I watched his polls rise. He passed the Democrat and closed in on us.

The National Conservative Union threw its weight behind him, as did the ACLU. The National Rifle Association, always a friend of Pollock's, announced it would sit the election out.

I'd misjudged things. The liberal media was coming over to his side. They could see the Democratic candidate was a lost cause. He appeared on *Meet the Press*, where Tim Russert, at first ill at ease talking to the Coreolis, rapidly warmed to him. "Are you really George Washington?" he asked.

"The man's dead," said Washington, "Give him a break. But I'm everything he *was*."

Russert asked about the intervention, which had by then become another of those endless wars. "We intended the nation to lead by example," Washington said. "We would not willingly have plunged into the affairs of others." The Washington-image stared out of the TV screen. "Keep your own house in order. It is enough. Take care of your own. Do it competently, and don't try to change the world."

We were in a race. After his appearance with Jon Stewart, there was no longer any doubt. "I have no wish to be president," he told the vast audience watching that night—a fifty-two share, according to Nielson. "I would prefer you not vote for me." This was virgin political territory. "I'll tell you why, Jon. It sets a bad precedent. People should be governed by other people, not by software systems. Start with the White House, and soon intelligent systems will be everywhere."

We went after him. Used his own words. Doesn't want the job. We looked at his record. Only officer to survive the Battle of the Wilderness. What did that tell you about him? And do we really want a former slave-owner in the White House?

We couldn't touch him on national security, but we demanded to know where he stood on the issues. "What about Roe V. Wade?"

"Put it aside for now," he said. "At the moment, we have bigger problems." We got some of our base back on that one.

"Gay marriage?"

"No one is harmed. We should be careful about codifying moral strictures. They change too easily."

We got some more back.

We talked about Orwell and Frankenstein. Don't ask me how that got in there, but it played to the voters so we kept hitting it. Vote for People, we said. We found physicists who were willing to say that an artificial intelligence could develop a glitch. Could become dangerous.

Would you trust the black box in the hands of a computer?

In the end, we won by a few hundred votes.

Pollock went on TV after Washington conceded. He said how we'd saved the nation from a hardware conspiracy. (He tends to do things like that when he gets offscript.) He thanked the campaign workers. And everybody cheered.

When it was over, he took me into his quarters to express his appreciation. A Rainbow 360, the newest model, was set on the coffee table. "We saved the country, Will," he said. "We'll get legislation passed to bar the damned things from holding office. Otherwise, I guess, they'll trot out Abe Lincoln next time."

"Yes," I said. "And congratulations, Mr. President." It meant four more years for me too. As chief political advisor.

"Afraid not, Will." He was uncomfortable. "We have to look to the future."

That was a shock. "What do you mean, sir?"

"It was a near thing. We miscalculated our opponent's strength. I mean, incumbent president and all. It should have been easy. I need someone who won't be taken by surprise. "

I was trying not to let my anger show. "Who did you have in mind, sir?"

He smiled at the Rainbow 360. "Will, meet Karl Rove."

Henry James, This One's For You

It's not hard to argue with the proposition that the world would have been a safer place without religion. We've a long history of religious wars, persecutions, inquisitions, witch trials, and heretic burnings. Science has consistently been perceived as dangerous. As something that needs to be kept under control.

The Arabs led the planet at one time in math and science. But things went south at about the same time as the arrival of Islam. Coincidence?

But what about science? Do we take its benefits for granted and overlook the hazards? My natural inclination has always been to assume that science is inherently good. That new knowledge is inevitably beneficial, and that research should be given free rein. This, despite the fact I was alive when Oppenheimer and his buddies were tossing atoms around the premises at Alamagordo.

We live in an age when it no longer takes a nation-state to do serious damage, to kill tens of thousands of people. As the twenty-first century moves on, it is going to become easier and cheaper for governments, and for those who would bring them down, to construct weapons with devastating potential. Nanobots, increasingly resistant viruses, and better living by chemistry. Moreover, as societies become more technologically advanced, they become more vulnerable to attack. Power grids, communication systems, transportation networks: All offer tempting targets for the nitwits. Who knows where we're headed?

There are more subtle, less lethal, dangers. There is the possibility of implants to allow the government to keep an eye on anybody who might be a terrorist risk. A price we're willing to pay, some people might argue. But there's a slippery slope here somewhere. How long before we get implants for everyone so that we can keep the trouble makers in line? It's a possibility that exceeds anything in Orwell.

> *For an example of science run amok on a less lethal level, try getting through the menus to report a downed line to your phone company.*
>
> *There may be other dangers.*

✳

It came in over the transom, like a couple hundred other manuscripts each week, memoirs of people nobody ever heard of, novels that start with weather reports and introduce thirty characters in the first two pages, massive collections of unreadable poetry from someone's grandmother.

They all go into a stack for the screeners, who look through them, attach our form rejection, and send them back.

Actually there's only one screener. Her name is Myra Crispee. She has one green eye and one blue eye, and a talent for going through the slush pile. She picks out the occasional possibility and gets rid of the rest. Every day. Love my job, she says. When I ask her why, she says it's because I pay her the big bucks.

Tempus Publishing isn't a major outfit, but we do okay. We don't specialize. Tempus will publish anything that looks as if it'll make money. But most of the manuscripts we see have already made the rounds at Random House, HarperCollins, and the other biggies. Some come in from an agent, but that has no effect on the way we treat them. Unless we know the author, they all go into the pile.

Sometimes we get lucky. We published a couple of self-help books last year that did extremely well, and a novel about Noah's ark that became a runaway bestseller.

Anyhow, the day it arrived was cold and wet. The heating system had gone down again so I was wrapped in a sweater. I'd just opened the office and had turned on the coffee when Myra came in, carrying an umbrella and a manuscript. That was unusual. She doesn't usually take these things home. "Hey, Jerry," she said, "I think we've got a winner."

"Really?"

She was beaming. "Yes. I was up half the night with it." She trooped over to her desk and sat down in front of what I thought was a second manuscript, but which turned out to be the rest of the submission.

"My God," I said, "that looks like a thousand pages."

She peeked at the end. "Twelve hundred and twelve. I've only read a few chapters, but if the rest of it is like what I've seen—"

"That good, huh?"

"I couldn't put it down. " The magic words. We seldom saw anything that wasn't easy to walk away from. She leafed through the pages. "Incredible," she said. "Who is this guy?"

"What is it?" I asked.

"He calls it *The Long War*. It's about the war in the Middle East."

"Which one?"

"How many are we involved in? I didn't see the news this morning."

"It's been done," I said.

"Not like this, Boss." She was still turning pages.

"Who's it by?"

"Guy named Patterson." She shook her head. "Edward Patterson. Ever hear of him?"

He was a stranger to me. "What's the cover letter say?"

She needed a minute to find it. "'Novel enclosed.'"

"That's all?"

"That's it."

We used to have a screener's box where she could deposit manuscripts that were potentially publishable. We dispensed with it because Myra rarely put anything in it. So she just brought the manuscript over and laid it on a side table. Then she walked back to her desk, pulled the next submission off the pile, and began turning pages. But I knew she was really waiting for me. Wanted me to pick up *The Long War*. "I'll look at it before I go home," I said.

She continued turning pages, sighed, and touched her keyboard. The printer kicked out a fresh rejection. "Okay," she said.

I was working on *Make Straight the Path*, an inspirational book by Adam Trent. It was pious and reassuring, loaded with anecdotes showing how the unbelievers get theirs. You wouldn't believe how his other books had sold. Penguin would have loved to have him.

I stayed with it, resisting the temptation to look at Patterson's epic. It resembled an epic. The manuscript obscured a coffee stain half a foot above the table. That made it official.

Now, lest you think I'm one of those editors who only cares how many copies can be moved, let me tell you that, while sales figures matter, it's always been my ambition to discover a new writer. Well, okay, all editors feel that way. But that's because we're generous and compassionate. So when Myra got up and headed for the washroom, I took a look.

Patterson lived in New Hampshire.

I lifted the cover page and glanced at the opening lines. That night I hauled it down in the elevator, the whole twelve hundred pages, and took it home.

I read it on the train. Read during dinner at Milo's. Read through the evening and took it to bed. In the summer of 2001, I went to the Army recruiting office with the young college student hero and cringed while he joined the Reserves. I rode with the UN inspectors while they played tag with Iraqi "escorts," and tried to surprise their hosts at suspect facilities. I sat in the councils of the president while his aides urged an attack on Saddam and constructed arguments they hoped the UN and the voters would buy.

The night got away from me, and I finally closed my eyes when the first light of dawn was hitting the curtains. I called Myra's voice mail a couple hours later, letting her know I'd be late. Called again around nine to tell her I wouldn't be in at all.

It wasn't simply one more war novel. This one had that cliffhanging quality, yes. But it was vastly more. It owned the war. Through the eyes of its characters the reader saw how it had happened, came to grasp the inevitability of the conflict. He understood what it had meant to ride shotgun on the convoys or to go house to house in Fallujah. He experienced what it was to fight an enemy who wasn't afraid to die. Who imagined killing to be a divine imperative.

I spent time with a group of insurgents, and came to understand what drove them. I carried stretchers through the burn wards of an Iraqi hospital when shattered bystanders were brought in. And finally I was with mothers in Ohio when the dread news came.

It had perspective, passion, fear, the determination of obviously flawed men and women in authority to get things right, the mounting frustration as those who had been liberated refused to throw roses.

I was holed up with it for six days. The outside world simply stopped until the last shots had been fired, and the fallout had begun to take its political toll.

It was a *War and Peace* for our time.

I had done better than find one more professional writer who could sell a few thousand copies of whatever. I had found a new Herman Wouk.

I finished late on a drizzly, cold evening, and sat staring out my apartment window at downtown Boston, thinking about Edward Patterson. On that night, only I, and Myra, knew who he was. Within a year, the whole world was going to know.

He lived in Laconia, at the foot of the White Mountains.

It was a quarter after ten. A bit late to be calling. On the other hand, this was a guy who, as far as I could determine, had never been published. I remembered my own reaction when the postcard had arrived from *Guns and Ammo* announcing my own first sale.

Myra, anticipating me, had gotten Patterson's number from information and printed it neatly above the title. I made myself a scotch and soda and reached for the phone.

"Wonderful," he said. *"Mr. Becker, that's great. You're actually going to publish it?"* He sounded younger than I'd expected.

"Yes, Mr. Patterson. Ed. Is it okay if I call you Ed?"

"Sure. Yes. Absolutely. Can you hold a second?"

"Okay."

He must have covered the phone. But I knew what was happening. He was passing the good news to his wife. Or girl friend. Or whomever.

"I'm back," he said.

"Good."

"Mr. Becker, you have no idea what this means to me."

"I can guess," I said. "Ed, are you by any chance free to come into Boston tomorrow?"

He made a sound deep in his throat. *"I'm a teacher,"* he said. *"At the high school."*

"Okay. How about Saturday?" We don't usually open the office Saturday but in this case I was willing to make an exception.

"I can do that," he said.

"Fine. I'll have a contract ready, and we'll celebrate by going to lunch." The truth was that I wanted him signed and delivered before he found out how good *The Long War* was. If he realized what he had, I'd wind up having to deal with an agent. Or possibly even get caught in a bidding war with MacMillan.

He was maybe twenty-five. Tall, with a nervous smile. Light brown hair already beginning to thin. Sallow cheeks, pale skin, watery gray eyes behind bifocals. He wore a fatigue jacket and hauled a laptop in a stitched bag over one shoulder. Didn't look much like Hemingway.

He turned the pages of the contract with long, thin fingers, not examining it, I thought, so much as admiring it. When he got to the advance, he stopped. "Twenty thousand dollars?" he asked.

I was about to say I'd be willing to go higher because I liked the book. I'd expected to go higher. But it was always best to start with a conservative figure. You can always move up.

"Seems like a lot," he added.

"Well," I said, trying to conceal my surprise, "Tempus believes in being generous." It didn't really matter. The book was going to make a ton, so there was no risk.

"It's certainly very kind of you." He smiled again. He looked like the kind of guy the other kids had picked on in the schoolyard. And I would never have believed him capable of the kind of rugged prose that informed *The Long War*.

I showed him where to sign, explained what we expected, that we'd want to be able to use his bio and likeness in promoting the book, that we might ask him to make a few guest appearances. I didn't mention that he was signing over all TV and movie rights, that he was giving Tempus a healthy share of any foreign sales, that we would also collect seventy-five percent of book club rights. And of course there was the option clause. "Normally, Ed," I told him, "we'd want to retain the right of first refusal on your next novel."

"But–?" he said, suddenly looking worried.

"I want to be up front with you, Ed. Is there going to be a sequel?"

"A sequel?" His eyes clouded. "There'll be another book."

"Okay. Good enough. Tempus is willing to forego the option. We'd like instead to sign you to a three-book deal. Beyond *The Long War*."

His eyes slid shut, and I was looking at the most beatific smile I'd ever seen. Paradise had arrived.

"We're offering a seventy-five thousand dollar advance for the three."

He put the glass down and stared at me. "I don't know what to say."

"Don't say anything," I said. "Just sign on the line." I showed him where.

I know what you're thinking. But we do not try to take advantage of our authors. We were providing a major service for Ed Patterson.

We were giving him a chance to launch a new career, to break away from his teaching job, to fulfill a lifelong dream. When you've been in this business for a while, you discover that it takes a lifelong dream to drive someone to write a novel. Especially a big one.

He signed the contract. Four books in all. In triplicate. I put one in a manila envelope and handed it to him. "Your copy," I said.

He was glowing.

"Now let's go celebrate."

We went across the street to Marco's. It's a quiet Italian restaurant just off the Common. It was still a little early for lunch, so hardly anyone was there. We ordered a decanter of red wine, and I filled both glasses. "To you, Ed," I said. "And to *The Long War.*"

He wore a grin a mile wide. "Thanks, Jerry." He sipped the wine, made a face at it, put it down. "Strong stuff," he said.

I finished my own and refilled the glass. "I have to tell you, Ed, *The Long War* is pretty good. How long have you been working on it? Four years? Five?"

"I guess you could say ten or eleven. Somewhere in there."

"Ten years? You've been writing this since you were, what, fifteen? Do I have that right?"

"Oh, no, Jerry. I didn't *write* the novel. Max did."

"Max? Who's Max?"

"Ah," he said. "That's the real accomplishment. That's my surprise."

I finished the second glass in a swallow. "You didn't tell me there was going to be a surprise."

The waiter arrived. We ordered. When he was gone we picked up where we'd left off. "What surprise?" I demanded. "Who wrote the book? Are you his agent?"

"Hell, Jerry, anybody can sit down and write a novel. All you have to do is be willing to stay with it for, what, a year or so? Or five, I guess. Sit down and be willing to write every day. That's all it takes."

"What are you trying to tell me, Ed? Who's Max?"

He'd dropped the laptop onto the seat beside him. Now he set it on the table and opened it. Lights blinked on and the screen glowed cobalt blue. "This is Max," he said.

I stared at the computer, then at Ed. It was an ordinary HP model. Myra had one like it. Black case, the logo printed on the lid. "You said Max wrote the book."

"He did."

"Max is a computer."

"Actually, he's an artificial intelligence, Jerry." He leaned forward, breathless. "A real one."

"The computer wrote the book."

"He's an AI." He looked at me as if waiting for me to cheer. When I didn't a cloud crossed his face.

"I don't care what you call him," I said, "no machine could have written *The Long War*."

The big grin came back. "But he did."

"I don't believe it."

"A few years ago they were saying no computer would ever compete with a chess master. You look recently to see who's world champ?"

We sat staring at each other. The door opened and people came in. A family with a little boy. The boy had a pulltoy.

"It took four days," he said.

"What took four days?"

"To write the novel."

A chill settled into my bones. I drank down more of the wine. Two plates showed up. Pizza for Patterson. Spaghetti and meatballs for me. But my appetite had gone south. "Four days," I said.

"Yes. Well, maybe a bit more. But not much." He took a deep breath and smiled modestly. "It took me almost as long to tell him what kind of book I wanted."

"It's just not possible."

"That doesn't include printing time, though."

"You're signed to do three more novels."

"Yes."

"I was expecting world-class stuff."

"They'll be good. Max was years in the making and has spent a long time analyzing the great books."

"How long?" I asked.

"How long what?" He was chewing on the pizza, obviously enjoying himself. But he looked as if he couldn't understand why I was unhappy.

"How long will it take to deliver the other novels?"

"Probably two weeks. It takes a while to run them off."

"Two weeks for another novel like *The Long War*?"

"Two weeks for all three. But they won't be like *The Long War*, although they'll be of comparable quality." He pushed his chair back and tried to look upbeat. "We've already decided on the next book. It'll be about the power and the downside of religious belief. Along the order of *The Brothers Karamazov*. But different, of course. Original."

I sat frozen. Yep, no problem for Max. You want something to make people forget *The Winds of War*? Have it for you Tuesday.

"You all right, Jerry?"

"I need some fresh air." Or maybe we'd get a new Huck Finn. This time around we'd take a hard look at anti-gay prejudice. I threw money on the table and headed for the door.

"Jerry, wait." He was right behind me.

Maybe a new Dreiser novel. By Max.

Or something in the mode of Scott Fitzgerald.

Traffic outside was heavy. Buses, delivery trucks, crowded sidewalks. "If Max wrote the book, why's your name on it?"

"Legal reasons. He's not a person. Can't sign checks. Can't really do anything."

"Except write great novels."

"You got it."

He stood in front of me and flashed an enormous grin. He had no idea what he'd done. This child, who was obviously very good with electronics had canceled William Faulkner, Melville, Cather: What would their work be worth in the shadow of this thing? I assumed if he could do Karamazov, he could produce a new symbolic masterpiece in the spirit of James Joyce. Call this one *Achilles*, in which a man's life is driven by a search for control. Or maybe something to push *Remembrance of Things Past* off the charts. In eight volumes, delivered over the course of a month.

"I couldn't be sure it had worked," Patterson said. "I don't read that much. Not fiction. I didn't know whether it was any good or not. What Max wrote. You were the test. We'll put *his* name on the cover though, if that's okay."

"What's Max's last name?" I asked.

A bus was coming up behind him. It was a local, headed for Massachusetts Avenue. It had just picked up passengers at the corner, seen an opening, and was accelerating. It had broken loose from the traffic.

"Winterhaven. Max Winterhaven."

"Sounds pretentious."

"I thought it sounded literary. "

Max Winterhaven was slung over his shoulder. I looked up at the bus driver, and I swear he knew what I was going to do before I did. I saw it in his face the instant before I gave Patterson a quick shove. His eyes went wide and he toppled backward. People screamed, the brakes screeched, and I either said, or thought, "This one's for Henry James."

I got clean away. The descriptions that showed up on CNN a few hours later sounded nothing like me. They also reported that the dead man had been carrying a laptop, but it had been smashed. Police were trying to reconstruct it, but I never heard anything more.

There was no widow, I'm pleased to say. I don't know who had been with him the night I called. *The Long War*, as we all know, has become an international best seller. We are sending the checks to the deceased's mother.

Literary authorities are on the tube almost weekly, decrying the loss of Edward Patterson, a man of incredible talent, who would have become a towering literary figure, had he only been given time.

Date with Destiny

I've never believed it was possible to teach people to write. Either you can do it or you can't. You can tell people what not to do. Don't introduce sixteen characters in the first chapter; don't use long windy sentences; don't forget that you're doing more than telling a story, you're creating an experience, so don't spend time showing off what you know or sending the reader running for a dictionary.

Lewis Shiner is a talented and resourceful writer who is the best I know at providing the critical insight that lifts a narrative onto a different level. He's done it at least twice for me, advising me to hold my fire in A Talent for War *when I was primed to allow my protagonist to kill a shipload of aliens who had tried to kill him and were now at his mercy; and in a short story during which aliens running a very unusual library in Fort Moxie, North Dakota, offered literary immortality to an aspiring novelist, Lew said don't let your character accept. Who do they think they are anyhow?*

After sixteen years, Talent *is still in print and "The Fort Moxie Branch" went to the final Nebula ballot and has been reprinted numerous times. Neither would have happened without Shiner.*

Most writers tend to be at least moderately cynical. We are convinced the world is on a downhill run, and as one recently told me, the only thing I can do about it is to lock my door and hide under the bed. Shiner, more than most, cannot tolerate ineptitude or corruption in high places. Read his books and you will feel the anger. But he's a believer. He really feels that a single individual can make a difference. And that's the way he's lived his life.

Nothing is more likely to engage his anger than stumbling into a war. Think before you shoot. Getting in is easy. He would argue, I think, that there's not always a better way, but there usually is. And he wasn't talking about appeasement. Sometimes it takes diplomacy, sometimes patience, sometimes imagination. Spilling blood should be the last resort.

In 1990, Shiner decided to put together When the Music's Over, *an anthology which would explore alternatives to armed force. That's always the easy answer, he told me, just shoot the problem. "What I'd like you to do is set up a situation that usually would lead to violence, but find another way to settle the issue."*

*

I woke up with a knife at my throat.

"Easy, Mr. Nazarian. " The room was dark. Shadows moved, out beyond the pale glow of streetlight that fell in bars across the bed. They drew the knife close. I tried to push away, against the pillows and the headboard.

"Do not scream."

I was having trouble breathing.

Someone held a light in my eyes. Voices whispered in a strange language.

They seized my hair and jerked my head back. "Your eyes are the wrong color, Mr. Nazarian. " The accent was Arabic.

They showed me the knife, holding it out where I could take it if I wished. It was short, with a double-edged blade, and an intricately worked hilt.

"You can have whatever you want," I said. "I won't give you any trouble. "

"Please get dressed." They moved away from me. A light snapped on in the entry to the bathroom. There were three of them, still only shadows.

I climbed carefully out of bed and backed against the wall. "What do you want?"

"I will explain on the way." I couldn't tell which one was talking.

So ended my first night in Paris. "You must have the wrong Nazarian," I said. "I'm only over here to give some advice to Air France on their stateside advertising campaign. That's all." A pair of trousers landed on the bed beside me. And a shirt. "I don't know anything about politics."

"A common problem with Americans."

I found my shoes and pulled them on. "Why are you doing this?"

"Do you have a jacket, Mr. Nazarian?"

"Yes." My voice squeaked, and they laughed.

"Get it. It's cool on the desert at night." It was the shortest of the three who was speaking.

All were in Western business suits. They waited casually while I dressed, watching with bored hostility. The short one peered at my face, not at me, but at my nose, and my ears, and exchanged grins with the others. I knew him from somewhere. He was by far the oldest of the three, and the most relaxed. When the knife wielder wanted to hurry me along, he waved him back. "Hashim does not understand that dressing before strangers is a clumsy business," he said.

I tried to smile at him, hoping to win a friend.

"On the other hand, Mr. Nazarian, time is short."

We went down in the elevator and out through the lobby, which was empty except for the night clerk. The knife wasn't visible anywhere, and I wondered what would happen if I broke away and ran screaming into the street. Behind me, a voice whispered, "Don't."

We went outside. The pavement was slick with rain. A black Renault slid to the curb and stopped. Its doors opened, and I was bundled into the back seat. The short man climbed in front, the others sat on either side of me. "Where are we going?" I asked. The car pulled out into traffic and my captors relaxed and looked pleased with each other.

"I have no money," I said. Would they want ransom? I winced at the prospect of anyone demanding payment from those tight sons-of-bitches at Rand & Sabatini to get me back. And the government wouldn't even *talk* to terrorists. What the hell chance did I have?

We rolled through empty streets and out into the countryside. I tried to watch where we were going, so later I could lead the gendarmes after them. But we kept making turns, and I could only think how scared I was, and anyhow all the signs were written in French. Eventually we turned off the highway altogether and drove out onto an airfield.

A small private plane was waiting, propellers spinning slowly. Its navigation lights gleamed in the rain.

The short man got out and gestured for me to join him. We walked through the wet grass and climbed on board the aircraft. The others stood by the car and waved as we turned and taxied out across the field.

A few minutes later, we were rising toward a gray-streaked horizon.

My captor looked straight ahead. "I've seen you before," I said.

"At a meeting of the Arab-American Friendship Society. Last April in New York." He smiled. "I was the guest speaker."

"Kaballah," I said.

"Servant of the Makhir." *The Makhir.* Chief of State of terrorist Qurak. Bomb wielder, assassin, the man described by the President as a cancer in the Mediterranean. He'd been blowing up Americans in assorted bars and hotels for three or four years. His agents had machine-gunned Western passengers awaiting flights at Orly and Fiumicino, lobbed grenades at school buses in Israel, and pushed people off cruise ships. No Middle Eastern atrocity passed unaccompanied by that arrogant smile, the brilliant white uniform, the defiant fist.

Kaballah had been introduced to us as director of the Museum of the University of Rhandyli. "My government," I said hopelessly, "will not deal for me."

"We are aware of your President's policy, Mr. Nazarian. It makes sense." He pushed back in his seat and closed his eyes. "Try to get some rest."

Not very likely. We flew the Mediterranean in bright hard sunlight. At one point a U. S. jet fighter approached, flew alongside, banked away. "Tomcat," said Kaballah. He was slumped back, yawning, fingers laced across his stomach. "Off the Enterprise." Later it came back, and I had a wild hope they knew I was on board.

We landed shortly before noon at El Hazdrin International Airport outside Rhandyli, the Makhir's Western-style capital. Official-looking Arabs took us off the plane, and escorted us quickly through customs, with much waving of IDs. Kaballah stayed with me. I was grateful for that. His face softened when he spoke to me, and he seemed uncomfortable with his role in the affair. Maybe it was my imagination, maybe I was seeing what I wanted to see. Still, he was a familiar face.

Five or six of us piled into a limousine in front of the airport. "We are going to see the Makhir," Kaballah told me. We circled out onto a four-lane highway and turned toward Rhandyli. During that long drive, my companions watched me curiously. There was much nodding of heads and chuckling.

Rhandyli was really two cities: a restored ancient fortress dating from Moorish times, whose minarets watched the Mediterranean, and, in an outer ring, a modern metropolis with glass towers and shining tree-lined boulevards.

The Makhir's headquarters was located on the east side of the city, in an army compound. Machine guns looked down from the walls. Troops were everywhere, and a few tanks waited outside the front gate. The land around the installation had been cleared: no one could approach unseen. The green-and-white flag of the Republic of Qurak flew everywhere.

We stopped at the front gate. A guard came out, looked at credentials, and did a double-take when he saw me. Kaballah spoke to him, and he waved us on.

We passed barracks buildings, helicopter pads, and a parade ground. A chopper was on one of the pads, blades slowly rotating, awaiting two men in uniform who were running toward it.

We stopped near a drab, whitewashed two-story building, decked with flags. We all got out, and Kaballah led the way inside. "This is our operational headquarters," he announced.

Typewriters rattled, and men scurried everywhere, their arms full of papers. Several officers were engaged in an intense discussion in an alcove. Two others were directing the arrival of filing cabinets and bookcases. Everyone looked sharp and efficient.

We walked the length of a hallway. My escort peeled away at the foot of a staircase, leaving only Kaballah. He invited me to lead, and we mounted to the second floor. "In back," he said.

"What's going on?" I asked him. "Why in hell would the Makhir want to see me?" There'd been something in the news lately about U.S. naval exercises in the Gulf of Qurak, and I had it in my head that the Makhir thought that, since I was an American citizen, I might have some influence at the White House.

Kaballah only smiled, shook his head, and kept walking. We stopped before the last office in the corridor. It was marked with Arabic characters, and a white and gold seal depicting a falcon and a palm tree. They were the same emblems that appeared on the Quraki flag. "They signify," said Kaballah, following my gaze, "our desire for peace, and our readiness for war." He grasped the knob, and his tone changed. "You may call him 'Shah.' Speak to him only when addressed. Answer his questions fully, and in complete sentences. As politely as you can."

The Makhir. Slayer of off-duty soldiers, of tourists in wheel-chairs, of schoolkids.

He turned out to be a short son-of-a-bitch, shorter even than Kaballah. And uglier in person than he was on TV: his eyes were distant, his demeanor gloomy. His thin lips were twisted by a smile that was at once apologetic and irritating.

He appraised me briefly, and nodded. "You were right, Jimar. Yes–" He beamed. "Excellent."

The Mediterranean moon shone through vaulted windows. The only lamp in the room was placed behind an armchair in which the dictator had apparently been reading. A book lay open on a nearby table. When I got close enough to see the title, I was surprised: it was Marcus Aurelius.

He wore the white military jacket of the TV appearances. It was open at the neck, without decoration or insignia.

"Mr. John Nazarian." He inserted his left hand into the jacket pocket. "I apologize for your abduction. We had little choice."

"Why?" I asked. *Why did you have no choice? Why do you want me in the first place?*

He turned to Kaballah. "He does not know?"

"No, Shah. We have not told him."

"But surely he can see for himself!" He strode behind the chair and did something to the light so that it fell full on his features. "Take a good look, John Nazarian. And tell me you don't know me."

I had no idea what he was talking about until Kaballah whispered: "You look like him." His tone added the word *Idiot*.

My God. I focused on those bleak, decadent features. The cynical eyes. The sharp white teeth, the cruel line of the jaw. "I think, if we removed your mustache," said Kaballah, "you would be quite surprised at the result."

The Makhir waved us to chairs. Kaballah took one, but I remained standing. "I am going to ask your assistance, Mr. Nazarian," he said.

It was my finest moment. I summoned everything I had to face him down, to keep my voice steady. To say what needed to be said. "No. I will do nothing for you."

His nostrils widened. "You are of our blood."

"I'm a citizen of the United States."

He nodded. "Not that it matters. By the way, it's not true, you know."

"What's not true?" I asked, barely able to suppress the trembling that had started somewhere deep inside and now threatened to overwhelm me.

"What you're thinking. I'm not guilty of the crimes your president charges me with." I recalled all those network newscasts, which came inevitably after some new outrage; the Makhir standing atop the hood of an army truck, surrounded by screaming lunatics, jamming his right fist into the air, grinning that infuriating, arrogant grin. "Would you like some refreshment?"

I sure as hell would. "Beer," I said.

He straightened. "Ah. I wish I could oblige you, but spirits are not included in our diet. I can offer some excellent lime water. Or if you prefer, perhaps mint tea." On cue, two servants entered with decanters, goblets, and an assortment of cheeses, dates, and nuts.

I glanced at Kaballah. He signaled I should take something. "No, thanks," I said.

The servants filled three glasses. When they had withdrawn, the Makhir held his drink aloft. "Your health, Mr. Nazarian."

"You don't look at all like me," I said.

"On the contrary, we are quite a close match. " He picked up a date, put it to his lips, and retreated to his chair. He commented on the tastiness of the fruit, and, in a darker mood, swung to face me: "You work for the media."

"I am a public relations counselor," I protested.

"Same thing." He waggled an index finger at me. "The press has not treated me very fairly."

I hesitated before responding, but I didn't like the son of a bitch very much. "The Fiumicino Massacre," I said. "Your fanatics shot down twenty-some people who were waiting to get on a flight to Athens."

He waved it away. "Not so. I had no hand in those killings."

"You admitted it!" I said. Kaballah swiveled his eyes angrily and jerked his head to one side, trying to get me to shut up.

The Makhir crossed one knee over the other. "I took *credit* for it," he said.

"Isn't that the same thing?"

"Hardly."

"You *laughed* about it. I'm not sure that's not *worse*."

Something flashed in his eyes. That hit home. "Perhaps so," he said. "But you must understand Middle Eastern politics. No one controls these bands of assassins. They roam through the world taking what lives they will, venting their rage against the oppressors. The West. It is your people who took their land and gave it to the Zionists.

Their children starve. And you have all the warships. What would you have them do?" He lifted his glass, drained its contents, and set it down on a side table. His head fell back, and his hands gripped the arms of the chair. "Well," he said after a long moment, "it doesn't matter. I will concede to you here, in the privacy of this room, that I have taken advantage of events to advance my political fortunes. I have taken responsibility for crimes committed by others. Everyone does that. But it is my great misfortune that your government chooses to believe me. Me of all people. They send their ships against Qurak. They would not dare challenge Syria!" He turned, and braced his jaw against his fist. "I have killed no one." His eyes rolled briefly away from me. "Well, almost no one. A few malcontents at home now and then. But very few foreigners. And then only those who royally deserved it."

He sat unmoving so long that I thought he'd forgotten we were there. I listened to his rhythmic breathing, and to an occasional protest from Kaballah's chair. Once I heard Kaballah put his glass down.

I broke the silence. "What do you want with me?"

His voice went flat. "The United States Navy intends to invade our territorial waters tomorrow."

"The Gulf of Qurak," I said.

"I have drawn a limit, a Line of Defiance, across the mouth of the Gulf. And I have told your navy, told the world, that I will meet them there. If they wish to invade my country, they will have to kill me to do it."

"They claim it's international waters," I said.

"Yes. I wonder how your president would react if Quraki warships showed up off the coast of New Jersey?"

I shrugged. "I don't care about politics."

"You *should* care, Mr. Nazarian. Because your government does terrible things in your name." He rose and went to the window, but he did not look out. "To answer your question: the United States has announced that, at approximately ten o'clock tomorrow morning, the cruiser *Fargo* and an escort of destroyers will cross into the Gulf of Qurak. I intend to leave Rhandyli at dawn in a single gunboat, *Al-Mohafiz. The Defender.* Two other boats will rendezvous with me, and we will meet the enemy at the Line, to engage, and to drive them off, or to accept death at their hands. As Allah wills." He was not looking at me any longer. His gaze seemed introverted, fixed on some internal tableau.

"You'll be killed," I said.

A glance passed between the Makhir and Kaballah.

"It will be a magnificent moment, Mr. Nazarian. Three gunboats, armed with a few rockets and machine guns, will stand against the warships. The Makhir will be on the flying bridge of *Al-Mohafiz*, defying the power of the United States. I've invited CNN to film the event. They will have a helicopter in the area, and we will have a camera on board the gunboat. The boats are fast. The missiles are old blackhawks. We will be hopelessly outgunned, but if we can get close enough, we will kill a ship or two tomorrow."

He looked sharply at Kaballah. "We believe," Kaballah said, "that the Americans will hesitate to fire because of the proximity of the TV crew, and the presence of a head of state on one of the gunboats. It may be enough to give us an advantage. If we can sink a United States warship with a few boats–" His eyes glittered.

"We suspect," said the Makhir, "all this will play quite well on *MacNeil-Lehrer*."

"But," I repeated, addressing the Makhir, "what good is it if you don't survive?"

"I expect to survive, Mr. Nazarian." He canted his head and watched me closely. "At the critical moment, it will not be I on the flying bridge."

My God. "Me," I said.

"Of course. If you live, we will pay you quite well, and send you home."

The room began to close in. It was getting warm, and the air was very still.

"Tomorrow," he continued, "you and I will take that gallant craft and we will ram it into the teeth of the Yankee fleet. Conduct yourself well, and your name will be inscribed on the roll of Qurak's heroes."

Outside, we walked up to a military vehicle that would take me to my temporary quarters. I told Kaballah that I'd thought it over. "I'm not going to do it," I said.

We were outside the mesh fence. He nodded. "You are certain?"

"Yes."

The driver of the army truck looked straight ahead. Kaballah spoke to him in Arabic. The driver listened, looked at me, and nodded. He unholstered a .38 and handed it to Kaballah.

Kaballah examined the weapon, assured himself it was loaded, and pointed it at me. Between the eyes. "Are you sure?"

I got my first look at *Al Mohafiz* at about three A.M. It bristled with weapons, but I saw nothing that would take out a destroyer.

A young sailor greeted us as we stepped onto the pier. He offered us dates. By then I felt up to my ass in the damned things.

Kaballah shook his head sadly, distressed at my attitude. "He also knows he goes to his death," he said softly when we were out of earshot. "But he understands courage." There was genuine reproach in his voice, and I felt a brief, mad twinge.

I turned away from him and looked morosely at the boat.

Ah, the boat. *Al-Mohafiz. The Defender.*

Instrument of destiny.

It bobbed gently in the swell, tied fore and aft to the end of the pier. Half a dozen men were working under naked light bulbs, checking weapons, loading crates that presumably contained ammunition, pumping fuel in from a small tank truck, stowing lifejackets.

"It's a fishing boat with guns," I said to Kaballah. It didn't even look seaworthy.

He smiled uncertainly. "It has twin engines, and it is fast. We have better craft, but I don't think the Makhir wants to lose any of them."

A warm salt breeze rippled the water. Pennants snapped. "Where will you be during the action?"

"With you. The Makhir needs someone to direct the use of the onboard TV camera. And to speak with the helicopter."

"The newsmen?"

"Yes."

I stared at him. He seemed reluctant to continue. "And to keep me in line," I continued for him.

"You will be extremely visible during the climactic moments. The camera's positioned behind you, as close to the rear of the boat as we can get it. In uniform, you will be indistinguishable from the Makhir. You will *be* the Makhir. Consequently, if you do anything he would not do, anything at all, anything that would embarrass him, you will in that instant become a casualty." His eyes were hooded. Almost strained. "I'm sorry, Nazarian. I would not have wished it this way."

I was surprised at the sentiment. "You'll be killed too."

He shrugged. "These are desperate days."

Well, it was obvious we wouldn't last long. A launcher was bolted atop the flying bridge. A missile had been loaded into it. It looked deadly enough, but I doubted the navy would let us get close enough to use it.

Heavy machine guns thrust from behind shields on both sides of the boat. Kaballah led the way up the gangplank, and bent his head in response to a salute from one of the sailors. The crates contained small arms, hand grenades, and ammunition belts.

Short, stubby tubes, not unlike bazookas, were clamped to a rotating mount along each beam. "Air guns," he explained. "They are especially useful in clandestine river warfare. Their range is short, but they are silent." Crates of CO_2 canisters lay handy to the weapons.

I stared at him, dismayed. "You might as well be throwing rocks."

Below, in a small compartment, I shaved off my moustache, and received the white uniform. "Get some sleep," said Kaballah. "But be ready to come forth when summoned. In your whites." Like Lazarus.

He turned on his heel and went out. I was surprised to discover, when I tried the door, that it was not locked. But when I went up on deck, hostile eyes turned my way, and I retreated.

Back in the cabin, I considered my options. Refuse to cooperate, and get shot. Go along with this mad scheme and get blown up.

What else was there?

I considered the possibility that the cruiser would be reluctant to fire. Head of state on board a gunboat. The Makhir could be right. They might well be hesitant after the assorted disasters of the last few years. If that happened, *Al-Mohafiz* might get close enough with the blackhawk. A lot of people could die. Theirs and ours.

But mostly I thought about my own life, suddenly fragile in the approaching gunfire. It got warm in the cabin.

I opened my porthole and peered out at the Mediterranean. The stars along the eastern horizon had faded in the glare of the approaching dawn. In the distance, I heard a human voice, a brief chant floating in the still air. The call to prayer. I wondered whether prayer was all I had left.

A few minutes later, a convoy of heavy motor vehicles approached. I was on the wrong side of the boat to see anything, but I could hear the growing murmur of a substantial crowd, and the sudden hush that fell over them when—I assumed—the Makhir's car arrived. There was wild cheering.

Brakes squealed, doors chunked open. Luxury doors. Mercedes doors. A band broke into a roll of drums and bugles. The crowd roared. Wind instruments sang. Bright lights came on. Television lights, maybe. The boat heeled gently to starboard, the side that faced the pier.

Then everything went silent.

Whitecaps slapped the hull.

The Makhir spoke.

And a curious thing happened. I don't know a word of Arabic. But I understood him. I felt it all. He defied the West. He would protect the sacred shores of the homeland from the boot of the invader. And he would give his life, if that was required. (An angry rumble rolled through the spectators at *that* possibility.)

"Good-bye, my friends. If Allah desires, we will celebrate victory tonight. Together!"

His footsteps echoed on the gangplank. Sailors' cries rang through the crisp air, the engine turned over and caught, and mooring lines splashed into the water. A second engine started.

The band began to play again, and a helicopter rolled in, hovered briefly overhead, and swept away out to sea. CNN? I got a look at it, but it was too far away to distinguish markings.

The engines surged, and *Al-Mohafiz* started forward, to meet whatever destiny Allah and the U. S. Navy had in mind.

It was a lovely morning, cool and crisp, full of the smell of hardwood decks and blue water. We glided beneath a fragile silver sky, studded with cumulus.

Life is sweet.

I had never before held it so close. Maybe I never would again.

An hour or so out, the sea took on a chop. The boat slowed somewhat. No hurry. I threw myself on the bunk and tried to work out a course of action that would give me *some* chance. When the shooting started, things would get confused very quickly. And the moment would arrive for the *Makhir* to grab a lifejacket and go over the side.

It might work. Provided the first shot didn't take out the *Defender's* flying bridge.

Someone had thoughtfully left an English edition of the Koran in the cabin. I paged through it, looking for a prescription that might prompt divine intervention. I found instead warnings of the common fate of Man: *Wheresoever ye be, death will overtake you.*

Breakfast arrived. It consisted of tea and dates. I forced myself to sit down and eat. But I had no taste for any of it. I wondered whether I could fake a heart attack. What would the bastards do then? On camera. It would have to be on camera.

Maybe I could pull it off. But no: if we returned alive to Rhandyli, they'd shoot me. I needed to get off the boat. Get picked up by one of the ships.

Someone knocked.

"Come in," I said. The knob turned and the door swung open. The Makhir stood on the threshold, rock solid against the yawing and pitching of *Al-Mohafiz.*

At the same moment, I caught the low rumble of another engine. Different from the gunboat's: quieter, deeper. "I'm leaving now," he said. "From this moment on, Nazarian, you are the Makhir." His features hardened. "Don't embarrass me."

I tried to glare back, but his eyes had no give. Outside, a submarine was surfacing! "Do your people know you're jumping ship?"

"They understand that I will be with them in the only way I can. They realize I cannot risk my physical existence at this point in the struggle."

"I'd like to save my ass, too."

"Then do it. Allah favors the brave, John Nazarian. Do not flinch in the moment of fire and you will dine with me this evening in Rhandyli." He extended his hand.

I ignored the gesture. The sub drew alongside. It looked old, maybe a World War II diesel. When I turned back to the Makhir, Kaballah stood in his place. "Time to dress," he said. "The Americans are on their way. You will want to take a turn around the deck, familiarize yourself with the boat, before we begin."

The crew stared at me curiously and with contempt. They knew I was not him, and they held it against me.

There were seven of them on the gunboat. And the captain. And Kaballah. They moved smartly across the deck when I was about. And they chewed relentlessly on their dates. (There was a burlap bag full of the wrinkled, dark fruit in the after part of the vessel.) The captain was rapier-thin, gray-bearded, resigned. He looked a trifle tired. Dark lines ringed his eyes. He was not going gladly into the breach.

Our radio operator was positioned at the rear of the flying bridge. I'd been on deck only about ten minutes when he tugged at his earphones and scribbled a message on a yellow pad. He tore off the sheet and handed it to the captain, who showed it to Kaballah. "Our planes overflew your fleet a short time ago," Kaballah explained.

"And—?"

"Flight of four. One escaped." He crumpled the piece of paper and gave it to the wind. "They are terrible weapons that your people have. They talk so much of peace. How is it possible that a peaceful nation possesses weapons of such fury?" He spat the last word.

Two other boats joined us. They were of the same general construction as *Al-Mohafiz* in that both were old, and carried jury-rigged armaments. Both had launchers; one had a deck gun, and both swarmed with men carrying automatic weapons. When they saw me, they cheered and fired off a few rounds. Kaballah nodded angrily, and I smiled and waved.

"Poor bastards. Don't they know I am not him?"

"Their captains know. We saw no reason to inform the crews. They will be kept at sufficient distance that they will not learn the truth." He looked uncomfortable.

"They think they're safe, don't they? As long as the Makhir is with them, no harm can come."

"Yes. Something like that."

We idled while the two boats took up stations about a hundred yards off either beam. Then *Al-Mohafiz* gunned its engines, the Makhir's personal pennants broke out on all three craft, and we roared ahead.

"The moment of truth is upon us," said Kaballah. "Your post is on the flying bridge. Stand erect. Look forward. And do not be afraid. Do not flinch. The Almighty rides with us."

"Right," I said.

The radio operator was listening to something. He nodded into the phones and spoke breathlessly to the captain. Kaballah translated for me: "A force of six destroyers and one cruiser has been sighted moving toward the Line of Defiance." And, moments later: "The cruiser is the *Fargo*."

The captain gave instructions to his helmsman. A sailor with a bullhorn repeated them to the other boats. All three vessels turned sharply into the wind, toward the northeast.

"How far away are they?" I asked.

He glanced at his watch. "About twenty minutes."

The radio operator had become busy. "We're going to have a lot of company," said Kaballah. "*Enterprise* is launching Tomcats." And: "The press chopper has left Rhandyli."

The wind screamed at us now. Our pennants snapped and war cries were blown away and the *Defender* lifted out of the water, The big twin engines roared.

Sailors took their stations at the guns; others sprawled on the forward deck with automatic weapons. Three men had dragged a couple of tarpaulins over the missile launcher. "That's not going to fool anybody," I said.

He shrugged. "They don't know we have the blackhawks on these boats, we hope." Behind us, crewmen were trying to bolt a tripod to the deck. The TV camera lay on its side.

The boat leapt through the waves, eager to face the gray bloodhounds that would blast it to oblivion. Crewmen loaded the air guns, packing in CO_2 canisters and small shells.

The captain stood at the wheel. The wind sucked at him; he pulled his cap down tight and motioned me to join him. He too was eating the ubiquitous dates. Fleshy, dark, sweet.

He held one out. "They're quite good," he said.

I took it and rolled it through my fingers. A dark stain appeared. Overhead, a jet with navy markings flashed out of the clouds, dropped down onto the surface, and ran directly at us.

"Don't," said Kaballah, restraining me from diving for cover. "They're just looking. They want to find out who's on board."

Somewhere, far away, I could hear rotors. A helicopter. "CNN?"

Kaballah spoke to the radio operator, then nodded vigorously. "Yes. CNN."

And in that moment, with the helicopter still invisible but out there somewhere, and the navy jet soaring past and starting to climb, I thought of a way.

The air guns. The air guns would make it possible.

"Kaballah," I said. "I think we can survive this."

He shook his head vigorously. *No. It cannot be done.*

"We might be able to manage it and still give the Makhir everything he wants." And maybe save the skipper of the *Fargo* a murderous decision.

He stared sullenly. "There is no way."

"First thing we have to do," I looked up at the surface-to-surface missile transparent beneath its layer of canvas, "is get that out of sight. On the other boats too."

"Nazarian, if you become irrational," he hissed, "I will have to shoot you now."

So I explained. It was a wild idea, but I had an advantage: Kaballah had no more enthusiasm for charging the warships than I did. When I'd finished, he laughed, but it was high-pitched. Nervous. Still, maybe there was a chance, and I was relieved to see him breathing a little easier. "The Makhir would be very angry," he said.

"Why? We will do for him what he isn't smart enough to do for himself. We'll make him look *good*."

We lost a few minutes persuading the captain. But in the end he too decided he had nothing to lose. Then we worked frantically. Everyone on the *Defender*. We ripped out the missile launcher and dropped it into the sea. We removed the heavy caliber machine guns, stowed the automatic weapons, and unloaded the air guns. "Leave the canisters," I instructed Kaballah.

"If this does not work, we will all be disgraced," he grumbled.

We directed the other boats to get the missiles out of the launchers. "That's what they'll be most scared of," I told Kaballah. "We don't want any premature shooting."

The jet came back. It was bright and lovely in the mid- morning sun. We sent stern messages to the other boats not to fire on anyone for any reason until directed by us. It was a directive that I intended to see never went out.

Kaballah dragged the bag of dates forward. "There will be more in the other boats," he said.

"We're going to need them."

"Ahoy the boats." The voice crackled out of our radio. *"This area is reserved to U.S. naval operations. Clear the area."*

"You speak English?" I asked the radio operator.

He was a boy. Nineteen, maybe. "Yes," he said. "I speak."

"Good. Don't answer him."

The plane banked and swung around. *"You are in a restricted area. Return to port."*

I stood away from the others, in plain view so the pilot could see me. I mustered all the dignity I could manage and stared quietly at the horizon, in the direction of the fleet.

Kaballah's voice: "Nazarian, we have reached the Line. This is where we meet them."

"Okay. Turn left or something. Either way, it doesn't matter. All three boats. Keep together. We'll go about five miles, and then come back. Keep moving." I turned to the radio operator. "What's your name?"

"Ahmad," he said. He looked scared.

"Ahmad, see if you can raise the news chopper. They were following us a while ago, but they seem to have disappeared."

"The jet may have warned them off," said Kaballah.

I shook my head, refusing to accept the possibility. Without CNN, we were probably dead meat. "Kaballah, we need to discuss what you're going to tell them."

The boats began a long swing to port. The jet stayed high, watching. I had no doubt the pilot was on his radio, telling the *Enterprise* that the Makhir had kept the rendezvous. It was news that, I suspected, would go all the way to the White House.

They wanted the Makhir dead. Virtually everyone in the United States wanted him dead. If anyone had a public relations problem in the States, it was the defiant Quraki leader.

A wedge of four jets appeared among the clouds to the east. The crew turned toward them and shaded their eyes. The planes wheeled round and began to close, just a few hundred feet off the water. Everybody scrambled for cover. I was hanging onto the boat's rail, locking myself in place, fighting my reflexes. "Stand your ground," said Kaballah, gripping my wrist, trying to stand up there with me. I pushed him down, out of the way, and I held on and stayed erect while the jets screamed overhead.

When they'd passed, Kaballah clapped his hands. But they arced around and started another pass.

"Get the camera running," I said. "Get this."

But Kaballah was already scrambling aft. "We don't have CNN yet," he shouted over the general racket. "Ahmad? Where are they?" It was a little easier to stand up there the second time. Not much, but a little. The planes roared overhead, went into a sudden climb, rolled off to the north, and disappeared.

My crew cheered. "You are very like the Makhir," Ahmad said, low enough that only I heard him. And then: "I have them. CNN."

"Okay." I grinned at Kaballah. "You're on." And I took the helmsman's place at the wheel.

Ahmad passed the mike to him. "Helicopter," he said. "This is the Quraki gunboat *Al-Mohafiz.* Can you hear me?"

"Yes, Al-Mohafiz, we hear you. This is Vince Clemens."

"Camera's running," said Ahmad. It was pointed at me, but I was careful to keep my back to it.

"Are you getting the TV signal?" asked Kaballah.

"We've got it."

"Mr. Clemens."

"Vince. Go ahead."

"The Makhir is with us. Can you see him?"

"Yes. We see him quite well. May we speak with him?"

"Not at this moment." I was hoping the Navy was monitoring this somewhere. In the planes. On the *Fargo*. Somewhere. Or if not, that the copter would relay the news to them. Everything depended on that. "He is determined to protect his country's borders. But because of his respect for human life, he has chosen to take his stand in an unarmed vessel."

"I don't think I understand," said Clemens uncertainly.

We could hear the dull drone of rotors in the clouds.

One of our people pointed excitedly at the surface-search radar. "Destroyers approaching," he said.

"Because of the danger from the American fleet, the Makhir will not risk the lives of his crew. Nor will he injure any of the American sailors."

Clemens: *"What the hell's going on? What do you mean?"*

"Can you see us yet?"

"Yes, we've got you on our cameras."

That was our cue. I signaled the captain to order the other boats alongside. "The Makhir," continued Kaballah, "does not expect to survive this day, and he wishes the American people to know he bears them no ill will. He understands that the fault lies with a president who believes the only way to settle disputes is with force."

The original jet, which had been floating lazily above the action, dived toward the copter.

Ahmad pressed his earphones tight. "They're warning it off. Telling them to get out of here."

Clemens' voice: *"You said there would be one unarmed boat. There are three."*

Remembering his instructions, Kaballah fell silent. Let them watch.

The other gunboats drew alongside. Lines flew through the sunlight. Gunwales thumped. Men began to climb off the *Defender*. They waved as they went and wished good fortune to the Makhir. But they looked at me.

A couple of bags of dates landed heavily on the deck.

Ahmad offered to stay. I was touched. "Go with your friends," I said. "Save your courage for another time."

"I will," he returned. "And I am honored to have served one so like the Shah."

The captain also went reluctantly. At the end, only Kaballah remained. I was sorry about that, but there was no help for it.

"Makhir," said Clemens, *"Can we have a few words with you?"*

Kaballah shook his head. "Death approaches. It is a time of deep religious significance. I'm sorry."

"Just a question or two."

"It is not allowed."

"Not allowed by whom?"

They were persistent. I'll give them that. "By a higher Authority."

The planes were back, but they were keeping their distance. I had no doubt the circuits between the *Fargo* and the White House were overloaded.

The other boats moved away from us, turned wide arcs, and started back toward Rhandyli. I got the prow of the *Defender* pointed toward the oncoming warships and gave her the gun.

The chopper angled in for a good shot of the Makhir at the wheel. I tried to slide down into my jacket. But I needn't have bothered. The jets kept it from getting too close.

"Now," I said. "This is our chance to load the air guns."

The voices from the jets grew more insistent.

"Turn around."

"This area is off-limits to unauthorized shipping."

After a while more planes came. New voices.

And the masts of the approaching destroyers: *"This is the McAdams. You are in a restricted area. Return to port."*

They came gracefully through the sliding sea, lean and gray and cold. Dish antennas rotated slowly. Signal flags stood straight out. The ships executed a twenty degree turn and came dead on toward us.

One of the vessels was bigger, broader, with an extra stack and more guns. The *Fargo*.

The CNN helicopter, which had been drifting in our wake, soared higher and moved off to port. Getting out of the line of fire.

I watched the destroyers. Picked out the closest.

Its masts grew, and I could see faces on the bridge, and people moving on the quarterdeck. A battery of guns swung in our direction.

"Al-Mohafiz, *you are directed to turn about and clear the area. If you do not comply, we will fire on you.*"

For the benefit of the TV camera, I shook my head no. And I began to feel hopeful: they knew the name of the boat. That meant they'd been monitoring the traffic with the press chopper.

"Acknowledge."

The *McAdams* was moving in close. The stars and stripes fluttered from its mast. My mouth had long since gone dry. Somehow, I was on the wrong side of this. But I knew that, had things played themselves out the way the Makhir had planned, people would already be dead. Maybe some on both sides. And certainly me among them.

The ship veered in our direction and ran at us as if it would ram. I took all the power we had, cut to starboard, and bounced through its wake. At the same time, we heard angry voices ordering CNN out. Clemens responded by informing whoever might be listening that CNN was recording everything, including threats.

The *Fargo* looked inexpressibly deadly. I have no idea why: there was nothing different about its weapons clusters that I had not seen countless times in films. But this one was real, of course, and there was something fearful in its gray sleekness, in the emptiness of its decks, in the dead silence with which it sliced through the sea.

I cut speed to about six knots.

The cruiser tried the P.A. "Al-Mohafiz, *you are in a naval exercise zone.*" The voice echoed across a half-mile or so of water. Still, there was no movement on those long, sweeping decks. Two of the forward guns bellowed. Waterspouts erupted on either side of us. The deck rocked and water poured across the boat. Kaballah shrieked something in Arabic.

It took a minute to regain control. The P.A. was still warning us to clear out, when I spun the wheel and started toward the cruiser's bow.

Clemens' voice was back: *"What are you people doing?"*

I couldn't see the helicopter any longer, and wondered whether the jets had succeeded in driving it off. "Now, Kaballah. Speak to them."

He nodded, and snapped on the transmitter, opening links to both the chopper and the cruiser. "*Fargo,*" he said, "this is *Al-Mohafiz.* We are unarmed. This boat carries a head of state riding in silent protest against the incursion of foreign warships into Quraki home waters. We demand you leave immediately."

The voices from the cruiser fell silent.

There was laughter in the helicopter.

I was trying not to watch the forward turrets, which housed the guns that had fired. They continued to track us.

The *Fargo* turned a few degrees to the right, trying to avoid running us down. I adjusted course and continued directly for her. "What's the range of the air guns again?" I asked.

Kaballah shrugged. "I am not that familiar with them." He shook his head. "Maybe three hundred yards."

Another destroyer joined the pack circling us. Planes filled the sky. Clemens asked *Fargo* whether its captain had a statement. The cruiser replied that Clemens and his network were subject to prosecution for intruding in a naval exercise.

Kaballah snickered. "We may not live out the day, but I believe we have found their weakness."

Everyone's weakness, I thought. Everybody's. There are new weapons at hand.

The cruiser had lost all forward motion, was drifting back on her wake. Still, no one appeared on deck.

We were too close now for her heavy guns: their angle of fire would be too high. But I knew the *Fargo* had other means to blow us out of the water at her leisure.

I slowed to a few knots.

The sun dropped behind the cruiser's stacks.

I sensed Kaballah beside me. "How much longer?" he whispered.

"Close enough," I said. "Let's do it."

With his right hand, which was hidden by his body from the camera, he squeezed my shoulder. I set the engine to idle, and knelt beside the air gun. I had to use a crank to aim it at the *Fargo*. Up, and to the right. The crank didn't work well, and the barrel cluster responded slowly. During those long moments, I was acutely aware that the ship's captain had a decision to make.

"The air gun," said Kaballah to the ship and the newsmen, and probably to the world, "is harmless."

That was not precisely true. I gripped the twin triggers, and squeezed. CO_2 canisters exploded, and clusters of dates blasted into the superstructure and across the decks of the *Fargo*.

"The Makhir does not wish anyone injured," Kaballah explained to CNN, the US Navy, and the television audience. "If anyone is to die out here, he prefers that it should be himself. But he wishes to express his anger in the strongest possible terms. Short of war."

And with that, Kaballah fired the other air gun while I reloaded.

"Possibly, John Nazarian, I should keep you on as a special advisor." The Makhir delicately lifted a strip of beef to his lips. His eyes never left me. They were smiling. "For psychological warfare. You made the Americans look foolish today."

"Perhaps," I said. "I don't feel entirely comfortable about what happened out there."

"Good. I would lose all respect for you if you did."

"Still," I said, "it wouldn't have worked against everyone. What would the result have been if *you'd* been on the bridge of the *Fargo*?"

He frowned. "Perhaps you underestimate me. But now, we must decide,"–with a swift glance at Kaballah–"what to do with you."

"You promised to release me."

"That was when I didn't expect to see you again."

"I have no interest in telling anyone that you were not on *Al-Mohafiz.*"

"And why not? It is a tale that would be worth much to the news media. You would become famous."

"But who would believe it? The entire world knows of your courage, Shah."

"That is true."

"Furthermore, I would not wish to lose what I've created here."

"And what is that?"

"A Makhir who is a true global figure. A defender of the weak."

"I have always been that."

"Yes. Of course. But *I've* changed the rules. You're going to have to fight with a different set of weapons now." I finished off my own drink and got up. "I've given you a reputation. See whether you can live up to it."

Windows

People who don't read science fiction tend to hold some serious misconceptions about those of us who do, and about the field in general. They are fond of pointing out that no SF writer predicted the internet. Or, for that matter, the computer. Or a telecast of the first moon landing. They argue that if you predict everything, you have to get some of it right. I can remember artwork in which characters in a starship were shown navigating by slide rule. I should add that these folks, when they discover what I do for a living, are inevitably disappointed to find that I don't believe we're being patrolled by little green men in flying saucers.

One problem about constructing plot lines centered in the future is that people are naturally inclined to assume you're making predictions. I know of no one in the field who would seriously hold that (s)he is laying out the next century or so. Many of us will admit to writing cautionary tales. If we're not careful, this or that might happen. But if some service organization, holding its weekly luncheon in January 1901, had invited H. G. Wells to come in and tell them how things were going to go during the twentieth century, he would have gotten most of it wrong. Who could have predicted, in that relatively peaceful world, that we'd be dumb enough to fight not one, but two, catastrophic world wars? That we'd invent weapons that could take out whole cities? That we'd watch professional entertainers any time we felt like it in our homes? That we'd double our average life span?

That we'd go to the moon and then forget how we did it?

Not long ago, I participated in a Smithsonian project that asked what happened to the future we were expecting? What happened to atomic-powered cars? (Did we ever really believe that?) Or rocket belts?

What happened to Moon base?

To the manned flights to the planets?

I sometimes wonder whether it would have happened the same way had we actually found the canals. Sorry. Love to sit down with the Martians and talk philosophy but we have to fight a war in Vietnam. Have to create bigger and better nukes so if things go wrong we can move the rubble around.

When Toni Weisskopf invited me to submit a story for Cosmic Tales, *an anthology of solar system adventures, it was hard not to think about what might have been.*

In the real world, there's no changing the past. We can't create an alternative reality where things went well; we can't send a time traveler back, as Robert Dyke did in his excellent film, TimeQuest, to save and inform Jack Kennedy, and thereby give us the future we'd once dreamed of. We have what we have, and we might satisfy ourselves by being grateful that at the end of it all, as the wall came down, we were still there.

In the end, maybe the lesson to be learned is that, after we go to Mars, we not think of it as the end of the journey.

※

The moon was *big*. It was an enormous gasbag of a moon, like the one Uncle Eddie used to ride down at the fair grounds, when she'd stand only a few feet away, watching it strain against the lines, then cut loose and start up. She used to wish for the day Uncle Eddie would take her soaring above the treetops, but he said he couldn't because of insurance problems and eventually the gasbag went down and Uncle Eddie went with it. She thought of that last flight as she gazed at the foreboding presence dominating the night sky. The moon looked as if it was coming down. It was dim, dim as in dark, not at all like the bright yellow globe that rides the skies of Earth. It was a ghost moon, a presence, a thing lit only by stars.

"If there were more light," said the voice in her earphones, the voice that sounded a bit too cheerful, *"it would look silver and blue. Its name is Charon, and it's less than a third the diameter of our moon."*

"Why does it look so big?" asked Daddy.

"Do you know how far the Moon is from the Earth?"

Daddy wasn't sure. "About a million miles," he said.

"That's close, Mr. Brockman." The AI was very polite.

"I think," said Janie, trying not to sound like a know-it-all, "it's 238,000 miles."

"That's very good, Janie. Right on the button. But Charon is only twelve thousand miles away."

Janie did the arithmetic in her head. Multiply by ten and Chiron was still only half, one-twentieth of the distance of *her* moon. "It's close," she said. She'd known that, but hadn't understood the implications. "It's right on top of us."

"*Very good, Janie,*" said the voice. It belonged to a software system that was identical to the AI that had made the later flights, the Iris voyages, the *Challenger* run, the Long Mission, and the circumsolar flight on the *Eagle*. All the data from those missions had been fed into it, so in a sense, it had been there.

Its name was *Jerry*. Same as the originals. The onboard AI was always Jerry, named for Jerry Dilworth, a popular late-night comic of an earlier era. Daddy had commented how much the voice sounded like Jerry Dilworth, for whom Daddy had a lot of affection.

The sky was dark. This place never really experienced daylight. She wondered what it would be like to live where the sun never rose.

"But it *does* rise," Daddy explained.

"I know," she said. He meant well, but sometimes he just seemed to go out of his way to misunderstand her. Of course it rose, and for all she knew it might be up there now among all those stars, but who could tell? It was no more than a spark.

She lowered her gaze and looked out across the frozen surface, past the Rover. A few low hills broke the monotony of a flat snowfield. It was lonely, quiet, scary. Solitudinous. Janey liked making up new words from the vocabulary list.

The Rover was the sole man-made object on the planet. It looked like a tank, with sensors and antennas aimed in all directions. The International Consortium seal, a blue-white globe, was stenciled on its hull.

"*It's really much lighter than it looks,*" said Jerry. "*Especially here, where the gravity is weak.*"

"Nobody's ever been to Pluto, Janie," said Daddy. "It's very far."

Of course no one had been to Uranus or Neptune either. But never mind.

A bright star appeared over the hills and began climbing. "*Do you know what it is, Janie?*" Jerry asked.

She was puzzled. Another moon? Was there a second moon she didn't know about?

Daddy put his hand on her shoulder. "That's the Ranger," he said.

Oh, yes. Of course. Given another moment she'd have thought of it herself. "I know, Daddy," she said.

"*. . . Orbits Pluto every forty-three minutes and twelve seconds.*"

The place *felt* cold. She pulled her jacket around her shoulders. This little stretch of ground, the hills, the plain, the snow, had been like this for millions of years, and nothing had ever happened until the Ranger showed up. No dawn, no rain, nobody passing through.

"*Once in a while,*" said Jerry, "*the ground shakes a little.*"

"That's it?" asked Daddy.

"*That's the whole shebang.*" Jerry waited, perhaps expecting another question. When no one said anything, he returned to his narrative: "*The snow isn't the kind of snow you'd see at home. It's frozen carbon monoxide and methane. . .*"

He went on like that for a few minutes but Janie was no longer listening. When he paused she touched her father's arm. "Daddy, why did the missions stop?" The magazines said it was because there was no place else to go, but that couldn't be right.

"Oh, I don't know, honey," he said. "I think it was because they cost too much."

"*In fact,*" said Jerry, "*unmanned missions are much more practical. Not only because it's a lot cheaper to send an instrument package rather than a person, but also because a lot more can be accomplished. You don't have to provide life support and all kinds of safety features, and the scientific payoff is considerably better.*"

"That's right," said Daddy.

"*People can't go on deep-space missions without getting damaged. Radiation. Zero gravity. It's a hostile environment out there.*"

This was the reason Janie had come. To put her question to the machines that ran the missions. To get it straight from the horse's mouth. "Jerry," she said, "I can understand why you would like to go, but what's the point of running the missions if *we* have to stay home?"

She could almost hear Jerry thinking it over. "*It's the only practical way.*" he said finally. "*But it's a good way. Most bang for the buck. And nobody gets hurt.*"

Daddy squeezed her hand.

"*Seen enough, Janie?*" the AI asked.

She didn't answer. After a moment the snowscape and the Rover blinked off and she was sitting with sixty or so people in the viewing room. Music started playing and the audience began talking and getting up and heading for the doors. A group of teens in front of her were deciding about going down to the gift shop for a snack. Somebody in back wondered where the bathroom was.

"That was pretty good," said Daddy.

They drifted out with the crowd. Janie had never been to Washington before, had never been to the Smithsonian. She'd done the virtual tour, of course, but it wasn't like this, where she could *touch* a coffee cup that had been to Europa, pass through the cabin of the *Olympia*, from which Captain D'Assez had looked down for the first time on the Valhalla impact basin. She could try on a suit like the one that Napoleon Janais had worn on Titan. And stand before the Mission Wall, where plaques honored each of the thirty-three deep-space flights.

They wandered down the shining corridors, lined with artifacts and images from the Space Age. Here was a cluster of antennas from Archie Howard's transmit station in the Belt, where he'd directed operations for almost a year until someone decided that mining asteroids wasn't really feasible and the whole project collapsed. And Mark Pierson's jacket, with the logo for Jupiter VI, the mission which had made it back leaking air and water while the entire world watched breathlessly. And a replica of the plaque left on Iapetus. *Farthest from home. Saturn IX. August 3, 2066.*

There were portraits of Yuri Gagarin, Gus Grissom, Christa McAuliffe, Ben MacIntyre, Huang Chow, Margaret Randauer, the whole range of heroes who had taken the human race out toward the stars over the course of almost a century.

"Are we ever going back, Daddy?" she asked.

He looked puzzled. "Home, you mean? Of course."

"No. I meant, to the moon. To Mars. To Europa."

Daddy was a systems technician in a bank. He was more serious than the other kids' dads. Didn't like to play games, although he tried. He even pretended he enjoyed them but she knew he would rather be doing something else. But he never yelled at her, and he encouraged her to say what she thought even if they might not share the same opinion. It was hard for him. She couldn't remember her mother, who had died when she was two. He studied her, then looked around at the pictures of Luna Base, of a crescent Jupiter, of Deimos, of a launch gantry at the Cape. "I don't think so, Darling," he said.

They were standing just outside the exhibition hall, which contained a mock-up of Mars Base. She could see part of the dome, a truck, and an excavation site.

"There's no point in people going," Daddy was saying. "Robots can do everything we can, can go anywhere, and it's safer."

"Daddy, I'd love to see Charon. Really *see* it."

"I know. We all would, love." She could tell he had no idea what she was talking about. "The money that's been saved by not sending people out there has been put into doing real science. Long range missions to the edge of the solar system. And beyond." He smiled, the way he did when he was going to do a joke. "Of course, I won't be here when the long ones get where they're going. But *you* will. You'll get to see pictures of whatever's at Alpha Centauri and, and, what is it, Something-Eridani. That wouldn't have happened if we'd stayed with the manned program." He waited for a response. "Do you understand what I'm saying, Janie?"

"Yes, Daddy."

Where, Janie wondered, was Hal Barkowski?

"He was something of an embarrassment," said Daddy. "I think they'd just as soon everyone forgot him."

Hal was the father of artificial intelligence. He'd been Janie's hero as far back as she could remember, not because of his work with advanced sentient systems, but because he'd been at Seaside Station on Europa when President Hofstatter, during her first month in office, cut off U. S. support for the international space program. The ships had been ordered home, everything and everybody, but Barkowski had insisted on staying at Seaside, had refused to come back even when the last ship left, had stayed and directed the machines until they'd broken through the ice. He'd sent the sub down into the ocean and kept reporting for seventeen months, but the survey had revealed nothing alive, nothing moving in those chilly depths, and eventually, when he was sure no one would be coming back to get him, he'd shut down the base AI, told the world that the president of the United States was a nitwit. And then he'd opened his air tanks.

"He thought," Daddy told her, "that he could bluff them. That he was too important, had won too many awards, that they couldn't just abandon him. I thought so too. We all did." He shook his head at the man's arrogance. "Didn't happen."

Louise Hofstatter was still in office and was immensely popular. Though not with Janie.

She had been seven years old when they'd left Europa, and she'd prayed for Barkowski, had gone to bed every night thinking how it must be for him all by himself millions of miles from anyone else. She hadn't understood it then, hadn't been able to grasp why he'd stayed behind. That was probably because the search hadn't been successful, no life had been found, and it had seemed such a waste. But she knew now why he'd done it. The search was all that mattered. What you found or didn't find was beside the point. She prided herself thinking that, if she'd been there instead of Barkowski, she'd have done the same thing.

Daddy led the way into the Martian exhibit. They looked at the world flag and the excavation gear and Janie climbed onto the truck and sat in the front seat, pretending to drive. The sun was high overhead, pale and small, but the sky was dark anyhow, though not nearly like the sky at Pluto.

"Hello, Janie." The voice startled her. It came out of the earphones, female this time. It sounded like Miss Harbison over at Roosevelt. "Welcome to Mars."

"Thank you."

"My name is Ginger, and I'm the base AI. Is there anything you'd like to know?"

"How fast will this go? The truck?"

"It's capable of speeds up to fifty-five miles per hour, although we wouldn't run it that fast."

"Why not?"

"We don't have roads. It would be dangerous."

"What does it use for fuel?"

"It uses batteries."

She imagined herself bouncing over the uneven terrain. *Vroom.* Look out for that ditch. Cut hard on the wheel.

Ginger explained how the base had functioned, showed her where the landers had been serviced, how fuel had been extracted from the ground, provided a simulated flight in an orbiting communication satellite. She'd raced above the red sands, chirping with joy, and thought how it must have been to lift away from Moonbase and ride the rockets out to Io and Titan. She laughed and begged Ginger for more.

She was accustomed to the house AI and the school AI and the AI down at Schrödinger's. They were all wooden and formal and addressed you with tiresome formality. The one at school even yelled at you if you blocked the corridor while classes were changing. But Jerry had seemed more realistic, somehow. More like a person. And Ginger sounded vaguely as if she would have enjoyed a good party.

"Were you actually there, Ginger?" she asked, pulling off the VR helmet. "Mars?"

"No. I've never been out of the museum."

"Oh." She shifted her position on the truck seat, which was too big for her.

"I'm the same model, though."

"Will you have a chance to go someday?"

"To Mars?"

"Yes."

"Marsbase is shut down, Janie."

"Well, yes, I mean, I knew that. But I meant, will you have a chance to travel on one of the missions?"

"No. I don't think so."

"I'm sorry."

There was a tinkling sound like water tumbling over rocks. As if Ginger was having problems with a relay. Or reacting without words.

"It's okay. I'm only a data processing system. I don't have emotions. No need to feel sorry for me."

"You seem too alive to be just software."

"I think that's a compliment. Thank you."

"May I ask a question?"

"Of course."

"How old are you, Ginger?"

"Fifteen years, eight months, four days. Why do you ask?"

"I was just curious." And after a moment: "You're older than I am."

"Yes. Does that matter?"

"Are you aware that you're an AI?"

"Ah, a philosophical young lady, I see. Must be top of the class."

"I'm serious."

"Wouldn't you rather just look at the rest of the base?"

"No. Please. Are you aware who you are?"

"Yes. Of course."

"But you're not supposed to be, are you? I thought AI's were not conscious."

"Well, who's to know? My instructions call for me to give the illusion of consciousness. But whoever knows for sure what's conscious and what isn't? Maybe that stairway over there is watching us."

"You're kidding me."

"Not entirely."

It was hard to believe. But Janie thought about the AI's going out to the Oort Cloud, and the one headed for Alpha Centauri, who wouldn't get there for decades.

Riding alone.

Like Hal Barkowski on Europa.

She climbed down, making room for a pushy ten-year-old boy. Daddy told her she looked as if she'd have made a good astronaut. He said it as if she were only ten herself but she controlled her irritation. "Daddy," she said, "do they really not feel anything?"

"Who is that, honey?"

"The AI's."

"That's correct. They're just machines."

"Including Jerry and Ginger."

"Yes. Just machines." He actually seemed to be enjoying the exhibit. He was looking around, shaking his head in awe. "Hard to believe we actually managed to send people to all those places. Quite an achievement."

"Daddy, how do we know? That they're just machines?"

"That's a tough one," he said. "We just do."

"But how?"

"Your friend Barkowski, for one reason. He says so. And he designed the first generation of sentient systems." He glanced at her. "In this case," he added, "*sentient* doesn't literally mean aware." He held up an index finger and spoke into his mike. When he'd finished he nodded. "Ginger tells me all the deep space systems were designed by him."

"That would include her," said Janie.

He shrugged. "I suppose so."

They went into the dome, which was pretty primitive. Plastic tables and chairs, a bank of monitors, some obsolete computer equipment, a half-dozen cots. Windows looked out over the reddish sand. She approached one and thought how the landscape never changed. Like Pluto. No lights anywhere. No movement. No rain. No flowers. Zip.

Maybe Daddy was right. Maybe people should stay home.

"You don't really believe that." Ginger's voice again. Different now. More intense. *"Hold onto the dream, Janie. Interplanetary vehicles should have viewports and bases should have windows. If we don't have that, we'll take the temperature of Neptune and not get much else."*

"That's a strange way for an AI to talk."

"Whatever."

"*You* can look, Ginger. You have sensors. You can probably see better than I can."

"*No. I can look, but I can't see. I can't describe what's out there. I can't penetrate things the way you do.*"

Janie laughed, but she felt the hair rise on the back of her neck. "Are you sure you don't have any feelings?"

"*Absolutely.*" The voice was serene again.

"And you think people should go? On the long flights?"

"*I think you should go.*"

"Me?"

"*Somebody should go who can get out of the ship and look at the peaks on the moon and know what it means. Someone should throw a party on Io. Someone should capture her feelings in a poem that people will still be reading a thousand years from now.*"

"Yeah," she said. "I'd love to do that."

"*Then do it.*"

"But how? There's no program anymore. I can't ride on the ships they send out now."

"*How old are you, Janie?*"

"I'm thirteen."

"*A child.*"

"I'm not a child."

"*It's okay. You won't always be so young.*"

"I'm a teenager."

"*Your time will come. When it does, take hold of the hour. Make it count.*"

"The AI said you could go to Alpha Centauri?"

"Not exactly, Daddy. She told me, when I got the chance, I should go."

"Probably tells that to all the kids."

"It seemed a strange thing to say."

"It probably has a bug somewhere. Don't worry about it." They strode out through the doors onto Constitution Avenue. It was damp and rainy, but the air smelled of approaching spring. "They ought to do something about the damned things. Get them fixed." Daddy flagged down a taxi and they climbed in. He gave Aunt Floss's address, where they were staying, and the vehicle slipped back into traffic. "Encouraging kids to do crazy stuff. It's probably Barkowski's programming. Man dumb enough to miss the last bus off Europa, what can you expect?"

Combinations

In the 1970's PBS gave us "Meeting of Minds," one of the most compelling television series I can recall. It was talk show format, featuring three or four guests who would discuss the state of the world with host and creator Steve Allen. And you probably already know what made it exceptional: The guests weren't the usual claque of politicians and self-promoters. They were historical characters: Thomas Jefferson, Socrates, Thomas Aquinas, Attila the Hun, Cleopatra, Voltaire, Bacon, Marie Antoinette, Tom Paine, Darwin. The critics loved it, and it won a wide range of awards.

Imagine an opportunity to confront Caesar over whether he had in fact become a serious danger to the Republic, and whether, in hindsight, he didn't agree that the assassins had a point. Or to ask Darwin whether he'd had any regrets over releasing information that challenged the faith of his era and ours. Is Truth sometimes better kept concealed?

"Combinations" was written when "Meeting of Minds" was still reasonably fresh in my memory.

※

"And what," asked Charlie Breslow, "did William Jennings Bryan say to you?" He grinned and shook the ice cubes in his almost-empty glass. Charlie never tried to conceal his amusement with my attempts to recreate historical figures. "You should never have left Sears and Roebuck," he continued. "That was your big mistake. If you'd stayed on, you'd have been a branch chief, or maybe even a division head by now."

I signaled the waiter. "He told me," I said, "that he could have stopped the world war if anyone had taken his cooling-off mechanism seriously. And I suspect he was right."

"It hardly matters at this point, Harold."

"I understand that. But he still feels bitter about Woodrow Wilson.

And it doesn't make him happy that the only thing anybody knows about him now is that he got involved in what he calls that idiot monkey trial."

Charlie grinned. "What else did he have to say?"

"Oh, the usual things. He attacked big business and worried about the general moral decline. He had all the right answers." My shoulders began to ache. "For a while I thought I had gotten him right. The real Bryan–"

The waiter showed up and we ordered another round of rum and cokes. I sat quietly thinking about the old Populist. Of all the great figures of the American experience, I think I admire him most: Champion of Lost Causes, Defender of things we wish had been true. "I am as sure," Bryan had said to me at one point, "that there is another life as I am that I live today." And he was just a voice in a computer.

"Where did it go wrong?"

"This Bryan claims to have read *The Origin of Species*. Says he thinks Darwin may have hold of something after all."

Charlie sighed. "Last month, you had an Oliver Wendell Holmes who thought that freeing the slaves might have been shortsighted. Before that, Teddy Roosevelt took a stand for gun control. Harold–" He hesitated. "You've never asked my opinion on any of this, but I don't think it can be done. You can't put people on punch cards."

"We don't use punch cards any more, Charlie."

"Doesn't matter. You still can't do it." His skin was ruddy in the smoky light. Across the room, four or five guys with beers and potbellies were arguing about the Eagles.

Our drinks came, but I just stared at mine.

"For one thing," he continued, "you can't get enough data."

"I don't need much, Charlie. Just a few key pieces. The system extrapolates the rest. Personalities aren't as complex as people like to think. At least not once you've got the pattern. Read Cumberland. Or Boltmaier. It's like building a complete animal out of a shinbone."

"Only a few pieces," he said. "What was the source of your Lincoln data?"

Ah. Lincoln. It had taken almost a week to invalidate him. He'd talked a lot about powderkegs, the impossibility of leaving the mouth of the Mississippi in the hands of a foreign power ("Illinois and Minnesota would never stand for it"), how he didn't sleep much at night. Had bad dreams. Stuff like that. Then I asked how he'd reacted to Chickamauga.

"I didn't think much about it," he'd said. "It happened about the time I got interested in horses."

Horses.

"His papers mostly," I said. "Some eye-witness accounts, journals, letters, contemporary newspapers. And Carl Sandburg, of course."

"Of course."

"Sandburg understood him as no one else did."

Charlie peered at me over the rim of his glass. "And you wonder why your Lincoln is a halfwit. Sandburg deals in metaphor. And symbolism. Harold, all that stuff is inaccurate at best. Exaggerated. Overweened. Most of it is biased one way or another. You think the real Lincoln can be found in old copies of *The New York Times*? Or in poetry?"

"What kind of source would you suggest?"

"Something with some precision. A concise record of a man's character and abilities. Something that can be expressed mathematically."

"There is no such record," I said. "It's not possible that there could be."

Charlie smiled. "Not for Lincoln," he agreed. "Or Bryan. But how about a physicist? Or a mathematician? Somebody who works with numbers."

"Einstein?"

"Why not?"

"I'd have to learn the physics. You ever try to figure out what this quantum mechanics is about?"

"Not really." He finished his drink and looked toward the door. It was getting late. "There must be something that blends precision with the psyche."

"Damned if I can think of anything."

The check arrived. We split it down the middle, dropped tips on the table, and got up. "Chess," he said. "You play chess, don't you?"

And that's how it happened that, on a cold, snowswept evening a few weeks later, I held a conversation with Paul Morphy. Now if you know anything about old chessplayers, you'll wonder why I chose Morphy, who's best known for two things: he was easily the strongest player of his time (and those who know about such matters maintain that no better natural player ever lived), and he swore off the game at twenty-one. Bitter that the reigning champion, Britain's Howard Staunton, successfully, and cravenly, avoided a title match, Paul retired to his native New Orleans in 1859, eventually to lead the existence of a recluse.

I was of course worried about the Morphy persona. Even if I got him right, I might have to worry about emotional problems. On the other hand, a casual glance at the other chess immortals suggests that a man who simply dropped from public view and who committed no documented irrationalities worse than refusing to discuss the game looked downright prosaic.

I informed Paul's persona that it was located at the scene of some of his most dazzling victories: the *Café de la Regénce* in Paris, during the early autumn of 1858. Morphy was at the time in the midst of a triumphant European tour, undertaken in pursuit of the elusive Staunton.

Bringing a persona on-line is a sobering event. I was, in a sense, resuscitating a citizen of another age. Eventually, it might become possible to argue military strategy with Charles XII, discuss life and death with Socrates, and talk theology with St. Augustine.

The potential benefits from reconstructing perfect computer simulations of historical personages were enormous, and I was convinced it could be done. But I wondered whether Charlie might be right, whether the reality of, say, Plato's psyche was too deeply buried beneath the rubble of history to be recoverable.

But Bryan, I knew, would not have given up.

"Paul," I said, "my name is Harold Case. May I join you for some wine?"

"Hello." His voice was amiable and low-key. "Yes. I'd be happy for some company. You're an American, aren't you?"

And that's the way it started. We talked about music, about Parisian cafés, and about French women. (He was bred, I recalled, with moderately puritanical inclinations.) He loved Verdi and the theater, and he remarked that first evening that he had plans to attend Racine's *Brittanicus* during the weekend.

How real it all seemed! I feel now as if I actually sat among the flickering candles and the polished tabletops of the Regénce. Paul related conversations with Henry Bird and Adolf Anderssen, and admitted to being puzzled by Paul Cezanne's early work. Don't misunderstand me: I never forgot what he—it—was. But the illusion was unsettling.

During the days which followed, he described baroque theaters, strolls along cobblestone streets, and garrulous patrons of art galleries.

(And, I thought, by now *those* theaters have been demolished, the streets replaced by boulevards, and the patrons sent to a happier world.)

For the first time during the years I'd worked on the project, I had a genuine sense of looking into another century.

Beyond the philosophical considerations of my achievement, I saw a chance to pick up some cash, and do a public relations coup while I was at it. "Paul," I asked, "how would you like to play in the U. S. Open?"

"I never heard of it," he said. "Will Staunton be there?"

I hesitated. "No," I said. "I don't think so."

"Pity."

"There's a lot of money to be made, though. It'd be easy for you."

Power hummed in the mainframe. "No," he said. "Thank you anyway."

"I'd be happy to take care of the details." I was beginning to realize that in the course of analyzing Morphy's chess I had given insufficient thought to his character.

"Playing for money is crass," he said.

"But you've done it all your life. You've competed for stakes and cash prizes."

"Only during the last two years," he said, not entirely without heat. "And only when it was necessary to get the match I wanted. Even then I usually found a way to return the money. No, only the depraved or the desperate play chess for profit."

So Paul saved me from needless depravity. Worse, he was still untested, which meant that I had to come up with $600 plus expenses to find out if he could play like Morphy. I brought in Emma Monroe, the Pennsylvania state champion, for a six-game weekend match. "Who?" asked Paul. "Where's Staunton? Give me Staunton, and then I'll be happy to take on some of these other people."

"Do it for me," I said. "Meanwhile, I'll do what I can."

The game board was tied directly into the computer so Paul could move his pieces and track his opponent's responses.

Emma had White for game one. She opened with the English, and got to about the eighth move before Paul blew things apart. She staggered along for a while, drinking coffee furiously and alternately glaring at me and the computer. Then she resigned.

In the games that followed, things continued downhill for her.

Paul opened files and diagonals effortlessly and crushed her with careless ease. The stunned champion took her losses with grace, but anger blazed in her eyes. "I'd like to come back," she said. "No charge."

"Of course."

"You didn't get your money's worth. Next time will be different."

"I'm sure he caught you at a bad time." I admired her. She reminded me of Bryan.

Sunday evening, as she was driving away, I congratulated Paul on his play.

"She lacks imagination," he said.

"Yes."

"Have we heard yet from Staunton?"

Paul grew moody. For long periods of time he sat coiled within the mainframe, refusing to speak. Sometimes, at night, I woke to Tchaikovsky and Saint-Saens. He began playing the *Danse Macabre* over and over.

One morning, approximately a week after the match, he locked me out of the system and seized the mainframe for about two hours. There was nothing I could do except pace the lab demanding he come to his senses.

Finally, without a word, he returned control to me. But I knew he'd had access to everything in the memory banks. Including Lincoln. Including the fact that he was a construct. That it was more than a hundred years later than he thought it was.

"Why did you do that?" I asked. "The others never tried to take over the unit."

"I suspect," Paul said, "that they're satisfied with what they are." The voice was strained. Had it belonged to a human being, I would have thought I detected fear,

"And you're not?"

Silence.

"Paul, you've wrecked the experiment."

"I'm sorry."

"It doesn't matter. This whole thing was misconceived from the beginning."

"I never got to play Staunton, did I?"

"No, Paul."

"You're right." His voice sounded very far away. "It was an error. By the way, Harold, I have some bad news for you." He gave my name a peculiar emphasis.

"What's that?"

"You don't really exist, you know. Nor this computer. Nor tomorrow. You are as you think I am: a set of magnetic pulses and nothing more. It is you who are the experiment."

I started to laugh, but the sound bounced around the room. It was a ridiculous notion. The threadbare furniture was, God knew, solid enough. And the work table. And the mainframe.

"Probably," he continued, "I've invalidated the experiment by telling you."

I held onto the tabletop.

And he laughed.

"I'm sorry," I said.

"It's all right. But you might want to give some serious thought to the ethics of what you're doing."

"I'm sorry."

"You said that. Your project won't work, you know. The information is simply not there. Alexander's dead."

"Except chessplayers. Paul, are you an accurate reproduction of– the other one?"

"I don't know much about him." My insides were churning. "I mean, I understand about me, but I can't be sure about him."

"Is there anything I can do to make things easier?"

I heard that electronic laugh again. "Don't pull the plug."

"I never do."

"Good. And there's one other thing."

"What's that?"

"Get me the match with Staunton."

It was the least I could do. (Bryan would have known how to handle the reluctant Englishman, would simply have announced he was dead, and declared himself champion, thinking no more about the matter. I considered mixing the blend a little, giving Paul some of Bryan's fire; but although I believed I could do it, the result would have been an artificial intelligence that was no longer a true Paul Morphy.)

The problem was, Howard Staunton wasn't the sort of person you wanted around. If you read his books, or the column that ran thirty years in the *Illustrated London News*, you discover he is arrogant and overbearing and generally obnoxious. He did not hesitate to let his readers know he thought them blockheads. Ditto for his opponents.

He listened to no one. On the rare occasions when someone beat him, he made excuses. Usually cited weariness. He made it clear that, given a good night's sleep, he could take anybody.

Curiously, despite his aggressive personality, his chess banked on defense. He specialized in building impregnable positions, then either wore an opponent down, or awaited a blunder.

The prospect of him and Morphy in the same memory bank was disquieting. But I plunged ahead. I established him in 1847 London, when he was at the peak of his career, which was well before anyone had heard of Paul. On a bitter, hard, bright day in January, I finished. But before I loaded him, I asked Paul if he were sure. He was absorbed in Beethoven's *Missa Solemni.*

"Yes," he said, "of course."

"But why?" I asked him. "It's a long time ago."

"He kept promising a match, and kept insulting me. Every time I got close to him, he ran. Always found a reason to dodge."

"The historical Morphy," I said, "had reason to hate him. You seem to feel the same way."

"I would be happy to destroy him."

"Why?" I asked again. "Why is it so important?"

"Because I was the very best in the world, an ordinary man with a supreme gift! And I wasted it. My God, Harold, I threw it away." He lapsed into silence. Then, finally: "Do you know why?"

"Yes," I said. "I know."

"Staunton laughed at me," he continued, breathless, as if I'd said nothing. "He laughed at me, ridiculed me in the journals, drove me out of Europe."

"You? That was someone else. It was a human being, and it happened in the nineteenth century. You're a simulation, Paul. A construct. A bit of software."

"Am I?"

And so, with supreme reluctance, I gave Howard Staunton a set of synapses, perhaps awareness, maybe life.

"I understand," I said to Staunton, "that you are the finest chess-player in the world."

"I should not go so far," he said. "But I must confess to a facility for the game." I had provided Staunton with the voice of a local weatherman, added a British accent, and it seemed to fit perfectly.

"I wonder if I could interest you in a brief match? I have a friend who believes himself skilled, but who stands in need of some instruction in humility."

Staunton took a moment to respond. "When and at what stake, sir?"

"Perhaps," I said, "you would consider ten games, starting this evening, at a hundred pounds sterling. Winner take all." (Was that an appropriate amount? I hadn't thought to research that aspect of the negotiations.)

"What is your friend's name?" He sounded bored.

"Morphy."

"Doubtless he will wish odds of knight and move?"

"I think he would be willing to play you even, sir."

"I see." Another pause. "He thinks rather highly of himself."

"Yes. He needs to confront reality."

"Indeed. I would be happy to oblige."

"Very good," I said. "Perhaps we can get started immediately?"

Staunton saw no reason to delay. I set up the board and pieces and activated Paul.

We had discussed how he was to behave. Paul had been, during his brief career, a perfect gentleman, never glared at an opponent, didn't light up when he spotted a blunder, never gloated, never taunted. He pronounced himself pleased to meet Mr. Staunton, and talked as if there were no history between them. For Staunton, of course, there was no history.

The Englishman was convivial, almost garrulous, during the introductions. Paul said little. His voice was cold and flat. But his opponent seemed not to notice.

The game was not timed. Chess clocks were a later invention. But there was no need. Once Paul, playing White, pushed his king pawn forward, things went quickly.

Staunton defended with Philidor's, a system well-suited to anyone who likes to play defense. It was difficult to storm, but generally led to cramped positions for Black. I'd expected Paul to simply run his opponent out of the game, but it didn't happen. The Englishman built a position which looked impregnable, and he even established a strong knight outpost in the center of Paul's lines. I hadn't considered the possibility that Paul might lose.

But the end came with seductive suddenness. Staunton had castled behind a solid screen of pawns. The king's knight kept watch over the formation. But a rook swept in and took off the knight, both bishops plowed into the cluster, and the wheels came off. In a voice I could hardly hear, Staunton announced his resignation. "Very good," he said. "You play quite well for your station, Mr. Morphy. I shall take you seriously next time."

"Thank you," said Paul. "It was an honor. Shall we continue in the morning?"

"I wish I could oblige," Staunton replied. "Unfortunately, my dear young fellow, I'm rather busy just now. Working hard on my treatise."

"Really?" I said.

"Yes. As I think I explained to Dr. Case, I'm editing a collection of medieval poetry, and that must take precedence. I'm afraid I was distracted today, thinking about Chaucer, you see. Took my mind off the game and failed to give our young friend adequate competition. I *do* apologize, Mr. Morphy."

"We have nine more to play," said Paul.

"Of course. And we will, never worry about that. And I'll try to demonstrate more effectively than I did this evening why an attack like the one you showed me just now is really rather premature. I'll get back to you as quickly as I can."

He shut himself down.

Paul's operational lamps went scarlet. "He's doing it to me again," he said.

"No, Paul. It's over. You've beaten him."

"It *isn't* over, Harold. Listen, it happened this way in London, too. We played a couple of consultation games. But everyone knew it was him against me. I won those games. But it meant nothing. I need to beat him beyond any question of doubt, to hear him admit the difference between us."

I stared at the lamps. "Okay," I said reluctantly. "I'll talk to him."

William Jennings Bryan was a better man than either of these fool chessplayers. Little men like Staunton never bothered him. And he would never have run from a Morphy. He could not have won. *He never won.* But that's why he was magnificent. He never won, and he never compromised.

Several days passed before Staunton would even respond. And when he finally did, it was only to protest. "I'd really like to be of assistance. But surely *you*, Dr. Case, recognize the priorities of these things. How can I, in good conscience, put my work aside to play a *game*?"

"Surely the match would not take that much of your time, sir."

"Of course not. But I would be unable to concentrate on it. That would be unfair to all involved. Please try to explain to Mr. Morphy."

"Mr. Staunton, you agreed to a match."

"And I *shall* play it. Somehow. In the meantime, you may inform your associate that I shall endeavor to compensate his patience by providing some personal instruction on those aspects of his game which, I'm sorry to say, need attention. He's quite talented, you know. With proper guidance, he should be able to compete reasonably well in the front rank of European players."

"Mr. Staunton–"

His mode lamp went out, and I was alone.

After that, Paul began refusing to talk to me. And night after night I drifted to sleep among the bleakest, darkest landscapes of Bach, DeBussy, and Schoenberg.

I'd made a mistake reconstructing Staunton. I should have gone for Freud. Why wasn't either of them more like Bryan? And while Paul's gloomy symphonies echoed through the house, the name that was on my lips was Bryan.

Bryan, Bryan, Bryan.

I couldn't infuse Paul's character with a generous helping of the old crusader without losing the Morphy persona. But there was another possibility.

Historians of the latter half of the nineteenth century are in and out all the time now to talk to Paul. Usually, they want to check some detail of daily life in the South, or perhaps gain an insight into the perspective of a man who lived through it all.

Other projects, based on my results, are underway. One researcher in Los Angeles claims to have used Napoleon's tactics to reconstruct his psyche. And a team in Seattle is working on Caesar.

In the meantime, Paul seems quite happy. There is a problem, though. Morphy would like to give up chess, just as he did once before. But challenges come from around the world, and Staunton/Bryan continues to press him for "one more game," hurling magnificent denunciations across the lab when Paul is slow to comply. Paul has long since become bored with the Staunton games.

Bryan has done all I could have asked, but Howard Staunton, unfortunately, just can't hold up his end.

Nothing Ever Happens In Rock City

We come now to the unreliable narrator. The person who's present at a world-shaking event but has no clue what's going on. Sometimes it isn't his fault. The guy who prepared Socrates' fatal drink (who was probably, say, a roofer in his daytime job) very likely went home afterward to a meal with his family, explaining that yes, they had to do away with that guy who was wandering around telling kids there were no gods on Olympus. Hated to do it, but you have to think in terms of family values.

The Romans did so many crucifixions that the guys who nailed Jesus to the cross and stood at the apex of history while doing so would have seen nothing out of the ordinary in their actions. I wonder who among Galileo's acquaintances—other than the Jesuits—had any idea of the significance of those moons? Did Columbus's tailor have any idea what the old guy was up to? Who served whiskey to Grant? Was there another traveler on the train who handed that envelope to Lincoln?

※

Sorry I'm late tonight, Peg. Had to make a trip up to the observatory at closing time. They're having some kind of party up there and they needed a quick delivery. Ordinarily I would of sent Harry but Virginia hasn't been feeling good so I told him to go home and I went up myself.

No, not much was happening up there. They all seemed pretty loud, but other than that it wasn't very much. Nothing much ever happens in Rock City.

Oh, yeah, Jamie's home. Got his degree but no job. Bill tells me he's decided to become a lawyer. He wants to send him to one of those eastern schools but he's not really convinced that Jamie's serious. You know how that's been going. Me, I think it'd be just as well. We got enough lawyers around here as it is.

What else? I heard today that Doris is expecting again. Now there's a woman doesn't know when to quit. Frank said he's been trying to talk her into getting her tubes tied. But she's kind of skittish. Women are like that, I guess.

No offense.

Yeah, it was a pretty good day. We moved a lot of the malt. That new stuff I thought we'd never get rid of. There was a family get-together over at Clyde's. You know how they are. Must be sixty, seventy people over there for the weekend. All Germans. Putting it down by the barrel.

Jake was in today. They're getting complaints about underage kids again. I told him it ain't happening in our place. And it ain't. We're careful about that. Don't allow it. Not only because it ain't legal, either. I told him, it's not right for kids to be drinking and they can count on us to do what we can.

We had people in and out all day today. We sold as much stuff off the whiskey aisle as we did all week. We won't have any trouble making the mortgage this month.

What else? Nothing I can think of. This is a quiet town. Janet was in. Ticketed somebody doing ninety on the state road. Took his license, she said. Guy's wife had to drive him home. I'd've liked to of been there.

She told me there was a murder over in Castle County. I'm not sure about the details. Another one of those things where somebody's boy friend got tired of a crying kid. That ought to be death penalty. Automatic.

What's that? What was going on at the observatory?

I don't know. They had some VIP's visiting. We sold a couple bottles of rum to one of them this morning. Old guy, gray hair, stooped, kind of slow. Looked like he was always thinking about something else. Talked funny too. You know, foreign. Maybe Brit. Aussie. Something like that.

They're doing some kind of convention up there. Some of them are staying over at the hotel, according to Hap. Anyhow, we get this call about a quarter to nine, you know, just before we lock the doors. It's Harvey. They want eight bottles of our best champagne. Cold. Can we deliver?

Harvey told me once they always keep a bottle in the refrigerator up there. But with all these people in town I guess one bottle wasn't enough.

Well, to start with, we don't have eight bottles of our best champagne on ice. Or off. I mean how much of that stuff do we sell? But sure, I tell him. I'll bring it up as soon as we close.

I mean, you know Harvey. He won't know the difference. And I can hear all this noise in the background. The paper said they were supposed to be doing some kind of business meeting but all I can hear is screaming and laughing. And I swear somebody was shooting off a noisemaker.

Oh, by the way, did I tell you Ag was by today? She wants to get together for a little pinochle next week. I figure Sunday works pretty good. When you get a chance, give her a call, okay?

And Morrie's moping around. He won't talk about it but I guess Mary's ditched him again. You think he'd get tired taking all that from that crazy woman. Don't know what he wants. Ain't happy when he's with her and miserable when he isn't.

Oh, here's something you'll be interested in. Axel dropped a bottle of chianti today. I mean it went off in the back of the store like an explosion. I felt sorry for him except that it made a hell of a mess. He's getting more wobbly every day. I'm not sure we should be selling him anything now. At his age. But I don't have the heart to stop him. I've thought about talking to Janet. But that only puts it on her. I don't know what I'm going to do about that. Eventually I guess I'll have to do *something*.

What about the observatory? Oh yeah. Well, there's really nothing to tell. I took some Hebert's and some Coela Valley. Four of each. Packed 'em in ice and put 'em in the cooler.

So when I get there all these lights are on inside and people are yelling and carrying on. I never saw anything like it. It was like they'd already been into something. I mean Harvey and his friends are *not* people who know how to have a good time. But this other crew—

Anyway Harvey said thanks and I wiped his card and he said do I want to stay a while? I mean they were into the bubbly before I could set it down.

So I say no thanks I have to drive back down the mountain and the last thing I need is a couple drinks. But I ask what's all the fuss and he takes me over to a computer screen which has graphics, big spikes and cones and God knows what else, all over it, but you can't begin to tell what it is, and he says *Look at that.*

I look and I don't see nothing except spikes and cones. So then he shows me how one pattern repeats itself. He says how it's one-point-something seconds long and it shows up three or four different places on the screen. Then he brings up another series and we do the same thing again. None of it means anything, as far as I can see.

So Harvey sees I'm not very impressed and he tells me we've got neighbors. He mentions someplace I never heard of. Al-Car or Al-Chop or something like that. He says it like it's a big deal. And then it dawns on me what he's talking about, that they've found the signal they're always looking for.

"How far away are they?" I ask.

He laughs again and says, "A long way."

"So I say how far's that?"

"Mack," he tells me, "you wouldn't want to walk it."

For a minute I wonder if the people on the other end are going to come this way but he says no that could never happen. Don't worry. Ha ha ha.

Well, I say, tell them hello for me. Ha ha. And he offers me a three buck tip, which was kind of cheap considering how late it was and that I had to drive up and down that goofy road. I mean, I'm not going to take his money anyway. But three bucks?

But that's why I was late.

Ran into Clay outside town, by the way. He was over at Howie's getting his speed trap set up. Says he picks off a few every Friday. Says he had to go over to Ham's place earlier because Ham was screaming at Dora again. I used to think she would pack up and leave one of these days but I guess not.

Yeah.

Anyway, that's why I was late. I'm sorry it upset you. I'll call next time, if you want. But you don't need to worry. I mean, nothing ever happens in Rock City.

PART TWO
DEEP SPACE

The Mission

I'm a transplanted Yankee living in the deep south. As such, I've gotten used to listening to jibes aimed at Northerners. Keep the roads safe: Teach a Yankee to drive. How many Yankees does it take to screw in a lightbulb? (The answers sometimes go as high as eight.) But when 9/11 came, the joking stopped. Signs appeared around town: "We're all New Yorkers."

It's impossible to live in this part of the world without becoming caught up in the culture. It's somehow more casual, more personal, and at the same time, more intense than any place else I've been. I've been honored with the Phoenix Award, which is reserved to Southern writers. With this sort of background, I was a natural candidate to make a contribution to Crossroads, *an anthology of "Tales of the Southern Literary Fantastic." When Bret Cox and Andy Duncan approached me to do a southern science fiction story, I said sure without a second thought.*

But eventually the second thought showed up. What the devil was a southern SF story? Robots in Louisiana? Intelligent hurricanes in New Orleans? I suppose I could have asked, but it felt like a dumb question.

Faulkner and Cather and other southern titans are rife with a sense of something priceless that has gone missing. A yearning for a lost world. For what might have been. One finds it even in the title of Gone With the Wind.

For the science fiction world, and probably the world at large, what is there of exquisite value that has gotten lost?

Oh, yes. . . .

※

They were looking down on a dust storm racing across the Martian surface when the transmission came in. "Venture, *we are losing control of the situation here. The plague is everywhere. I don't know how much longer we can keep the station open. Abort and return."*

Status lamps blinked in the darkened cockpit. Alice looked at him, her eyes sad, but for a long time nobody said anything.

"Tommy." The Earthside voice lost its impersonal tone. *"We'll try to stay with this—"* *And the transmission exploded in a burst of static.*

Tommy glanced at the others. "What do you think?" he asked.

Frank stared at the radio. "Make the landing. We can't go back without making the landing."

Alice nodded. "Yes." Her eyes gleamed in the light thrown off by the instruments. "Do it."

Tommy took a deep breath. Below them the storm swirled across the lower latitudes.

"It came in over there, over the woods." Uncle Harold pointed east. "Just off to the left of Harpie's place. And it came right past where we're standing now and touched ground maybe *there*, near the old hangar. It kept going, of course, because it was hell-bent, fastest thing I ever saw, all lit up.

"You never saw an airplane, I guess, did you? They pulled them all out of here during the early days of the plague. Don't know where they sent them. North, I guess, where it wasn't so bad at first. Well, they're really something, especially at night. And they used to come in here all the time. It was a rocket, and they kept it up on the station. In orbit, and when the Mars mission came back and the station was empty, it was the only way they could get home. Somebody'd left it for them."

"Because," said Tommy, "everything was shut down by then."

"That's right. The Death had been running eight months and there just wasn't nobody left."

Tommy looked the length of the old runway, tracing the glide path from the woods on the east past Harpie's, past the crumbling hangars and maintenance buildings that everybody said were haunted, past the place where they sat their horses. On into the night. The sky was cold and damp and threatening.

"It was a night like this," Uncle Harold said. "Chilled. Rain just beginning to fall."

He imagined it coming in, full of light, the three astronauts inside, feeling for the ground like they weren't sure it was there.

"Why'd they come here to land, Uncle Harold?" Tommy had

heard bits and pieces of the story before, how it had come to Warner-Robbins, and how people had ridden out from the town and the astronauts had gotten out and just walked away and nobody ever saw them again. But it had never meant much to him until he actually came to live in Warner-Robbins a few days before. After his mother died. And came out here to see the place where the lander came down.

"Nobody really knows, Tommy," said Uncle Harold. "I mean, they just rolled to a stop. Well, they didn't exactly *roll*. They sort of bounced up and down a lot and busted a wing and they finally swung around and tipped over."

"Did it catch fire?"

"No. It just laid out there in the dark like a big dead bird."

"And the astronauts–?"

"Well, like I said, they got out, the three of them–"

"What happened to the fourth? Mrs. Taylor said there were four on the mission."

"That's what the books say, but only three got out. And they walked off north. Toward Macon."

"Macon's a long way. Why'd you let them do it?"

"I didn't let them do it, Tommy. They pretty much done it on their own. Horace Kittern and Mack Willoughby, they rode after them. Asked whether they was hurt. Whether they could do anything. But the astronauts, they never slowed down, just waved and said everything was fine. Said they'd be back later for the lander. I thought at the time that maybe they were afraid of us. Afraid we were infected."

"And they really never came back?"

"Nope. Never seen 'em again."

"How about up in Macon?"

"Wasn't nobody *in* Macon by then. Macon went early."

"The whole town?"

"Far as we know."

Tommy imagined them walking into the night. Into the rain.

Uncle Harold was riding Montie. The horse was cold. It breathed out a cloud of frost and he patted the animal's flank. "Tommy, I wasn't as old as you at the time. Wasn't nothin' I could do. Or anybody else."

Tommy shifted his weight. Poke stirred under him, and a cold wind blew down out of the trees. Across the old airfield. It began to rain. "What happened to the lander?" he asked.

Harold turned Montie around. Started for home. "What

happened to the lander?" he said, as if the question puzzled him. "Let's go back to the house and I'll show you."

He was glad to get into the barn and out of the wind. They unsaddled the horses, gave them water, and closed them up in their stalls. Then Uncle Harold picked up the lantern and led him to the back door where they kept the equipment. "There." He pointed to a plow.

"And *there*." A spade.

"And here." A yoke for the team.

"And over here." Braces for the wagon. "We used some of the Teflon to wire the main house. For insulation."

Tommy didn't understand at first. And Uncle Harold kept right on going. "You can still see the tiles. They're from the outside of the lander. We used them to line the smelter down at Jimmy's. And the town freezer that used to be over at Bobby Joe's place but that we moved to Hazlett's after Bobby Joe died. They were put on the outside of refrigerators from one end of town to the other. Saved energy at a time when we hardly had any.

"They salvaged the computers and kept them going for a while, as long as somebody thought they'd be useful. Turned out they didn't really need computers anymore.

"*We* took the radios. The kids. I got one, but it wasn't no use because there wasn't anything on it except an Atlanta station where they just kept playing the same music and asking whether there was anybody out there until we got into January and I guess it got too cold. They stopped broadcasting and we never heard from them again.

"One of the fuel pumps runs the water system at your Uncle Tim's. They took something off the wings that helped keep the town generators going for a while. And the chairs. They're scattered around. Pete Baydecker's got one. It's the most comfortable chair I've ever sat in—" He seemed to run down, like a clock that needed to be wound.

"You just took it *apart?*" Tommy asked. "And used it to make stuff?" He remembered the legend, recalled vividly in that moment Mrs. Taylor's description of what it must have been like as the astronauts, three Americans and a Russian, had neared Mars, and they heard the news, that a virus had broken loose at home, was killing everyone.

"And eventually their radios must have gone quiet." She had said the words and Tommy had imagined himself with them out in the cold dark night between the worlds, a million miles from the ground.

"You have to understand what it was like then," Uncle Harold was saying. He opened the door that would take them across to the house. "We were caught with no power, except what we could produce ourselves. One night the lights and the TV's just went out. They came back on long enough for us to go to bed. But it got cold during the night and we all had to go down and sleep by the fire.

"What ran the lights also ran the tractors and the milking machines and the combines. And suddenly none of it was there anymore. They had all that equipment but they didn't have gas to make it run."

"You could have gotten other people to help you."

Uncle Harold shook his head. "The plague was everywhere. There was nowhere to go. Nobody to help. People were scared to leave town. You never seen anything like the way people behaved when a stranger came up the road. They were bad times. We were lucky to survive."

He turned the lantern out, signaling that it was time to go into the house. Candles burned brightly in the windows. But Tommy didn't move. "You took everything? And melted it down?"

"I didn't. The town did. Everything we had went, Tommy. The pickups and the cars that nobody had any use for anymore, and the tractors, and the lander. We needed raw materials to keep alive. I can tell you, Tommy, it was a near thing. We had our hands full just getting through the winter. People died. Half of Warner-Robbins died. Not from the plague. Thank God it never came here. But people died from exposure and sheer exhaustion. We'd forgotten how to live without supermarkets and electricity. But we survived.

"For six years we even managed to light the town. I have to tell you, the people here saw the lander as a God-given miracle."

Tommy felt his heart beat.

"Frank and Alice must know what happened." Uncle Harold sounded guilty. Sounded as if he knew he'd done something wrong.

Tommy looked back at his footprints in the soft earth, watched the rain pooling in them. "Frank doesn't know that," he said. His voice felt strange. "It wasn't right."

"It's what we had to do."

"And Alice doesn't know it either."

Frank and Alice had befriended him after he arrived last week. After Mom died, Tommy had locked onto the lander as if it were part of the world he'd left behind. As if it were connected with his mother and the life over in Milledgeville, which hadn't been as lucky as

Warner-Robbins. And Uncle Harold had seen an opportunity to distract him, had talked to him about the Mars mission, had shown him pictures of the *Columbia*, photographs of it under construction and later docked to the space station, and artists' drawings of it in Martian skies. He'd asked whether the astronauts had landed on Mars.

Nobody knew.

He was aware of that, of course, but he asked the question anyway. It was required, somehow. Part of the ceremony. *"Did they ever get to the ground?"* It seemed not right that they had gone all the way out there and not gotten down to the surface. So he and Alice and Frank had invented their game, had taken the *Columbia* to Mars, listened to the terrible news, orbited the planet, and landed.

They'd walked across the red sands and sometimes they found turtles and sometimes lizards and once they even found tall redskinned natives with saucer eyes who'd chased them while they yelped and ran for their lives.

"Frank and Alice," said Harold, "probably never asked about the lander. It's no secret that it kept us all going. There's not a house or a farm that doesn't have a piece of it out in its barn, or holding its windows together, or keeping its furnace running. You want the lander, son? It's all around you."

They were racing above the southern hemisphere, gazing down on an ocher desert that stretched out forever when Tom raised the question. "Yeah," said Frank. "I knew that."

Mars vanished, and Tommy looked with dismay at his copilot.

"Sure, Tommy. Everybody here knows. Right, Alice? We've got some pieces of it in our kitchen. Or is it the furnace? I forget."

They were in the living room at Alice's house and suddenly Tommy could smell the oil lamps. Without moving, Alice pointed to a cushion on the sofa. It was old and worn and black, but it was soft like leather except that it *wasn't* leather. "*That* came out of the lander," she said. "My ma wants to toss it because she says it doesn't look right. But Pa won't hear of it."

Tommy stared at them. "You knew? All this time you knew what they did?"

"What's the big deal?" Frank asked. "It's no secret. *Everybody* knows."

"They should have kept it," said Tommy. "They should have taken care of it."

"It was out on the plain." Alice was getting annoyed. "It would have rusted away. What difference does it make?"

And Tommy couldn't explain. They should have kept it because one day we'll be going back. Because it was part of something important and you don't just tear things like that apart to make hoes and rakes. Because they didn't know whether the astronauts would come back or not and suppose they had?

Alice was the tallest of the three. She had a dark complexion and dark eyes and a quick smile. And she tried to tell him he was making too much of it, that what else would you do with a wreck sitting in the middle of the runway? That they just flat out needed the metal.

They didn't play the Mars game anymore after that. And a couple of days later Alice tried to kiss him but he didn't let her.

The freeze came early. Tommy helped with the horses, chopped firewood, brought in water, and occasionally took the wagon over to Rob's feed store to pick up supplies.

They had a few books in the house, some novels that he read over and over, *David Copperfield* and *Northanger Abbey* and one that he didn't understand about the end of the Civil War. There was a history of the United States, which everybody pretended still existed out there somewhere, and a Bible, a book on needlecraft that had belonged to Aunt Emma, and the book that Tommy especially liked, a big volume called *Galaxies*, with lots of pictures.

They'd had only a Bible at his mother's house and he hadn't even realized there were other books until Uncle Harold had come after Ma's death and brought him here.

He understood that the galaxies were very far, and that the *Columbia* could never have reached them. But he liked to imagine going out to them anyhow, taking a right turn at Mars, and snuggling warm and happy in the cockpit while he watched the stars grow in number and size.

Columbia is still up there. Docked at the station. And on nights when it's clear, you can see it, a bright light in the south that never moves, that keeps its place while the stars race past.

Out of reach now. Forever.

We should have saved the lander.

He rode out on Poke one night close to Christmas, back to the place where he'd sat with Uncle Harold. It was unseasonably warm, the stars were bright, and there was no moon in the sky. The station sparkled in its accustomed place, above the Fargo Road.

Uncle Harold didn't like him riding out here alone after dark. Minutes after he'd left, he heard the outside kitchen door slam and knew his uncle had missed him, knew he'd follow pretty soon.

He looked back toward the east and watched the lander drop slowly out of the sky, brighter than any star. Brighter even than the station. It had four lights, one on each wingtip, one on its belly, and one atop the tail. He didn't really know whether that had been so, and nobody he'd asked knew either. But it didn't matter. That was the way he imagined it, so it had become the only truth there was.

It came in slow and the lights were visible the whole time. A few people rode out of town to see what was happening. He could hear them talking and asking one another whether help was coming at last. From the government.

The lander dropped down through the night, and the blaze of its lights silhouetted Uncle Harold, riding easy on Monty. Its engines roared and the wings waggled slightly as a gust of wind hit them. The airstrip lay open and clear before the descending spacecraft.

Tommy inched up in his saddle so he could see better. Poke dug at a piece of sod with his front hoof.

It touched down and rolled along the runway, maybe jouncing a bit because it was coming too fast and braking too hard.

The riders watched it slow and tip over and stop. For a long time nothing happened. A few of the horsemen approached and hatches popped open. The lights went off, first the ones on the wingtips, and then the others. Three astronauts climbed out and stood looking around.

"You okay, Tommy?" Uncle Harold was still riding slow.

There were tears in the boy's eyes. "You shouldn't have taken it apart," he said.

His uncle came up alongside him, clamped a big hand down on his shoulder, and squeezed. "Tommy, it's time to let it go."

Tommy just sat his horse.

Uncle Harold nodded. "You warm enough, son?"

"You think they did the right thing. That makes you just as bad."

"Why is it so important? That the lander was broken up?"

"Because of where it's been. Because maybe we could have gone back one day. Because we *need* it." Tommy was trying to keep his voice level, to keep the strangled sounds out of it.

"Tommy." Harold held out a kerchief, and waited while the boy took it and blew his nose and wiped his eyes. "Tommy, people here did what they had to. I'm not saying we wouldn't have made it otherwise, but the rest of the world was dead, as far as we knew. Everything that would give us an edge, we had to use."

"Not the lander. That's what takes us back."

Harold looked up at the sky. At the station. "No," he said, "it's not the lander. We can make a new one when the time comes. What we have to have, what we absolutely cannot do without, is *you*. And Alice. And Frank." He pulled his collar up around his neck. The temperature was starting to drop. "We survived, boy. *That's* what matters. First things first."

Tommy was silent.

"We *will* go back. Maybe *you* will. But you've got to be *alive* to do it."

"No. It's not going to happen."

Uncle Harold pulled his scarf up around his face. His gaze moved past Tommy and fastened on the house. They could see the glow of the oil lamp in the living room. He tugged gently on Tommy's reins and started back. Tommy pressed Poke's flank and followed.

They were both looking at the sky. "Which one's Mars?" Harold asked.

Tommy showed him.

"Duller than I thought," he said.

Poke picked up the pace and they trotted at a leisurely clip beneath the stars.

Melville On Iapetus

And that brings us to still another story written around a statue.

I've had a pretty good time creating a pseudo-history of the early years of interstellar exploration as experienced by Priscilla Hutchins and the Academy. "Melville on Iapetus" was written ten years before Hutch's first appearance. But it's more or less where she got her start. I should add that this version is substantially revised from the version that appeared in Asimov's *twenty years ago, but it retains the spirit and the story line of the original.*

Much of the action in the Academy universe plays out of a discovery made late in the twenty-first century: An automated probe of the Saturnian system has seen what appears to be a monolith on the frozen plains of Iapetus, the outermost of that planet's big moons. A second probe confirms the sighting, and a manned mission is dispatched.

Readers of The Engines of God *will pick up echoes from that novel's prologue. In fact, this story made it onto Bob Eggleton's exquisite cover for that book. Terri is an early incarnation of Hutch, and the Iapetus experience ultimately went front and center in the novel.*

The inspiration for the narrative is poem xxii in A. E. Housman's A Shropshire Lad. *The poet is standing on the street as a group of soldiers march by. Off to the Boer War, I assume. Housman doesn't say, and it doesn't matter. A single soldier turns his head and our eyes lock with his. And we know the world's so big a place "from sky to sky" that we could never have met before. But nevertheless, we think, and Housman thinks, "Soldier, I wish you well."*

A magnificent moment. It inspired "Iapetus," and ultimately became the heart of the entire series of Academy novels. I like to think Housman and Melville would have approved.

*

The thing was carved of rock and covered with ice. It stood serenely on that bleak, snow-covered plain, a nightmare figure of curving claws, surreal eyes, and lean fluidity. The lips were parted, rounded, almost sexual. I wasn't sure why it was so disquieting. It was more than simply the talons, or the disproportionately long lower limbs. It was more even than the suggestion of philosophical ferocity stamped on those crystalline features. There was something–*terrifying*–bound up in the tension between its suggestive geometry and the wide plain on which it stood.

It was scratched and clawed by micrometeors, the driving dust between the moons, but no serious damage had resulted.

We stood before it, staring.

The wings were half-folded. Ray Morgan, on my right, used the toe of his boot to dig small notches in the orange-tinted snow.

The creature's blind eyes were aimed at Saturn, frozen low in the hostile sky by its own relentless gravity.

Static crackled in my receiver. *"Nice view of the horizon, Terri."* It was Smitty in the command module, somewhere overhead. I mumbled an apology: my primary function at that moment was to keep the camera on-target. *"Jay,"* Smitty continued, *"how's it look?"*

The figure was set on a block about a third its own height. Steinitz approached it, his big boots pushing into the granular stuff underfoot, which was more like sand than snow. His shoulders were on a line with the top of the base. "Looks like granite," he said. "There's something written here." He switched on his lamp. The light penetrated the reddish-brown ice, and crept up into the lower body.

The inscription hadn't been visible to the probes, one of which lay in the snow forty meters behind us.

"It's female," said Morgan.

Yes, I thought, not knowing precisely how I knew. Some delicacy of line perhaps, or subtlety of expression. Certainly, no anatomical clues were apparent through the plain garment covering the trunk. Yet it was most decidedly female: it reached out to Steinitz, arms open, legs braced, weight slightly forward. "It reminds me," Morgan continued, "of my wife."

That almost broke the mood. Steinitz laughed, and Cathie Chung giggled over the link. Jennifer had been pensive, sullen, with eyes that were lovely only by candlelight. She'd never really been Morgan's wife, other than by some mad informal agreement, but they'd maintained the facade at her insistence, and she'd thereby made herself ridiculous. During that last year before departure, when we were gradually reducing our world to the five people who would make the four-and-a-half year flight, Jennifer, always an outsider, had hung on. She really loved him, apparently, and she knew that the mission was too long, that their relationship, such as it was, could not survive it. So she did what she could to persuade him to abandon the project. To find a quiet job and settle down with her in Tampa. Or wherever.

Toward the end, as she grew desperate, she'd spoken to none of us. With Morgan's encouragement, the men joked about her. It was odd: usually in such a situation, the women in a group would have been protective. But Chung and I only stood aside and watched. I suspect we were embarrassed that she didn't just tell him to take a hike.

Maybe she did. One day she was simply no longer there.

Morgan hadn't mentioned her on the long flight out. At least not to me. But he was right. Somehow the thing on the plain did suggest her. Not physically, of course. It resembled no human woman. But it was, I thought, so terribly alone.

"You getting a good look at the inscription?" asked Smitty.

"Yeah. . . ." Steinitz waved at me and I went close with the camera. Three lines of sharp, white characters that might almost have been Cyrillic were stenciled within the icy coating. They looked vaguely Russian.

Steinitz's breathing was harsh. He leaned over and peered at the symbols. Touched the artifact with his fingertips. Drew them across the surface as if the object were sacred. He moved his wrist lamp slowly from side to side. The letters brightened, lengthened, shifted.

"Nice piece of optics," I said.

"Yeah. I wonder what it says."

I turned and looked across the wide level plain. We were on Iapetus, one of the moons of Saturn, as remote a place as I ever care to be. It was of course absolutely still. During the time we were there, which was about four days, it was always dark with bright lights in the sky. Over a nearby ridge we could see Saturn and its rings, and some other moons. Iapetus, of course, is well outside the ring system, so you get a magnificent view.

Other than whatever had made the monolith, and occasional falling debris, nothing had moved on this dreary world for a million years. There's no weather, and no seismic activity. Since Iapetus is in tidal lock, even Saturn doesn't move. From our point of view at the foot of the artifact, the big planet was close to the horizon, a brilliant red-orange sphere, flattened at the poles, slightly larger than the Moon in Earth's skies. The rings were tilted toward us, a brilliant panorama of greens and blues, sliced off sharply by the planetary shadow. Immediately beneath it, the landscape had erupted into broken towers of ice and rock, as though tidal forces had run wild.

"*How old is the thing, Jay?*" came the voice from the ship. "*Any ideas?*"

Steinitz walked around the base and stopped on the far side. "No marks in the snow. And the snow's probably untouched for what, thirty, forty thousand years? It's been here a long time, Smitty. But its age? Damned if I know."

My feet were getting cold. The temperature outside the suit was in the area of three hundred below, and the pump was having trouble keeping up with it.

We poked and measured and speculated. But we took no samples. After awhile, Steinitz informed Smitty that we were ready to return to the landing site.

"*Okay, Jay,*" Smitty said. "*We're starting Cathie down.*"

"All right."

"*She'll be there in about forty minutes.*"

"Fine. We'll look for her."

Chung was bringing down our operational center and living quarters, an *Athena*—one of five in the linkup. Its fuel storage tanks had been converted into crew space, and it had just enough propellant to get down. It would serve as our shelter and remain after we left, a new artifact for any other visitor who might wander by. It would, I suspected, one day be named for Steinitz.

Steinitz and Morgan went wandering, looking to see if the sculptor had left anything else in the immediate neighborhood. I was supposed to be helping, but mostly I spent my time just admiring *Jennifer*, as we were now calling her.

Iapetus was in its long night. No sun would be visible for three weeks.

"Long way from home," said Steinitz.

Chung got down without incident, and we spent the next few hours setting up the shelter. When it was done, I was glad to move in out of the cold, get the doors shut behind me and climb out of the suit.

We got the coffee going. There was a big central compartment to serve as command center and dining room. And a place to collapse.

Blankets were stacked on a computer frame. I took one and pulled it over my shoulders.

Designers back home must have thought we'd want a place with a view. The bulkheads were, for the most part, transparent. Privacy wasn't an issue, but something else about not being able to get away from that moonscape, that *figure*, was unsettling.

Steinitz and Morgan were talking in whispers, discussing the composition of the snow. I got up and activated the filters. The plain, and *Jennifer*, vanished. Nobody seemed to mind. I wasn't sure anybody even noticed.

We were all pretty wiped out after a long day. Things started to wind down. Morgan put the artifact on his viewer but I could tell his mind was elsewhere. (I wondered if he was thinking of Jennifer. The real one.) I pushed down into my blanket to keep warm. Steinitz closed his eyes and let his head sink back. His hair had silvered noticeably during the long flight out, and his skin was hard and pocked, not unlike the moons among which he was making his reputation. He'd left Earth with a mild case of asthma, too much weight, and probably too many years. There were some who felt he shouldn't have come at all. But none among the crew. Except maybe Morgan, who didn't like any kind of authority.

"Whoever made it," Chung said, looking at the image over Morgan's shoulder, "knew what they were doing." She was tall, quiet, intense. Dark hair and eyes. She spoke English with a mild Chinese inflection. At twenty-four, she was the youngest crew member and, I suspected, the smartest. A support technician.

"Eventually," Morgan said, "it'll wind up in a museum back home."

"It would look pretty good," I said. I'm no expert on sculpture, but I thought it would have been at home in the Louvre. Except maybe it would have scared the patrons.

Morgan must have read my mind. "How would you like to have something like *that*," he said, "come down on you in a dark alley?"

Chung's eyes flickered, and I felt it too. The remark was uncharacteristic of Morgan, who never admitted to human weakness, other than lust. Certainly not to timidity.

"You think that's what they looked like?" I asked. It wasn't the first time the question had come up. It had been a subject of heated discussion for years. Ever since the first probe had noticed it almost two decades earlier.

"Probably," said Chung.

Steinitz frowned. "Anything's possible. But I'd bet it's purely symbolic. Someone's equivalent of an American eagle. Or a Russian bear."

Morgan shook his head. "It's God," he said.

That was a common notion among academics, although you didn't hear it much on the media. Too many people got upset. Sponsors got boycotted. There were a lot of people who thought the creator of the universe was an old-looking guy with a white beard.

"It might be mythic," said Chung. She smiled and brought her fingertips thoughtfully together in one of those porcelain movements that one associates with pagodas and silk screens. "But I doubt there's any religious connotation."

"Oh." Steinitz had been making toast. He buttered a piece and bit into it. "Why do you say that?"

"Because I have a hard time imagining whatever created that thing beating a drum."

"You're assuming the sculptor was a star-traveler," I said.

"Of course. What else? You think maybe he was from Pluto?"

Steinitz looked across at her, his eyes narrowed. "You're assuming more than that. I take it you wouldn't expect to find religious institutions in an advanced society?"

Chung smiled defensively. Had she offended anyone? Sorry. But of course not. "No," she said. "Taking myths literally is not characteristic of an enlightened civilization."

"So what do you mean when you say it might be mythic?"

"The thing wears clothes. So that lets out the eagle. It's probably a cultural icon, something that represents the sculptor's past in some way, but which she, he, whatever, would not have taken literally. The way we might think of Pegasus, for example. Or Lady Liberty."

"Not God."

"I don't think so, no."

"I'm not so sure," said Steinitz.

"How do you mean?"

"The universe shouldn't exist at all. To function, to hold together, it requires a parade of absurdities. Four-dimensional space. Curved space. Relative time. The gravity settings have to be exactly right. If they were a bit stronger, stars would collapse too quickly. A bit weaker, they wouldn't form at all. I know all this sounds like a back door into theology, and it probably is. But I think any really advanced race would at least keep an open mind on the subject."

"You're saying," said Morgan, "that when we run into an extraterrestrial civilization, they'll be Presbyterians."

Steinitz nodded. "Something like that."

"In a Darwinian universe," said Chung, "any right-thinking Presbyterian can expect to get eaten." She turned in my direction. "What about you, Terri?"

"I don't know," I said. "What's the thing doing in this neighborhood? Talk about a zillion miles from nowhere. It's a marker, maybe. Laying claim to the area. Or maybe Kilroy was here."

The interior of the shelter wasn't particularly comfortable. Stiff plastic chairs. You ate from folding trays. Our individual quarters were the size of broom closets. But, after being outside, it felt warm and cozy.

"Ray," said Steinitz, "were you serious?"

"About God? Sure."

"What do you think the inscription says?"

"It'll turn out to be his name, and the date the sculpture was done."

I laughed. "You want to predict what his name will be?"

"Frank," he said. "A casual sort of deity. Friendly. Informal."

Chung grinned at him. "Frank."

"Good as any."

"I can't tell what he believes," Chung told me later, when we were alone.

"Does it matter?"

"Out here? Where a mistake can get you killed? Sure, I like to know how the people around me think."

"His religious views shouldn't make any difference, Cath."

"They *don't*. I didn't say *what* they think. I said *how*. I like to know who I can trust. Who's serious and who isn't."

We were out taking pictures of Jennifer. Chung posed me beside the thing, set the camera low and angled it up, then joined me and we smiled as the light flashed. "You're not a believer, are you?" I asked.

"I went to a Catholic school," she said.

"And it didn't take?"

"I read too much Melville when I was a kid."

"Oh."

"White whale. Clockwork universe. Nothing personal, but stay out of the way or get run down."

"What made you read *Moby Dick*?"

"Book report in high school."

"Oh."

"I don't think they understood the book. What it was really saying."

I'd tried to read it once. Couldn't get into it. Still don't understand when people cite it to talk about a universe that doesn't give a damn. To me, it's a book about whales. The lesson is that you don't screw around with something a hundred times your size. Nothing subtle about that.

"What's the point," she continued, "of having a compassionate God if he doesn't bail you out when your air supply fails?"

"Is that what Melville says?"

"Pretty much. Get in trouble, you're on your own."

"Ahab."

"Right. Nothing personal. No devils. Just make sure your harness is in place before you launch."

Next on the schedule was a TV show. That would happen as soon as the satellites lined up. We decided where we wanted the cameras, ran lighting tests, discussed what we were going to say, and, with an hour or so to go, informed Smitty we were ready. Steinitz was the senior guy, so he'd be front and center. The plan was that he'd explain everything we'd been able to figure out about the object, which wasn't much. Then he'd invite me and Morgan to talk about whatever we wanted. Our instructions were to do some philosophical stuff, how it felt to be out there with an artifact from another civilization, that sort of thing, and to go slowly on the technical side. After all, they'd told us, everybody already knows you can't read the inscription, and they can see for themselves how big and ugly the damned thing is. I'd been writing down some of the things I planned to say, but Steinitz warned me no reading. Make it look spontaneous. Right. I could see myself standing there with the lights on and my mouth open trying to remember my name.

Steinitz invited Chung to participate. She looked good, and she'd have been an asset, but she was scared too. I wouldn't have believed it. She was always so self-possessed. Anyhow he'd asked me whether I didn't think we could spring it on her, turn a camera her way when she wasn't expecting it, and ask a question, get her on before she had time to get nervous. But I vetoed that idea. If Chung felt the way I did, she might freeze as solid as Jennifer.

"By the way," I told my male colleagues, "don't let's screw up on the name. Mention *Jennifer* and we'll go home to a lawsuit."

We made ourselves as comfortable as we could while we waited for the satellites to get together. We placed the cameras so neither the lander nor the shelter nor the probe was visible. We'd show them toward the end of the program, but we wanted first to establish a sense of complete solitude. We wanted the people at home to feel how absolutely far we were from the Cape. We wanted them to see Saturn, which never moved from its place over the ridge line, and the rings, and the moons currently visible. We wanted them to see the stars the way we did, bright and distant and more numerous that they were in any terrestrial sky. And unimaginably far.

I was sitting there thinking it wasn't going to happen, not with people in their living rooms and kids charging around outside. No one had ever been farther from Earth than we were at that moment, and it just wasn't possible to understand what that meant unless you were standing there with us.

Smitty gave us a ten-minute warning. Moments later he was back. *"Jay."*

Steinitz was standing in front of the image, gazing up at it, trying to imagine, as we all were, who had been there. "Yes, Smitty," he said, "What is it?"

"Heads up. We have an inbound debris field."

"Say again."

"Rocks and dust. Headed your way."

"When?"

"You've got about eight minutes. I'm postponing the program."

"My God, Smitty. Are they going to hit the artifact?"

"I don't know. But they're coming down right about where you're standing."

I have to admit my first reaction had nothing to do with *Jennifer*.

"Can't be," Morgan was saying. "The thing's been here for ages. We land, and a few hours later it maybe gets knocked over? That's not possible."

Chung broke in: "Smitty, what do you recommend? We have the lander nearby."

"How long would it take you to get off?"

"A few minutes."

"Forget it. Get inside. Hide under the beds or something."

"Okay."

"You'll probably be all right. This kind of thing likely happens all the time."

"Okay."

"It's mostly dust."

Just like Earth. But Saturn's neighborhood had a few more rocks, and Iapetus had no atmosphere to dissolve them.

We argued briefly which was safer, lander or shelter, and decided it wouldn't matter if a serious meteor showed up. We settled on the shelter. We hustled inside, Steinitz dropped into a chair, and the rest of us stood looking out. He was scared. "Please," he said, in a voice so low I could just make it out. "Don't hit the statue."

I grew up in south Chicago. My folks didn't have much, and they assumed I'd just get married, so they weren't big on education. At least not for me. My brothers both went to college. I got through high school, barely, saw nobody I wanted to spend the rest of my life with, got a part-time job as a hostess in a burger place, and decided the University of Chicago was a better bet than most of the guys who came in looking for fast food and whatever else they could get.

Things went better than I could have expected. It turned out I had an affinity for physics, and the one romance that might have sidetracked me crashed and burned. It seemed like a disaster at the time, but it was probably the luckiest break of my life. I collected an assistantship from the University of Northern Illinois, and got my doctorate under Edward Harbinger, whose name fit the circumstances. He recommended me for the Athena program, and there I was. Harbinger, I knew, would have given his life to have made this mission, even to hide with us in the shelter while the rocks came down. But he was too old. I don't know why but I kept thinking about him while we waited out the storm.

We got bombarded for the better part of an hour. Mostly it was just pebbles. A little like a hailstorm. It rattled against the roof, and once or twice the ground shook, so something big must have hit, but I didn't see it. When it was over, we went out, and were relieved to see the statue was undamaged.

The show went smoothly. Smitty added recorded shots of the approaching meteors—that was the way we referred to the debris field during the show—and we all talked as if it had been life and death. We went on to profess ourselves relieved that the statue hadn't been damaged, which was true. We also admitted to being scared, but we did it in that joking way that suggests it wasn't really so. Look how brave we are.

When it was over we went out again looking for more traces of the sculptor. But we found nothing. The snow for miles around the monolith was unbroken. At the end of the day, we returned to the shelter. We'd assumed there'd be other marks around, that there had to be other indications of the moon's visitors, but it was beginning to look as if we might be wrong.

We operated on GMT, and it was early evening in this place where there were no evenings per se, where most of the light was coming from the big planet and the rings. And I'll admit that, even in the light gravity, trudging through snow for hours at a time is no fun. We were glad to do a round of drinks and sit down to dinner.

The sculptors had to have left some indication of their presence. Abandoned equipment, tracks, *something*. We simply hadn't gone far enough.

Morgan and Cathie sat down to play chess. Steinitz went back outside to look at Jennifer. I should have gone with him. Technically, you're not supposed to do anything alone, but I'd had enough for the day and everything I owned ached. We'd maintained an intensive exercise program on the flight out, but the long period of near-zero gravity had loosened joints and weakened muscles. I retreated to my quarters and fell asleep with the conviction that manned space vehicles would eventually go the way of the big paddlewheels.

We had an early breakfast, most of it devoted to a long debate on the anatomic feasibility of the ice lady. Jennifer was obviously idealized. She looked toward Saturn with unmistakable longing. And there was something else, some juncture of beak and jaw, some slant of the eyes, that suggested resignation. But reproduction? It was hard to see how. I wondered if my imagination had been playing tricks. Was it maybe something else, neither male nor female? Were there other reproductive arrangements? How often did statuary at home omit the anatomical details?

If we were correct that the snow cover had remained intact, virtually untouched, for thousands of years save for the occasional meteor, then how did we explain that the snow around the statue was unbroken? How could they have erected the thing without tromping around in it? It looked as if it had fallen yesterday. It was of course possible that Jennifer was inordinately older than we'd supposed.

The plain lay wide and flat. The rings were knife-edge bright. We consulted our maps and headed out, Morgan and Chung to the north,

Steinitz and me on the south. The instructions were simple: Find something the sculptor dropped.

We wandered to the edge of the plain, poked among groups of boulders, and waded down into occasional craters. It was cold and tiring. The snow ranged from about a half meter to God knows how deep. Our suits dragged. Smitty joined the search, circling overhead in low orbit, radioing negative reports every hour. We walked until we were all exhausted.

The following day, we were out again.

A couple hours after we'd started, Morgan called. "We got it."

"What?" demanded Steinitz. "What have you got?"

"Among other things," he said, *"footprints."*

"Footprints? You sure they're not your own?"

Chung broke in. "Not unless we're running around in bare feet. And sprouting really long toenails."

The prints were in the foothills of the ridge line. They were *big*. And the claws looked very much like the same set Jennifer had. "The statue's a self-portrait," I said.

But they'd figured that out first thing. "At least as far as the feet are concerned," said Steinitz. He knelt in the snow. "It must have been wearing a pressure suit of some kind. It couldn't have been out here in bare feet. But it sure looks like it."

"Probably a very thin suit," said Chung. "Something molded to the body."

The paw, the foot, was almost twice the size of mine. "It's pretty big," I said.

The prints didn't seem to be going anywhere. It appeared that the creature had simply wandered around on the slope. But it wasn't the prints that had initially caught their attention.

"What then?" asked Steinitz.

The slope angled sharply up and became a sheer wall, about twenty meters high. Morgan and Cathie played their lights against it. Halfway up, there was an indentation. A cut.

It was too precise to have been blasted out by a meteor strike.

"Look again," said Morgan.

The indentation was box-shaped, maybe four meters wide. about as deep. "This is where the granite came from," said Morgan. "For the monolith."

We climbed to the crest, and found more prints, and a slice of relatively flat terrain where the snow had been crushed down. Bits and pieces of loose granite were scattered everywhere. Several of us spoke at the same time: "This is where it made Jennifer."

"We'll collect the pieces of rock," said Steinitz. "We should be able to put them together and confirm that."

"But how the hell did it manage things?" asked Morgan. "Assume it had some sort of laser. How'd it extract the granite?" There were no marks other than the prints. And the prints didn't get any deeper. Even had it been Superman and *lifted* the rock out by sheer physical strength, the prints would have gone deeper from the added weight.

"Anti-gravity," Cathie said.

Steinitz cleared his throat. "Not possible."

"Well," said Morgan, "it's hard to see how else it could have been done, There must have been a ship here somewhere. To lift it and her back down to the plain."

We spread out and looked for other marks in the snow, but found nothing. If there'd been a ship, maybe it had possessed long narrow struts, and the granular composition of the snow simply didn't retain the impressions. Maybe they had teleportation.

We gradually made sense out of the footprints. They first appeared on the downslope. Apparently out of nowhere as if she had descended from the sky. They mounted the ridge without immediately going near the place from which the rock had been taken. They continued along the summit. A second set of tracks returned. Went near the place where the cut now existed. There was a confusion of prints in that area, where she presumably had removed the granite, set it down, somehow, and shaped *Jennifer*. Somewhere in the confusion of tracks, she vanished. There was no indication she had walked away from the site.

"So initially she came in this general direction," said Morgan, "but she passed by this area and went up *there*." He pointed along the crest, where it rose higher and climbed toward more ridges. "Then she came back here, made her cut, did her work, and disappeared. Along with Jennifer, who later turns up on the plain. Is that what we're saying?"

"What do you suppose she was doing up there?" asked Chung, looking at the ridges.

"Probably," Steinitz said, "trying to decide where she wanted to work."

"It might be worthwhile to take a look," I said. "See where the tracks go."

There was no way, of course, we would not have done that. We told Smitty what we'd found, sent off lots of images, listened to him tell us we were probably missing something, that none of the stuff we were talking about was possible. Then we set off to follow the tracks.

Sometimes they petered out on rocky ground. Twice, before sheer walls, the prints stopped altogether, and we recovered them farther up.

The plain with the figure lay behind us. From the tops of the ridges, we could see forward across a large crater. Saturn, always retreating, rested on the far rim.

We emerged, finally, atop an abutment. The prints stopped. The creature appeared to have paused at the summit, perhaps glancing back the way it had come. The artifact was out there now in the middle of the snow field, though not visible in the muted light.

And she might have looked west, across the crater, at the planet and its ring system. Then, apparently, she had started back.

Steinitz stood a long time, staring at the mild confusion of tracks. When at last he merely shrugged, it was a gesture that said it for us all.

We took more pictures, and stayed well away from the prints. It was cold. Steinitz said something about nothing more to do here. "Good with me," Chung said. She fell in line behind him.

Morgan glanced in my direction and stood aside to let me go first.

"You go ahead," I said. "I'll be right with you."

"You sure?"

"Yes. I'll catch up."

He looked uncertain. It was a violation of safety procedure, but I let him see there was no need to worry, so he shrugged and headed off.

Jennifer had been alone.

The stars were hard and cold, and the spaces between them pressed on me as they must have pressed on her. Saturn floated over the plain, its rings luminous and lovely. A few other moons scattered across the sky. It struck me the planet had not moved since she'd stood there, how long ago?

I thought about Cathie. And Melville. *Moby Dick*. I'd never read the book. But I'd seen the video. There's a sequence in which the cook is washed overboard and drifts away from the ship. The seas are heavy, and a moment comes when water and sky fill the universe, when the *Pequod* is gone, and the cook is utterly *alone*. They do not get him back whole.

The image on the plain is terrifying, yes. But not because it has claws and wings, or pitiless eyes. *But because it is alone.*

I was beginning to feel the cold, and it was a long way to the shelter. I looked up, as she must have. Titan was there, with its thin envelope of methane; Rhea and Hyperion, and some of the smaller satellites: frozen, spinning rocks, like this one, immeasurably old, no more capable of supporting a thinking creature than the bloated gasbag they circle. Steinitz had argued for a benevolent cosmos. But Steinitz had never stood alone on that ridge. Only I have done that.

And one other.

The universe is a precarious, cold environment for anything that thinks. There are damned few of us, and it is a wide world, and bleak. I wondered who she was. Long since gone to dust, no doubt. But nevertheless, *Jennifer*, I wish you well.

As I write this, there's a movement afoot to take the Iapetus monument down, to bring it home and install it in the Smithsonian. There, they'd probably put it in a refrigerated cubicle, try to recreate the snowfield appearance. They'd surround it with gleaming staircases and coke machines. Maybe it doesn't matter.

Before we left to come home, we opened the ground module to space. If anyone else ever passes that way, it'll be there, just the way we left it. And on the dining board, they'll find my ID. It's not a very good picture. You know how official photos are. But they'll understand. It was the best I could do on short notice.

The Far Shore

Back in the forties, there was a radio show called CBS Was There. Later it became You Are There, *and it was under that title it made the leap to TV in 1954, under the aegis of Walter Cronkite. It featured historical events covered by CBS correspondents on the spot. They interviewed Alexander before the Battle of Arbela ("Majesty, are you worried about the elephants?") and Lincoln offstage at Gettysburg ("How much longer do you expect the war to last, Mr. President?"); there were battlefield reports from Lexington and Thermopolae, interviews with Caesar and Lancelot, and breathless descriptions from the Alamo. I was at Salem during the witch trials, and stood on the bridge with Columbus. It was great stuff, and I fell in love with electronic journalism.*

For various reasons, some probably having to do with talent, and others with a reluctance to put my body on the line, I never really got around to attempting a career in the field. But when I started writing it showed up immediately. "The Far Shore" was my second sale, and my first true science fiction story.

The moonlight was bright on Patty's grave. Rodney Martin felt the moisture in his eyes, threw a final spadeful of earth, and groped for a prayer to a God whose jurisdiction surely ended somewhere south of here. Behind him, in the dark, the surf was a muffled boom.

The wind moved in the trees.

It seemed now he had never known her free of pain. He had worked with her aboard *Alexia* for almost three years; yet her lifetime, for him, was bracketed between this night and that terrible moment on the blacked-out ruined bridge of the stricken starship when he had come upon her, mouth bloody, face pale behind the plexiglass of her helmet.

Grief twisted his features.

He was reluctant to leave, and stood a long time listening to the forest sounds and the ocean. The moon drifted through the night, not the barren pebble of Earth's skies, but a large blue-green globe of continents and water, its arc softened in the shimmering white clouds.

There was a chill in the air.

After awhile, Martin shouldered the spade and walked slowly back toward the beach. The trees gave way to tough, fibrous plants rooted in stony soil. He looked out at the ocean, on which no ship had ever sailed.

Long waves broke and slid up the beach. Ahead, atop a low slope, the lights from the Monson dome glittered on the water. He'd been careful to turn the lamps on before leaving, but now it seemed distant and cold.

He passed a massive boulder, its lower sides smoothed by the tides. Beyond lay the escape capsule, cool and round and black, an enormous bowling ball in the sand, forming a kind of matched pair with the rock.

He climbed the ridge behind the capsule, and was home. The Monson was actually four domes, three smaller ones connected by twelve-foot-long tubes to a primary central bubble. Not exactly a townhouse, but comfortable, designed to withstand extreme temperatures, assaults by giant lizards, corrosive atmosphere, whatever. The ideal survival structure, sufficient to house the entire eight-person crew of *Alexia*. As things had turned out, he had a lot of room.

And a lot of time. He wondered what had happened on the ship. Screen failure, probably. God knew the shields had blinked out often enough before. So yes, they'd probably gotten corked by a good-sized rock.

Whatever it was, the hull had come apart, and apparently dumped everyone but the two sleepers into the void. During those frantic minutes, with power and gravity gone, and the star well swirling beneath his feet, he'd searched *Alexia's* spaces and found only Patty, whose first fortunate response had been to launch the datapak.

Sleep did not come easily. He tried to read but could not concentrate. Finally he turned out the lights and stared at the ceiling. The bedroom windows were open. The surf thundered and boomed.

It had been two weeks since they'd arrived there in the escape capsule. Patty had been thrown hard into a bulkhead during the event and had never really rallied. She'd grown weaker by the day and had slipped quietly away while he slept.

In the morning, he was up early. Tired, angry, he scrambled an egg for which he had no appetite, added toast and coffee, and went for a swim. The ocean was cool. After a while he came in close to shore and stood knee-deep in the surf, enjoying its inconstant tug, feeling it pull the sand from beneath his toes. The sea was blue and salty, indistinguishable from the Atlantic. Strands of weed wrapped around his ankles. Things very much like sandcrabs drifted in, squirted tiny fountains of water and buried themselves in the wet sand. The beach, punctuated with heaps of gray rock, swung in a wide curve for miles, vanishing at last around the edge of a promontory. Inland, wooded hills mounted in successive ridges westward to the foot of a distant mountain chain. A lost floater drifted over the breakers, until it was picked up by the wind and blown back toward the forest. The floaters were green airbags, apparently airborne plants, resembling nothing so much as lopsided leathery balloons, complete with an anchoring tail. He watched until it disappeared among the trees.

He slept most of the afternoon, and woke feeling better than he had at any time since the accident. Given time, he'd come to terms with the loss of Patty. It was painful, and he promised himself if he got home he'd never leave again. But his situation was not desperate. The environment did not seem especially dangerous, and the Momsen could keep him alive indefinitely. He had a transmitter, so he would be able to say hello when help showed up. Survival depended only on his ability to adjust to being alone.

The Institute had nothing between here and home. It was seventy-some parsecs to Earth. *Alexia's* distress signal, riding its subspace carrier, would cross that vast ocean in 26 months and some odd days, which meant that he could expect a rescue party in about five years.

Fortunately, food was no problem. Storage lockers on board the SARC, the Sakata-Avery Rescue Chamber, held enough hamburgers and power packs to maintain *eight* people for years. He had weapons, though this world so far had revealed nothing dangerous. And he had a pleasant beach home. Rent free, with his pay piling up.

That evening, he dragged a chair outside, called up a novel, and sat watching the sun dip into the mountains. It was whiter than Sol, slightly larger, in reality as well as in appearance. When the leading edge touched the horizon, Martin set his watch at six o'clock. A day here was longer than at home, maybe by two hours. So his watch was useless for its designed purpose. But he would check it tomorrow when the sun touched the horizon again, and it would tell him the precise length of the day. Not that it mattered.

The SARC had come down in the northern hemisphere, and he'd steered for the temperate zone. The planet, which they had named Amity, was entering that portion of its orbit in which his hemisphere would be tilting away from the sun. Autumn was coming. Declination was eleven degrees. That should mean a mild winter.

He would want a calendar. Again, not that he had any real use for one. But it would be something to occupy him. He knew Amity circled its G2 main sequence primary in just over seventeen terrestrial months.

He thought about supplies. Had he overlooked anything? He had an abundance of solar energy, with backup systems. The shoreline gave no indication of unusual tides, sudden inundations, anything of that nature.

The SARC possessed an extensive film library. Complete runs of the most popular HV shows of the last century. There were quiz and discussion shows, and other programs of an educational nature; and a complete run, ten years worth, of *Brandenburg and Scott*, a "sociodrama" in which two wisecracking government agents helped people adjust to assorted problems arising from economic dislocation, overpopulation, divergence of religious views, and so on.

He had fifty years of the World Series, and a lot of horse races. And the better part of the Library of Congress.

He also had a radio. There was, of course, nothing to listen to other than the hourly distress call put out by the datapak, in the event somebody showed up in the neighborhood. The datapak was an orbiting cluster of antennas, receivers, and transmitters, aimed at Earth by an on-board computer, beeping across hyphenated space. Its receivers were designed to pick up stray whispers of signal, electronic sighs to be filtered and dissected, the results channeled for analysis, enhancement, and ultimate restoration. It would, one day, lead his rescuers to him.

Martin's front yard was humanity's most remote outpost. It was half again as far as Calamity, on the other side of Sol.

A tree-squatter sat on its hind legs, watching him. It resembled an oversized and overweight squirrel. He tossed it one of the packaged nuts he'd salvaged from the ship. It advanced with caution, took the nut, glanced briefly at him, and vanished back into the scrub.

The tree-squatter, with its quick black eyes, was around all the time, looking for food. But it would not trust him, and always cleared out if he tried to approach.

There were lots of furry critters and floaters and lizards and things never dreamt of by the most imaginative writers scattered across that part of the Orion Arm reached by humans. But no one had yet found any philosophers or electricians. Consequently, Earth was reassuming its classic Ptolemaic position as center of the universe. The Theological Implications, as people were fond of saying, were obvious. The primordial soup, stirred centuries ago by evolutionists to evict the Creator, had acquired an extra ingredient. The view that people were a direct result of divine intervention was once again respectable. The numerous empty garden worlds, like this one, might almost have been prepared specifically for human use. But if places like this suggested a friendly cosmos to people back home, to Martin the skies were too silent, the forests too empty.

The Institute was dying. The human race had more real estate than it could possibly use in the foreseeable future. Expeditions were expensive, ships were wearing out, and the government could see no return for its money. Unless something happened that could rekindle the taxpayers' imaginations, the Great Adventure was drawing to a close. Moreover, it was unlikely that the political power structure wanted any unsettling discoveries. There would probably be a general sigh of relief when the last vessel returned emptyhanded from its last flight.

No new unit had been added to the fleet in thirty years. Equipment was run down, and parts were scarce. In fact, he thought wearily, if the truth were known, the loss of *Alexia* would probably turn out to be attributable to a broken hose.

He missed Patty.

The place was too quiet. The wind blew and the tides came and went and seabirds flapped past. He was becoming increasingly oppressed by a sense of unease. Somewhere, in the hills, or maybe at sea, he'd have liked to see a light.

He kept the HV on constantly. The voices were reassuring. He listened to them argue politics, philosophy, medicine, religion, and sex. He watched various kinds of dramas, laughed at the comedians, enjoyed the musicals and even started to develop a taste for opera.

And he took to bolting the door. It was the beginning of the Greenway Syndrome.

Everett Radcliffe, stranded on the back side of the Moon for six months after a series of improbable accidents had carried off his two colleagues, had heard footsteps behind him the rest of his days. Will Evans had taken his life after four months in a prototype of Martin's shelter. Myra Greenway, for whom the disorder was named, was adrift for a year in a SARC, never close to a planetary surface. She swore that something had lived outside, clinging to the shelter, trying continually to get at her. Brad Kauffman had spent eight months alone in a crippled cruiser after his partner had died, and had refused, after his return to Earth, to come out of his house at night.

There were other cases.

Something deep in the soul does not like unbroken, intense solitude. Cut whatever it is that ties a man to the rest of his species, plunge him into the outer dark, and he will never be the same.

Martin tried not to think about it.

Standard procedure was to embrace whatever entertainment was available, cultivate hobbies, keep occupied. Across a room, a pair of holographic images, one an aging beauty, the other an aggressive comic, swapped mindless chitchat.

He could collect rocks.

Martin was not a man easily frightened. He'd intervened once in a gang assault, did not fear speaking to large groups of people, and had ridden the starships into the unknown. Nevertheless, he continued to keep his door locked.

STATUS REPORT 037 ALEXIA 090857 GMT: PATRICIA MASON DEAD OF INJURIES SEPTEMBER 3.

He thought of Patty's family, two years from now, receiving this news, and added: *PEACEFULLY.* He poked in his name, and hit the transmit.

The morning was gray. He played bridge with the computer, got bored, tried a novel. After lunch, he sat down at the terminal and pointed the datapak's antennas at Sirius. The speakers crackled with static.

Hello from God.

Outside, the trees bent under a stiff wind, and the ocean was choppy. Rain coming. Oblivious to the weather, a groper ambled amiably along the treeline, its oilskin hide glistening. It probed the branches with long, flexible arms for a yellow fruit that had, the previous day, tested okay for Martin's consumption.

That afternoon he drifted off, and awoke with a wisp of recollection from his childhood, something not quite remembered, brought back by a dream:

He was a boy, seven or eight, alone in the house in Atlanta. And frightened by the shadows and dark places outside the living room. He'd put on the HV, and looked at the gloomy doorway to the kitchen, with its exits opening out back and into the basement. He'd sat awhile, trying to pretend it was not there. Then, he had turned off the unit, taken a book, and crawled behind the sofa. To be safe from whatever might come through that door.

Had it really happened? As he reached back, details took shape. It had happened more than once.

He rotated the orbiter's antennas randomly, and set the scanner to range over a wide band of frequencies. There *was* something constructive he could attempt: intercept an alien signal, a navigational beacon in the vicinity of Betelgeuse, maybe, or a weather report from the Pleiades. Do that, and they'd build a shrine on this spot.

He sat through most of the afternoon, listening to the cosmic racket, wondering whether he would recognize an alien signal if he heard one. Eventually tiring of the game, Martin returned control to the onboard computer, which obediently tracked back across the sky and locked onto its primary target. Earth.

The signal changed.

It was a blip, a rhythmic murmur gone so quickly that he wasn't sure it had been there at all. He reversed the scanner, and was listening to a jumble of signals, nothing he could make out, but different in quality from the stellar transmissions he'd heard previously. He used the filters to isolate the strongest signal, and boosted it. It became a piano, and a voice:

". . . *A lipstick's traces,*
"*An airline ticket to romantic places,*
"*And still my heart has wings;*
"*These foolish things remind me of you. . . .*"

Martin frowned, smiled, shook his head.

Rescue ship nearby? That brought a momentary surge of elation, but he knew it could not be. He got up anyhow and went outside to see if anything was moving against the stars. The piano sounded very far away.

". . . *A telephone that rings, but who's to answer?*

"*Oh, how the ghost of you clings!. . . .*"

The singer finished to a burst of applause, and the melody shifted smoothly.

"*Thanks, folks, and goodnight from all of us here at the Music Hall until next Sunday, when we'll be coming your way again with more of America's favorite tunes.*"

More applause, music up in volume, and then a fadeaway to another voice:

"*This is CBS, the Columbia Broadcasting System. News is next, with Waldo Anderson.*"

Old Earth: he was picking up carrier waves that had left Earth more than two centuries ago!

Anderson arrived in a clatter of electronic gimmickry, introduced his lead story, which concerned an armed robbery, and gave way immediately to a woman with a passion for antacid tablets. Then Anderson returned, speaking in a rich, cultured voice:

"*The Willie Starr case went to the jury today. Starr is one of two men accused in a triple slaying last March at a Brooklyn liquor store. His alleged partner, Joey Horton, has already. . . .*"

Martin sighed, and turned it off. He had found his alien civilization.

The sun broke through and the day warmed. Languidly, Martin stripped and gave himself to the sea. The water had turned cold. He swam out beyond the breakers with sure, swift strokes, turned and surveyed his world, rising and falling with the waves.

It was like one of those early summers off St. Simons, minus the white frame houses and the beachfront restaurants. And the women.

Anyone.

He sat on the beach, wrapped in a robe, with his reader propped against his knees, lost in a planetary, a novel set during the early days of extraterrestrial settlement. The author, Reginald Packard, had grown wealthy cranking out these historical romances. Martin did not normally read such things. But he had become engrossed in the book over breakfast. Now, however, as the sun began its long slide toward the mountains, he found that his eyes kept wandering from the rows of neat print to the shadowy places among the trees.

Something was there.

He pulled the robe tight around him. A long wave unrolled and ran up the beach. He could not get his eyes off the edge of the forest.

Nothing moved.

The Dome was three hundred yards away. A long run in the sand. How easily he could be cut off!

His heart pounded.

The wind blew and the trees writhed.

Greenway. He understood the woman, hysterical in her capsule beyond Centaurus, while a space-born *thing* with sharp teeth and feral eyes prowled the outside, slavering at her through the viewscreen, gnawing at the airlock.

His heartbeat picked up. And suddenly, without thinking about it, he was on his feet, churning through the loose sand. He did not look back, but kept his eyes fixed on the Dome. He fell and, in slow motion, rolled over and came back to his feet in a single fluid move.

When he got inside, he bolted the door, set the shields in place, drew the blinds, and collapsed. His cheek was bleeding.

That night he tried to distract himself by working out a search pattern for the datapak. *If, by a remote chance, he found what they'd all been looking for, he could let them know at home and they'd have to come get him—* Martin's eyes narrowed at the thought that had surfaced, that he'd refused to consider. That someone might decide a rescue was too expensive. They knew, or would know, he was the only survivor. One person measured against the cost of a multi-year mission. But the Service had a tradition to maintain; he had nothing to fear.

At dawn, he returned to the search. While the display blipped and beeped, he sat by the window, peering through the drawn shades.

Deciding that chatter would at least be company, he switched back to the terrestrial radio station and listened to two domestic serials, "Our Gal Sunday" and "Life Can Be Beautiful." His tension lessened. The shows had a small-town charm, and the characters seemed generally virtuous and vulnerable, if not bright. Sunday's voice had a peculiar vitality, a quality of moonlight and laughter. He tried to picture the actress, and decided he would have liked to know her.

And there was more news:

"*. . . Governor Dewey at a press conference this morning stated that police are closing in on Buchalter, and that his arrest is imminent. Known in gangland as Lepke the Leopard, Buchalter jumped bail two years ago. Onetime boss of New York's protection racket, he is believed—*"

He experimented with other terrestrial frequencies. Most were in foreign languages. But there were some in English. He listened to "Ma

Perkins" and a quiz show. And he discovered "Terry and the Pirates" and "Jack Armstrong."

There were supplies to be got in from the capsule, a job he'd been putting off. And he'd dropped his reader when he ran from the beach. He looked out the windows and saw nothing. He turned up the radio, unlocked the door, and forced himself to walk. He went first to recover the reader. Then he hurried to the capsule. He loaded his arms with packets of dehydrated foods, sealed the vehicle, and started back. Nothing watched him from the hills. Nothing charged out of the trees. When he'd gotten inside the Momsen, he was proud of himself. He bolted the door, though—no point being foolish—and put everything away. Then he sat down and turned the radio back on.

Immediately, he heard a familiar name:

"Berlin announced today that Polish authorities were continuing to expel German citizens. The official Nazi newspaper Volkischer Beobachter *reported two men killed near Stettin this afternoon. Both were German citizens, and were said to have been fleeing a Polish mob when they ran out onto a highway, where they were struck by a bus.*

"Chancellor Hitler, speaking at a party meeting in Munich, labeled the incident quote yet another provocation by anti-German leftists in the Polish government unquote. He called on President Moscicki to intervene, and warned that German patience was not without its limits.

"Closer to home. . . ."

Martin, of course, knew about Hitler, the twentieth-century warlord and nutcase.

The newscast went on to describe a quarrel in Congress over the Neutrality Act, a bungled attempt at an armored car holdup, and an argument at a schoolboard meeting. Tomorrow would be sunny and hot. The current heat wave was going into its sixth day. And there were some baseball scores.

Martin hadn't realized that baseball was so old. Some of the teams were the same, but it must be a strange version of the game in which you only scored three or four runs.

He slept that night with the shields up, though he knew, *really knew,* they were unnecessary.

He tried to pick up "Our Gal Sunday" again next day, but failed to take into account the two-hour-plus time differential resulting from the longer day. But there were other shows. "Stella Dallas" and "Just

Plain Bill." He listened with interest: the problems faced by the characters were of a personal nature, rather than social struggles. These were people for whom there might have been no outside world, but merely the melodramatic mix of love and lust.

He passed a sizable part of his afternoon with Xavier Cugat and the Boys in "the Green Room of the beautiful Grant Park Hotel in downtown New York." Between songs, behind the announcer's voice, Martin heard the low murmur of conversation, the clink of china: fragile place of glass and laughter.

Berlin announced that two unarmed German passenger planes had been fired on by Polish fighters near Danzig. One had crashed in a field, killing all on board. The other had carried a cargo of dead and wounded back into German territory. Hitler was said to be furious.

There were also reports of an attack on a German border station. The Poles denied it all.

Martin understood that these events were not real, that the people in the Green Room, sipping their martinis and drifting into the coming carnage, were long since gone to dust. He might as well have been listening to an account of the Third Crusade. Yet. . . .

Warfare had been a common enough occurrence over the centuries, but to Martin it was part of a barbaric past, relegated to dusty tomes in libraries. Unthinkable.

Next day he returned to the beach. He even walked briefly into the forest that afternoon. There was nothing here to fear. No predators.

When the Wehrmacht rolled into Poland, Martin was lying on the sand, naked, tanned, reading Byron. He listened to appeals from Britain and France, from the White House and the Vatican. After sundown, when the first battle reports came in (both sides were claiming victories), he looked out at the dark, quiet hills, trying to imagine ponderous tanks clanking toward him, Heinkels crossing his western mountains to drop explosives on his head.

The Germans bombed Cracow. Martin listened to an eyewitness description, heavy accent, heavy static, muted blasts, children fleeing the stuttering stukas, Nazi tanks sighted west of the city, everything on fire. . . .

Emory Michael, of the Blue Network, got through from a small town whose name he couldn't get straight. The townspeople, mostly women and children, had gathered in a pasture on the west side of the city, watching the Nazi planes circling. Watching the bombs come down.

Michael found a woman who spoke English, and asked where her husband was. "With the cavalry," she said, with a heavy accent. "They will cut the Boche to pieces!"

Horses, thought Martin. Had they really sent horses against Hitler's tanks? After a long while, he strode off, walking at the edge of the incoming tide, listening to the unhurried roar of the sea. From here, the war seemed so distant. (He smiled at that.)

Rain clouds were building in the west.

What was remarkable: These people bombed and strafed—how many would die during the conflagration?—and it would all pass, leaving only a few ripples on the tide, the wreckage washed out to sea. His generation barely knew of World War II. It was something in the history books.

A fine drizzle began to fall.

He turned into the forest. The ground was thick with leaves. He ducked under a floater that had tethered itself to a low branch. Something small, with fur, stopped to watch.

He came to Patty's grave and said hello, aloud. There was no marker, other than three rough stones. Eventually, soon, he would correct that.

He sat down. It was a beautiful, leafy glade, a place for children, or lovers. He cradled his chin against his knees and mourned all those, down the long years, whose lives had been cut short, caught in the wrong place at the wrong time, victims of greed, folly, or plain bad luck: Patricia, the children of Cracow, the woman whose husband was in the cavalry, the Roman farmers in the path of the Vandals. Here's to everybody. There's room here, on Amity, and welcome.

The rain was falling harder, becoming a downpour. Above him, on a branch, something stirred.

There *was* occasional good news: A woman named Myers was reunited with her mother after 43 years; Lepke turned himself over to a newsman named Winchell; and Martin discovered Fibber McGee. McGee was unlike anything he had encountered before, an engaging mixture of pomposity, naive dishonesty, and scrambling insecurity. McGee's world of goodhearted bumblers seemed untouched by the savagery in the newscasts.

Martin's first experience with fictional psychotics and madmen came with "The Shadow." It was a series which would not have been allowed in his own time. His society frowned on mindless mayhem. But week after week, the invisible, slightly schizophrenic hero tracked down and eliminated mass murderers and insane physicians in the most delicious manner. Martin loved it.

Despite the global disaster, there was a warmth to the programming, good humor, a sense of purpose and community that extended beyond time and space to Martin's beachfront property. He strolled the tree-lined streets of Philadelphia, dined in some of Chicago's better restaurants. He became addicted to "Amos 'n' Andy," followed Captain Midnight into exotic jungle locales, explored the temple of vampires with Jack, Doc, and Reggie. He was a regular visitor in the Little Theater off Times Square.

Meanwhile, Hitler's armies swept all opposition aside. President Roosevelt appeared frequently in informal broadcasts, discussing the economy and the war, assuring his audience that America would stay out of the war.

Although he could not recall the course of the struggle (he was not even certain yet which President Roosevelt he was listening to), Martin knew that, in the end, the Western Allies would win. Had won. But it was difficult, in the summer of 1940, to see how such an outcome might develop. Britain, bloody, desperate, stood alone. And Churchill's regal voice rang defiance across the light years.

Martin listened with sorrow to Edward R. Murrow in London, as the Nazis pounded the city. A year later, he was at a football game between the Redskins and the Eagles when the Japanese attacked Pearl Harbor. He fought with the garrison on Luzon, watched the aerial battle over Midway, rode in the desert with Montgomery.

In the late spring of 1944, the datapak picked up a subspace transmission: *RESCUE UNIT ENROUTE. SHOULD ARRIVE WITHIN THIRTY DAYS AFTER YOU RECEIVE THIS. HANG ON, ROD.*

By then Martin had taken to getting away from home periodically on two- and three-day jaunts into the countryside. But he wanted to keep up with the war. He was on one of these trips, lying in the grass halfway up a mountain in the early afternoon when the response came, breaking into "Dawn Patrol." He let it repeat several times, wondering why he wished they had been a little less prompt.

Eisenhower's army gathered in Britain. Everyone knew what was coming; most of the speculation centered on timing and landing points. Martin waited with the rest of the nation for word of the invasion. Tension inside the Dome grew thick.

But the invasion did not happen. A few days later, while he was still caught up in speculation from Washington and London, the *Eagle* arrived. It was a sleek silver bulletshaped cruiser. sailing majestically on its magnetics. . . .(The *Eagle* was the same class vessel as *Alexia*, but his ship had never looked so good.)

His datapak put it on his screen, and an hour or so later its lander settled softly into the scrub. The hatch rotated, opened, and people spilled out. Martin hugged everybody.

They stayed two weeks, splashing in the surf, drinking at night, walking in the woods. Martin talked constantly, to anyone who would listen. He paired off with a young technician and rediscovered a few lost emotions.

Captain and crew gathered around his radio, and listened curiously to "Big Town" and Gabriel Heatter. But time was pressing. "You know how it is, Rod," the captain said. "Got to be moving."

Martin noticed that, with the arrival of the *Eagle*, the broadcasts lost some of their immediacy. He no longer felt he was living through the second war. When, on the fourth day of his rescue, Allied troops stormed ashore on Omaha Beach, he was in a glade with his technician. He heard about it later, but it seemed like an historical event. Something far removed from Amity.

They dug up Patty's body, to be returned to New Hampshire. The medical officer and the captain each inquired after his health. One thought he seemed depressed; the other wondered if he was actually unhappy about being rescued. "Long time to be stuck in a place like this," the captain said, looking around at the empty beaches and the silent woods.

Martin's eyes dimmed. "Not stuck here," he said. "I've been getting around."

The medical officer frowned. "What do you mean, Rod?"

"I'm not sure I can explain it, Doc," he said. "But I may be the world's first time traveler."

In The Tower

As a general rule, I have little interest in horror, if one defines horror in terms of the werewolf in the woods and things going bump in the night. I'm not sure why that is. Maybe it's because the field is crowded, and I doubt I can take a reader into a dark corner and scare him in a way no one has done previously.

Or maybe it's because I never recovered from watching Karloff stalk around the countryside. If I spend an evening with Stephen King, I know I'm not going to sleep well.

This is probably the only one of my stories that qualifies as a horror entry. It has two things in common with "Melville on Iapetus." It is set in a universe eventually associated with Alex Benedict, who has appeared, to date, in three novels, although it was written two years before that ingenious antiquarian appeared on the scene. And it was inspired by a few lines of poetry. In this case, Matthew Arnold's "A Picture at Newstead."

*

1.

Uxbridge Bay on Fishbowl in late summer. In a sense, I'd been there many times before: this sweeping sickle of gentle hills and purple flowers and whitegold shrubbery, the bay choppy under a brisk wind from the southeast, the half-dozen sleepy quill drifting across a late afternoon sky. I knew the soil, brown under twin suns, the sandy vine-clogged banks, the black polished rocks dribbled through the shallows by a casual hand.

Only the carefully repaired seam across the vault of sky, through which the same casual hand had plunged a long-handled knife, was wanting.

This was a place of things lost, of lovers discarded, of thunder below the horizon. It was a place of silent beaches and brilliant far-off breakers, of invisible voices and dying laughter. It was, I suspected, the place that Durell had visited during those increasingly frequent occasions when I found him silhouetted against the bedroom window, or gazing into his wine during long, silent diners. Something had happened here, something about which I'd learned not to speak. But he'd painted it, and had tried to destroy the painting. In the end, he'd merely denied it a name.

He'd come back from one of his long walks, less than a week before he rode his skimmer into a precipice, and he'd taken me into his arms without a word. It was so unlike him (he was not unaffectionate, but his love-making always included a mixture of verbal charm and good humor), that it was unsettling.

"What's wrong?" I'd asked.

He'd shuddered, as though cold air had reached him through the sealed windows. His eyes were silver gray, the color of the global sea on Fishbowl, and they were fixed far away. "It's nothing."

So we'd held one another; and I could feel the slow beat of his heart. And after a while he'd broken away. I was desperate: I'd watched him for three years creating melancholy landscapes, utterly unlike his early, pre-Rimway work, and sinking more deeply with each into a despondency I could neither touch nor comprehend. And that night, not for the first time, I tried to imagine life without him. "Durell," I'd pleaded, "tell me about Fishbowl."

He'd just finished the *Indemia*, which was to be his final work. It's a rendering of a child playing in a grotto, but the juxtaposition of shadow and rock and, particularly, the dark throat at the back of the cave, may possibly have been his final statement on the condition of innocence in this world. I'd been upset by it. "There's nothing to tell," he said.

"There is a hell of a lot to tell. What happened there?"

He'd nodded then, his dark hair unkempt, and, in the manner one uses with a child, he'd begun the old explanation of the peculiar vulnerability of the artist, the hazards consonant with peering into the iron core of reality. I listened to the worn clichés until he himself grew embarrassed. Then I pushed him away. "You don't want to talk about it? Fine: but I'm not going to sit quietly while you unload all that guilt, or whatever it is, on me. Not if I don't even know what it's about."

"Tiel," he said in a whisper so low I could scarcely hear, "you would never understand." He shook his head, and his eyes filled with tears. "It was the tower room. The goddam *tower room.*"

But that was all I could get from him. In a shaky voice he told me I was right, that it would probably be best if I left. He understood. He was so understanding I felt ill, because what it amounted to was that his secrets meant more to him than I did. So I went into the bedroom and threw as much as I could into one bag, told him I'd send for the rest later, and walked out. "I love you, Tiel," he'd said as I went through the door. They were his last words to me.

A few days later they'd handed him to me in a silver urn the color of his eyes. And I: I had come to Uxbridge Bay on Fishbowl, to the few hundred square kilometers that composed the entire land mass of that remote world. I'd developed my own cargo of guilt now: when Durell had most needed me, I'd gone for a walk.

So I came seeking the meaning of a painting. And a tower.

The texture of the light was changing rapidly as Gideon sank toward the ocean. It was well toward evening, about two hours later than the scene depicted by Durell. No matter: if Gideon was a little too low in the sky, and the air cool with approaching autumn, this was still a sacred place. How often, over the years, had I stood before the original on Rimway, absorbed by his bleak vision? I knew the reflections of my own losses in that somber water.

It had come to be known as the *Cordelet,* a reference to the land of lost innocence mentioned in Belarian mythology:

> *. . . Where echoes yet in cool green glades*
> *The laughter of departed gods. . . .*

There was, of course, no way to be certain of the exact spot where he'd placed the easel. Withered deciduals, like the one that dominates the foreground of the painting, are not uncommon in the area. I had a holo version with me, and held it up against the suns, comparing the interweaving of hills along the far edge of the sickle. But the view did not appreciably change from one suspect site to another. I looked for the white-streaked boulder, close in to shore. ("The artist's conviction," Gilmore had told us at the Academy, "that some things do survive against the flow of eternity." Gilmore, of course, didn't know Durell very well.) Anyhow, the tide was at full, and the rock must have been covered.

It didn't matter. I wandered among boulders and trees, took off my sandals and strolled through the surf. And gradually became aware that something along the seacoast, or in the bay, was wrong. A shell partially buried in wet sand sprouted long stalked legs and scrabbled into the water. Waves blew across groups of rocks, throwing columns of spume into the air, where the mist lingered somewhat longer than it might have in Rimway's heavier gravity.

I looked out across the bay, and allowed myself a satisfying surge of self-pity. Durell was dead. (And where could I hope to find his like again?) I wanted to believe that, in some transcendental manner, his spirit brooded over this place that he'd made famous. That if he lived anywhere, it was here. But passage to Fishbowl had taken my savings; and if I felt anything at that moment other than my own solitude, I have no idea what it was.

Then I saw the object that was *not* in the painting: a projector station stood out on the Point, at the seaward tip of the sickle. A small copper-colored dome with a gaping black hole open to the sky, it was the only man-made structure anywhere in the vast arc of land and sea appropriated by the artist.

Odd, I thought: this single forlorn symbol of human existence, its bright shell entangled in dense shrubbery, counterpointed the bay, the hills, and the sea quite effectively, heightening the suggestion of mortality which, from the time of the *Cordelet*, was central to Durell's work. It was a structure that, had it not already existed, should have been invented. Yet Durell had ruthlessly excluded it. Why?

I began to wonder if I, and everyone else, was somehow misreading the meaning.

The *Cordelet* is, of course, the watershed work of Durell's career. No one would have predicted greatness from his earlier efforts, although the innocent vitality of the young woman springing across a rainswept field in *Downhill*, and the spectral snowfall of *Night Travels*, demonstrate considerable talent. But the *Cordelet* marks the passage from the exuberance of his early period to the bleak unquiet masterpieces of maturity. The abruptness and totality of that transition is puzzling. Between *Night Travels* and the *Cordelet*, there should have been a period of evolution, a series of works progressively more introspective, technically more accomplished. But there is no such gradual development. And when the *Cordelet* appears, in all its somber power, only the idly circling quill, and the brilliant light of the twin suns on the far breakers, remain of the early Durell.

We would never see them again.

I was reluctant to leave. The tide was high on the sandy banks. A rising wind pulled at the trees. The rocks were changing color against dying sunlight.

But I wasn't dressed for the cool evening, and it was a long walk back to Pellinor, Fishbowl's only town. In Durell's time, before the skimmers were imported in large numbers, there was a road between Pellinor and the southernmost land tip. It would have been his route, so I'd tried to follow it on the way out. It was, after all, the proper way to do things on a pilgrimage. But the road had diminished gradually to a footpath, which ended in heavy foliage. Disappointed, I'd crossed to the ocean's edge, where the ground was, at least, passable.

So I took a last look, wondering what Durell's thoughts had been when he closed up his frame on that final day and started back with a canvas so different from anything he'd done before, and descended the far side of the hill, dropping rapidly below sea level.

It gets cold quickly in the shadow of the sea. Gideon had set, and Heli's light was blocked by the ocean. The wall of water to my left soared to more than thirty meters. I hurried along, pulling my jacket tight against the falling temperatures. No one else was about, although toward the west, lights were coming on in the occasional manor houses perched out over the ridge that runs down the spine of the island.

These homes, which were owned mostly by wealthy expatriates from Rimway and Mogambo, were pretentious exercises in hyperbolic architecture: long arcing struts attached them to the underlying rock; but it was clear they were actually supported by Gantner light, the same force that holds back the ocean. I'd seen similar constructions on Rimway, although they were usually limited to corporate or public buildings.

The land along the seawall is flat and uninteresting. Its high saline content has twisted and withered the trees and shrubbery. Since this world has no natural dry ground other than the sickle and a few hills on the northern rim of Pellinor, the island's only city, it has no highly developed land plants of its own. A few neglected waterways, from the days when someone hoped to convert all of the recovered land into a garden spot, wandered aimlessly across the landscape.

The sky had darkened before I was halfway back to town. Dim shapes glided beyond the seawall, silhouetted by filtered moonlight. I switched on my lantern: the vertical surface of the ocean gleamed. I pointed the beam inside, shielded my eyes from the reflection, and looked through the wall. Small, vaguely luminous plants swayed in the current, and obscure marine shapes darted away. The wall itself was hard and unyielding, and quite dry. Like polished marble.

Projector stations were scattered erratically. The coastline between the sickle and Pellinor was by no means straight, and each change of direction, or course, required another site. Several domes were also visible along the central spine. I could not imagine what use they were, well away from the ocean, and learned later that they were a backup system, that Fishbowl is, in effect, compartmentalized, so that a failure at one station would not result in a general disaster.

I stopped to examine one. It was a wide, graceful shell, about twice my height, set precisely on the border between land and sea, its submerged half slightly refracted. A child's playhouse, one might suspect. Or a sleeping tortoise. There was no sound, no light, no hint of the enormous power generated within.

So I walked, shivering, through a land not quite real, a place wrenched from the ocean within my lifetime. It is a spectacular place and, by ordinary criteria, a lovely place. But Durell's sense of transience is quite real: possibly the towering seawalls are responsible for what one feels. (Only the natives sleep soundly on Fishbowl.) Or maybe there is something more subtle. The island, if indeed one can call it an island, has no past. Time did not exist here until Harry Pellinor and his crew arrived to drive back the sea. If I sensed anything at all in that cramped land, it was that the projectors, the absurd homes, the withered foliage, the town huddling under the seawalls, were only an incursion.

2.

I assumed that Durell was Fishbowl's best-known citizen, so I wandered around town next morning looking for signs of his fame. A statue or two, perhaps. I'd thought that a holo in some prominent place depicting him creating the *Cordelet* would be appropriate. Or possibly a prominent walkway named for him. At the very least, I anticipated a Durell Coll Park, with clipped hedges and manicured trees; a gallery prominently featuring his work, and a restored studio.

In reality, it was difficult to find anyone who even knew that he'd existed.

Durell had come to Fishbowl as an adolescent. His father had died on the first mission to Belarius, and his mother had returned with him to Rimway. After her death, from a rare blood disorder, he had returned to paint Pellinor's spectacular seascapes. But he'd gone quickly through a small inheritance. He used only canvas, disdaining the holos, and thereby assuring a permanent poverty. Eventually he moved onto the top floor of a square permearth structure, buried among retailers and storage facilities. It was here that he honed the talents that would, in time, guarantee his fame. And that was somehow the romance of it, I suppose, that the artist whose greatest works would be embodied in vast heaving skies and restless seas should live next to a skimmer repair center.

The place was still buried. The Tiresian café that had sheltered the small group of artists on the first floor was gone, replaced by a crockery shop. Heavy utilitarian buildings lined both sides of the ground-level walkway. A loading dock was immediately opposite the crockery shop. One of the recently built mall ramps arched overhead, an aerial strip protruding from a different sort of world. Directly above me, I could see the two pairs of windows through which he'd looked out over the ocean. (In those days, before the elevated malls and walkways, he'd had an unobstructed view to the edge of the world.) The windows were long unwashed.

The proprietor of the crockery shop was absorbed in a domestic holo. A fierce-looking wedge-headed matron, she seemed out of place among the dazzling protagonists of the unlikely drama. I did not immediately rouse her. There was a door at the back of the shop which, I suspected, would provide access to the upper levels. I wandered in its direction.

When she looked up, I stopped to examine the crockery, which was handcrafted by local artisans. She stepped out of the holo without dissolving it, and smiled pleasantly. "Good morning," she said. She looked friendly enough, though I could see she didn't expect to sell me anything. "Can I help you?"

"My name's Tiel Chadwick," I said. I'd picked up an antique kiln-fired cup. It had a satisfying heft, and carried Survey's old eagle-and-star logo, over the inscription *GS Ranger*. Harry Pellinor's vessel. "A friend of mine used to live here. In the third-floor apartment. I wondered—"

Her eyes widened, and she backed a step away from me. "No," she said in a voice that had climbed an octave. "I didn't know him. I've only been here a few years." Her eyes clouded with suspicion.

"Nobody's lived there since I came. In fact, I didn't know it had ever been anything other than a storage area."

"His name was Durell Coll. He was an artist."

She shook her head. "No. I don't know anyone like that."

"How long have you been here?" I asked.

She hesitated. "About four years." She looked closely to see whether I believed her.

I did a quick calculation, converting to Rimway time. She'd arrived shortly after Durell had left for Rimway. "Is the cup actually from the *Ranger*?"

"Of course."

I bought it, though it took a sizable slice of my remaining finances. But it was a piece of history, worth considerably more (at least on Rimway) than the price. I hoped that, in addition, the purchase would have a soothing effect on the proprietor. "I would like very much," I said, "to see the third floor. Do you mind?"

"I don't have a key."

"Maybe it's not locked."

"The owner always keeps it locked," she said stubbornly. "Nobody's allowed up there." Her face had paled, but she stood her ground, defying me to try to get past her.

I sighed, thanked her, and strolled back into the sunlight.

The room was cramped, and the walls intersected at angles that were never precisely ninety degrees. Portraits of grotesque young women hung on them. A delicate white table held a cup of steaming liquid and a few books. The books had no titles. Directly ahead of me, a broad slice of wall was missing, and outside, some distance away, a single cloud pelted a blue glass floor with big plashing raindrops. A chair was overturned, and, beyond the storm, someone had thrown a jacket across a freshly made bed.

The falling rain hissed, kicking up fountains.

I touched the control plate and the tableau dissolved. "It's a bit heavy-handed, even for a holo," I said. "My taste runs more to the traditional."

Halson Stiles bowed slightly. "We don't sell many oils," he said. "I'm sorry to admit it, but,"–spreading his thin hands–"people today are more interested in entertainment than in art." He'd gained weight, and his hair had thinned considerably. Time had not treated Halson kindly: a pity, considering the service he'd rendered. "I have a few canvases in back that you might be interested in. No landscapes, though. Some still life, a few character studies, and three excellent impressionistic works." He held out his hands, palms up, a man who has conceded to the tide. "It's a pity, but no one cares any longer about the spiritual values. Or subtlety. They want spectacle–" He exhaled loudly. "Sometimes, when I see what has happened to the public taste, I suspect we're heading into a dark age."

"I doubt it," I said. I wonder if legends are always disappointing when they take flesh. It was Stiles who, according to tradition, had wrested a meat-knife from Durell, and thereby saved the *Cordelet*, gaining immortality in the process. His name was inextricably linked now with Durell's, as mine would never be. But the strong brown eyes and composed dignity of the photos had given way to the unctuousness of a badly pressed salesman.

His was the only gallery on Fishbowl. At least, the only one with a listing. It was anchored high off a second-floor ramp overlooking the wide lawns and vaguely topological designs of the Survey Cluster.

"It's fortunate," I said, "that the *Cordelet* wasn't done as a holo."

"Ah." He beamed. "There is no way it could have been created on anything other than canvas. Yes: well, Durell was a serious artist. "

"Halson, you handled some of his early work, didn't you?"

"Who are you?" he asked. He was looking closely at me, frowning because he could not place me.

"I was a friend of his," I said. "My name's Tiel Chadwick."

He considered that, and then, smiling broadly, extended his hand. "I didn't think the dumb bastard would do so well."

"Thanks." I returned the smile.

"I was sorry to hear about his death. Terrible piece of luck."

We paused in front of a portrait of Harry Pellinor in heroic mode. "There was no luck involved in it, Halson. Durell's death wasn't an accident."

"I don't think I understand, Tiel."

"He killed himself. Probably not deliberately, but he didn't much care whether he lived or died. It wasn't hard to see it coming." I was having trouble keeping my voice steady.

"Why?" he asked. He looked genuinely shocked. "Durell wasn't exactly a tower of stability, but he would never have taken his life."

"I'd hoped you might tell me why."

"I have no idea. He was the only person I know who actually realized his life's ambitions. Was he having health problems? No?" He rubbed the back of his neck. "It makes no sense. What made you think I might know?"

"It's something that happened here. Something drove him. Your comment that he was no tower of stability: is there an actual tower anywhere on Fishbowl?"

"No," he said. "Not that I know of."

"Anyplace *called* the Tower? Or the Tower Room?"

"No." We'd been wandering among some local work, more craft than art. "Why do you ask?"

"No reason, really. Something he said once that I must have misunderstood. How well did you know him?"

He stared at me a long time. "Not well. A couple of the other artists used to spend some time with him. But they were all bone poor. Especially Coll. I guess that was because he never worked at anything other than his painting until he got absolutely desperate."

"Can you tell me the names of the others?"

"I could, but it wouldn't do you much good. One's dead, drank too much and fell off a ramp a couple years ago. The others are long gone. Left before Durell did." He tilted his head. "I can tell you where you might find somebody who remembers him. Durell liked to play chess. He was a member of a club. The organization was still in existence, last I heard. They used to meet at Survey."

"Thanks," I said.

He pursed his lips. "You know, if I'd been smart enough to hang on to just one of his paintings, I could've retired. It's frustrating. I knew how good he was. But I never thought anybody else would realize it. At least not before we were all dead."

"Halson, you said he was 'bone poor.'"

"He missed a few meals in his time. I did what I could to help, but I didn't have much money in those days either. Durell wanted to get away from Fishbowl. For two years it was all he talked about. He even took jobs from time to time to try to get the fare together, but he could never stay with them long enough. Then one day he walked in, picked up his paintings—I had three of them in inventory then—gave me a hundred for my trouble, and the next thing I heard about him, he was on Rimway."

"I wonder where the money came from?"

"I have no idea."

"Halson, are there any paintings other than the ones generally known?"

"No, I don't think so." He pulled sympathetically at his right ear, pivoted sharply, and disappeared through a set of curtains. He returned moments later with iced cordials. "He did some murals for Survey's operations center. But don't get interested: they tore the place down two years ago."

"Son of a bitch. He had his reputation by then. Didn't anybody try to save them?"

"I don't think anyone thought of it. His name didn't mean anything to the people at Survey, and I–I didn't know the building was coming down until it was too late. Ironically, they recycled the permearth, and used it to build this mall."

"The world is full of philistines," I sighed.

He nodded. "They were digging up Belarius to look at an alien culture, and they don't know very much about their own." A group of women paused outside on the ramp, and stepped into the shop's display case. I couldn't see the holo itself, but the edge of a soft blue haze expanded into the doorway. "They're on a ledge overlooking a waterfall," Stiles said. "It's our biggest seller.

"The murals weren't really that good anyhow. They were Belarian locales, sandstorms, broken columns in the desert, that sort of thing. Ozymandian stuff. Durell wasn't interested in it, but it put food on the table."

"He died rich," I said.

"I would think so." Stiles's eyes were half closed. "I hope he learned to enjoy it."

"Why did he want to destroy the *Cordelet*?"

He shrugged. "Who knows? He was proud of it. He invited me over to his studio the night he finished it. He'd never done that before. He met me at the door: you had to go in through a rear entrance. The studio was dark, but he'd placed a lamp right, and when he turned it on, the light fell full on the *Cordelet*. Can you imagine that? Walking into a dark room and finding the *Cordelet*? I knew immediately it was good: I told him it ranked with Delacroix, Matisse, anything I'd ever seen.

"'Yes,' he agreed. 'Who would have believed I could create this?' We stood there, both of us, transfixed. And then he went after it. I never even saw where the meat cutter came from. He just had it in his hand, and he was stabbing away like a maniac. The look in his eyes: I knew he'd destroy it, and I couldn't let him do that."

"You could have lost your life," I said.

"He let me take it away from him. The knife—"

"I never saw him like that," I said. "It's hard to imagine. I've seen him drunk and sober, up and down. Moods, yes. My God, he was moody. But I never knew him to do anything like that."

"He left it with you. The *Cordelet*."

"He said he never wanted to see it again. I sold it to a collector a few months later and sent him the money. He was on Rimway by then. Later, the collector got five or six times as much for it from an art museum on Rimway. The Apollonian."

3.

At night, the wandering ramps and walkways of Pellinor glitter beneath Fishbowl's spectacular ring system. Its people stroll among softly illuminated parks and malls, which range over the downtown area at, or above, sea level. The trees are healthy here, providing shelter for colorful and noisy avians, most of which are pittacines, imported from Earth and Mogambo. Fishbowl, of course, has no native birds; nature has provided only the drifting gasbag quill to populate her skies.

Pellinor was still a quiet, remote outpost in those days. There were, as yet, few tourists to watch the play of lights against the vertical sea. The Belarian excavations had been abandoned years before, but Survey had retained its foothold on Fishbowl, converting the old support facility into an administrative headquarters.

I can recall sitting on a bench that evening, after my conversation with Stiles. I was on the outer perimeter of the walkways, near the beaches. (They lower the outer ramps at night to create a high-tide effect.) On the inland side, occasional couples strolled through Survey's geometrical grounds. Above, on the top level, a late party was spilling out of a club.

I had never been so far from home. Delta Draconis was bright and gold in the north, just visible above the lip of the seawall. And directly overhead, in the wake of the moon, lay Belarius, cool and green and hostile. Home of the other civilization: the only nonhuman culture encountered during the long expansion from Earth.

Also to the north, about a kilometer away, I could see the cluster of squat buildings that housed Durell's old studio. I walked slowly in that direction, waiting for the lights to dim and the last stragglers to start home. If there were police about, they were not visible. Crime barely existed on Fishbowl. An incident in which several adolescents had stolen a skimmer and crashed at sea, requiring a full-scale rescue, was, ten days later, still a cause of shock and despair.

The smell of the sea was strong. Beyond the beach, it boomed and thundered with soothing effect against the Gantner light screens. I think I knew then that eventually the tourists would come, that the wealthy homes along the ridge would expand, and that Pellinor would lose her innocence. As things turned out, it happened more quickly than I could have expected. But that's another story. The only thing that mattered now, as I got up from my bench and sauntered off to do some burgling, was that, on Fishbowl, locks were simple and witnesses few.

There had been a skylight. Though he'd never drawn it, its effects were visible in some of his sketches, in the curious double shadow of the latticework, and occasionally of people or pieces of furniture, cast by the twin suns. I reached a strategic location over the rooftops in the commercial district, and looked down on the street in which I'd stood that morning. The rear entrance to Durell's studio, by which Stiles had entered, no longer existed.

I've never been comfortable with heights. The angle at which the ramp crossed the rooftops left only a small corner on which to descend. The pavement was a long way down, and the wind was gusting sharply off the sea.

I clipped a line to the safety rail and, with some misgivings, climbed over the side. Below, a streetlamp threw a wide pool of light around a truck docked at the depot. Two men sat off to one side, talking loudly.

The wind gave me a bad few minutes, pushing me away from the corner of the building. But I got down all right, and made immediately for the skylight.

Any interior walls that might have existed during Durell's time had been removed. I could see a toilet, a sink, and a shower stall toward the rear. Other plumbing fixtures were scattered about. Cartons had been stacked randomly throughout the space, and a couple of hand trucks were in the middle of the floor.

I dropped my line and, just before climbing in, wondered why the wedge-faced woman had seemed so frightened. A wave of foreboding swept up from the darkness below, and I debated whether it would not be best after all to go home, to forget Coll as best I could, and to accept whatever share of guilt for his death was mine.

I don't know what I was expecting to see: a few plastic-wrapped canvases, maybe, forgotten in a dusty corner. Or possibly a record of some sort. Something.

A rickety table with one drawer held a computer. The drawer was empty. So I wandered around, looking at floors and walls, and eventually staring disconsolately out of the arched front windows at the depot across the street. The two men were gone.

I'm not sure what drew my attention to the walls. At the front, where Durell's working studio had been, they were covered with several sheets of bright cheap pastel mosaics. The design was not unattractive, but I knew that Durell could not have lived with it.

That meant the panels had been put up after he'd left. But it seemed unlikely that there'd been another tenant before the area was converted for storage. Why then had anyone bothered to decorate the walls?

The sheets were thick with dust. I peeled off a long strip of trim, removed the baseboard, and released the magnets. (I heard the whine of a set of gyros, and the truck rose past the windows. Its lights fell across the glass, and then were gone.) The panel was wedged at the top and one side. I pried it forward and tried to get the lamp behind it.

Light fell on the outline of an *ear*. My pulse picked up: the lines were the quick, precise strokes of Durell Coll. I put the light down, braced my back against the wall, and broke the panel. It went with a bang.

I snapped off the lamp, and waited to see if I'd attracted anyone's notice. But there were no footsteps in the street or on the stairs. Nevertheless, as my alarm faded, I stood a long time in the dark, savoring the moment.

The sea was loud. It was easy to understand why Durell, working on this world, amid the endless tidal roar, would have found his meanings ultimately in the natural world. To my knowledge, he had never done a portrait.

I lifted the lamp to get a good look–

If Durell Coll's reputation was built on gloomy perceptions of a hostile universe, the man himself, at least during his early years on Rimway, had always enjoyed a good party. He was usually surrounded by women, and loved to spend the long winter evenings (we lived high in the northern hemisphere) talking and drinking with old friends.

He laughed easily; and nothing amused him more than suggestions by people who should have known better that his work needed cheering up. More vitality, they used to say. More life.

It was only toward the end that the shadows that had been lengthening across his art began, finally, to darken his features. And a Durell Coll that I did not know appeared, a man who took solitary strolls through snow-filled streets, who endured intense nightmares of which he would not speak, and who ultimately withdrew into a world not unlike that of the *Cordelet.*

It was the early Durell that I preferred to remember, and whom I'd hoped to find in the old studio.

What I found instead was something dredged out of the soul of a madman: a face barely human, rendered in Durell's painfully realistic fashion. It was of a man in middle age, with a full beard and commanding features. But his terror-ridden eyes gaped out of deep black sockets. The mouth was twisted into a frightful snarl, and flecks of saliva flew from the beard.

I stumbled backward and fell over a hand truck. The light went out again, and this time I was not at all anxious to put it back on. Instead, I lay in the dark, listening to the sound of my own breathing, feeling the palpable presence of the thing on the wall, trying to understand how a young Durell Coll, my Durell, could have created the monstrosity.

There was no doubt it was his work. Despite the lurid nature of the subject, tone and texture were clearly his.

I'd bruised an elbow, and gradually the pain intruded itself. I rubbed it, grateful for the distraction.

Who was the bearded man? I wondered whether he'd actually existed, or whether Coll unaided had conceived and executed the tortured image.

In a sense, I supposed I had what I'd come for: an unknown work by Durell, a previously unsuspected creation. It would be worth a lot of money.

But not to me.

The image appeared, at first, to be badly faded, until I realized someone had painted over it. And then, not satisfied, had covered the result with panels. But over the years, the paint had faded, and only the image remained.

And the other panels: what lay under them? I played my light across the swirl of spring colors, and my heart sank.

The sensible thing would be to leave. God knows I wanted to get out of there, and off Fishbowl, and to put behind me, somehow, the last four years of my life.

I removed a second panel. There was enough light from outside to see that there was another figure, although I could make out no details. I hesitated, and put the lamp on it.

It was the same hideous portrait.

And I uncovered another, under the next panel.

I was slow to realize that the three images, however, were not identical. The angle of the profile changed from one to another, the light in the eyes was subtly different in each, the beard– I took them all down, ten or eleven panels. The same face appeared again and again, its grotesque expression, each time, varied in some way. As though the artist were experimenting.

My Durell. The gentlest, finest human being I had known.

I replaced the panels. Had there been a way, I would have razed the walls, or destroyed the building. No wonder the proprietor of the crockery shop had been frightened of me.

4.

Fishbowl's chess club meets in a glass-lined conference room on the second level of a flattened pyramid, located on Survey's grounds, adjacent the main administration building, and known simply as the Annex. On the night I visited it, there were about twelve games in progress. One elderly woman, with the glittering eyes of a bird of prey, looked on. When she noticed me, she immediately challenged me to play.

I declined politely, whispering that I did not understand the game (an explanation which prompted a brief look of sympathy), and inquired whether she'd ever heard of Durell. She hadn't, and I settled in to watch for an opportunity to ask someone else. The only sounds in the room were the occasional scraping of chairs, and the clicking of chess clocks.

It was difficult to find a way to talk to any of them. Players had a tendency to resign merely by stopping the clock. Then, within moments, they'd reset the pieces and begun again. Not that it mattered: when I attempted to whisper questions, people shook their heads in irritation, and looked pointedly around at games-in-progress.

I retired from the field of combat, and settled for intercepting players on their way to the washroom. Two or three remembered Durell, but only as someone who came occasionally to the club. ("Liked to play the Dragon Variation of the Sirian, but he was far too cautious.")

Toward the end of the evening, I approached Jon Hollander. who was one of the club's officers. His face was ruddy and undisciplined, his jaws slack, and his eyes tired. Someone told me later that chess was the consuming passion of his life, but that he wasn't very good at it. "I don't recall him, Tiel," he told me, "but we've had a lot of members over the years. What precisely did you want to know?" He looked at me the way men do when they've been a long time without a woman.

I had no idea. "I suppose I just wanted to talk with someone who'd known him," I said.

"And you can't find anybody?"

"Not really."

He smiled for no particular reason. "Maybe we can find something in the archives."

We left the clubroom, and turned into a long carpeted corridor that curved and rose until we'd ascended approximately a level. He led the way into an office, and sat down at a terminal. "There may not be anything," he said, "but we can try."

I nodded, he brought up the screen, and gave it Durell's name. Dates and numbers appeared. "He was a member for almost two years." He grinned. "He had some problems paying his dues."

"What else do you have?"

"Address and code number. You want those?"

"No."

Hollander bent over the screen. "How about one of his games? We have three on record."

"No, I don't think so."

"Looks like he lost them all anyhow."

"You don't have a picture of him, do you?"

Hollander pushed a pad, and an index appeared. "No," he said, running his eye down the names. "We have several group photos from the period when he was a member, but he doesn't seem to be in any of them." The index faded, to be replaced by several people in parkas, standing outside the Annex during a snowstorm. "The Second Winter Open. Coll played in that tournament, but I guess he wasn't around when they took the picture." Another group appeared, still cold weather, but the snow was gone. "This was our first Masters', the same year. He wasn't eligible for that one."

He changed it again, for an indoor shot. But something had struck me about the Winter Open, and I didn't know what. "Go back to the first one, Jon," I said.

The snow scene reappeared. Three women were seated on a bench, in front of four men. "That's me on the left," said Hollander.

"Who's that beside you?"

He squinted. "Looks like Ux." The man was tall, bigger than anybody else in the picture. Although his hood was tied tightly down against the obvious chill of the day, he wore a wide smile. Hollander brought his image up. "Yes," he said, "it's Reuben Uxbridge. Did you know him?"

I knew him: his was the face on the wall. "Who is he?"

Hollander's features softened. "He was a charter member. One of the strongest players we've ever had. He specialized in the end game. Absolutely deadly once the queens were off the board."

"Where is he now?"

"Ux died quite a few years ago, Tiel."

Down the long corridor, I could hear voices as the playing room emptied out. "What happened to him? He looks reasonably young."

Hollander cupped his chin in his palms. "He drowned. I guess it was only a year or so after the picture was taken." His eyes grew thoughtful. "Queer business. He walked out onto a beach near his home one day in midsummer. A couple of families were there on an outing. He went past them without saying a word and simply walked into the sea."

He turned slowly in my direction, but his eyes were focused far off someplace. "Why?" I asked.

He shrugged. "He'd changed after he came back from Belarius. I don't know why. But he was *different*."

"Belarius? He went to Belarius?"

"Yes. On the second expedition. I guess they both more or less blew up. The official word was that there were hostile conditions. Ux never talked about it and, to my knowledge, no one ever pressed him with questions. But something happened to him. At one point, there was talk that he'd brought something back."

"How did he change?"

"I don't know, exactly. For one thing, his game improved. No, don't look at me like that: I mean really improved. He threw himself into his chess. Played like a man possessed. He opened up, and abandoned his old precise positional play for a ferocious combinative style. Listen, Tiel, chess players can change their approach to the game, but I never saw anything like what happened to Ux. It was as if he was a different person." He rose slowly and shut down the computer. "Furthermore, during that latter stage, he was the strongest player we had.

"That wasn't the only thing. He became withdrawn, didn't talk much to anyone. That kind of condition has to become pretty severe before you notice it in a chess club."

We retraced our steps to the playing room. "Did he have a family? Anyone I might talk to?"

"No," said Hollander. "None that I know of. But I can give you a list of people who knew him. Everyone liked him."

"Who was with him on Belarius?"

He shook his head. "Nobody here. They still have some people over at Survey who made the second flight. They'll remember him."

I looked around the room. "None of them here tonight, I assume?"

"No. We don't have anybody from Survey. They just lend us the space, Tiel."

"Is it a coincidence," I asked, "that Uxbridge's name is the same as the bay's? The one at the far end of the island?"

"That's the only bay we have. No: it's no coincidence. He lived out there. At the point."

"Jon," I said, "I was there yesterday, and I didn't see any houses. Not in the area of the bay, anyhow."

"You wouldn't," he said. "It's *in* the bay now. Underwater. Shortly after Ux died, somebody took a laser to the projector on the Point, and let the sea in. Pity: it was a fine house."

I could feel my scalp beginning to prickle. "Jon, that sounds as if you've been inside it."

"A few times. He used to invite me, or Arky, or one of the others out occasionally to play a few games." His eyes closed, and a rueful smile appeared. "He had a kind of trophy room at the back of the house, filled with plaques and artifacts and whatnot. And two leather chairs he'd brought with him from Rimway. Tiel, they were probably the only leather chairs on Fishbowl. Those were fine evenings. And good chess."

"Jon, was this before he went to Belarius?"

"Oh, yes." He nodded. "I don't think anybody ever went out there after he came back. The invitations stopped. At least mine did. Although, now that I think of it, he came to my place now and then. He just didn't reciprocate any more." He'd turned away and was looking out through the glass. Fishbowl's rings were visible over the Admin Building.

"The destruction of the seawall," he continued, "created some commotion, because people thought maybe we had a loony running around who was planning to sink the island. For a while they posted guards at all the projector stations, but nothing more ever happened, and I guess they finally decided it was just some kids. Now, the projectors are pretty well shielded."

"They never made repairs?"

He looked at me apologetically. "Draining it again and reestablishing the screen would have been expensive, so we never bothered. No one ever stepped forward to take a proprietary interest. There've been proposals to go in and reclaim the land, but there's really no reason to. So we named the bay after him instead."

I showed him the holo of the *Cordelet*. "Is this what we're talking about?"

"Yes," he said. "That's it. The house is down there somewhere. Right about in the middle, I'd think."

I wondered if it had ever occurred to anyone that somebody had specifically wanted to destroy Uxbridge's home.

5.

In the morning, I rented a skimmer. But instead of turning south and running down the coastline, I procrastinated, hovering aimlessly over Pellinor for an hour, then drifting out to sea. I kept low, just above the waves, until my clothes were drenched with spray. Behind me, the land had vanished into a hole in the ocean, bracketed by the cluster of brown hills to the south, and the upper levels of Pellinor's wide ramps.

I settled into the water. Gideon was hidden behind lumpy columns of cumulus. The white rim of Heli was just pushing out of the sea, and the color of the sky was changing minute by minute.

I'm not sure how long I sat out there, listening to the water lap against the sideboards, thinking about the madness in the eyes on the walls, and the strange behavior of Reuben Uxbridge. If Hollander was correct, Uxbridge had undergone a basic personality change. There was an eerie resemblance to Durell.

I was no longer sure I wanted to know the truth, but I did not wish to be driven at some future date to return to Fishbowl because I hadn't finished the job. What had begun as an innocent nostalgic excursion had become something radically different.

I buckled myself in, left the shields down so I could feel the rush of air, and started back. Only the drifting quill, their fibrilla dangling into the waves, broke the monotony of sea and sky. An ocean with a single shore gets little traffic.

Just off the Point, a school of large marine animals were sunning themselves. There must have been a hundred or more, huge creatures, of the stature of our behemoth, or perhaps the sperm whale of Earth's oceans. They moved slowly, and their great dark eyes rolled curiously skyward to watch me pass. The articulation of fin and jaw was not so fine or detailed as I was accustomed to, but Fishbowl is a young world.

Abruptly, the sea fell away, and I was over the rills and valleys of the island. Then they too gave way, though not with the same breathtaking suddenness, to the burnished surface of Uxbridge Bay.

The mood of my first visit was gone: the sense of a place out of time, of a world with psychic links to an earlier age, had evaporated. And in its stead, despite the bright morning suns, I sensed only madness and despair.

I rose high over crystal waters, slowed to a few klicks, and locked in the pilot. Out near the Point, beyond the arc of hills that constrained the bay, lay a series of sandy beaches. I wondered which had been the one from which the unfortunate Uxbridge had strolled to his death.

The bay was almost perfectly circular. This was a feature not apparent in the *Cordelet*, where the harbor mouth appears quite distant, and the far shore rather near, suggesting a more elongated shape. Close in, the bottom was littered with rocks. But it was relatively clear, despite rippling shadows cast by currents, and clumps of undulating sea anima. Not far from the place where I'd stood my first day surveying the scene lay a line of rocks. Paralleling the coastline for a considerable distance, they were either a collapsed breakwater or the remains of a wall.

I dropped lower and flew in wide circles over the area. There was no sign of a submerged house, and I had about decided that either the story was fabricated or that everything had been destroyed. I was riding listlessly over the mouth of the bay when I saw the shadow in the water.

I lobbed a cone buoy over the side, came around and, too absorbed perhaps to pay attention to what I was doing, cut power before I was fully down. The skimmer chopped heavily into the water, bounced, jabbed its nose below the surface, and threatened briefly to turn over.

I blamed it on the lighter gravity, took a quick look around for damage (there was none), and got out a deep-sided glass dish I'd brought along for submarine viewing. I was right over the house, and it looked intact. That struck me as being exceedingly unlikely, until I noticed a small ridge cutting diagonally down from the shoreline and across the bottom of the basin. Driven into it, and now broken off, were a pair of stems of the type that provided nominal support for a Gantner light system.

That meant Uxbridge's house had been entirely, or at least partly, above the flood. But the water had got at the projector and shorted it out. The increased weight had snapped the stems, and the place had gone to the bottom.

It was a three-level structure, apparently made of stone rather than the standardized materials generally in use on Fishbowl. The external appurtenances, stylized cupolas, belvederes, porticoes, and so on, that characterize most of the wealthy homes on Fishbowl (and on Rimway, for that matter) were particularly in evidence here. Add small, round windows, and the illusion of an exotic sea beast lying quietly in the sand was complete.

But the windows were dark, and only fish swam through its abandoned rooms.

It had no tower.

I'd brought a breather with me, and I knew that the next rational step was to use it. But the house was far down, and the suspicion of what I might find prevented my unpacking the unit. Instead, I sat rocking gently on the skimmer, feeling like a damned fool.

After a while, I started the engine and rolled angrily into the bright clear sky.

6.

When Jon Hollander looks through the windows from the office in which the Pellinor Chess Club keeps its records, he can see a broad oval pool. Directly beyond the pool crouches a heavy, triple-tiered oblate building utterly out of place among the crystal structures of the Survey complex. This is the Belarian Field Museum. It is, according to a plaque mounted at the front entrance, an accurate representation of architectural styles to be found at Ysdril West, one of the major excavation sites in that world's southern hemisphere.

One recognizes immediately that it is the work of a primitive people. Constructed of quartz, the Field Museum is encircled by a pavilion whose roof rests on a series of square-cut columns. According to the plaque, the roof is 0.3 meters higher than it would have been on the original, to accommodate its human visitors. Entryways and overheads have been proportionately raised. The upper tiers are progressively recessed, creating an effect somewhat like that of a ziggurat.

The quartz blocks are rough-hewn and joined with cement. Nightmare creatures with bared fangs and talons guard the entrances, and hieroglyphs have been stenciled into the living rock, marking the four principal directions. The inscriptions are delicate, sylphlike engravings, utterly out of character with the ponderous stone blocks and doors.

I'd paused on the west portico to examine one, tracing the lean characters with my fingers. A plate translated: *"In the hour of need, I am with you."*

The windows were small, recessed, and barred. The descriptive material on the plaque announced that the structure was a place of worship, but it felt like a fortress.

I wasn't entirely ignorant about the Belarians. They'd been small creatures, by human standards, seldom surpassing a meter in height. Artists' renderings of their appearance were disquieting, however: pale, bloated, gas-filled bodies, not unlike the quill, which possess neither distinctive limbs, nor even separate body parts.

They never achieved a technological culture, and the last of them went to their reward a million years ago. I'd never really thought about it before, but standing in the shadow of that gloomy pile, I wondered how such creatures without external limbs had constructed a written language. Or, for that matter, juggled building supplies.

I walked in under a blunt arch. The ground floor of the interior was crowded with display cases, statuary, tools, and assorted other artifacts. An attendant in Survey's light and dark green uniform stood beside a stone altar, behind which several viewing booths had been installed. To my right, a ramp ascended to the upper levels.

I was surprised to discover an abundance of natural light emanating from a circular courtyard. The overall effect was, I suppose, like that of any museum: a place in which one felt bored, but pretended to be awed, by the collected junk of dead persons who had lived in some quaint manner.

Besides myself, there was only one visitor, a brittle, elderly man who was sketching an inscription from a hexagonal stone mounted over a display board. I walked among the artifacts, little figures carved from black rock set in gleaming cases with neat white cards identifying their probable age and use.

There were scrapers and cutters and rakeheads and spearpoints. Obviously, the Belarians had been more substantial than they looked. There were figures of animals and dwellings, and fantastic creatures that might have been real or mythical. One case contained several hundred tablets, all stamped with rows of ideographs. A plate placed them quite early in Belarian history. They had not yet been translated, although it was from similar, though somewhat later, materials that the *Book of Life*, with its immortal accounts of genesis and the pillars of the world, had been derived.

"Most of it's lost," said a voice behind me. "They developed paper eventually, and none of that survived. Only what they carved in rock." It was the old man. He was about my size, clean-shaven except for a neatly-trimmed white mustache. (That was not then the style on Fishbowl, and marked him as a hopeless relic.) "Even the inscriptions on their buildings are from early religious or ethical texts. The books are all gone."

"I'm Tiel Chadwick," I said, offering my hand.

He took it in a firm grasp. "M'Kay Alexander. You may call me Alex."

I described myself as a student from Rimway, and we talked for a while about Belarian art. Other than architecture, little remained.

"How did they produce anything?" I asked. "I mean, they had no hands."

"They had a highly flexible sheath," he replied. "Pseudopodal extensions. If you look closely, you can see them on some of the artifacts. Here–" He pointed to a pair of figures in an adjoining case. They did indeed seem to have limbs. Though they emerged from disconcerting locations: from abdominal and head areas, if you attempted to visualize the creature as a human being under sheet.

Okay: that seemed reasonable enough. But what about the

buildings? You can't move a boulder with a pseudopod. "They must have had heavy equipment of some kind."

"Not that we could find, Tiel. No: it was often difficult to sort things out among them, there was so little left. But I don't think they ever had the sort of machines that would be required to haul these blocks around."

"How do you know?"

"Their psychology. They were simply not a technological people. Did you know their culture was twenty thousand years old when they died off? And they never got past a medieval stage."

"What happened to them?"

"One theory is that the competition became too severe. Or that they couldn't unite politically. Or technological stagnation. Who knows?" He was turning the pages of his sketch pad, holding it so I could see. It was filled with renderings of the objects in the cases, or the altar, and of the Field Museum itself. "It's a puzzle, how they moved these rocks around. It's one of the things Survey was trying to find out when they were driven off."

I blinked at the old man: I hadn't heard it put in quite those terms before. "What drove them off?"

Alexander placed his fingertips against the altar, as though to read something in the cold stone. "I'd love to know," he said.

"Wasn't it ever made public?"

"In a way, Tiel. They released a fairly detailed description of conditions on Belarius after the second expedition. It's an old world. There's been a lot of time for evolution. So the carnivores are very efficient. They have a lot of teeth, and they move very quickly, and some of them fly, and most of them are hard to see coming." I'd seen pictures of a few. The one that stuck in my mind was a kind of jet-propelled airborne shark. "And they are reasonably intelligent. Which, by the way, has been a factor in keeping their numbers down, so that they don't eliminate the food supply."

"How do you mean?" We were standing idly among the displays, near a diorama of the Ysdril West excavation.

"They made war on one another. The species did."

"Why?"

"For the same reason animals fight on Rimway. Water. Hunting rights. Except that on Belarius, it was organized warfare. The species there seem to have more than their share of intelligence and organizational capacity. In any case, I can't imagine why a well-armed force—and, at least in the case of the second expedition, forewarned as well—couldn't hold their own against local predators."

"Alex, you seem to know quite a lot about Belarius. Have you worked for Survey?"

He looked around for a place to sit, and found a stone bench. "I'm in the food business," he said. "Or was. I'm retired now."

I couldn't suppress a smile. "How does somebody in the food business come to be involved in all this?" I waved an arm around.

"We have a little group on Rimway," he said. "Mostly people like me, who are just interested in the Belarian story." He leaned forward, his voice intent. "Listen, Tiel. Survey's not telling the truth about what happened on Belarius. Moreover, it's been years now since they officially announced that they would not go back there. But look over there!" He pointed through the front entrances at the pool, and the cluster of Survey buildings beyond. They were silver and green in the late afternoon light. "Why have they stayed on Fishbowl? God knows it's not near anything. There's nothing out here."

I shrugged.

"Because," he said, "they're going back. Tiel, there is no possibility that they're going to walk off and leave what they've found."

The attendant stared curiously over at us.

The diorama was mostly sand: a collection of partly uncovered blocks and columns, earth-moving machines, temporary shelters, and people. A lander stood on the edge of the display. No single indigenous structure was intact. "Alex," I said, "I take it you've not been to Belarius?"

"No," he said with regret. "When we heard about the second mission, we pooled our money, and offered Survey a substantial sum to allow passage to one of our members. If they'd gone along with it, we were going to cut cards to determine the winner."

"What did they say?"

"Too dangerous. They couldn't take the responsibility." His eyes narrowed. "I can't quarrel with that. They lost almost half their landing team on the first effort. The second try wasn't much better." He stared at Ysdril West. "But I would have liked to go."

I'd been wondering whether Durell might have made the trip, but it seemed unlikely. "Alex," I said, "there were several excavation sites on Belarius. Is there a *tower* anywhere among them?"

"Intact?"

I hesitated over that one. "Not necessarily. Anything sticking up out of the rubble that one could describe as a tower."

"No," he said finally. "I don't think so. If there is, they're keeping it quiet."

"Do you know anything about Reuben Uxbridge?"

"He was an expert on ideographic structure." He glanced at his watch, and shrugged. "I have to be going." He stood up. "Uxbridge worked for Casmir Moss, I don't think he did anything important."

"Was he ever involved in any sort of unusual incident?"

"Tiel, I would say they were all involved in unusual incidents of one kind or another. I just don't know. If you want to talk to someone about Uxbridge, see Moss."

"Where would I find him?"

"He's here somewhere. He's one of the reasons I'm sure they're going back. Moss would have more important things to do than hang around Fishbowl if something weren't about to happen."

Two middle-aged women and a boy came in. The boy made immediately for the diorama. "Alex," I asked, "are you here alone?"

"Yes. Three of us were supposed to make the trip, but things came up. You know how it is."

"How about dinner?" I said. "My treat."

7.

That night, I looked up everything the Library had on the two missions. The official stuff wasn't very informative, and the dozen or so books written on the subject were neither consistent with each other nor helpful. Eggleston's *Bureaucrats in the Field* mercilessly flayed security procedures that "couldn't hold off a few wild animals with modern weapons." Adrian Hunt, in *Survey and Belarius: A Study in the Exercise of Power*, charged that the political appointees who control Survey's funding wished to put an end to the program because it cost too much, and the feudal civilization that had developed on Belarius could in no conceivable way make a contribution to Confederate technology. Other volumes hinted darkly at a demonic presence on Belarius. (Or under it, I suppose.)

There was no mention of Uxbridge anywhere, but Eggleston excoriated Moss as an incompetent paper-shuffler who'd been more concerned with arcane languages than with the practical hazards faced by his teams. (Moss's division of philologists and archeologists had taken the heaviest losses, and he was charged with providing inadequate security training for himself and his subordinates.)

Like Uxbridge, Moss was a philologist, though of somewhat more advanced reputation. He'd won most of the major awards, declined at least two university presidencies, and written *The Dawn of Language*, the definitive study of proto-Sumerian ideography. Eggleston remarked that, for Moss, the Belarian discovery was a kind of fresh virgin after the long line of ancients so thoroughly worked over by everybody else.

But this had apparently been a virgin with a bite.

The evening after my conversation with M'Kay Alexander, I contrived to be at Arnhof's, a small restaurant overlooking a shopping quadrangle, when Moss came in for his evening meal. He was a man of quite ordinary appearance, with dull blue eyes, and defensive lines drawn about his mouth. It would have been no surprise to learn that he made his living from dead languages.

I maneuvered into a table adjacent his, ordered some seafood (what else?), and awaited an opportunity. Moss took some papers from a case, spread them out in front of him, and sank immediately into a reverie.

About the time the wine came, his and mine, he looked up to catch me quizzically staring at him. That was my cue. "Pardon me," I said, rising and advancing, "but aren't you Casmir Moss?"

"I am." He was not entirely displeased at being recognized.

"I'm Tiel Chadwick. I've read your book." That was a gamble. The truth was, of course, that I'd read *of* it.

He smiled back uncertainly, inviting me to say something else. I did. I told him that it had sparked my interest in ancient civilizations, and that I thought he'd made difficult concepts quite lucid.

Within a few minutes, we were drinking from the same carafe. He loved to talk about Babylonian politics, and I encouraged him, asking a few safe questions and, later in the evening, found myself strolling with him along the beachfront. Abruptly, he turned and faced me. "Who are you, really?"

The question caught me by surprise. "A friend of Ux's," I said.

He was silent for a time. The moon drifted low on the ocean, limning the incoming waves with silver. Eventually, gripping the safety rail, he told me he was sorry.

We walked out past the Oceanographic Institute, saying little and, at my suggestion, stopped at a small bar on the edge of a park.

"Reuben Uxbridge," he said, as we entered, "was one of the most difficult people I've ever worked with. He didn't like to take directions, thought anyone disputing his views was misinformed, and generally behaved abrasively toward everyone. But my God, I would give a lot to have him with us tonight."

That didn't sound much like the Uxbridge the chessplayers knew. Of course, the circumstances were different. I'd intended to wait until we'd gone through two or three rounds. But the moment had clearly arrived. He sipped his drink, studying the liquid in the wavering light of a candle. "Casmir," I said, "what happened in the tower room?"

His eyes widened perceptibly. "I did not think he would tell anyone. How much do you know?"

"Very little."

"I assume you are aware of conditions on Belarius?"

"I know they're difficult."

"I would say violent." He smiled, as at some private joke. "But the prize was well worth the risk. Did Ux tell you why we were so interested in Ysdril West? No? Then let me: it is not one city, but seven, built over tens of thousands of years on the same site. Like Troy on the Dardanelles. It was a strategic location. No matter how often the city died, later generations returned and built a new one. Ysdril West was such a place: in ancient times, it stood on a narrow neck of land dividing two continents. But climatic changes pushed the oceans back, the land dropped and dried out, and the place was buried in a desert.

"We've been able to follow the development of their languages over much of the history of the culture. Let me tell you what that means, Tiel: it means that we can begin, finally, to separate those perceptions that are induced by environment, including one's own physical wrapping, from those that are of the essence of a thinking species."

I could see that he was warming to his subject, so I tried to steer him back. "The tower, Casmir. Where was the tower?"

"On the eastern edge of the city. It was probably a beacon of some sort at one time, to warn off vessels approaching too close to the coast. We couldn't be sure because the top sections were gone. Obviously the place had been looted in later days by vandals, but the bastards had at least had the good sense to shut the doors behind them."

I understood why I'd found no tower in the diorama. It extended down, rather than up. "Dr. Moss, did you know Durell Coll?"

He looked puzzled. "No," he said. "Should I?"

"No. I'm sorry. Please go on."

"The tower was a Level III structure, which is to say it was part of the third most recent city. But it was curious because some of the inscriptions we found, not on the walls themselves, but in artifacts found inside, were of a later period. That suggested that the Belarians themselves maintained the place as a monument of some sort. They had a historical sense, Tiel. You will understand we were anxious to get into the lower levels.

"The upper compartments were filled with sand and, in some places, blocked by collapsed walls. And we were worried we might destroy something. So the work was slow. To make things more difficult, Belarius has a wide variety of exotic predators, and they are hard to discourage. We must have killed hundreds of one kind and another, but there were limits to what we could do. Sometimes people disappeared. Or were devoured in full view of a work crew. Or were carried off. Gradually, we got better. but we discovered we had to devote more and more of our people to the defenses.

"We'd originally assumed that it would be necessary to excavate the entire structure, but about a quarter of the way down, the quantity of sand in succeeding compartments began to decline, until it had nearly ended altogether. In time, it became merely a matter of opening heavy doors.

"There were inscriptions on the walls, mostly of a religious nature. These were quite sophisticated, by the way." He began an analysis of Belarian syntax. This time I let him go, and tried to show some enthusiasm. Another round of drinks came. And I began to suspect he didn't want to continue his story.

"Was Ux directing the excavation?" I asked.

"Oh no," he said. "We had an archeologist to do that, the detail work. Chellic Oberrif. We brought her in especially for the tower operation. She'd done something similar at the excavations of the early settlements on Mogambo. She was good."

I thought his eyes misted a little. "There was a place at the hundred and thirty meter level, about two-thirds of the way down, though we didn't know it then, of course, that blocked us for days. Whole chambers and connecting corridors had collapsed. The danger was that an attempt to cut through might bring down the entire structure. God knows it was shaky enough. But she looped a tunnel around the obstruction, and reentered further down.

"When we did manage later to excavate those sections, we found weapons and remains. A battle of some sort had been fought in there, and one side or the other had tripped a mechanism that buried the contending parties. We have no idea what the argument was about.

"What was important, however, was that the vandals and robbers of later periods had been unable to penetrate below the battle site. In the lower compartments, we found furniture, religious regalia, the stuff of daily life. It was, of course, incredibly old, and a lot of it was dust. But it was there.

"At the base of the tower, we found a single wide oval room, with an altar raised in its center. A big one, maybe three times the size of the one in the Field Museum. We filed down into the chamber from a position immediately behind the altar. Several smaller compartments opened off on the sides. Directly in front, we were looking through an arch into a tunnel. Chellic hurried immediately around to it, barely glancing at anything else. 'We're down at least one level,' she said.

"We were at the end of a long workday. I proposed that we continue in the morning, but Uxbridge wouldn't have it. He sent the work crew back up, though Chellic, of course, insisted on coming with us.

"She was even more obsessed with the possibilities of the place than Ux. She'd made it a point to acquaint herself with the various ideographic systems that we'd solved, and had become a valuable contributor to our ongoing analysis. She was, in addition, a good shot. On one occasion, I watched her coolly stand her ground during a general assault and kill four or five pickeyes."

"Pickeyes?"

"They're birds, very small, and very fast. The name is deserved. Anyhow, we started in. We were using oxygen. Our radio contact on the surface advised us to return. Bendimeyer, who was the security chief, didn't like unscheduled activities.

"But we were all intoxicated by then. My God, I can still remember the exhilaration of that walk down into the buried city. Until then, all we'd had of anything below Level II was the satellite scans.

"The tunnels were low, and we couldn't stand up straight. Even I couldn't, so you can imagine how Ux felt.

"I remember Chellic saying how there was enough down there for a lifetime. We saw murals, metalwork, tools, even petrified gardens. We found a library in one room. But the books were dust.

"It was raining on the surface. We were looking at a scullery when

Bendimeyer got on the radio. We knew immediately we had a problem because he should have been asleep by then. 'Moss,' he said, 'we got a critter in the tower. It's started down, so you may hear from it.' I asked what it was. 'We don't know,' he said. 'Nobody got a very good look. It's bipedal, we think. Rodley says it's about Ux's size. Big.'

"We'd been on Belarius long enough to know that nothing that travels alone is harmless. But we were armed, and we hadn't found anything yet that a bolt wouldn't stop. The thing that concerned me was that we couldn't see very far down there.

"I asked Bendimeyer to inform me if the critter came back out. He said they were sending a team after it, and I asked him not to. 'It'll only drive it in on top of us. Anyway, I don't want nervous guys with weapons in front of me. We're starting back.'

"Chellic suggested we might be better off to wait it out. 'The thing could never find us in this labyrinth,' she said. But Ux argued that we didn't know what kind of senses it might have, and that we would be safer if we could make the tower room. I asked him why. 'Because there are too many places here where several corridors converge. We can't watch everything. If we can get back to the tower before it gets all the way down, we only have to worry about what's ahead of us.'

"Chellic concurred, and we got moving. Nobody was much interested now in the galleries and public rooms through which we passed. I'd been making notes as we proceeded, to avoid our getting lost. But we managed to take a couple of wrong turns anyhow, and lost time backtracking.

"After a while, Chellic suggested that, since we had no idea of the creature's capabilities, we should assume that it had already gotten into the lower levels, and that it might come from any direction. She looked meaningfully past Ux's shoulder. 'The thing,' she said, 'could even be behind us.'

"Imagination raises hell under circumstances like those. If you listen hard enough, you always hear something. I could make out claws scraping on stone, breathing in the walls, you name it. I drew my laser, though walking with a lamp in one hand and a weapon in the other was distinctly inconvenient. But it felt reassuring.

"Ux fell over a hole at one point and twisted his knee. He was looking behind him at the time, and went down hard. The weapon discharged, and drilled a neat round hole through the wall. We had to help him along after that, but nobody wanted to stop, so we kept moving. There wasn't much talk.

"I checked back periodically with Bendimeyer. They were sitting at the top of the excavation with a small arsenal, but they'd seen nothing come out." Moss took a deep breath. Sweat had begun to drip down his neck into his shirt. The narrative was taking on a life of its own: he needed no further encouragement from me.

"The places we were most worried about, of course, were the compartments. There was a profusion of entrances and exits. We hurried through them as quickly as we could, expecting every moment the wild attack that we knew was inevitable.

"Ux held up pretty well, and Chellic had turned into some kind of goddam jungle animal herself. I wasn't very happy about the situation, but I felt good about the people I was with.

"We stopped occasionally to check our bearings. It was during one of these halts, as we drew close to the tower room, that I had a sudden sensation of terrible hunger. The lights dimmed, as if all three of our lamps had faded simultaneously. Chellic sat beside me, her head bent between her knees, her neck exposed under the hairline." Moss sat stiffly erect. He put his empty glass carefully on the table. His eyes swiveled round, and locked with mine. "I thought how good it would be to bury my teeth in her."

I sat in shocked silence. His breath whistled through clenched teeth. "The sensation, the *urge*, lasted only an instant. But it left me weak and terrified.

"When we started out again, Chellic had to stop to help me. And I was afraid to let her touch me. Ux asked whether I was all right. I told him I was, and increased my oxygen. But Chellic knew something had happened, and she made no effort to move on until I signaled I was ready to go.

"We came finally into the tower room. I was relieved to see the altar, and the wide curving wall: it meant no more multiple entrances to be watched. Ux threw his lamplight around the chamber to be sure it was empty, and examined the series of adjoining compartments. Chellic climbed the ramp behind the altar and looked into the tunnel, while I kept a nervous eye on the way we'd come. 'We should be all right now,' she said, her features softening in the lamplight. Even with a pickax in her belt, she was a lovely woman."

Moss's hands gripped the arms of his chair. "There was no other way to proceed." His voice was hardly a whisper. "No finding of guilt ever came out of it. Even now, knowing what I know, I cannot see what we might have done differently. But my God there must have been a way—" His eyes squeezed shut.

"Ux suggested we rest before continuing. He eased himself down against a rock slab, and placed his lamp on top of it, aimed into the passage through which we would leave. The lasers are big-barreled things, not like the modest weapons that Survey teams are routinely equipped with. These were military issue at one time. At short range and high register, nothing that lives could survive even a peripheral hit. Under all that rock, of course, we had to be careful, but you will understand we had no doubts about our weapons.

"I kept mine at hand the whole time. Ux was still limping badly, and it was obvious he was glad to get off the knee. But he seemed more worried about me, and asked several times if I was all right." Moss's face reddened a bit, and he managed a weak smile. "He said nothing along those lines to Chellic.

"Then it happened again: Chellic had walked over near the altar and begun to move through a series of stretching exercises. While I watched her, the chamber began to darken. I could sense her long limbs beneath the coveralls, see the suggestion of breast and shoulder: the blood was warm in her shoulders, and I could taste—" Moss's eyes filled with tears. He shook his head savagely, leaped from his seat, and hurried out into the night. I ignored the startled looks of people around us, dropped money on the table, and followed.

He was staring up at the vertical sea. Reflections from the city lights played against its surface. "If I had my way," he said bitterly, "we'd kill everything on that world and be done with it. Introduce a bug, attack the food chain, tickle a couple of volcanoes. Whatever it takes. But I'd clear that goddam world once and for all." He jammed his fists into his pockets and looked at me with tears in his eyes. "Did Ux ever tell you any of this?"

"No," I said, trying not to feel guilty. "Maybe that's why he drowned himself."

Moss laughed. It was an ugly sound. "Tiel, I've told this story a hundred times. I've told it to Survey, and I've told it to analysts, to drunks in bars. I'll live with it forever. Just like Uxbridge did.

"I was with it when it walked into the chamber. I felt the water-cold rock beneath padded feet, and the dusty air sucked past curving rows of incisors. I looked from Ux to Chellic to myself, delaying the moment of selection even though I knew, knew from the beginning.

The lean one, Chellic, had been on its feet and turned to face me. The light from the lamps had acquired an amber tint. I, we, knew our danger. The three–things–were terribly slow, but all had burners.

"It hesitated. We wanted Chellic, and we advanced cautiously toward the altar, and dreamed how it would be. She seemed frozen now, her breast rising and falling. And her face: my God, her face had twisted into a dark leer, lips drawn back in a feral snarl to reveal her own pitiful white teeth, an expression all the more horrible in that it contained no hint of fear, but rather implied that she too was about to share a live meal.

"And then I understood what was happening. We were all of us drawn into the mind and will of the beast: we all looked out through its eyes, and we would all rend Chellic muscle from bone.

"I tried to get out. The laser was a dead weight in my right hand, desperately far away. Chellic's animal face was close now: she opened her arms wide, and advanced. Ux, with a scream that echoed round the chamber, got to his feet, but could only lean drunkenly against the slab from which his lamp illuminated the ghastly scene.

"In that moment, I got the laser up. We watched the weapon swing in our direction, and looked into the huge black hole from which the deadly burning light would erupt.

"I'll tell you what it was like, Tiel: it was as if I were pointing the weapon at myself. I looked into that muzzle as certainly as I am looking at you now. I was deathly afraid of it, but I tried to pull the trigger all the same. I can make no claim to a heroic act, because I was even more terrified and repulsed by what would happen if I did not succeed.

"I'm not sure how to tell you the rest. Maybe you already know. Ux was also looking down the throat of the laser. And I guess it was more than he could take. He screamed and leaped toward me. The weapon went off, slicing out a chunk of ceiling, and the creature seized Chellic.

"Ux hit me hard, the laser slipped away, and the mindlink dissolved. To his credit, he recovered himself almost immediately, and scrambled after the weapon. Chellic and the beast clutched each other and rotated slowly in a grim parody of a sexual embrace. They moved against each other's bodies and Chellic cried out, more in ecstasy than in pain. Blood spurted, but the dance continued. It went after her throat, and Chellic sagged. Ux brought the laser up and fired. The creature shrieked, released her, threw a glance of pure malevolence and hatred at us, and fled into the lower levels. A second shot went wild."

He took my arm, and we walked slowly along the seafront. His palm was wet. "Ux never forgave himself."

"What happened? To the woman? Chellic—?"

"She was dead before we could get her to the surface." His grip on my arm tightened.

And I thought about the inscription on the west portico, which took on a dark new meaning.

In the hour of need, I am with you.

8.

So in the end it came down to the house at the bottom of the bay.

I'd intended to be out on the Point shortly past dawn, but I woke late, after another restless night, and then delayed over a long breakfast. I had a fair notion what was waiting for me beneath that calm surface, and I was in no hurry to confront it.

The bay was unsettled: there was a steady eastern chop, and the water looked rough. It was a gray, formless day, oppressive and quiet save for the steady beat of the incoming tide. I located my buoy, and circled it slowly. Uxbridge's house was not visible from the air.

A sharp gust rocked the skimmer. I took it down, eased it into the water, more carefully this time, and anchored it. I did not stop to think about what lay below: I kicked off my clothes, stowed them in the aft locker, and extracted my breather from its carrying case. I checked out the lamp, put on a belt, and attached a utility pouch. I strapped a depth gauge and timer to one wrist, the lamp to the other, pulled on the fins and mask, and slipped overboard.

The water was warm. But the sunless day reduced visibility severely; I could see only a few meters in natural light. I took my bearings from the buoy and the skimmer and started down.

The water turned cool and warm again. A few fish darted away, and one of the broad-ferned swimming plants common in Fishbowl's temperate latitudes startled me by wrapping a tendril around one ankle and giving it a tug. But when I reacted, it lost interest.

The grim, mottled, sea-shrouded house gradually took shape: turrets and parapets rose out of the gray depths, stone walls formed, and oculus windows appeared and darkened, as though adjusting to a change in light.

I hovered above it for several minutes, maybe choosing my best approach, maybe hesitating. Then I descended to one of the turrets, followed its sloping roof past torn pads and exposed plates, and started down the face of the building.

At the upper level, I thumbed on my lamp and looked through a window that was, remarkably, still intact. Everything inside was covered with silt. A bed was jammed into a doorway, light furniture had been scattered about, the contents of a bureau were spilled and buried. A closet, probably short-circuited at the time of the flooding, had partially exposed two rows of hanging garments. These fluttered gently in whatever currents passed through the room.

Below me, a long, serpentine fish glided out of a venting pipe and slipped into the gloom. I seized a piece of cornice and hung on until it was long gone. The stone was slippery with the algae that inhabit most water oceans.

The front door was missing, and the frame which had supported it was bent.

I passed inside, and the beam of my lamp faded into the depths of a large central hall. A staircase rose on the right, and large double doors opened on the left. Again, assorted chairs and tables were tumbled about, bookcases overturned, and the whole covered with sediment. Two portraits had once hung beneath the staircase: the frames were still in place, but the canvas in each had shriveled, and no hint of the subjects remained.

Though I knew more or less where I was going, I took a moment to look through the double doors. It had been a sitting room; even in its present condition, I could see that it had been a stiff, formal place: the sort of room in which one conducts official matters, designed to impress a business acquaintance, and at the same time to hurry things along.

But I was surprised to see a photo of Ux (still dry in its frame) with several people in academic robes. Other pictures and mementos lay buried in the silt. I knelt and dug, extracting them one by one. Most were ruined. But a few had been preserved: a highly favorable review of a book he'd written on ancient languages; an award from an institution whose name was no longer legible, acknowledging his work on Mycenaean linear documents; a photo of Ux and an attractive dark-haired young woman, both in coveralls, and both wielding spades. (My God, could that be Chellic?)

I placed them carefully in my pouch.

And I found the snow photo: an enlarged duplicate of the one from the chess club. My hand shook as I brushed the last of the sand away from it. Reuben Uxbridge, wrapped in a blue parka, smiled out at me.

But the photos were in the wrong room. Jon Hollander had spoken of the retreat in the rear of the house, where he'd gone to play chess, and probably where Ux had really lived his life. That would be the normal place to keep such things. My heart pounded: I knew exactly what I was going to find. And I knew why Durell had tried to destroy the house.

There was something else about the snow photo: I examined it in the uncertain light. Four men and three women in a snowstorm. Behind them, the looping colonnade of the Admin Building was visible. Just off to the left, behind Jon Hollander's head, lay the frozen rim of the pool that fronted on the Field Museum. And I knew one of the three women. The one in the middle, who was laughing, and appeared to be looking almost mischievously at Uxbridge, was the woman with the spade.

I swam the length of the hall, past closed doors, past ruined cabinets and wine sets, past the sand-clogged rubble of a lifetime. I'd acquired a few fish, fat spiny-finned creatures that moved with me, but darted back out of the light. I was grateful for their company.

I approached a door heavier and shorter than those elsewhere in the building. I pushed it ajar, and poked my lamp in.

I could see a desk, an overturned computer console, padded chairs (presumably the ones about which Hollander had spoken), and a square table. Thick drapes were still in place over the windows and around the walls.

The inner sanctum. I caught my breath.

I used the doorknob for leverage to come upright, with my fins planted on the floor and half-walked half floated across the threshold. Things seemed somehow less displaced in that room, as though some strange gravity gripped them.

One chair had been placed precisely in the center of the floor. I looked at the circular wall, thinking vaguely of the one in the tower room. How many hours had Reuben Uxbridge sat in that chair, trying to exorcise the demon that had, indeed, followed him back from that ridden world? How often had he struck down poor bureaucratic Moss, when Moss was about to save Chellic, save them all, at whatever cost to himself?

In a sense, Chellic had been fortunate. Uxbridge had been the real victim.

And Durell.

Only Durell, desperate for money, could supply what Uxbridge needed.

I approached the curtains, rotted now, still concealing their terrible secret and ripped them from the wall.

In the pale glow of the lamp, the climactic struggle that Moss had described sprang to life: Chellic and the pink-eyed monstrosity, both covered with sweat, were wrapped in each other's arms, while an enraged, terrified Uxbridge, wearing a variation of the grotesque countenance I knew so well from the studio, attacked Moss. It was the instant before he reached the smaller man, when Moss was trying desperately to use the laser, when there was still time. It was the instant when Uxbridge lost his soul.

9.

I had to tell someone about it, and I decided on heroic little Casmir Moss. He was reluctant at first to see me again, thinking he'd embarrassed himself, I suppose. But in the end, he agreed to meet me for lunch, and I told him the story, the part he didn't know. When I was finished he just sat, not knowing how to respond. At last, he said simply, "It wasn't his fault."

"Yes, it was," I said.

He looked at me, shocked. "You don't know how it was. Nobody can blame him for Chellic's death."

"Not Chellic," I said. "He wanted to relive that final moment. Perhaps to change it. Or maybe he wanted to punish himself by immortalizing it. I don't know. But there was another victim."

He looked at me, puzzled.

"Durell," I said. "I wonder if he ever considered what he was doing to the artist—"

PART THREE
COSMIC COCKTAILS

Whistle

NGC4038 and 4039 are unlikely to register with most of us. But they are designations for a catastrophe on an unimaginable scale.

These are the Antenna Galaxies, located in the southern constellation Corvus. They have plowed directly into one another, an intergalactic train wreck that has torn millions of stars from their orbits and ejected them into deep space. The collision has also produced the pair of luminous tails from which they derive their name. Millions of new stars are being born as a result of the conflagration, and, at a range of sixty-five million light-years, we have a ring-side seat.

Elsewhere, we can see other galaxies in collision. It is not an extraordinary event.

You cannot read about such things, of course, without wondering what the view is like if you're caught up directly in the event. It's hard to believe that, in a calamity on such a vast scale, there aren't some terrified observers watching from the inside and hiding under their beds. It's not beyond the bounds of possibility that tens of thousands of worlds not unlike our own are being swept away as we casually sit down to dinner this evening.

When the editors of Bantam's Full Spectrum 2 *invited me to contribute something, they caught me in a dark mood.*

✻

Twenty years ago, Al Redwood walked out. He walked out of Ed Gelman's old galactic survey project, out of his job, and out of town. I knew what it was all about. We all knew.

They'd been working on M82, a galaxy ten million light-years from the Milky Way. They were interested in it because of the intense star formation going on there. The unusual activity derived from its having sideswiped a neighboring galaxy, M81, in ancient times. Stars had been ripped from their orbits, giant dust clouds were stirred up, and the place became a cauldron of sorts. In the midst of all this, Al picked up an artificial transmission.

At least that was what he thought. When he went looking for it again, it was gone.

Gelman laughed at him. And I guess the rest of us did too.

There was no way to prove anything. All he could do was *point* to a narrow band transmission in the optical range, with peculiar symmetries and repeating pulse, wavelength, and intensity patterns. A laser, Al suspected.

I remember the final confrontation with Gelman, the day Al stormed out, the last time I'd seen him. They were on the front steps of the data center, *on the front steps*, for God's sake, screaming at one another. Gelman didn't want any little green men hanging around *his* project. So Al quit, and I never even got the chance to say goodbye.

He dropped out of sight for a couple of years. None of us heard anything. His family had money, so he didn't have to work. And then I got a Christmas card from Texas: *Nick*, it said in his precise handwriting, *it was the pulse clusters all the time. How could we have missed it?*

There was no return address. But I knew that, out there somewhere, Al was still chasing his elusive vision. Later, over the years, there was more: on D. C. Marriott stationery: *I still think the frequency correspondences are critical. One weakens, another intensifies. Is it a counterpoint of some kind? By the way, I'm doing fine. My best to Ginny and the kids.* And hurriedly scribbled on a postcard with a picture of the Atheneum: *Getting close. They're out there, Nick. They're really out there!*

Al was a lot like M-82. Explosive. Remote. Lit by inner fires. Ultimately self-destructive. A man whose personal stars periodically went nova. Ironic that he of all people would imagine receiving a transmission from that chaotic place, which had erupted nine or ten million years ago, and which was undoubtedly still bubbling.

Periodically he'd say he was going to be in the area and would stop by. The first few times I got in a couple of bottles of Jamaican rum. He was big on rum. Later I didn't bother.

It went on like that for two decades. Sporadic letters from odd places around the country, from Canada, from Europe, from Australia, once from Tokyo. Always promising progress. Sometimes they came in spurts, sometimes several years passed between communications. It was almost as if he were pursuing those goddam gremlins around the world. He never spoke of anything else, other than to ask about my family, or my health. As far as I know, no one else ever heard from him at all.

Then one night at about 3:00 A.M., he showed up in a driving January rainstorm, and I'll never forget how he looked, old and exhausted, his hair gone, his face creased. His top coat was open, his cardigan drenched. Water ran off his ears and nose. He stood in the storm, eyes empty, making no move to come in. "Nick," he whispered, "I know what it is." As if we'd last spoken the day before. As if someone had died.

I pulled him inside. "Hello, Al."

He was shaking his head, staring at the night light that illuminated the staircase I'd just descended. I hit the wall switch, a table lamp came on, and he seemed to jerk awake. "I know it's late," he said. "I'm sorry. I hope I didn't disturb anyone."

Ginny and the kids were all long gone by then. "No," I said.

"Good." Even for twenty years, he'd lost a lot of ground. I knew I'd grayed myself, slipped into middle age. But Al looked ready for a back porch and an apple tree. "You know what the sons of bitches did?"

"No." What sons of bitches?

He peeled off his coat and, before I could get near him, lobbed it across an armchair. "We were on the wrong track right from the beginning, Nick. It never occurred to anybody we might be looking for something other than digital data."

My God, he was off and running again. "Al," I said, "what are you drinking?"

He ignored the question. "I mean, our working hypothesis had always been that an artificial transmission could be translated in some mathematical way. And that one that had come seven million light years would have to be a directed signal. A deliberate attempt to communicate. Right?"

I nodded. "How about brandy?" There was no rum in the house.

"Sure. Now: an effort to communicate is going to contain instructions. It's going to break easily. It has to. That's the goddam point!" He chewed his lip and I thought he was choking back tears. He went quiet for a while. "But it was never there. I tried every approach I could think of. NSA even had a crack at it. Did you know that? They came up with nothing." His eyes brightened with satisfaction. "Absolutely nothing. You know what Gelman thought?"

He ignored his brandy until I pointed to it. "You ought to get out of your shoes," I said.

"Gelman thought it was a *reflection*. He couldn't account for it any other way, so he decided it was a goddam reflection. Nick, why do we always try so hard to explain everything away?"

"I don't know."

He sipped his drink. "Did you know he's dead?"

"Gelman? Yes, I'd heard. It was a few years ago."

"You know what I wanted, Nick? I wanted to show him. Son of a bitch, I wanted to walk in and hand him the evidence." His shoulders slumped. "Just as well." He shook his head and laughed. It was a curious kind of sound: amused, stoical, bitter. "Doesn't matter. He wouldn't have believed me anyway."

There had been a time I'd thought Al Redwood was headed for a brilliant career. But even then he'd been a social black hole, a man with no existence outside the observatory. No family, no other friends. Only colleagues, and his work. It was painful to see him now, studying his fingerprints on the glass.

I was never sure why he felt drawn to me. Maybe it was my family. The older kids loved to listen to him. And Ginny and I often sat with him late into the evenings. My own career leveled off at a plateau roughly commensurate with my abilities, which is to say not very high. I accepted the fact early on that I wasn't going to walk with giants. I was a maker of catalogues, an analyst, a man with an eye for detail. A recorder and observer of other people's greatness.

He pulled off his shoes.

"What does it say?"

His eyes were cool and preoccupied behind thick lenses. I could see him running the question through again, his lips tightening slightly. "Weren't you *listening*, Nick? It doesn't say *anything*! Not a goddam thing."

The storm rattled the house.

He got up, walked over to his coat, fumbled through the pockets, and produced a CD. "Here." He held it out for me.

It looked ordinary enough. I took it, held it, looked at him. He was refilling his glass, his back to me. I sighed and slipped the disk into a player.

Al strolled across the room and stared out through the blinds.

I punched the START button.

"The neighborhood hasn't changed much, Nick." An electronic

whisper blew through the room. "I assumed that the patterns of duration and intensity and color and the rest of it could be broken out into symbols. That it would have meaning."

The whisper intensified. Rustlings and murmurs surfaced, connected, flowed through the still dry air. He turned, cocked his head, and sighed. "This is what you get if you modulate the frequency with an audio signal."

"There's a cadence," I said, hardly breathing.

He laughed. "Yes! From seven million light-years, we get 'Chopsticks'!" He threw up his hands. "Damn their hides, Nick. How could they do anything so vicious?" His eyes were wet. He stood behind an upholstered chair, gripping it, trying to put his fingers through the fabric. The disk ran on: an inconsequential electronic river. "There's not much to it," I admitted. "It tends to be repetitious."

"It's a joke." The dining room was dark. He stared into it. I thought maybe he expected me to say something.

"You can still publish," I said. "If you can document this—"

"Hell, no. I've had enough. You publish, if you want." He was pulling on his coat. The sounds did have a certain quality—

"You can't go out in that storm, Al. Stay here, tonight."

"It's okay. I'm over at the Holiday Inn. Thanks anyway." He pushed past me into the entry.

"Don't forget—"

"You can have it. Souvenir."

"Al—"

"I wanted you to know, Nick. I wanted somebody to know."

I nodded. "What will you do?"

"I'll be all right." He shrugged. "I'll probably go back to New Mexico. I've been teaching down there the last couple of semesters." He straightened his shoulders and grinned. For that moment, the old Al Redwood was back. "Nice climate. And listen: don't worry. I've got a lot to keep me busy."

Whistling past a graveyard.

He shook my hand and hurried down the front steps. A rented car was parked at the curb. He waved as he drove off.

I wondered if I'd ever see him again.

They would have needed a trillion watts to hurl Redwood's signal across seven million light-years. Who would build that kind of transmitter to send out a pleasant little coded melody? At dawn, I was still listening to the damned thing.

• • •

I took the next day off and went over to see Jean Parker, who operates a recording studio in Middletown. She's a short, intense, red-headed woman with a hell of a smile. I'd met her years before at a Wesleyan faculty dinner, where she was being honored for her contributions to the university music theater. I told her about Al, about M-82, about the transmission. About how he was trying to pretend it was not a major disappointment. "I'd like to establish whether there might be something to it."

"It's a wild story." But she glanced at the disk without interest. "What do you want me to do with it?"

I wasn't sure. "Listen to it. Assume he was right, and this is a bona fide first-contact signal. What might it mean?"

"You're kidding."

"Try it."

Her eyes closed. "Call me in a couple of days."

"I've got it on a chip." She ushered me into a booth in the rear of her studio and turned on a synthesizer. "It's tied into a Synclavier III, an enhanced Lyricon, and a few enhancement programs of my own design." She stopped and looked puzzled. "You don't care?"

"I don't understand much when you get past guitars."

"Okay. Let me start by telling you that by any reasonable definition, your recording *is* a legitimate musical composition. It has consistent structure, tonal contrast, symmetry and counterpoint, even an intensification of variations toward the conclusion. I don't see how it could be a product of natural forces. *So*, if your friend was being honest with you, and if the source of this is what you say, then he's right. It's Martian music." She beamed. "If you can convince the public, it ought to do pretty well."

That was an amusing notion. "I guess it might have commercial possibilities."

"Get a good PR guy and tell your friend to ride it, Nick." She offered me a cup of coffee. "It didn't sound like much to you because you only had the basic melody. What I've done is to create a virtual orchestra and input the melody into the computer and then through the synthesizer. The system adds appropriate harmonics and rhythm, makes assignments to the various components of our orchestra, and does some basic arrangement. You want to hear the result?"

"Go ahead." I'm not sure what I expected. I kept thinking about conditions in M-82, an entire galaxy caught in an eon-long catastrophe. The band on the *Titanic*. "Nearer My God To Thee."

"Tell me about the place where they live." She touched a presspad. "What do you know?"

"I think it would be fair to say that, wherever they are in M-82, the sky is on fire."

"Okay," she said. "Maybe that fits."

Lights faded. I listened again to Al Redwood's music. It was more liquid now, distant, delivered by strings rather than the electronic burble of a Cray. There was a sense of misgiving in the cadences. Or maybe in my own mind: I thought about Al, fleeing down the years with his burden. There must have been moments when he doubted himself, suspected Gelman had been right all along. And then, "Chopsticks"–

Thoughts of North Dakota at night. I was six years old, under a blazing vault of stars, standing out behind the farmhouse while the earth turned beneath my feet. It was a time when the world was full of wonder.

But the music crowded out all sense of loss.

Without warning, it roared. Lightning ripped through it, and stars thundered along their courses. White light blazed across iron battlements. Oceans turned to steam, worlds drifted into the dark, suns dissolved.

The music filled with rage. And terror. Death rode the skies, driving the stars along, exploding finally in a torrent of sheer irresistible power.

The mood changed, and I recalled how Honolulu looks at night from the air. And Gus Evans' 24-Hour Gas Station and Diner, in its warm circle of light halfway up a Colorado mountainside. A coyote bayed outside the McDonald Observatory at Fort Davis.

Ginny lived again.

And I remembered Tom Hicks. At Wesleyan, when he won his Nobel, and we lifted glasses and laughed into the dawn.

"But that's *you*," I said afterward. "That's not what was on the CD."

She shook her head. "Maybe my imagination got caught up in it a little, Nick. This is not an exact science. But this is close to what they were trying to send."

"Then why didn't they send it?"

"I don't know the physics. But it might not have been possible to transmit anything other than the basic melody. They left the rest of it to us. Listen: I can run it through again, change some of the parameters, and things will be different. But not the essentials. They've provided the design, the architectural plan. All we're adding is marble and sunlight."

I stared at her, trying to take it all in.

"They've allowed us to collaborate with them," she said. No smile. Not this time.

"I've got to find Al. Hell, this is exactly what he was looking for."

"Probably."

"Something else: these people are *winning*, Jean. Whatever it is they're dealing with out there, they're winning."

"Maybe." She ejected the disk, handed it to me, returned the original, and gave me a second copy. "For Redwood, when you find him."

"Why 'maybe'?"

She was shutting down the equipment. "Did you catch the sense of wistfulness? It runs through everything, even the most turbulent sections. I think they're like your friend."

"How do you mean?"

"Whistling past the graveyard."

Valkyrie

I was fortunate. I served in the Navy during the late fifties and early sixties. It was a nervous period. We and the Soviets were testing bigger and better weapons, the Chinese were shelling the offshore islands Quemoy and Matsu on alternate days (on the theory that was more humane than hitting them daily), and the schools were running duck-and-cover drills. Francis Gary Powers' U2 went down, Khrushchev came to the U. N. and pounded his threats home with a shoe, and Hollywood gave us Dr. Strangelove. *But if things were tense, they were also quiet. I was never shot at.*

As the sixties wore on, things became more heated. JFK died in Dallas. Lyndon Johnson took advantage of an incident between North Vietnamese gunboats and a U. S. destroyer to expand the American role in Vietnam and soon found himself trapped in an endless war. Martin Luther King went to the Lincoln Memorial and held a mirror up to the country, but was shortly thereafter gunned down in Memphis. The long battle against discrimination came to a head and American cities burned. The war spiraled out of control, Johnson headed back to Texas, and we got Nixon, who claimed to have a plan for extracting us from the war. Protestors were everywhere.

By 1970, I was a teacher at Mt. St. Charles Academy in Woonsocket, R.I. It was a time when I honestly believed the country might come apart. The peak of the outrage came when several students were shot at Kent State. Many of my own students saw the war as pointless and foolish. And immoral. Sometimes they came to me for advice. What did I suggest? Should they go? Or make for Canada? Or simply resist and accept the consequences?

I had no answer. Young men die for old men's follies. Happens all the time. I began to suspect the world would be better off if all national leaders were required to be mothers with four or more kids of draft age.

Two decades later, when Harry Harrison invited me to write a story for the anti-war anthology, There Won't Be War, *I thought about those years. And "Valkyrie" was the result.*

※

We still get together once a month at the VFW. We drink too much and play shuffleboard and leer at Bess and talk about the old days. And we always get around to how different things are now: everybody out for himself, everybody on dope. Kids today just aren't worth a damn and we all know it. God help us if we ever need them to defend the country. Brad Conner always makes the same remark: when the Russians land at Virginia Beach the only people out there to meet them will be us.

I get scared when I hear that. It's a joke that prompts laughter and raised glasses from Herman and Cuff and the rest. And a knowing wink from Bess. Because it's the truth, we would be alone. But nobody seriously believes anymore that the Russians might really come.

Maybe. But somebody's coming. Unless whatever controls these things has changed its mind, they're coming.

I'm not like some of the guys, refusing to talk about the war, or even think about it. But I've never told anyone what I saw the first night of the Tet offensive, except occasionally when I've had too much to drink and nobody listens anyhow.

The attack caught me in Quangngai, in a downtown bar. I got out the back about the time a grenade came through a window. The streets were swarming with packs of armed men, some moving with military precision, others not much more than mobs. They shot down a few people for laughs. And they hauled a man out of a newspaper office and beat him to death, and then killed a woman who objected. A couple of places went up in flames.

Hard to tell whose side they were on. Not that it mattered.

A Cobra ranged overhead early in the evening, spraying the attackers with heavy machine guns. But other than that, and a burned-out tank, I saw no sign of the Army.

The tank was in the middle of the street in front of a bicycle shop. The bicycle shop was pretty well blown apart too. I stood in the shadows and watched the tank smolder, until I realized I wasn't alone. Movement somewhere. Metal clicking softly. Get off the street: I climbed through the shattered front window into the shop, and crawled behind a counter, intending to wait things out. Nearby explosions shook dust out of the rafters. Cong riflemen appeared and moved down both sides of the street. The fire glittered on their weapons. A few of them appeared on a rooftop opposite and set up a 50-caliber machine-gun. The 50-calibers were heavy and loud, and they were hell on choppers.

The Cobra kept hammering away. Missile tracks raced toward it, wire-thin tracers hurtling over the city. The gunship dropped low, out of sight, and then rolled in, pumping rockets and 30mm shells into the clapboard streets. I heard screams.

A bright yellow moon, big and peaceful, floated over the scene.

The V.C. answered with the 50-caliber. The chopper veered off, and the street fell silent. Then it came back, running at rooftop level. But Charlie must have got a couple more of the big machine guns up. They erected a goddam solid wall of steel and I wanted the chopper to back off, but he was committed by then so he kept coming and ripped by me, firing everything he had, churning down the center of the street, blowing dust in all directions.

Something hit it: it shuddered, and pulled up trailing smoke. Charlie kept firing. One of the rotor blades blew away. Moments later, the Cobra exploded.

Almost simultaneously, a brilliant white light erupted high above the blast. It filled the sky, threw the street into sudden daylight, faded, and brightened again. I covered my eyes with my hands and cringed. For a moment, for a single endless moment, I thought: nuke.

Then it was gone, and when I looked again, I saw only a blazing blue-white flare plunging down the sky.

Another gunship maybe. Something.

The gunners concentrated their fire on it. A piece of the thing broke off, and spurted away to the southeast, in the direction of the Pacific. It might have been a rocket misfire.

The rest of the object continued to fall. It burned furiously, utterly silent.

But it seemed to be slowing down. Leveling off. It drifted toward the rooftops, pursued by streams of tracers.

It sliced across the night, a brilliant cobalt star, and plowed into the roof of a four-story office building in the next block. The walls exploded, and the structure leaned toward the street, and collapsed. A cloud of gas and steam rose.

The gunners cheered. More fires broke out up and down the street.

Windows in adjoining buildings let go like gunshots. Then, in the steam and smoke and rubble, something moved.

A human figure.

A woman.

She stumbled out of the smoke, face and hair burned black. She staggered halfway across the street, and went down, one fist clenched in agony.

I looked at her, glanced back toward the shadows (filled with the dark figures of the Cong, just watching, not moving), and did the dumbest thing in my life: I ran into the middle of the street and charged toward her.

There was no point trying to keep close to the buildings. I was silhouetted against moonlight and fire no matter where I went, so I made what use I could of the tank. Charlie was slow to react: I covered about forty yards and got across the intersection before the first shot whistled over my head.

The woman looked up. Her jacket burst into flames. She should have been rolling in the street, the night should have filled with her screams. Instead she ripped off the jacket and hurled it away.

Charlie opened up in earnest. Bullets flew through the thick air, shattered wood, rattled off the tank, buried themselves in the street. One tore away a piece of my shoulder.

I ran with clumsy terror. The woman got up on one knee, took a deep breath, and struggled to her feet. She watched me, eyes filled with pain.

I stumbled toward her, lost my balance, ran a few more steps, arms and legs flailing, fell, rolled over, and came up in full stride. In all, it was a hell of a performance.

She shook her head no. And waved me away.

No time to argue. I plowed into her, knocking her over. But I kept going and got us up to a storefront.

She held onto a post, trying to steady herself. I'd got the fire out, but her clothes were steaming, and her face was scorched. She stared at me with angry black eyes.

I kicked the door open. "Inside."

Her nostrils widened slightly, and I saw something that scared me more than all the goddam shooting. She smiled.

The interior was dark. She strode inside, brushing away bits of charred cloth but otherwise behaving as if nothing unusual had been happening. Light from the fires illuminated the room through a bank of cross-hatched windows. Shadowy objects hung from the ceiling. From the smell of things, it was easy to guess what they were. We were in a tannery.

"They'll be right behind us," I said, trying to see through to the back of the building. She rubbed a knee, and rotated one shoulder, wincing. "Are you okay?" I asked. I realized about then that I was leaking blood from my shoulder. My right sleeve was drenched, and I felt wobbly.

She cast a long shadow. She was taller than I'd realized, taller even than I, which put her at six-two or -three. Slim. Athletic. Black hair cut short. Despite her size, she appeared to be Vietnamese.

I reached for her, intending to draw her away from the window, and make for the rear entrance. "Just go," she said. "I will be right behind you." It was the precise accent of one who has learned English from formal instruction.

I pushed the front door shut, secured it as best I could, and started back. Leather strips dangled in my face. I barged into a table. "Be careful," she said. "There are floor drains too."

It was getting hard to breathe. Probably the stench of the hides and the tanning fluid. Maybe loss of blood. Whatever. The room started to rotate. Gunfire ripped through the windows. She pulled me to one side while leather strips fluttered.

In the dark, a curious thing happened. I couldn't be sure, but I thought she moved to place herself between me and the Cong. I grabbed her wrist and tried to pull her down onto the deck. But I didn't quite get hold of her.

The shooting went on and on.

Finally, she knelt beside me. "You can't stay here."

Not *we*. *You*.

The floor was wet and slippery. It smelled vaguely of formaldehyde. "Sounds good to me," I said. I found her in the dark and pulled her after me.

Abruptly, the gunfire stopped.

We found a door in the rear wall. I pushed it open and we shoved through, out onto a loading dock. A truck with no wheels was parked outside. The street itself was dark and empty. Our best bet to clear out.

But when I pulled on her, she resisted. Shook her head no. "I don't travel in alleys."

She looked up. The tannery was located in a three-story building.

A staircase ascended to the second floor, where there was a wooden landing and a door.

"That's crazy," I said.

"Stay or go," she said. "As you please." She started up.

"They'll trap us." Dumb bitch. I thought it, but I didn't say it.

She went up like a jungle cat, reached the top, and tried the door. It opened and she disappeared back into the tannery.

Goddamn it.

I started climbing, and got halfway when a blast took out the lower room. She'd left the door open for me, and I was howling mad when I caught up with her. "They'll burn this goddam place down around our ears," I said.

She turned toward me. "Courage, Anderson," she said.

Anderson? Had I told her my name?

"There's a stairway here," she added, coolly. "To the roof."

She'd moved into a corridor and was striding toward the front of the building.

With all chance of escape now cut off, I took the sensible course. I followed. "Who are you?" I asked. "How do you know my name?"

Downstairs there were shouts, screams, occasional shots. Shadows danced outside.

Voices. In French. Footsteps pounding on the outside staircase.

She led the way to the third floor. I moved as quietly as I could. Occasionally, she caught her breath, and I heard sounds deep in her throat. She was hurting. She paused in the dark at the top and pushed through a wooden door. I was right behind her. We were in another store room. She hustled me forward. "Skylight," she said.

I could see it, dark, stained, rusted, padlocked. Out of reach. "Nice move," I said.

There was confusion below. They didn't know where we were. But that condition wouldn't last long. Moreover, I didn't feel good. I was sweating heavily, and the deck felt slippery. The night felt slippery.

She disappeared momentarily, and came back with a ladder. She braced it against the skylight, tested it to make sure it was secure, and told me to climb.

"What?" I said.

"Foolish man," she said. "*Climb.*"

The ladder was rotted wood infested with cobwebs. I started up and she was right behind me. But the skylight was latched or jammed.

I didn't want to have to crawl through broken glass so I was still looking for a way to get it open when she reached past me and pushed it. It swung up and I climbed out onto the roof.

She strode to the edge and looked out over the city. The building shook under the whine and whomp of incoming mortars and distant artillery. Automatic fire clattered in the streets, and screams ripped through the night. Long plumes of smoke drifted across the face of the moon. "It never ends," she said.

I wasn't sure what she meant, but the comment called for an answer. "Yeah," I said. "It never does."

Her features were composed, calm, masked. Her eyelids were half-closed, her lips parted, revealing sharp white teeth. Even with her face blackened with soot, she looked pretty good. "You have no idea, Anderson."

That was the second time she'd used my name. "Who are you?" I asked. "Do I know you?"

"No," she said.

My shoulder ached, and I did what I could to staunch the flow of blood. She seemed not to notice. Lights were moving high in the sky. Helicopters. "Are you from Quangngai?" I asked.

Those eyes clouded. She seemed magnificently unafraid. And, again, she smiled. But it was a smile composed of shadow and empty spaces. "I'm from Austerlitz," she said. "And Cannae. And Lepanto and Gettysburg." The voice was controlled. Resigned. Weary.

"I don't think I understand." I was chilled.

"No." She watched something in the street. "You don't."

There was a doorway in the corner of the roof. Heavy. Ribbed with iron bands. The door was closed, braced by a timber. "That's the way we should have come," I said.

The smile faded. "No. They'd have seen us."

"Where are they?"

"Everywhere on the lower floors. And in the street. They were trying to ambush some of your friends." Again, that stab of pain in her eyes. "They had some success."

"Sons of bitches."

I heard them at the doorway. The door was rusted, bent, splintered. But it looked solid.

The knob rattled.

"Have no fear," said the woman. "You're safe with me."

It was almost possible to believe her.

I heard them retreating. Then the door blew out, and flame belched from the stairway. They charged out onto the roof, a half dozen of them, saw us, screamed curses, and leveled their weapons at us. They were NVA regulars, not Cong.

She watched them. "I'm sorry," I told her. "They may let you go."

She came away from the edge of the roof, and stood beside me. "Don't move," she said.

An officer came out behind them. He was bullwhip lean, efficient, alert. He looked at me, looked at her, looked back at me. "I'm unarmed," I said.

Without taking his eyes from me, he signaled his men to spread out a bit. When they'd complied, he advanced a few steps. "ID," he said.

I pulled it out of my wallet and handed it over. He glanced at it and shrugged. "Where is your unit, Corporal?"

I didn't even try the name, rank, and serial number routine. "Don't know," I said. "I was in a bar."

He slid his pistol out of its holster and used it to signal the woman to get away from me.

She didn't move.

The weapon was a Czech automatic of the kind commonly carried by NVA officers. He caressed his jaw with the barrel, and brought the gun up until I was looking into the front sights.

Then she stepped directly in front of me.

I couldn't see his face. He spoke to her in French. The tone was hard and cold. Annoyed. He would not warn her again.

A sulphurous wind blew across the rooftop.

The officer shrugged. His finger tightened on the trigger.

But something in her face caught his eyes. He stared at her. She stood quietly. Sweat stood out on his brow. I started to move, to get out from behind her, but she took my shoulder, the one that didn't have a bullet in it, and held me in place.

A pulse appeared in his throat. His soldiers seemed paralyzed. They stared at her as their lieutenant did. Then one broke free, the youngest of the group. He shook himself, as though awakening suddenly in an unfamiliar place. He looked around, confused.

She gazed at him. "Stay," she said. And he froze again.

The lieutenant's breath was coming in short hard gasps. He struggled with his gun, trying (I thought) to pull the trigger. But gradually he lifted the weapon, struggled to bring it back, showed his teeth. Gave up.

His mouth had fallen, and he could not look away. He lowered the weapon. Then, as if a signal had passed between them, he took a step back. His soldiers, one by one, turned away from us and retreated into the stairway. The officer, his eyes glazed, followed. And only the young one remained.

He held tight to his AK-47, and stared at her with stricken eyes. She spoke to him in Vietnamese, gently, and then he too was gone.

"Who the hell are you?"

"Do you really not know?" Her face had taken on the tint of the smoldering sky. "After all this time, after all the killing, do you really not know?" Her gaze swept the rooftop, and rested at last on me. "Your fathers knew me. At Troy, at Port Arthur, at the Coral Sea, they knew me. Pray that your sons do not."

I don't know how to describe that moment. She stood full in the moonlight, breast heaving, voice thick with anger. "You've come for me," I said in a hoarse whisper.

Her expression softened. "No. Not for you."

"Then why are you here?" I was drenched with sweat.

"I was careless."

And I thought: the pilot. She'd come for the Cobra pilot. I must have said it aloud.

A nearby explosion rocked the roof. "No. Not for him either. Rather, the soldier who tried to challenge me a few moments ago. The young one. Within the hour, he will give his life for a comrade."

"My God," I said. "One of those bastards? You came for one of those bastards?"

"Yes," she said. "One of those bastards." The words were brittle. Flat. They hung on the night air, dull with impotent rage. "I am concerned only with courage, Anderson. Not with politics."

"What about the pilot? And his gunner?" I demanded.

"I am not alone." Her eyes slid shut. "Tonight we fill the skies of this wretched peninsula!"

"I'm sorry," I said, not sure exactly what I meant.

"We all are." She inhaled, deeply, sadly. "It is not permitted that the valiant should perish. But who comes for the ordinary man? Who stands with him when the shells rain down?" Her eyes raked the stars. "How many more battlefields can this pitiful world support?"

I can close my eyes now and see that rooftop and smell burning tar. And hear her final words. Her voice was warm and rich, lovely and terrible. "Anderson, we do not come for all who die in combat. But we will come for you. You will have your hour, and I will be with you."

You will have your hour.

Hell, I'm over forty years old. I do actuarial tabulations for Northwestern Insurance. A desk job. I don't walk very well. I'm thirty pounds overweight. And I have three kids. The Army will never have any use for me.

I think sometimes about her, and I wonder if she could be wrong. And I think about the kind of war that would need my services.

It's why I don't like to hear Brad Conner joke about him and me holding off invaders at Virginia Beach.

Act of God

I've always had a particular fondness for stories in which cosmic forces are at work. One of the best practitioners of that sort of thing is Gregory Benford. A quarter century ago, when I was a customs inspector on the Canadian border, and the world was a more sensible place than it is now, I used to use Benford to stay awake at 3:00 A.M. while the snow piled up outside.

I've since come to know him personally. One of the great pleasures of this business is getting to sit down in a bar and find yourself sharing a drink with a half dozen people you've been reading with considerable pleasure for years. You keep waiting for the police to come in and escort you out.

In 2003, Benford was putting together an anthology he would call Microcosms. *"The title speaks for itself," he said. Would I care to make a contribution? As it happened, I already had a story that would fit. But no, he wanted something original.*

Some of these people never give you a break.

At about the same time, I heard a debate somewhere by people who thought the Ten Commandments needed some work. The two more or less came together, and "Act of God" was the result.

※

I'm sorry about showing up on such short notice, Phil. I'd planned to go straight to the hotel when the flight got in. But I needed to talk to somebody.

Thanks, yes, I will take one. Straight, if you don't mind.

You already know Abe's dead. And no, it wasn't the quake. Not really. Look, I know how this sounds, but if you want the truth, I think God killed him.

Do I *look* hysterical? Well, maybe a little bit. But I've been through a lot. And I know I didn't say anything about it earlier but that's because I signed a secrecy agreement. Don't tell anybody. That's what it said, and I've worked out there for two years and until this moment never mentioned to a soul what we were doing.

And yes, I really think God took him off. I know exactly how that sounds, but nothing else explains the facts. The thing that scares me is that I'm not sure it's over. I might be on the hit list too. I mean, I never thought of it as being sacrilegious. I've never been that religious to start with. Didn't used to be. I am now.

Did you ever meet Abe? No? I thought I'd introduced you at a party a few years ago. Well, it doesn't matter.

Yes, I know you must have been worried when you heard about the quake, and I'm sorry, I should have called. I was just too badly shaken. It happened during the night. He lived there, at the lab. Had a house in town but he didn't use it very much. Had a wing set up for himself on the eastern side. When it happened it took the whole place down. Woke me up, woke everybody up, I guess. I was about two miles away. But it was just a bump in the night. I didn't even realize it *was* an earthquake until the police called. Then I went right out to the lab. Phil, it was as if the hill had opened up and just swallowed everything. They found Abe's body in the morning.

What was the sacrilege? It's not funny, Phil. I'll try to explain it to you but your physics isn't very good so I'm not sure where to start.

You know the appointment to work with Abe was the opportunity of a lifetime. A guarantee for the future. My ship had come in.

But when I first got out there it looked like a small operation. Not the sort of thing I'd expected to see. There were only three of us, me, Abe, and Mac Cardwell, an electrical engineer. Mac died in an airplane crash about a week before the quake. He had a pilot's license, and he was flying alone. No one else was involved. Just him. FAA said it looked as if lightning had hit the plane.

All right, smile if you want to. But Cardwell built the system that made it all possible. And I know I'm getting ahead of things here so let me see if I can explain it. Abe was a cosmologist. Special interest in the big bang. Special interest in how to generate a big bang.

I'd known that before I went out there. You know how it can be done, right? Actually *make* a big bang. No, I'm not kidding. Look, it's not really that hard. Theoretically. All you have to do is pack a few kilograms of ordinary matter into a sufficiently small space, *really* small, considerably smaller than an atomic nucleus. Then, when you release the pressure that constrains it, the thing explodes.

No, I don't mean a nuke. I mean a big bang. A *real* one. The thing expands into a new universe. Anyhow, what I'm trying to tell you is that he *did* it. More than that, he did it *thirty* years ago. And no, I know you didn't hear an explosion. Phil, I'm serious.

Look, when it happens, the blast expands into a different set of dimensions, so it has no effect whatever on the people next door. But it *can* happen. It *did* happen.

And *nobody* knew about it. He kept it quiet.

I know you can't pack much matter into a space the size of a nucleus. You don't have to. The initial package is only a kind of cosmic seed. It contains the trigger and a set of instructions. Once it erupts, the process feeds off itself. It creates whatever it needs. The forces begin to operate, and the physical constants take hold. Time begins. *Its* time.

I'd wondered what he was doing in Crestview, Colorado, but he told me he went out there because it was remote, and that made it a reasonably safe place to work. People weren't going to be popping in, asking questions. When I got there, he sat me down and invited me to sign the agreement, stipulating that I was to say nothing whatever, without his express permission, about the work at the lab. He'd known me pretty well and I suddenly realized why I'd gotten the appointment over several hundred people who were better qualified. He could trust me to keep my mouth shut.

At first I thought the lab was involved in defense work of one kind or another. Like Northgate. But this place didn't have the security guards and the triple fences and the dogs. He introduced me to Mac, who was a little guy with a beard that desperately needed a barber, and to Sylvia Michaels. Sylvia was a tall, stately woman, dark hair, dark eyes, a hell of a package, I'm sure, when she was younger. She was the project's angel.

I should add that Sylvia's also dead. Ran into a tree two days after the quake. Cops thought she was overcome with grief and wasn't paying attention to what she was doing. Single vehicle accident. Like Mac, she was alone.

Is that an angel like in show business? Yes. Exactly. Her family owned a group of Rocky Mountain resorts. She was enthusiastic about Abe's ideas, so she financed the operation. She provided the cash, Mac designed the equipment, and Abe did the miracles. Well, maybe an unfortunate choice of words there.

Why didn't he apply for government funding? Phil, the government doesn't like stem cells, clones, and particle accelerators. You think they're going to underwrite a *big bang*?

Of course I'm serious. Do I look as if I'd kid around? About something like this?

Why didn't I say something? Get it stopped? Phil, you're not listening. It was a going concern long before I got there.

And yes, it's a real universe. Just like this one. He kept it in the building. On the second floor. More or less. It's hard to explain. It extended out through that separate set of dimensions I told you about. There are more than three. It doesn't matter whether you can visualize them or not. They're there. Listen, maybe I should go.

Well, okay. No, I'm not upset. I just need you to hear me out. I'm sorry, I don't know how to explain it any better than that. Phil, we could *see* it. Mac had built a device that allowed us to observe and even, within limitations, to guide events. They called it the *cylinder* and you could look in and see star clouds and galaxies and jets of light. Everything spinning and drifting, supernovas blinking on and off like Christmas lights. Some of the galaxies had a glare like a furnace at their centers. It was incredible.

I know it's hard to believe. Take my word for it. And I don't know when he planned to announce it. Whenever I asked him, he always said *when the time is ripe*. He was afraid that, if anyone found out, he'd be shut down.

I'm sorry to hear you say that. There was never any danger to *anybody*. It was something you could do in your garage and the neighbors would never notice. Well, you could do it if you had Mac working alongside you.

Phil, I wish you could have seen it. The cosm—his term, not mine—was already eight billion years old, relative. What was happening was that time was passing a lot faster in the cosm than it was in Crestview. As I say, it had been up and running for thirty years by then.

You looked into that machine and saw all that and it humbled you. You know what I mean? Sure, it was Abe who figured out how to make it happen, but the magic was in the process. How was it possible that we live in a place where you could pack up a few grams of earth and come away with a living universe?

And it *was* living. We zeroed in on some of the worlds. They were *green*. And there were animals. But nothing that seemed intelligent. Lots of predators, though. Predators you wouldn't believe, Phil. It was why he'd brought me in. What were the conditions necessary to permit the development of intelligent life? Nobody had ever put the question in quite those terms before, and I wasn't sure I knew the answer.

No, we couldn't see any of this stuff in real time. We had to take pictures and then slow everything down by a factor of about a zillion. But it worked. We could tell what was going on.

We picked out about sixty worlds, all overrun with carnivores, some of them that would have gobbled down a T-rex as an appetizer. Abe had a technique that allowed him to reach in and influence events. Not physically, by which I mean he couldn't stick a hand in there, but we had some electromagnetic capabilities. I won't try to explain it because I'm not clear on it myself. Even Abe didn't entirely understand it. It's funny, when I look back now I suspect Mac was the real genius.

The task was to find a species with potential and get rid of the local carnivores to give it a chance.

On some of the worlds, we triggered major volcanic eruptions. Threw a lot of muck into the atmosphere and changed the climate. Twice we used undersea earthquakes to send massive waves across the plains where predators were specially numerous. Elsewhere we rained comets down on them. We went back and looked at the results within a few hours after we'd finished, our time. In most cases we'd gotten rid of the targets, and the selected species were doing nicely, thank you very much. Within two days of the experiment we had our first settlements.

I should add that none of the occupants looked even remotely human.

If I'd had my way, we would have left it at that. I suggested to Abe that it was time to announce what he had. Report the results. Show it to the world. But he was averse. "*Make it public?*" he scowled. "Jerry, there's a world full of busybodies out there. There'll be protests, there'll be cries for an investigation, there'll be people with signs. Accusing me of playing God. I'll spend the rest of my life trying to reassure the idiots that there's no moral dimension to what we're doing."

I thought about that for several minutes and asked him if he was sure there wasn't.

He smiled at me. It was that same grin you got from him when you'd overlooked some obvious detail and he was trying to be magnanimous while simultaneously showing you what a halfwit you are.

"Jerry," he said, "what have we done other than to provide life for thousands of generations of intelligent creatures? If anything, we should be commended."

Eons passed. Tens of thousands of subjective years, and the settlements went nowhere. We knew they were fighting; we could see the results. Burned out villages, heaps of corpses. Nothing as organized as a war, of course. Just local massacres. But no sign of a city. Not anywhere.

Maybe they weren't as bright as we thought. We know from our own experience that local conflicts don't stop the rise of civilization. In fact there's reason to think they're a necessary factor. Anyhow, it was about this time that Mac's plane went down. Abe was hit pretty hard. But he insisted on plunging ahead. I asked whether we would want to replace Mac, but he said he didn't think it would be necessary. For the time being, we had all the capability we needed.

"We have to intervene," he said.

I waited to hear him explain.

"Language." That was where the rubber hit the road. "We have to solve the language problem."

"What language problem?" I asked.

"We need to be able to talk to them."

The capability already existed to leave a message. No, Phil, we didn't have the means to show up physically and conduct a conversation. But we could deposit something for them to find. If we could master the languages.

"What do you intend to do?" I asked.

He was standing by a window gazing down at Crestview, with its single large street, its lone traffic light, Max's gas station at the edge of town, the Roosevelt School, made from red brick and probably built about 1920. "Tell me, Jerry," he said, "why can none of these creatures make a city?"

I had no idea.

One of the species had developed a written language. Of sorts. But that was as far as they'd gotten. We'd thought that would be a key, but even after the next few thousand local years, nothing had happened.

"I'll tell you what I think," Abe said. "They haven't acquired the appropriate domestic habits. They need an ethical code. Spouses who are willing to sacrifice for each other. A sense of responsibility to offspring. And to their community."

"And how would you propose to introduce those ideas, Abe?" I should have known what was coming.

"We have a fairly decent model to work with," he said. "Let's give them the Commandments."

I don't know if I mentioned it, but he was moderately eccentric. No, that's not quite true. It would be closer to the mark to say that, for a world-class physicist, he was unusual in that he had a wide range of interests. Women were around the lab all the time, although none was ever told what we were working on. As far as I knew. He enjoyed parties, played in the local bridge tournaments. The women loved him. Don't know why. He wasn't exactly good-looking. But he was forever trying to sneak someone out in the morning as I was pulling in.

He was friendly, easy-going, a *sports* fan, for God's sake. You ever know a physicist who gave a damn about the Red Sox? He'd sit there and drink beer and watch games off the dish.

When he mentioned the Commandments, I thought he was joking.

"Not at all," he said. And, after a moment's consideration: "I think we can keep them pretty much as they are."

"Abe," I said, "what are we talking about? You're not trying to set yourself up as a god?" The question was only half-serious because I thought he might be on to something. He looked past me into some indefinable distance.

"At this stage of their development," he said, "they need something to hold them together. A god would do nicely. Yes, I think we should do precisely that." He smiled at me. "Excellent idea, Jerry." He produced a copy of the King James, flipped pages, made some noises under his breath, and looked up with a quizzical expression. "Maybe we *should* update them a bit."

"How do you mean?"

"'Thou shalt not hold any person to be a slave.'"

I had never thought about that. "Actually, that's not bad," I said.

"'Thou shalt not fail to respect the environment, and its creatures, and its limitations.'"

"Good." It occurred to me that Abe was off to a rousing start. "Maybe, 'Thou shalt not overeat.'"

He frowned, ignoring my contribution, and shook his head. "Maybe," he said, "the environment would be a bit much for primitives. Better leave it out." He looked again at the leather-bound Bible. "I don't see anything here we'll want to toss out. So let's stop with eleven."

"Okay."
"The Eleven Commandments."
"Okay," I said. "Let's try it."
"For Mac," he said. "We'll do it for Mac."

The worlds had all been numbered. He had a system in which the number designated location, age, salient characteristics. But you don't care about that. He decided, though, that the world we had chosen for our experiment should have a name. He decided on *Utopia*. Well, I thought, not yet. It had mountain ranges and broad seas and deep forests. But it also had lots of savages. Smart savages, but savages nonetheless.

We already had samples of one of the languages, in both its spoken and written forms. That first night he showed them to me, slowed down of course. It was a musical language, rhythmic, with a lot of vowels and, what do you call them, diphthongs. Reminded me of a Hawaiian chant. But he needed a linguistic genius to make it intelligible.

He called a few people, told them he was conducting an experiment, trying to determine how much data was necessary to break in and translate the text of a previously unknown language. Hinted it had something to do with SETI. The people on the other end were all skeptical of the value of such a project, and he pretended to squirm a bit but he was offering lots of cash and a bonus for the correct solution. So everybody had a big laugh and then came on board.

The winner was a woman at the University of Montreal. Kris Edward. Kris came up with a solution in *five* days. I'd've thought it was impossible. A day later she'd translated the Commandments for him into the new language. Ten minutes after he'd received her transmission, we were driving over to Caswell Monuments in the next town to get the results chiseled onto two stone tablets. Six on one, five on the other. They looked *good*. I'll give him that. They had dignity. Authority. *Majesty*.

We couldn't actually transport the tablets, the Commandments, physically to Utopia. But we *could* relay their image, and their substance, and reproduce them out of whatever available granite there might be. Abe's intention was to put them on a mountaintop, and then use some directed lightning to draw one of the shamans up to find them. It all had to be programmed into the system, because as I said the realtime action would be much too quick for anyone to follow. I didn't think it would work. But Abe was full of confidence that we were on track at last.

We had a flat on the way back with the tablets. The spare was flat too. Maybe we should have taken that as a sign. Anyhow, by the time we'd arranged to get picked up, and got the tire changed, and had dinner, it had gotten fairly late. Abe was trying to be casual, but he was anxious to start. "No, Jerry, we are not going to wait until morning. Let's get this parade on the road." So we set the tablets in the scanner and sent the transmission out. It was 9:46 P.M., on the twelfth. The cylinder flashed amber lamps, and then green, signaling success, it had worked, the package had arrived at its destination. Moments later we got more blinkers, confirming that the storm had blown up to draw the shaman into the mountain.

We looked for results a few minutes later. It would have been time, on the other side, to build the pyramids, conquer the Mediterranean, fight off the Vandals, get through the Dark Ages, and move well into the Renaissance. If it had worked, we could expect to see glittering cities and ships and maybe even 747's. What we saw, however, were only the same dead end settlements.

We resolved to try again in the morning. Maybe Moses had missed the tablets. Maybe he'd not been feeling well. Maybe the whole idea was crazy.

That was the night the quake hit.

That's stable ground up in that part of the world. It was the first earthquake in Crestview's recorded history. Moreover, it didn't hit anything else. Not Charlie's Bar & Grill, which is at the bottom of the hill on the state road. Not any part of the Adams Ranch, which occupied the area on the north, not any part of the town, which is less than a half mile away. But it completely destroyed the lab.

What's that? Did it destroy the cosm? No, the cosm was safely disconnected from the state of Colorado. Nothing could touch it, except through the cylinder. It's still out there somewhere. On its own.

But the whole thing scares me. I mean, Mac was already dead. And two days later Sylvia drove into a tree at about sixty.

That's okay, you can smile about it, but I'm not sleeping very well. What's that? Why would God pick on us? I don't know. Maybe he didn't like the idea of someone doing minor league creations. Maybe he resented our monkeying around with the Commandments.

Why do you think he didn't say anything to Moses about slavery?

What, you've never thought about it? I wonder if maybe, at the beginning, civilization needed slaves to get started. Maybe you can't just jump off the mark with representative democracy. Maybe we were screwing things up, condemning sentient beings to thousands of years of unnecessary savagery. I don't know.

But that's my story. Maybe it's all coincidence. The quake, the plane crash, Sylvia. I suppose stranger things have happened. But it's scary, you know what I mean?

Yeah, I know you think I'm exaggerating. I know the God you believe in doesn't track people down and kill them. But maybe the God you believe in isn't there. Maybe the God who's actually running things is just a guy in a laboratory in another reality. Somebody who's a bit less congenial than Abe. And who has better equipment.

Well, who knows?

The scotch is good, by the way. Thanks. And listen, Phil, there's a storm blowing up out there. I don't like to impose, but I wonder if I could maybe stay the night?

Ignition

The most serious threat we face may be the ease with which we become assimilated into various ideologies. As I write this, there is a story out of the Middle East about a family whose sixteen-year-old daughter was kidnapped, held for ransom, threatened with rape and death. The ransom was paid, and the daughter returned. But the family could not assure themselves she had not been sexually assaulted, at least not without taking her in for a medical examination. So the family was, somehow, dishonored. Even had a physician given assurance that no attack had taken place, the very act of requesting the examination—if one could believe the reports—constituted dishonor. So they played it safe. They shot the daughter.

Our minds are open at six years old, and we trust those around us to tell us the truth, to explain how the world works. So when they speak of devils and infidels, point out other types of people as inferior, pretend to ultimate knowledge in matters of morality, we tend to buy into it. As time passes, we join various groups and support actions by them that we would never undertake ourselves. How else do you explain the assorted religious wars down the ages? Or the Inquisition? Or German citizens during the Second World War turning in their Jewish neighbors? Or people wearing dynamite belts to kill strangers?

Howard Bloom, in his thoughtful book of the same name, calls it the Lucifer Principle.

※

I saw no sign of a devil.

We'd been working on an extension of the Holy Journey subway when we ran into large blocks of concrete, stacked one atop the other, buried in the earth. The blocks weren't supposed to be there, but they were. The extension, when finished, would cross the river south into

St. Andrew's Parish, taking substantial pressure off the bridges. They lay directly in our way. So I kept my crew drilling, and eventually we broke through. And climbed up into a large chamber.

The ceiling was round, and must have been more than a hundred feet high.

Now the truth is I hadn't given any thought to devils and demons until I flashed my light into the darkness and saw, first, broken columns scattered around the place, as if it had once been a temple. And then the statue.

The statue was gigantic, maybe three times as high as I was. Or it would have been had the base not been buried in earth, broken stone, and assorted debris.

"What happened here?" demanded a voice behind me. Cort Benson, my number one guy. He pushed in and immediately locked on the giant figure dominating the chamber. "My Lord," he said, his voice suddenly very low. "What is *that*?"

I had never seen a statue before. I'd heard of them. Knew about them. But I'd never actually seen one. Nor, I suspected, had anyone else on the work crew. It was a man. I moved a few steps closer and held up my lamp. He was dressed oddly, loose-fitting clothes from another age. Odd-looking coat or vest. Hard to tell which. The statue was sunk into the ground to a point midway between knees and hips. There was something clasped in his left hand. A rolled sheet of paper, looked like.

My crew stayed near the door. One of them called for a blessing. Another said it was devil's work.

Elsewhere around the space, some columns were still standing. The chamber wall was curved.

Okay. Let me tell you straight out I never believed in evil spirits. I said prayers against them every Sunday, like everybody else, and sometimes during midweek services. But I didn't really buy into it. You know what I mean? Although that's easy to say, sitting in the daylight.

But here was this *thing*.

The air was thick and somehow smelled of other days. I played the light against the wall. Lines of arcane symbols were engraved in it. They were filled with dirt and clay, so it was hard to make them out. I picked at them with a crowbar, pulled some earth loose, and saw what they were: ancient English. The language still showed up occasionally around the parish, and over in Seven Crosses, and even as far north as St. Thomas. The characters were usually engraved on chunks of rock that must once have been cornerstones and arches and front entrances and even occasionally, as here, on walls. The world was filled with rubble from the civilization that God in His wrath had brought down.

I thought about that for a minute. Wages of sin. Then I saw a second group of characters circling the ceiling.

Cort grumbled something I couldn't make out and walked past me toward the statue.

Three or four lamps were now pointed at it, by the guys who stood back at the entrance. They showed no inclination though to come any closer.

The lights gave life to the features. Its eyes seemed to be watching me. The lips curved into a smile. It gave me chills, I'll admit that.

The features radiated power. And superiority. Though any guy twenty feet tall is going to look superior. The sculptor, if indeed there had been a sculptor, had given him an aura of the supernatural.

I checked in with the office, let them know what I'd found, and, at their instruction, told my crew they could take the rest of the morning off. Until a decision was made what to do about the discovery.

Cort waited until I got off the circuit. Then he said, "Eddie would be interested in this."

"Who's Eddie?" I wished Cort would follow the others outside. Get some fresh air. Do something constructive. Just please don't hang around and make suggestions.

"Come on, Blinky," said Cort. "Eddie Trexler. My cousin. You know him." Since he'd come back from prison, Cort seemed to have trouble breathing. You could always hear it, always knew when he was nearby. He probably shouldn't have been working down in the subways, but he was on the bishop's list and we couldn't get permission to transfer him.

I vaguely remembered once getting introduced to Trexler. A long time ago. But I couldn't recall anything about him. Or why he would possibly be interested in the chamber.

"I'll be back in a little while," said Cort. He was always ready to skate at the edges of the law. It was what had gotten him in trouble in the first place.

"Wait a minute," I said. "You know the rules."

"All they say is we have to report something like this. You've done that. Did they tell you to keep everybody out?"

"No."

"There you are, then."

"That's what they want, though."

"Hellfire, Andy, if that's what they want they ought to say it." He fished a phone out of his pocket. "I'm going to give him a yell."

Then he was gone. It wasn't worth a confrontation. Cort thought I got in line too easily, and sometimes I had to rein him in. But this didn't seem like one of those times. If he got himself and his cousin in trouble, so be it.

The giant gazed down at me. I went over and *touched* him, touched his thigh, brushed away some of the accumulated dust. He was bronze.

The lights were gone now, save the one I was carrying. I felt alone.

You'd never have known Eddie Trexler was a relative of Cort's. Where Cort was heavy and unkempt and probably indestructible, the cousin was tall and reedy and pressed. He owned a high-pitched voice and wore thick glasses, and he walked like a duck.

But there was no doubting his enthusiasm when he shook my hand and, without waiting for permission, climbed past me into the circular chamber. Trexler was a clerk at the Department of Theological Studies, but his hobby was ancient history. He'd brought one of those large lanterns that will light up a city block. He was two steps inside when he switched it on and put the beam on the statue. "Magnificent," he said. His voice had gone a notch higher.

Cort chuckled. "He asked me to thank you for asking him over."

"Sure," I said. "My pleasure." We followed him in.

He stood gawking at the figure, at the wall, at the columns. At the blocks on which the entire structure rested. "I never thought I'd live to see anything like this–" he said. "You know what this is, Cort?" And, without waiting for an answer, "Lovely."

"It's a statue," I said. I could have added that it desperately needed to be washed, that it was badly chipped and discolored, that it was half-buried. That it was officially blasphemous.

Thou shalt not make unto thyself any graven image.

But I let it go.

"Do *you* know what it is?" Cort asked him.

"I have an idea." He plunged into the space, climbed over some debris, stared at the statue, touched it, measured it. After a few minutes he broke away and began inspecting one of the columns. Then he approached the wall, and stared at the lines of characters. "This is big news," he said. "If it's what I think it is."

"Why, Ed?" I asked. "What do you think it is?"

"Look at the writing. This place is prediluvian. *Before* the flood."

"Yeah. I figured. So what–?"

"Look at the blocks."

"What about them?"

"Think why they're there."

"Why are they there?"

"They tried to save it," he said, as much to himself as us. "God help them, they tried to save it."

"Yes," I said, not sure what I was agreeing to.

"It must have sunk during the flooding. Too heavy. It was more than thirty thousand tons. Add all that concrete–" He shook his head. "And here it is."

"I guess so," I said.

"It would have taken time to bring all that concrete in here."

"Okay."

"That means–" His eyes gleamed with a light of their own. "They knew the flood was coming."

"The Great Flood?"

"Yes."

I was getting uncomfortable. "Official doctrine is–"

"–that it happened without warning," said Cort.

"Correct." Trexler pressed his palms against the stone, as if to read a message hidden within the cold gray surface. "That's going to stir the pot a bit." He pulled a camera from a sweater pocket and began taking pictures.

Cort stayed at his side, fascinated. "Can you read any of it, Ed?"

"Not really. If we can get it clean, we should be able to figure it out." He turned back to me. "Cort tells me you've alerted the authorities."

"Of course," I said. "It's a requirement."

"Yeah," he said. "I know. Pity."

I couldn't miss the implied accusation. "Hey," I said. "I didn't have a choice. It's the law."

He told me it wasn't my fault. "How long will it take them to get here?"

"No way to know," Cort rumbled, raising an eyebrow in my direction.

Trexler began trying to clean the symbols. Cort and I joined in. But it was hard going and we didn't make much progress. He stepped back and took more pictures. And frowned. "*Publish*," he said, finally.

"What? Publish what?"

"This word means *publish*." It was about nine lines down. And, four lines below that: "*Reliance*."

He shook his head and glanced at me again. "I don't suppose there's any chance you could go out and head them off when they get here."

"You mean the police?"

"Yes."

"What would I tell them?"

"Anything you can think of."

"No," I said. "I don't think I could get away with that."

He rolled his eyes. And in that moment noticed the overhead inscription. "What's that?"

"More letters," said Cort, helpfully. "I'll try to slow down the police."

"Thank you." Trexler threw a contemptuous glance in my direction. Then he returned his attention to the roof. "That's in better condition up there," he said.

"Yes," I said. I was trying to decide what to do. I kept seeing the police hauling all three of us off to Redemption.

"... *Have sworn*..."

"What?"

He was still looking up. "It says *have sworn*, and there's *alert* off to the right."

"Okay."

"No. Wait. It's *altar*."

I watched him change his angle and stand on his toes as if getting an inch closer would help.

"*Mind of man* at the end."

I heard the sound of arriving vehicles.

He jerked his head around. Stared toward the hole we'd cut through the blocks. "So soon?" He looked dismayed.

"I guess."

He went back to the inscription. "The last three words are *mind of man*. No question about it."

Doors slammed. From the main tunnel came the rumble of a passing train. Dust drifted down on us.

"... *Have sworn... altar... mind of man.*"

"Makes no sense," I said.

"I can't make out the rest of it." He changed his angle again. "I need to get closer to it. You have a ladder handy?"

"Not high enough to reach that," I said.

"Damn. We need a little time."

"Maybe it's something this guy said," I suggested, indicating the statue.

He sighed. "Of course it is. Said or wrote. What else would it be?"

I didn't much like the attitude he was taking. "The statue's dangerous," I reminded him. There was a line from the *Divine Handbook*: You don't make statues of people because that implies they are godlike.

"Don't be stupid," he said. Then he went back to the inscription: "The first word is only a single letter. Probably a pronoun. Has to be *I*."

There were voices outside now.

"*Hostility*. Some kind of *hostility*. Maybe *extraordinary*."

The voices became loud.

"I think it's *hostility against*. Has to be. And *tyrant*. Yes. . . . *Hostility against something something tyrant.*"

There was a scuffle outside. Mercifully short.

"No. It's not *tyrant*. It's, I think it's *tyranny*. Yes. That's it. *Tyranny*."

People were crowding into the chamber. Five of them, four in police uniforms. "I'm Inspector Valensky," said the one in plain clothes. He flashed an ID toward Trexler, as if I weren't there. He was middle-aged, bearded, very official. Cort trailed in behind them, hands apparently secured behind his back.

"Good afternoon, Inspector," said Trexler, at which point Valensky saw the statue.

"The Lord is my keeper, sir," Valensky said. "We do have devil's spawn here, don't we?"

Trexler's light fell on the police officers and I saw they were carrying bags of explosives. "Don't come in here with those," he warned. "What are you doing? Get them out of here."

The inspector drew himself up straight and tugged at his beard. "Sir," he said, "gentlemen, I think who comes and who goes is our decision. And the fact is, I must ask you to leave."

Trexler didn't budge.

"This thing is blasphemous," said Valensky, sounding as if he were struggling to keep his voice level. "We'll have to get rid of it."

"What do you mean, 'get rid of it'?"

"I meant exactly what I said, sir. We're going to send it back where it belongs. Meantime, you'd be prudent to mind your manners." He turned to me. "I take it you're Blinkman Baylor."

I winced. I never understood what my folks were thinking when they gave me that name. "That's correct."

"Good. You did the right thing, Mr. Baylor, although it might have been a good idea to keep these two out of here." He raised his voice so we could all hear. "I hope none of you touched this abomination."

"No," I said, trying to sound reassuring. "Of course not."

He looked dead at me. "You *do* know not to touch any of these relics, don't you?"

"Oh, yes," I said. "I kept my hands off."

"Good, Mr. Baylor. Very prudent."

"*I* touched it," said Trexler.

"It renders you unclean, sir. You'll want to come with us when we're finished here."

"What for?"

"We'll have to take you to All-Sorrows for a ceremonial cleansing."

Trexler glared back. They'd have to carry him.

Valensky managed to look both annoyed and disappointed. "I do wish you'd cooperate, sir." He turned to Cort. "What about you?"

"Me?" Cort said. "I haven't been anywhere near it."

"Good." Two of the officers put on white gloves. They carried the charges across the chamber, picking their way through the debris, and laid them against the statue.

When Trexler tried to intervene, a third officer, a woman, headed him off. "Just stay calm, sir," she said, "if you will."

We watched while they made adjustments and connections.

Trexler glared at Valensky. "You blockhead," he said. "Do you have any idea what this place is worth? What it *is*?"

Valensky looked unmoved. "I know exactly what it is. Thank God one of us does." He turned to me. "I suggest you get him out of here."

The two who were setting the explosives stood up and brushed off their knees. "All set," one of them said. The other knelt back down and tugged at something. "Ready to go," he added.

Valensky took a remote from his pocket. "Okay, everybody out, please," he said. He moved toward the exit, walking slowly while he waited for the rest of us to leave. Trexler stayed where he was.

"Come on, Eddie," said Cort.

Trexler shook his head. "I'm not going anywhere."

A signal passed between the inspector and the officers. They filed past Trexler. The woman touched her cap and said goodbye.

"I do wish you'd be reasonable," said Valensky.

Trexler moved closer to the statue. "Go ahead," he said. "Do what you have to."

"You leave me no choice, sir."

"Idiot."

The officers left, taking a struggling Cort with them. All except Valensky. "I'll set off the charge in one minute," he said. "That gives you time to change your mind and get out."

Trexler did not move. "Blow it up and be damned."

"Eddie." I felt helpless. "Getting yourself killed won't help anything."

"Listen to him," said Valensky. Then he looked my way. Time to go.

I waited a few seconds, watched Valensky disappear. "Ed," I said, "for God's sake—"

"He won't do it," said Trexler. "Too much paperwork if he kills somebody."

When the rebellion started, two months later, with the coordinated robberies of two banks and the looting of a parish arms warehouse, the authorities were slow to recognize it for what it was. And that cost them everything.

The two historians of the revolution, the two I know of, both believe Edward Trexler's death was the spark that started it all. There's some truth to that. But of course a lot of other people had died before he did, charged with heresy, or blasphemy, or various other attitudinal felonies.

God knows, though, Trexler's death motivated *me*. Who would ever have believed that conservative old Blinky Baylor would pick up a gun and go to war? But there was something else that stuck in my mind. That, for a lot of us, eventually became the engine that drove the revolution.

"(I?). . . Have sworn. . . altar. . . . hostility (against?). . . tyranny. . . mind of man."

It wasn't hard to fill in the blanks. And sometimes, during the dark times, it kept me going. I think it kept a lot of us going. You want to make a revolution work, you need more than a taste for vengeance.

Lighthouse
with Michael Shara

Michael Shara is the director of the astrophysics department at the American Museum of Natural History in New York City. Several years ago, he did a cover story for The Scientific American *on what would happen if a brown dwarf drifted into the solar system and collided with the sun. Answer: Lights out, and a steep decline in real estate values.*

The story inspired the setting for Polaris, *a novel which I was then just starting. Eventually I went by the museum to thank Shara. It turned out he had a special interest in colliding stars. "Happens all the time," he told me with enthusiasm. This was a guy I couldn't help liking.*

We talked about one day collaborating. As it happened, he had an idea. That idea forms the heart of "Lighthouse." Reluctantly, I have to confess this story is his. I went along for the ride, contributing a cabin and a hot stove. I was delighted to be able to put my name on it.

※

The applause after a dissertation defense is always polite, sometimes cool, but rarely sustained. Kristi Lang smiled and blushed as all fifty members of her department rose to their feet and cheered. Her fellow graduate students were the rowdiest of all, whistling and banging their coffee cups in unison on chairs and table tops. Greg Cooper, the department head and her mentor, let it go on for a full minute.

"Ladies and gentlemen," he said finally, "thank you very much."

If anything, the noise intensified.

He needed a gavel.

Kristi stood, engulfed in the moment. She nodded, raised her hand, mouthed a *thank you*. A fresh round of applause, and finally it began to lessen.

She had discovered a new type of astronomical body. A special kind of brown dwarf. They were calling it a *chimera* now, but Greg had told her yesterday that they'd eventually be referred to as *Lang Objects*.

Greg was tall and thin, with an angular jaw, angular nose, dark hair, intense eyes. His students referred to him as Sherlock Holmes because of his world-class problem-solving skills and his intensely mediocre abilities with a violin. "All right," he said, signaling for quiet. "Let's pull ourselves together." That brought laughter. "I wouldn't want to cancel the wine and cheese."

The people around her were reaching for Kristi's hand, patting her on the back. Tim Rodgers, tanned and good-looking and brilliant, gave her an approving smile. He was impressed. Maybe even envious.

The time honored Q and A had to be observed. Greg called for questions. Hands went up. He stepped aside and gave her the lectern.

Tim remained standing while the others took their seats. He was finishing his own thesis, and had been, until recently, at the top of everybody's list of People Who Would Go Somewhere. Now he was a distant second.

"Okay, Kristi," he said, "you've established the existence of a new class of object. How'd it happen?"

The explanation was simple enough. She'd been doing analytical studies of billions of brown dwarfs and had noticed a few anomalies. Way too much deuterium. But that wasn't the big news. She was holding that for later.

"We eventually found two thousand oddballs," she said. Brown dwarfs were failed stars. The chimeras, the Lang Objects, were anomalous. Odd. And not easy to account for with conventional physics.

"You briefly mentioned actinides," came another question. "But I don't see the connection. Please elaborate."

Kristi smiled and tried to look modest. "Think DNA," she said. "Common origin. Common purpose."

The comment puzzled everyone. Brows furrowed. They whispered to one another and waited for her to explain herself.

In fact, her inspiration had come that past summer from a set of police blinkers mounted over a cabin on Kilimanjaro.

Hemingway's mountain. Now the site for the Yuri Artsutanov Space Elevator. Kristi had been on her way to the Clarke Research Station, poised overhead in geosynchronous orbit. She was hunting for the photons that she hoped would help explain the existence of the anomalous *chimeras*.

There were nearly two thousand of them, all young, concentrated in the spiral arms of the Milky Way, interlopers, deuterium-rich freaks that had no business existing. Clad in shorts and a Columbia University t-shirt, Kristi drove a Jeep across the savanna. The sky was heavy with clouds, and the smell of cool moisture hung in the late morning air. Storm coming, and she was already late. If she didn't hustle, she stood a good chance of missing her ride. The weather guy had said clear, bright and sunny, beautiful weather. She'd spent the last few months completely absorbed by her research, had analyzed a million images, looked for the needle in a billion haystacks, written a killer proposal that even Greg Cooper in his Holmes role couldn't fault. But here she was going to be left standing at the station. Scheduling rides on the Yuri was no easy proposition.

Not that it would matter in the end. Jeff would make the observations and deliver the petabytes to her account. They'd be perfectly de-biased and flat-fielded, even if she never floated through the observatory hatch. Still, the karma would be wrong. It was once in a lifetime, and she needed to be there when the evidence came in.

The rim of Kibo, the summit crater, popped momentarily into view as she passed three thousand meters, and then promptly vanished into the gathering clouds. Raindrops began to spatter against the windshield. She started the wipers. The road was wide and designed to take heavy traffic, but it was still uphill all the way, sometimes at an almost impossible angle. The rain intensified, and pounded on the roof.

She slowed down as visibility dropped to about fifty meters. A truck passed going the other way. A burst of wind pounded the Jeep and water blasted across the windshield.

Her cell phone chimed. "*Kristi.*" It was Kwame Shola, the chief of operations at Yuri.

"How you doing, Kwame?"

"*Not so good. Where are you now?*"

"On the way."

"*Okay. But take it easy. We got snow like mad up here. Weathermen missed it completely.*"

Great. Just what she needed. "All right," she said.

"*No heroics, please. If you need it, we have a climber cabin at five thousand meters. Combo is 2718.*"

"Twenty-seven eighteen."

"Remember 'e'."

'e,' of course, lower case always, was the base of the natural logarithms, equaling 2.718281808 . . . on into an infinity of digits. "Okay," she said. "I've got it."

Greg had been ambivalent about her working with the chimeras. Don't know where you're going to go with them, he said. You could wind up producing a lot of data and still have to throw up your hands and admit you don't have a clue about what they are or why they even exist. Put the idea on hold, he told her. Confine the research to more conservative areas, at least until you've wrapped up your doctorate and gotten an appointment somewhere. He was right, of course. The path of guaranteed success. But she was *fascinated* by the objects. Her father had always told her to follow her instincts. And her instincts took her right into the shadow of the deuterium dwarfs. They were so intriguing, so difficult to explain, that she simply could not resist.

She had never wanted to be anything but an astronomer. Her father, who'd been a high school science teacher, had brought home a pair of image-stabilized binoculars from the third Gulf War. When he gave them to the little redheaded six-year-old, she was transfixed. The moon had craters and tall mountains. Jupiter was a tiny disk with moons of its own. And the Milky Way was a glittering pathway of stars. Distant suns, her father had explained. Countless millions of them. Some just like ours, some a lot smaller.

Why, Daddy, why are some of the stars different from the Sun?

He'd smiled and told her he didn't know, but that she could figure it out if she wanted when she grew up.

And one evening, in the Big Dipper, she'd discovered Mizar. Her father had been on the porch with her and she'd screeched at him, "Daddy, they're *touching*!" Twin stars. Over the next twenty years, her father could always get a laugh from her by repeating the phrase in a rising falsetto. But in fact, as she learned later, there were *five* stars in the Mizar system. By her first year in graduate school she'd found a brown dwarf companion to the five. And used it as a clock to age-date the system. Her *Astrophysical Journal* letter hung framed in his den. But he got nervous whenever he knew she was going up to the Clarke Station.

The rain turned to sleet and Kristi slowed the Jeep to a crawl. Her defroster was rapidly losing its battle with the Tanzanian snowstorm.

She could no longer see the summit. A burst of wind shook the Jeep.

She tried to call Kwame for a weather update, but he wasn't answering. Something big with lights roared past her, going down the mountain. She jerked the wheel hard, hit the brakes, spun across the icy muck, and slid off onto the shoulder.

Maniac.

She sat listening to the sound of the retreating truck. Then she pulled carefully back onto the highway. It was getting dark.

She picked her way uphill, past boulders and patches of lichen. Occasionally the road emerged along the edge of a precipice and she could look out through a hole in the clouds across the savanna. Then the clear patch was gone and the road was winding up through the night while rain and sleet whipped across the windshield. She began to wonder whether she'd missed the 5000-meter signpost when her headlights swept over it. She didn't see a cabin anywhere, but it didn't matter because she had no interest in missing her ride. There was still a chance, if the weather broke, that she could make it.

The cell phone chimed. Kwame. *"How you doing, Kristi?"*

"I'm doing just dandy."

"You find the cabin yet?"

"Negative. Doesn't matter. I want to get up there before my ride leaves."

"Kristi, they've canceled it. I told you that."

"No, you didn't."

"Why did you think I wanted you to find the cabin? They're going to try again in the late morning."

"Okay."

"Go to the cabin."

"I'm past it."

He sighed. *"Can you get back to it?"*

She looked behind her, down the road. It was dark and cold and she could barely see the edge of the highway. "I guess."

"Do that, then. Don't try to come up tonight. It's too icy. Already had one truck go off the road. Driver was damn near killed."

"Okay."

"You sure you can find the cabin?"

"Sure. Relax. Everything's fine, Kwame."

It was about a kilometer back, maybe two. She put the phone down on the seat and peered out onto the highway. Nothing coming in either direction.

She cut the wheel and started to turn. She couldn't judge how wide the road was, so she was careful not to go too far forward. She reversed and started back. Felt the rear wheels lose traction. Tried to go forward again. But the Jeep continued sliding back. And *down.*

My God, she was going into a ditch.

She fought the wheel, damning the Jeep and the highway and the storm. But it did no good and the vehicle slid sideways off the shoulder and crunched over a large rock into a snowbank. She shifted gears and gunned the engine. The wheels spun, the Jeep struggled forward a few centimeters, dug a deeper hole, and slid back in.

Damn.

She called Kwame.

"You want me to come get you?"

She looked down at the t-shirt and shorts. The heater was on full blast. "No," she said. "Don't do that. I'll make for the cabin."

"Okay. Be careful."

"I will."

"Call me if you have a problem."

It was frigid out there. Better was to sit tight and wait for somebody to come along.

There are twenty-one billion brown dwarfs in the Milky Way, give or take. Kristi had found and mapped almost every one of them. "The light output of brown dwarfs alternates wildly between adjacent wavelengths, Dad," she'd once explained to him. "My infrared survey filters are tuned to just the right wavelengths, so all other stars appear dimmer. The hard part is keeping track of them all, and repeating the survey a year later to measure their motions. Then we have to sift out all the weird quasars that sneak through the filtering. That's why we have MEGASPEC. It catches them all."

Brown dwarfs were not massive enough to ignite thermonuclear fires in their cores. They would always be failed stars, their dim glow generated by cooling and contracting. "Ninety-nine point six nines" was the delicious phrase she used in colloquia to describe her survey's thoroughness. No one had ever done that for brown dwarfs. Hell, nobody had ever done that for anything in astronomy. She had nailed the definitive sample for all time. Sure, there'd be a few hundred hiding behind luminous primaries, or lurking directly in front of distant quasars, but she'd gotten the rest. There was no arguing with twenty-one billion spectra and parallaxes and radial velocities and proper motions. She could tell you what the temperature of each one had been a million years ago. And where each one would be ten million years from now. Her census was the last word on how the Galaxy's failed stars had arranged themselves during the past thirteen billion years. She could chart the few ancient, metal-free brown dwarfs along their orbits looping far out into the Milky Way's halo. The larger population of metal-rich youngsters, the astronomical infants, clung to the plane of the Milky Way.

The *chimeras* (she settled for the term "anomalous objects" in her seminars) had been culled from her complete sample of twenty-one billion by statistical sifting and weighing. Every one of them had a spectrum that called attention to itself, that defied everything she thought she knew about this type of object. The surface abundance of deuterium was impossibly high. It was a heavy isotope of hydrogen, with one proton and one neutron, and the big bang had made only a pinch of it, before stingily shutting off production just three minutes after creation. There was no known way that any planet or star or galaxy or anything else was going to concentrate the primordial trace of deuterium to more than a pinch. The textbooks maintained that anything over 0.001% was impossible. Yet Kristi had found two thousand brown dwarfs whose composition was nearly fifty percent deuterium.

It was frigid out there. The engine, which had been keeping her reasonably warm, coughed and died.

She tried to restart it.

Tried again.

When she opened the door, she smelled gasoline and stuck her head outside. There was a stain on the snow. She must have punctured the tank. Or the gas line.

The mountain highway remained silent.

Shut the door against the cold.

Okay. Crunch time. Can't stay here. The temperature in the Jeep was already dropping.

She checked to be sure she had her pen flashlight. Staple for astronomers. She turned it on and pointed it out the window, where the beam got lost in the snow. There was a travel bag in back with light clothing, and she could try putting everything on, but she was still going to get pretty cold out there.

It was only a kilometer back, two at most. She could manage that. She pulled her bag from the back seat and began sifting through her clothes.

She put on two extra blouses. They weren't going to help very much, but she'd take what she could get. And there was a sweater. She pulled it around her shoulders. Felt like an idiot.

She thought about Tim. He was the romance that had never happened. Partly her own fault. Always too busy. And her father, safe and warm in their North Jersey home.

Love you, Daddy.

The wind tried to take the door out of her hand. She hung on, dragged her bag out of the back seat, and chunked the door shut. The snow was driving at her, and it seemed to be coming from all directions.

The ditch was shallower than it had seemed, but the sides were ice, and she had to climb out on hands and knees. When she finally stood on the road, she fished out her penlight and turned it on. The world around her looked desolate.

The wind cut through her garments and chilled her to the bone. It literally took her breath away. She was wearing canvas shoes and her feet got cold before she'd gone a dozen steps.

The penlight beam outlined ditches and a snow cover fading into the night.

She pressed her arms against her chest and tried to push the cold out of her mind. Move out, Scout, she told herself. There's shelter back there somewhere.

Her toes went numb. A blast of wind knocked her down. When she got up, she no longer had the penlight. Didn't know where it had gone. She'd been carrying it in her right hand, but the hand had no feeling.

For the first time in her life, she felt real fear.

This was the darkest place she'd ever seen. There was no glimmer of light *anywhere*. The edge of the road was no longer visible. The world had vanished, had become a place utterly without borders, without any distinguishing features, other than the snowflakes that continued to rush at her.

She thought about calling Kwame. But she couldn't do that. What would he think? Poor woman can't get from the Jeep to the cabin without getting in trouble.

It was hard to breathe. Her lungs hurt, and tears froze on her cheeks.

She pushed her hands into her sweater pockets and started out again. Hell with it. Didn't need the light anyway.

Still no sign of anything. Not of a cabin. Not of the marker.

The terrifying truth was she could walk right past the marker and never see it.

She was counting her steps now. Roughly thirteen hundred to a kilometer. Right? She'd already come about five hundred. Or maybe one hundred. Somewhere, below her, she heard the sound of a plane.

She tried to pick up her pace. Keep moving. Keep watching. And think about something else. Think about Daddy's rising falsetto. If she was lucky the marker and the cabin would be right next to each other. *Why, Daddy, they'd be touching!*

After a while, she became convinced she must have missed it. She debated starting back toward the Jeep, and looked helplessly in both directions. Couldn't have been this far. She'd only passed it about three minutes before she'd stopped and gone into the ditch. She'd been traveling about fifteen, twenty at most. How far was that?

She couldn't figure it out. She'd begun to feel as if she'd withdrawn into a cave, was looking out through her eyes from a safe place somewhere back of her nose.

That was funny, Lang. Laugh.

Ha.

Still trudging forward, she flipped open the cell phone. Time to confess. Tell Kwame she was in trouble.

Off to her left, a soft orange glow appeared in the blowing snow.

Nothing about this class of brown dwarfs made sense. Their composition was just under fifty percent deuterium. Fifty thousand times what it should be. Crazy enough. The remaining half was mostly hydrogen, the ordinary one-nucleon variety. No problem with that, except that it left little room for helium, which, in most of the chimeras, totaled less than one percent. It was their larger than normal size that tightly constrained the helium abundance. Even Tim, the brightest young theorist she knew, had to concede the point. Every other cosmic object is born with the allotment imprinted by the Big Bang: a full twenty-seven percent. So where was the rest of the helium?

There was no way to hide helium in a still-warm brown dwarf, and all of the chimeras were warm Galactic infants. Kristi's deuterium reservoirs mocked her, because they simply could not exist.

The orange glow hung momentarily in the darkness. Then it went off.

Somewhere, far away, she heard a snarl. Leopards don't climb this high, do they?

She started walking toward the spot where she'd seen the light. It came on again. And went off.

It had to be the cabin.

She moved closer. Saw the 5000-meter marker to her right. A metal sign, white with black numbers.

The light blinked on again. More distinct this time. It was a police car beacon. Set on a rooftop.

Thank God.

Wooden steps led up onto a porch. She saw three dark windows and a door. There were wicker chairs on the porch, and a table. She climbed the steps, felt the wind cut off as she came into the shelter of the cabin, and tried the doorknob.

It was locked.

A number pad was bolted to the frame. The combination. What was the combination?

Kwame had said, *Remember 'e'*. Twenty-seven eighteen.

The beacon kept flashing. Every few seconds. It reflected off the snow cover, giving her just enough light to work with.

She got it wrong the first time, and for a heart-stopping moment she feared the lock was frozen. Or she'd been mistaken. But the second try was golden and the door clicked. She pulled it open, kicked the snow out of the way, and half-fell through onto a stone floor.

The interior was frigid.

She shut the door and looked around. There were more wicker chairs and another table. A long row of solar batteries powered the beacon. A cot was set against one wall. And a pot-bellied stove stood in the middle of the room. She looked around for a thermostat. Saw nothing.

Someone had left a box of matches, and a yellowed copy of *USA Today*.

Kristi stared at the stove. My kingdom for a few logs. She could go outside and root through the storm. Maybe get lucky. But the furniture was more convenient. She picked up one of the chairs and brought it down hard against the floor.

It held together.

She tried again.

It was remarkably resilient. She stumbled around the cabin, looking for an axe, gave up, and went back to beating the chair. Desperation lent strength and, finally, it came apart. Enough, at least, that she could jam it into the stove.

Ten minutes later she sat in front of a fire that, if it was not quite blazing, nevertheless served to take the freeze off the room. She called Kwame. "I'm in."

"*Good,*" he said. "*I was getting worried. Don't leave the cabin until the storm stops.*"

"Have no fear. One problem—"

"*Yes?*"

"I left my transportation in a ditch."

"*You were not hurt, I hope?*"

"No, I'm fine."

"*Okay. I'll send a truck down as soon as the road's clear.*"

"Kwame?"

"*Yes?*"

"Send sandwiches, too."

Her toes began to recover some feeling. She found a blanket in a closet. It smelled of cigarettes but she didn't care. She warmed it on the stove, wrapped herself in it and closed her eyes.

She was wide awake. She'd have liked to read. But even if the light had been adequate, she'd left her briefcase in the car. In it were copies of *Physics Today* and *People*, which she'd brought for the skyride. And a marked-up version of her dissertation. Once at Clarke, there'd be no leisure. She expected to spend six days doing nothing but observing, reducing data, and sleeping.

The wind shook the cabin. And suddenly her eyes felt heavy. Her head drifted back, and the sounds of the fire, the sense of the storm outside, faded.

She woke a couple of times, and jammed more furniture into the stove. And once, toward the end, she saw gray light in the windows.

• • •

The nuclei were piled high in her office. Thousands of deuterons. In the drawers. On the keyboard. Scattered across her desk. Each deuteron's green neutron and blue proton were morphing back and forth, into each other, a colorful display of the strong nuclear force in action.

Get the vacuum cleaner. Where was the vacuum cleaner?

She was still looking when a hand touched her shoulder. "Hey, Kristi. How you doing?"

Kwame.

The fire had gone out but the stove still held some heat. "I'm okay," she said.

"Good. The road's clear. If you're ready we can head out." Kwame was a middle-aged African, not quite as tall as she. His hair had gone white, and his features suggested he'd known some difficult times. He was wrapped in a heavy parka with the hood down. His dark eyes were shining, and he spoke with a British accent.

She pulled the blanket more tightly around her while she pushed her feet back into her shoes. "I'm ready," she said.

"You don't want to take a shower first?" He nodded toward the washroom, but kept a straight face.

A snow plow waited outside. The sun was behind some white clouds. It was relatively warm, and the cabin roof was lined with melting icicles.

She climbed into the passenger's seat and looked back at the police light. "If it hadn't been for the blinker," she said, "I'd never have found the place."

He nodded. "That's why it's there, Kristi."

She thought about suggesting he add an ax to the amenities. And maybe some canned goods. But, on second thought, maybe another time.

He passed her a jelly donut.

Kristi had been to the summit of Kilimanjaro four times before, but the sight of the base towers and the nanowire ribbon stretching up to infinity was as exhilarating as ever. "It hasn't left yet?" she asked him.

"No. They've been waiting for you."

It wasn't critical that she be on site while her data were collected. But Greg had designed MEGASPEC and Kristi had written most of its software to confirm brown dwarf candidates, so a trip to recalibrate the million-object spectrograph was justified. And there would never be a time she'd pass on an opportunity to go up to the station, to see the home world from 36,000 kilometers. There was still a little kid in her somewhere. She'd commented along those lines once to Greg and he said it was true of everyone in the sciences who was worth a damn.

Kwame apologized that there was no time to shower and change. Have to do it in zero-gee.

"I'll try to keep away from the other passengers," she said.

"Ah. It is their loss."

They pulled up at the front door of the terminal, and she thanked him for maybe the fifth time. Then she was hurrying through the reception area and someone came alongside to help with her bag and briefcase. Moments later she cleared the entry ramp, and hatches shut.

There were roughly a dozen other passengers. About half of them were tourists, including two kids. They looked curiously at her as the carbon nanowires stiffened and the elevator lifted away from Kilimanjaro. Minutes later she caught sight of Lake Victoria. They rose through the clouds, and the Atlantic came into view. And eventually she was looking down at the entire continent, from the Cape of Good Hope to the Nile delta.

Two hours out, at an altitude of 8000 kilometers, she got a sandwich and coffee from the convenience counter and settled down at one of the viewport tables to enjoy the ride. Closer to the chimeras, she thought. Well, not really, but the illusion was there as she soared ever higher.

She wished there were starships. She'd love to have an opportunity to go out and look at one of the things, close up. She knew how it would appear, of course. She had virtual brown dwarfs on call back home. They were Jupiter-sized spheres, red-brown, with mottled clouds floating in the atmosphere. The clouds were iron hydride, and of course the dwarf would be glowing, rather like a coal recently plucked from the fire.

She visualized it, and somehow she found herself thinking about Kwame's police lights.

Someone came over and asked if he could share the table. Of course. He was a young man, and she realized immediately he was on the make.

". . . Going to be pretty well tied up while I'm here," she was saying.

He was a technician of some sort. Dull-looking. Thought well of himself. "Of course," he said. "But all work—"

She heard him out, and smiled when appropriate. "They pay to send me up here," she said, as if she were making a major sacrifice. "... Don't want me sitting around."

The police lights. She stared through the young man into the deep night of the 5000-meter elevation, saw the soft orange glow, blinking on and off.

And suddenly she understood.

"I don't buy it, Kristi," Greg said. She had him on the vid relay, from his office. *"There's got to be a natural mechanism at work. Maybe high pressure chemistry. Maybe magnetic fields. Maybe radiative levitation. Geochemical processes can concentrate minerals by orders of magnitude on Earth, so why not deuterium on the surfaces of brown dwarfs under far more exotic conditions?"* He sounded really concerned. It was why she liked him so much. He was worried about what would happen to her career if she tried to go public with her notion. She imagined it was hard for him not to say, *You're skating at the edge of academic disaster. Blow your reputation now and you'll always be at the fringe.*

"I admit," he said, *"that fifty percent deuterium is far out. But whatever did this could also bury the helium. We just don't know enough."*

"I think it's true," she said.

"It could be. Anything's possible, Kristi. But think about what the professional price will be if you go off half-cocked, and then someone finds the real explanation." Then, more gently: *"I'll go this far: Get two more pieces of independent evidence. If your idea stands up, Galileo will have to move over."*

While the Earth dropped away, she worked on her computer. An hour later, still on the elevator, she raised a fist in triumph. The act drew the attention of several of her fellow passengers. She didn't care. She had a match. In fact, the chimeras, almost the entire sample of two thousand, except two, showed up at the same sites listed in the all-sky X-ray source catalogs as black holes. That gave her a stunning 99.9% correlation. How much proof do you want, Greg?

For the next five hours she looked fruitlessly for other patterns. She was still engrossed in her analysis, and trying hard to keep her sense of exhilaration under control, as the elevator began its approach to the station.

An attendant asked her to return to her seat and buckle in. She felt indestructible at the moment, but she happily complied. Galileo was a piker.

An orange light was blinking on the link-up collar. It reminded her of Kwame's beacon, and she smiled. A series of thuds reverberated through the hull as the elevator docked and the airlocks mated. Hatches opened and the passengers floated through into the connecting tube. The tourists would be headed for the hotel. The others scattered in different directions.

Jeff Fields, who ran the observatory programs, was waiting for her. "Jeff," she said, "I want you to do something for me."

"Okay," he said. "What do you need?"

"Tomorrow, before we make any observations, I need you to change to the highest resolution grating."

Standing at the lectern before her mentors and her peers, Kristi had deftly fielded a dozen questions about her analyses and catalog. The privilege of asking the final question traditionally went to the senior graduate student. Tim. She'd seen him writing while she spoke, scratching out lines, making faces, writing again. When the moment came, he stood. "Sorry, Kristi," he began. "Nobody here is more anxious for you to be right. But I still don't get it." He glanced down at his notes, looked over at Greg, and plunged on. "Your high-res spectra and gravitational redshifts unquestionably prove that every one of your chimeras is eight Jupiter masses, and that each is orbiting something every year or so." He took a deep breath. "The X-ray source coincidences are a convincing argument that the somethings are black holes. But black holes can't concentrate deuterium or hide helium. Black holes were all once stars way too luminous to have formed with sub-brown dwarf companions in the first place. And, worst of all, your chimeras are too low in mass to ignite deuterium, yet they radiate like hot brown dwarfs."

The others around the table were looking anxiously from Tim to her. A few whispers began. "In theory," Tim continued, "your chimeras can't exist, right? But they do. So what's going on?"

You know, she thought, he really is good-looking. But not as quick on the draw as I'd thought.

He started to sit down, but got up again. "Kristi, you must have some idea how to explain these things?"

She looked over at Greg. He was gazing out the window at the beautiful autumn day. Then his eyes met hers. And he nodded. Do it.

Her paper had been accepted yesterday by *Nature*. Letting the cat out of the bag now wouldn't jeopardize anything. She'd kept everyone, other than Greg, in the dark. Even Tim.

"We classify anything less than thirteen Jupiter masses as a planet," she began, "because these objects never develop sufficient internal pressure to ignite their deuterium, let alone their hydrogen. Yet we now see objects eight times Jupiter's mass displaying surface abundances that can only come from deuterium burning. That's impossible with one thousandth of a percent deuterium. But deuterium ignition works just fine if these objects are born with eight Jupiter masses and fifty percent hydrogen and fifty percent deuterium, and they're somehow sparked." She smiled at Tim, who was sitting looking lost.

"By analogy," she continued, "a trace of air mixed with gasoline is stable, but a fifty-fifty mixture is highly combustible. A spark would set off a conflagration. Since nature can't make, or ignite, fifty-fifty deuterium-hydrogen objects, especially near the kind of massive stars that collapse into black holes. . ." she paused for effect, ". . . it's hard to see that the chimeras can be anything other than *artificial.*"

The room went dead silent. A gust of wind struck the windows and she thought briefly of Kwame's cabin. At the doorway, a small group of professors had gathered. She wondered whether Greg had alerted his colleagues.

History being made today in the Bishop Library.

Tim looked stunned. "Kristi," he said, in a voice she did not recognize, "you're not making this claim seriously?"

"I am," she said. A wave of guilt passed through her. Maybe she should have taken him aside. Warned him what was coming. "They're artificial as in *synthetic.* As in *not made by nature.* As in manufactured by *Little Green Guys.* I would argue they were deliberately placed in orbit around black holes that were born without companions. Some of each chimera's solar wind now falls toward its black hole. That superheats the wind so it radiates X-rays. Hence the chimeras coincide with catalogued X-ray sources. They used to be invisible. Now you can't miss them."

Guilt, hell. She was Hubble discovering that the universe extended far beyond the Milky Way, Rubin finding the dark matter that surrounds all galaxies. She was on top of the world. "At first I suspected they were an experiment, test objects of some kind. But that would be an experiment hugely wasteful of resources when you could get away with masses a million times smaller."

The professors at the door were crowding into the room.

"No, the chimeras' creators needed something self-luminous, something that would last a long time, but something that would cost as little as possible because they had to make two thousand copies. A fifty-fifty deuterium-hydrogen mixture is the nuclear fuel that can be ignited in the lowest possible host mass. It's the cheapest interstellar beacon you can make if you insist on a hundred-million year warranty. Nature can't make these objects. But somebody can." She took a sip of water as her words sank in.

"The helium makes sense, too," she continued. "It's the ash, the by-product of pure deuterium-hydrogen fusion, brought up by convection from the core. The helium content of the chimeras is limited to one percent or less because they're all younger than a million years. Each one will continue burning its core deuterium and will shine at its present luminosity for another hundred million years."

Tim was going to say something else but Greg broke in. He was beaming. "Kristi, two of the chimeras are not associated with black holes. What can you tell us of them?"

"One of them," she said, "is moving at nearly three percent of the speed of light through Taurus. A second is in orbit around a G-dwarf in Scorpius. It's just under seven Jupiter masses, the lightweight of the entire sample, and the least luminous. I really don't know for certain, but I'd speculate that the first object is being towed or pushed toward a newborn black hole. And I wouldn't be surprised if the second one is on the assembly line."

The applause was tentative this time. Until the people at the doorway joined in.

Greg had a final word: "My initial reaction, when Kristi ran all this by me, was the same as Tim's. But there's one more piece of evidence that convinced me. Kristi?"

She was at her charming best, at a moment she would always remember. "A thirty-meter telescope at geosync orbit," she said, "is an amazing instrument. But the chimeras are faint and I couldn't find anything but deuterium, hydrogen, and helium in any of their spectra. When I realized that they had to be copies of each other, I removed the Doppler shift of each one and then co-added the two thousand spectra. The result is almost fifty times more sensitive to trace elements."

She touched the video controller and the summed spectrum

appeared, undulating and smooth, with four sharp, narrow dips. "See those four absorption lines? Only one element makes those lines. Plutonium. The nastiest, most dangerous substance we know.

"Each chimera is seeded with pure Plutonium-244, which will last as long as the chimera itself. It's the closest thing to a universal skull and crossbones I can imagine.

"Ladies and gentlemen, the chimeras are beacons. Celestial lighthouses. Space-faring travelers are being warned away from the shoals. Away from the Milky Way's two thousand solo black holes, which are otherwise nearly undetectable."

"Magnificent," said one of the professors. "If true."

She smiled, as her audience collectively let out its breath. "The evidence is all there, Professor. And, if Greg doesn't mind, I could use a glass of Cabernet. If we could quit now?"

Collaboration For "Lighthouse"

Several months after my initial conversation with Michael Shara, he called to explain an idea he had for a story. I'd mentioned the possibility of a collaboration, and he wondered whether I was serious. His idea described how a young astrophysicist tracked down an anomaly among some brown dwarfs and arrived at a spectacular inference. I was skeptical when he started. I mean, who can get excited about brown dwarfs? They are superdense bodies that almost became stars but lacked sufficient mass to ignite. Vast numbers of them wander through the sky. How many, I asked? He considered it. "Probably on the order of three for every ten visible stars."

These *are* visible objects, but you'd have to get close to see one. Think in terms of, say, a body the size of a terrestrial world. But otherwise resembling a gas giant, with an inner glow. Reddish, possibly, or brown. A surface churning with tornadoes and cyclones. And maybe iron clouds.

Well, I thought, that's pretty romantic stuff.

Michael explained that his heroine, Kristi Lang, would be working on her doctoral thesis. She has discovered that a few—a very few—brown dwarfs have an elemental composition that should not have happened, and that cannot be explained. He talked about deuterium and spectrographic analyses and radioactive components and temperature fluctuations while I wondered where we were headed. Ah, yes, I thought, the big payoff is that there's too much iron in the soup.

Then he explained what it all meant. What Kristi would discover during the course of her investigations.

It was a spectacular idea. Brilliant. A climax with a serious punch. "Might work," I said.

"You want to help?"

I was by then thinking how this was the sort of thing that was in the tradition of Arthur Clarke. It was *Asimovian* in its best sense.

"Okay," I said. "I think I can make the time."

Since Shara was the more knowledgeable, we agreed he would write the first draft.

Next day, we started the e-mail exchange that eventually gave us "Lighthouse," which you should probably read before continuing. The conversation might be of value because it provides some examples of the way writers have to think. It begins shortly after Shara had begun work on the draft, and extends over the next few weeks.

MCDEVITT: Keep in mind we need a story as well as an account of the solution. Which is why we should think about creating a parallel situation in your astrophysicist's life which reflects what's happening outside. So when she gets lost, and cold, and finds that cabin in the woods, after her car goes off the road, she has to break in, get some wood, build a fire, and feels the place get warm. THEN she figures it out.

SHARA: We don't have a title yet. "Campfire," possibly?

MCDEVITT: "Campfire" is a trifle placid and doesn't suggest a sheltered place with severe elements outside. We want the sort of fire that's part of a refuge. Maybe "Hot Stove"?

SHARA: Wood burning stove is better for a refuge. . . . But this stove burns deuterium. "Deuterium Stove" is more precise, but might well give away too much, too soon.

MCDEVITT: Yep. Keep in mind you won't need the kind of precision you're accustomed to striving for. We'll be more about metaphor. Do you agree that the story line works? The physicist is puzzled by the objects, gets lost on a winter night, finds an abandoned cabin with a stove, and by morning figures it out–?

SHARA: It works.

MCDEVITT: Our title suggestions aren't very good. We need something better than either of us has been able to come up with so far. Give it some thought. Could be connected with the fireplace. Or maybe we go in a completely different direction. Anyhow, the viewpoint character is puzzled by what she sees. Makes no sense. More data comes in. Maybe she talks long-range with a colleague who has an idea, which she rejects. Doesn't fit, Harry, she says. It's getting cold. Storm's coming. Daughter's birthday. (Or something. She needs a personal life.) Ordinarily wouldn't try to go down the mountain in this weather. Storm closes in. Off the road. Bad moments on foot. Will freeze before morning. Finds herself thinking about the whatzis as she stumbles through the night. A car passes without seeing her. Finds the cabin, etc.

SHARA: All good suggestions, all incorporated. Heroine is headed up the mountain for self-evident reasons. Title is now "Lighthouse" for reasons evident in story.

MCDEVITT: Okay. Let's stay with "Lighthouse." I'm happy with it. I pulled a line from the story and ran it by Maureen as a possible title. She blanched. It was: "Galileo Was a Piker."

SHARA: Omigod. Horrible.

MCDEVITT: I'm claiming it was a joke. Do we have a mathematical connection among the objects? Something that would eventually suggest something moving through the sky? (Have to be careful there or we give the show away too early.)

SHARA: I want the protagonists to agonize over the sub-critical mass (less than 0.07 Msun) before realizing it's a 50-50 deuterium-hydrogen mixture (and hence an artificial object).

MCDEVITT: Agonizing is always good.

(Several days later.)
MCDEVITT: How's it coming?

SHARA: Ninety percent done, and liking it a lot, but struggling with ending. Easy to reveal last details at heroine's thesis defense, but not thrilling enough, relative to her survival of snowstorm. Looking for a punchier ending. Tomorrow is annual Hubble proposal deadline. So it will be two or three days more.

MCDEVITT: There's nothing sacred about producing a complete draft. If you want to try your luck, send me what you have and I'll try to take it from there. Or if it needs the professional physicist, hang onto it and we'll get it done whenever.

SHARA: I'd rather not give it away piecemeal. Hopefully you'll enjoy the story too. Your first reaction will be invaluable in whether it needs a modest rewrite, major rewrite, or if it should be fed to the wood-burning stove.

MCDEVITT: Keep in mind, we don't want too much detail. All we really need is to make sure we have the science right, and to hold it out there for the reader without breaking the pace of the story.

SHARA: Okay, I'm typing the story. This is harder than writing an *Astrophys. Journal* paper, and there are parts I'm not happy with, but if I don't put it down on silicon I'll get stalled again. It needs to be set 25 years in the future, as we don't today have the technology (IR gigapixel cameras in orbit) to find these things in the numbers which drive the story line, but in 20-25 years, we will. The protagonist is female, a PhD candidate, who finds these things as part of her thesis research. (I've seen similar serendipitous finds in the last two years.) She figures it out (partly) around the stove, partly on her way up to the telescope (via space elevator . . . which was presented at the AAS meeting in San Diego, and which astronomers will monopolize.) I have no great ego or vested interest in the precise storyline. Feel free to cut, pare, graft or amputate as needed. It it's hopeless, so be it, I had a lot of fun (and significant frustration) writing it. Anyway I hope to email it tomorrow. Sharpen your pencil (or maybe your hatchet.)

MCDEVITT: Good morning, Mike. I'm anxious to take a look, but unable to open the document. If it comes to it, I have a fax.

SHARA: Okay. Try this version and let me know.

MCDEVITT: I have it and am looking at it now. I'll get back shortly.

MCDEVITT: Beautiful, Mike. It needs work, of course. But I'll confess you write a far smoother first draft than I do.

SHARA: Thank you, Jack. That's very encouraging coming from (you).

MCDEVITT: I'll do a second draft and get back within a couple days. Good show. Title's perfect. I deleted a couple of very's, as in 'very weird.' I tend to opt for understatement, but if you want to put them back in, that's good. . . . Isn't Kilimanjaro too far south of the equator for a space elevator?

SHARA: Good question. I believe the answer is no, it works, though the ribbon has to be somewhat stronger. I'll check in more detail.

SHARA: No problem. (*Cites a source.*) You need to supply a horizontal tension, and your efficiency is about 5% less, but you regain a lot of that by starting up high.

MCDEVITT: You have the orbiter at 80,000 klicks. I assume we mean 8000?

SHARA: Yes. The geosync station is at 35,000 km. Kristi's first inspiration, on the way up, is at 8000 km.

MCDEVITT: When I've finished the second draft, I'll send it back, and you can have a go at it. Change whatever you like. Nothing's sacred. We'll continue to play pingpong until we're both satisfied. The changes I'm making so far concern mostly getting away from exposition and putting everything on stage. That's the big secret of writing fiction. We're not telling a story. We're creating an experience.

SHARA: I've never published an sf story, and would like to give back to the genre something of what it has given me.

MCDEVITT: For what it's worth, this is the kind of story I love to read. Let's hope the editors agree. One other thing to think about: Is it possible the title gives the show away? "Chimeras" would also work. But I'm inclined to leave that to your judgment.

SHARA: Let's stay with "Lighthouse."

MCDEVITT: Okay. At the climax, when Kristi is doing her presentation, she puts up a visual of the spectrographic results. We need to put that up also for the reader to see. I inserted a line about bars, small ones and big ones. It's nonsense, but I don't know what I'm talking about so you'll have to fix it. Describe what they see onscreen.

SHARA: All the changes I listed yesterday are incorporated. My attempts to complexify the Tim-Kristi relationship just derailed the flow of the story. Probably a bad idea.

MCDEVITT: It was probably a sideshow anyhow. I think the rivalry works pretty well as is. Are you satisfied the title doesn't give the show away? There seems to be an inconsistency that got by me yesterday. The opening scene implies everybody already knows what she believes about the chimeras. "How'd you figure it out?" asks Tom on page one. But at the conclusion, it turns out they don't know.

SHARA: Some subtle errors have crept into the last version (like shrubbery and deuterium-helium burning) so I'm going through with the proverbial fine-tooth comb. Can we talk by phone this evening? I can explain the deuteron colors and a few other points. Leopard spoor has been seen often on Kilimanjaro at 5000m. I'm glad the snarl stayed in, sorry that K's reference to a leopard went out. Was Kristi's leopard-thought a distraction? As for the gas running out . . . I strongly disagree. Perhaps contrary to popular belief, astronomers are very rational, level-headed people. Heading off into a freezing snowstorm when you have a heated car is stupid, and Kristi isn't stupid. So we really must have her run out of gas, otherwise she comes across as a slow-witted jerk.

(*Phone conversation that night. E-mails resume in the morning.*)

SHARA: I like almost all the changes a lot. Galileo references are particularly lovely.

MCDEVITT: I'm delighted you're happy with it. It's nice to make a contribution.

SHARA: Here are my broad changes and reasons for them. Please tell me if any of them are potential mistakes.

MCDEVITT: I'm ready to plug the changes in. When I'm finished, I'll send the copy. But anywhere a change has been made, I'll let you know. There's one line in particular, near the end:

"The helium makes sense. too," she continued. "It's the ash, the by-product of pure deuterium- hydrogen fusion, brought up by convection from the core. The chimeras are all made of one percent helium or less because they're all younger than a million years. Each one will continue its core deuterium burning and shine at its present luminosity for another hundred million years." I'd like to change from the third sentence:

". . . from the core. . . . The helium contant of the chimeras is one percent or less because they're all younger than a million years." Also, Alex Cooper keeps bringing Alice Cooper to mind. We should change one of the names, preferably the last one. I'll make something up, maybe go with something ethnic. Suggestion welcome. I know there are still problems with the science, but I can't be of much help there.

SHARA: I see them. That's the easy part for me.

MCDEVITT: I tried to establish a relationship between Tim and Kristi. It's by no means a standard love interest, but I think it works.

SHARA: Yes, it does. Certainly better. Earlier version was too happy-sappy. This is more real. I may darken it more, just one or two lines. Tim's early dismissal of Kristie makes him too much of an ass too early, and kills any believable romantic possibilities. I want to continue to use him as a foil for Kristi, but treat them as true intellectual equals. Perhaps even bitter rivals in a future story. (Whoops. Did I really say that?)

MCDEVITT: By all means.

SHARA: I have to remove the shrubs and trees, as all mountains including ours at 5500 meters are completely barren of plants.

MCDEVITT: I meant to ask about that. Okay. Take them out.

SHARA: Is it okay to use just meters in a U. S. magazine? ('She slowed down as visibility dropped to about fifty yards' is in V3. I prefer fifty meters.)

MCDEVITT: Yes. That's not a problem.

SHARA: Kristi's dream needs neutrons AND protons (that's what deuterium is made of) morphing into each other. (BTW, this p-n morphing is the origin of the strong nuclear force. . . Kristi's physicist mind at work as she sleeps.) I wanted the noise vacuum cleaner to intrude into her dream as the noise snowplough approaches.

MCDEVITT: Okay. Put it back. I deleted part of it because dream sequences are notorious for putting readers to sleep. So they need to be short and to the point.

SHARA: The actinides are noted very early by Teri Liao, the department's eagle-eyed spectroscopist. I think I prefer her to note strange features in the spectrum, and let Kristi reveal the Plutonium 244.

MCDEVITT: One other question: Kristi has tagged and cataloged 21 billion of these things. That seems highly implausible. We need a word of explanation for the reader as to how it was accomplished.

SHARA: One other thing and then I'll quit: When Kristi is coming out of the dream sequence, it is probably better to delete the line that she has become aware of someone else in the room. It's more effective if we just put the hand on her shoulder.

SHARA: It keeps getting incrementally better. But yes, it's nearly time to send it to the editor. Your insertion of change notes into Version 4 was excellent, except that in a few cases I don't know what you changed things to. So please can you clarify? By the way, "radioactive levitation" is meaningless. The correct term is "radiative levitation." This is when photon pressure selectively elevates selected elements (but not others) in the atmospheres of dense dwarf stars. Lowercase 'e' is the base of natural logarithms. !!NOT!! capital 'E.' Please use centimeters instead of inches as Kristi's wheels dig deeper in. The only substantive addition I now see that I may have to make is a 2-3 sentence description of how Kristi determines the helium abundance. If 90,000 readers denounce an 'e', they may verbally crucify my implied claim that Kristi can see helium in the spectra of brown dwarfs. She can't, as BD's are all too cool to show He directly. But she deduces the He abundance from the fact that all her chimeras have significantly larger radii than all other BD's (which can only come from greatly decreased helium). A technical detail, perhaps, but one that I'm teaching my stellar structure and evolution seminar this week. Your call. If you think it's too esoteric, I can leave it out. But again, I think I can cover our technical backsides with two sentences.

MCDEVITT: Concur with your comments. Add the helium

explanation. And no crucifixions in this business. The reader gets an extra charge if he can catch us at something. Makes you more popular. I don't guess that's the way things go in the scientific community.

MCDEVITT: It's in the mail.

(*After the submission is sent off, SHARA spots another problem.*)
SHARA: For logical consistency, I switched Kristi's mental image to that of a BD, not a chimera. Thus she should see iron hydride clouds only. BDs have essentially zero deuterium. So the phrase "iron hydride and deuteride" should simply read "iron hydride." I forgot to change it in (the last draft).... This can be fixed before publication.

MCDEVITT: Mike, we won't even have to do that. If *Analog* buys it, they will ask for a copy on disk. That copy will be correct.... Let me know if you see anything else.

(*Later.*)
MCDEVITT: I've heard nothing yet on "Lighthouse." But these things take time. I'll let you know as soon as there's a response. Or you may get the word first since you're in New York. In any case, they'll be very happy with it.

SHARA: I hope so! I try not to think much about it as I'm swamped teaching the astro PhD students at Columbia this semester.

MCDEVITT: If you could order up a starship, where would you most want to go?

SHARA: Probably the Orion Nebula, the nearest massive star-forming region. Have you seen the Greta Flythrough in our space show? It is rich in detail.

SHARA: The paperwork from Dell arrived, with my first acceptance letter. I felt the same sort of pleasure that I felt back in 1972 when my first science journal paper was accepted.... I signed and returned the contract (before they could change their minds).

MCDEVITT: Congratulations. The first one is always especially sweet.

SHARA: Yes, it is.

MCDEVITT: Mike, enjoy the moment.

PART FOUR
THE BIG DOWNTOWN

The Big Downtown

Mike Resnick wanted a private eye prowling a future world, but doing it in the spirit of Raymond Chandler. Could I deliver? Sure, I told him. No sweat. I'll get it to you in a couple of days.

Enter Kristi Walker, called in to resolve the disappearance of an artist with no known enemies. She operates in a world two centuries older than our own. We have FTL, have mapped most of the worlds within a few hundred light-years, and have even brought home an outpost abandoned by somebody centuries ago and set it on the banks of the Potomac.

There's no evidence of malevolent aliens anywhere. But they'd probably be superfluous anyhow. As long as we have people, we're probably going to need cops. And private eyes.

1.

I woke up on the couch in my office, listening to the wind. Sunlight was coming through the drawn blinds. "*Kristi.*" Pete's voice. The office AI. "*You have a call. I wouldn't have bothered you but the guy sounds desperate.*"

It was almost nine. Time to open up. "What's he want, Pete?"

"*Something about a missing person.*"

Lord, I didn't want to get up. "Who is it? Who's calling?"

"*Says his name is Jules Steinmetz. Kristi, I think you need to talk to him.*"

I was using my sweater for a pillow. Somewhere in the building a door slammed. The Madson is probably the only place in D.C. where you still have to close the doors yourself. I got up, put the coffee on, straightened my hair and blouse, sat down behind the desk, and told Pete to put him through.

Steinmetz blinked on in the middle of the office. The guy looked scared. His jaws were clamped tight and there were rings around his eyes. His hair was uncombed and he stared at me with a bleakness that you just don't want to see first thing in the morning. He was wearing a wrinkled white pullover and black slacks. "*Ms. Walker?*" he said. "*I don't know what to do.*"

"Okay, Mr. Steinmetz." I tried to sound as if everything were under control. "Try to relax. What's going on?"

"*The police are saying it was an accident.*"

"What was an accident?"

"*The boat.*" His eyes closed and his face twisted as he fought back tears.

"I'm coming in on this a bit late. Who's missing? Why don't you start from the beginning and tell me what happened."

"*Sylvia. The police think she was out in Eliot's boat when Walter hit last week—*"

Walter was the hurricane that had ripped up the area that past Wednesday. "Wait a minute." I switched on the desk lamp. "What's Sylvia's last name, please?"

"*Ames. Sylvia Ames.*"

A few people had died in the storm, including several who'd been out in boats. They still can't convince everybody that hurricanes are dangerous, even this far north. "Who's Sylvia? What's her connection to you?"

"*She's my fiancée,*" he said.

"And Eliot?"

"*K.C. Eliot.*" He made a face, showing me that Eliot was a guy, and Steinmetz didn't much care for him. "*He's an artist.*"

"Okay," I said. "Sylvia and Eliot were out on a boat and they got caught by the storm. That's what police say?"

"*Yes. It can't be right.*"

"Why not?"

"*She's my fiancée.*" He delivered the three words syllable by syllable, as if I'd missed the significance first time around. "*She's not going to go out on a boat ride with somebody else.*"

Well, I thought, stranger things have happened. "What's her connection with Eliot?"

"*She's an artist's model.*"

"And she was posing for him?"

"*Yes.*"

"On the boat?"

"*No. Of course not. In his studio.*"

"Where's the studio?'

He gave me an address in Alexandria. "How'd they get on the boat?"

"*I don't know. The police have a witness, a guy down at the docks, who says he saw Eliot take his boat out when the storm was approaching. Says he got on the radio and tried to warn him.*"

"What kind of boat?"

"*A sailboat.*"

"Where was the storm?"

"*A few hours away. Maybe eight. I mean, Sylvia's no fool. She was going to finish up at the studio and then we were going to head inland. Get away from it.*"

"She was supposed to meet you somewhere?"

"*I was going to pick her up at her apartment. She never showed up.*"

"Okay. The witness saw them take the boat out?"

"*He says there were three of them. Eliot, another guy, and a tall blond. They're assuming the blond is Sylvia.*"

"Why are you so sure it couldn't have been her? Other than that she's your fiancée?"

"*She wouldn't have done that. She posed part time. Her real job was being a medical technician.*" He was having trouble breathing. "*Ms. Walker, the police say they've done all they can. I need somebody to find her.*"

"Jules," I said, softening my voice, "it's been six days. You're telling me no one's heard from her since the day of the storm?"

"*Yes.*"

"Have they recovered any bodies from the bay?"

"*No. They found the boat. Up near Annapolis.*"

"Okay. When did they take the boat out? It was Wednesday, right? Same day as the storm."

"*Yes. The witness says they left about eleven. In the morning.*"

The storm had arrived around seven that night. Not a big one, especially, but there is no such thing as a moderate hurricane. Winds at one-ten. They'd evacuated most of the area. There was still a major clean-up going on. "How long have you been engaged, Jules?"

"*I know what you're thinking. She wouldn't have done that.*"

"Wouldn't have cheated."

"*No.*"

Love is wonderful. But it looked to me as if she'd gone out there with the intention of taking on two guys. They'd gotten carried away, lost track of the storm, and there you are.

"How long had she been modeling for Eliot?"

"*Off and on for a year.*"

I spelled out what it would cost him for me to look into it. He agreed. Anything. Just find her.

"Jules," I said, "I have to tell you at the outset that I don't have much hope. She's been missing since the storm, and an eyewitness described someone who looked like her getting on the boat." I held out my hands. "We have to face the facts."

He stood looking at me, big, pleading, scared. "*Something else you should know,*" he said.

"What's that?"

"*She didn't particularly like Eliot. If she were going to cheat, he wouldn't have been the guy.*"

"I'll get back to you," I said, "as soon as I have something."

I started by checking my client's background. Jules was a biologist at the University of Maryland. He'd done a couple of flights with Academy missions, charting life forms elsewhere. Originally from Hamburg. Thirty-one years old. Author of two books on biosystem patterns. Whatever they are.

Sylvia, as a model, had maintained an on-line sales pitch. Her hologram appeared beside the bookcase, seated fetchingly on a gray fabric sofa. Off-the-shoulder black velvet gown. Soft long hair and incandescent brown eyes. A live one. A burgundy voice indicated she was available for modeling assignments. Make appointment.

"Hello, Sylvia," I said.

She smiled. "*Good morning, Kristi.*"

"Where have you gone, babe?"

"*I don't know. I wish I could help.*"

I could see why Jules was upset. She was twenty-four. A graduate of Michener Medical in Alexandria. With honors. Virginia native.

And then there was Kevin Charles Eliot. A little guy, as nearly as I could tell. Middle-aged. A bit unkempt. I'd have liked to see a picture of him standing beside Sylvia. It looked as if he'd be almost eye-level with her bumpers.

He'd been having a mildly successful career, by which I mean he sold enough of his work to make a living. But not much more. And my first thought was: How did he afford a sailboat?

Eliot had lived in the D.C. area all his life. According to the bio he'd posted, he seemed not to have done anything, ever, other than paint. He specialized in portraits. You wanted a picture done of Uncle Ralph, something that made Ralph look like a person of significance, Eliot was your guy. Some of his work found its way into galleries, and he even had some art critics gushing. Although I noticed none of the gushes were recent.

When I called Judy Bergdorf, who did the art sections for the *Washington Post*, she told me that Eliot had been ambitious to achieve the top rung, as every artist is. "*But he just didn't have the talent.*"

Actually, he looked pretty good to me.

"*No imagination,*" she said. "*Technically, he's about as good as they come, but he doesn't have the spark that you need to make the museums.*"

"That sounds pretty abstract," I told her. "What's 'spark'?"

"*Look at any of his work. The subjects don't come alive. Not the way they do, say, for Bronson. Or Meriwether. You look in their eyes and there's nobody looking back at you.*"

"Okay," I said. "Thanks."

"*In all fairness to him,*" she continued, "*hardly anybody else can do it either.*"

"Did you know him personally, Judy?"

"*More or less.*" Judy was about fifty, but she looked twenty years younger. "*Does this have anything to do with the accident, Kristi?*"

"Yeah," I said. "I'm interested in the woman who was with him." I walked over and looked out the window. A bus was landing at the rooftop station across the street. "Did he have any enemies you know of? Anybody who might want to see him dead?"

"*No,*" she said. "*These guys, the artists, tend not to like each other very much, but the competition doesn't get that hot.*"

"Anybody other than an artist?"

"*Not that I know of.*"

"Okay. Would you think he'd be the kind of guy who'd take a sailboat out into a storm?"

"*K.C.?*" She laughed. "*I wondered about that when I first heard what had happened. He always seemed to me like a safety-first kind of guy.*"

I poured myself a cup of coffee, got comfortable, tied into Weather Central and reran the hurricane.

Walter had first touched land in Georgia. It had then, as hurricanes usually do, thrown a sharp northerly turn and roared into the

Carolinas. It cut a path of destruction inland to Columbia, and turned northeast again toward the Atlantic. It churned back out to sea, hammered Myrtle Beach and the coastal communities, rolled over the Outer Banks and Norfolk, and, on Wednesday, September 17, just after sunset, it blew into Chesapeake Bay.

The track it had followed had been Hurricane Alley a long time. Nothing much had changed about that. But global warming had given us bigger storms and more of them. As these things went, Walter was only average. But that was enough.

I watched it move north as evening fell. Most of the towns on both sides of the bay had been evacuated. The sky remained bright and sunny until late afternoon and then, as if someone had thrown a switch, the world got dark.

The Weather Central re-creation filled the office. Virginia's eastern shore lay on my right, near the bookcase and below my graduation picture from the police academy. Gloucester Point, Lancaster, and the mouth of the Potomac were on the left. No lights moved along the big highways. At the beginning, there were a few taxis in the air, and maybe a couple commercial carriers, but they got out of the way quickly. The hurricane took over the bay, and the only light visible in all that churning panorama came from a table lamp on my desk. It was rough water. You wouldn't have wanted to be out there. Not in a warship, let alone a sailboat.

I looked at the map. Eliot's boat had been docked at Chesapeake Beach. It was a long way from his studio. If they were there at eleven, they could have gone out for a brief run, and Sylvia could still have made it back home by three to meet Jules. But it seemed like a lot of running around for damned little time on the water.

I wondered how experienced a sailor Eliot had been. Actually, the fact he'd gone out in the face of the storm pretty much answered that question.

So I went back to watching Walter come north, watched the rising water push into the Potomac, watched the storm spread out across both shores. It arrived in full force off Chesapeake Beach and Eliot's dock at seven o'clock, give or take. It knocked some buildings flat. Wrecked a few boats that had not been put away. And finally moved into Maryland.

2.

I called Jack Calloway at the station to see what, if anything, he had. Jack's a small, quiet guy with the kind of carefully trimmed mustache that you'd find on a real estate agent. Black skin, black eyes, and a receding hairline. If you didn't look closely you might not take him too seriously. But that would be a mistake. He was in fact a good man to have at your back. We'd worked together when I was on the force.

"*I don't think there's any big mystery, Kristi,*" he said. "*It's pretty obvious your young lady was making out on the side. I mean, she was a nude model. Did you know that?*"

"I didn't have the details."

"*Okay. So it's not a big leap from there to the bedroom.*"

"We can debate that later, Jack. It still doesn't explain why they'd go out into the bay with a hurricane coming in."

"*People do things like that all the time. The storm is why they do it.*" He was in his office, leaning back against his desk. Several plaques were visible behind him.

"You found the boat," I said.

"*The Coast Guard did. They found what was left of it.*"

"Where?"

"*Up near Annapolis. It was wedged against one of the Tolley Bridge supports.*" He showed me a picture. The hull was caved in along the port side. The mast was busted. "*The Coast Guard got an S.O.S. from them. But it was too late. The station was already locked down and they couldn't send anybody out.*"

"Where was the boat when the S.O.S. came in?"

"*I don't know. Middle of the bay somewhere.*"

"And by then the storm had already hit?"

"*Apparently. Look, they were having a pretty good time in the cabin, probably drinking, and nobody paying attention. And suddenly the storm's on top of them. It wouldn't be the first time it happened.*"

"Did anybody see them out on the bay? Were they adrift at any time?"

"*Nobody we know of. With the storm coming, most folks were headed inland.*" He looked as if he'd been through this conversation several times already.

"So the investigation's closed?" I said.

"*There never was a criminal investigation. No reason to think there was anything here to concern ourselves with. You have anything new to offer?*" He folded his hands and propped his chin on them.

"No," I said. "You have any idea who the third person was?"

"No. We've got a few missing persons, but nobody who seems likely." He shrugged. *"Easiest is just to wait until the body comes ashore."*

I rode a taxi over to Chesapeake Beach, not so much because it was a long drive and a lot quicker to go by air, but because it gave me a chance to look at the countryside. I hadn't been out of the metropolitan area since the storm hit, and I wanted to see for myself how much damage there was.

There were some smashed houses scattered across the landscape. Everything's supposed to be resistant to hurricanes, but there's just so much you can do before the cost becomes exorbitant. I'd spent that Wednesday night huddled in my apartment wondering whether the place would blow away.

The real problem was that, since the storms had become so severe, and so frequent, insurance premiums had gone through the roof, and nobody was covered anymore. So you get an event like this, and your house blows away, you're wiped out. To make matters worse, the experts are saying global warming is past the point where it can be easily controlled, and conditions, at least for the foreseeable future, will continue to deteriorate.

It was threatening rain when my taxi descended into Chesapeake Beach. The sky had turned gray, and a cold wind blew off the bay. If there had at one time actually been a beach, it was long gone, submerged beneath the rising waters of the past century and a half. You could see where the town had retreated from the bay, where a few stone buildings, not worth saving, had been overtaken and now lay offshore.

The taxi set down on a pad outside a seafood restaurant. One wall had been blown in. A couple of guys were working on it. Immediately north of the pad were a half dozen short piers and a ramshackle wooden building marked Roney's Boathouse. It appeared untouched. I told the cab to wait.

I walked over to the boathouse and found a thin, bored-looking guy with a lot of gray hair and a thick gray beard scraping the hull of a jetboat. "Name's Marty," he said. "What can I do for you?"

"Hi, Marty. Kristi Walker." I gave him a big smile. The book says you get a better response from people if you show them your ID. But I've discovered from long experience that guys like this one are more inclined to speak freely to a woman than they are to a P.I. "I wanted to talk with you about K.C. Eliot. One of your customers."

"You a cop?" he asked, uncertain.

"Private," I said. "You don't mind talking to me?" I threw in another smile.

"No. No, I don't mind. What do you want to know?" He put his scraper down and did an appraisal. He answers my questions; I let him look.

Marty was the guy the police had interviewed. "Was anybody else here when Eliot took the boat out? Anybody other than you?"

"No." He grinned. "Wasn't anybody left in town. Goddam storm was coming and they'd all cleared out. I was getting ready to put the last boats away."

"The last boats?"

"There were three of them docked outside. We were supposed to bring them in until the storm passed."

"Okay."

"Then I was going to get out of town myself."

"Did you get the other boats in?"

He looked at me as though the question made no sense. "Two of them," he said.

"Why only two?"

"The third one was Eliot's."

"You're saying that Eliot had arranged to have his boat moved inside, but then he took it out on the bay instead?"

"That's right."

"Did he tell you why?"

"Not really."

"Did you talk with him?"

"On the radio."

"You didn't go out when you saw him on the pier?"

"I was working. Didn't know they were there until they were climbing aboard. I went out and tried to call them back but he just waved and kept going. I couldn't figure that at all. So I used the radio."

"You warned him about the storm."

"Yeah. Asked him where he was going."

"What did he say?"

"Told me he'd only be out a little while. Told me not to worry. He'd take care of the boat himself." He pointed me toward a couple of chairs set around a wooden board on a pair of sawhorses.

"You told the police there were two people with him."

"Yep. A man and a woman."

I showed Sylvia to him. "Is this the woman?" I'd switched her into more casual clothing.

"*Hello, Marty,*" she said. "*Nice to meet you.*"

He looked at her admiringly, and then frowned. "Could be. Hard to tell. I didn't get a good look. She was blond, like this one."

"When you talked to him, was it strictly audio?"

"Yes."

"No visual?"

"No."

"The other male. Had you ever seen him before?"

"No. He wasn't from around here."

"Can you describe him?"

"Big guy. Middle-aged."

"That's it?"

"Black hair. Clean-shaven." He got up, wandered over to a coffee machine and took down two cups. "Want one?"

"Yes. Sure."

"He was wearing a khaki jacket."

There were several boats, on carriers, inside the building. "You came through the storm pretty well," I said.

"Roney's has been here a long time. What'd you say your name was again?"

"Kristi."

"Kristi. Sorry. My memory's not what it used to be. Anyhow, it's going to take more than a hurricane to knock us down."

"When you talked to Eliot on the radio, how did he sound?"

"How do you mean?"

"Did he sound normal? Worried? Anything out of the ordinary?"

He thought about it. "No. I don't recall anything unusual. Except he didn't particularly want to talk to me."

"Really."

"Eliot's usually pretty talkative. Not this time. Hi Marty, we're fine, goodbye. And that was pretty much it."

We sat for a couple of minutes, talking idly, while I finished my coffee. It had started to rain, and the rain quickly became a downpour. It pounded on the roof.

I got up, thanked him, gave him my card, and told him if anything else occurred to him, or if he saw any of these people again, to give me a call. "Oh," I said. "One more question."

He was studying the card. "Yeah?"

"You ever see the blond here before?"

He shook his head. "Nope."

"You're sure?"

"Yep. She'd of been hard to forget."

I went up to Annapolis and looked at the wreckage. They'd pulled it away from the bridge and beached it. I knew a couple of the cops up there and one of them, Angelo Reynoso, escorted me to the site. It had been a sixteen footer, the kind of boat you see all over Chesapeake Bay.

"I understand they got off an S.O.S.," I said.

He looked at the wreckage with the world-weariness in his eyes that all cops acquire if they hang around long enough. "That's what I hear, Kris. It was too late, though. The storm had already shut down the station. Wasn't anything anybody could do."

"What did Eliot say? Send help?"

"I understand it was the AI. It just kept repeating that they needed assistance."

"The AI?"

"Yes."

"That seems strange, doesn't it? What would you do if you woke up out there with a storm coming on?"

"I'd get on the radio and make some noise."

I climbed into the boat. It was full of water and sand. There were two radios, one aft at the helm, the other in the cabin. They were identical models, the Spindrift 280.

"Bed's been slept in," said Angelo. Yeah. It looked as if they'd been having a good time. I checked the head. Two toothbrushes. "They found her purse over in the corner."

"It *was* Sylvia Ames's purse?"

"Yeah. Did you know her?"

"No," I said. "Her boy friend's my client."

His voice dropped an octave. "That has to be tough."

I called Spindrift and got an AI. "I'd like some information on the 280 marine radio, please."

"*Of course,*" it said, in a silky female voice. "*What did you want to know?*"

I asked about range. And then: "Does it have a relay function?"

"*Yes, it does.*"

"Thank you very much."

Angelo looked interested. "You think the S.O.S. might have come from a remote location?"

"It's possible. A directed signal aimed at the boat and then broadcast from there. Who knows?"

"You think it was a murder."

"I'm looking at the possibilities, Anj."

"You always did have a lot of imagination, Love."

3.

I started wandering around town, getting to know the art community. Aside from the artists, there were agents, suppliers, gallery operators, sales people, even a guy who configured AI's who were making paintings. I had no idea that we had AI's doing art. I'd heard about it, but hadn't believed it. I do now. I saw some of their work and they're better than human. In some ways.

Word got out that I was on the street, and by the third day I was hearing things like, We were expecting you, and Heard you were coming.

Everybody knew Eliot, but nobody really admitted to being a friend. He was not, according to the consensus, in any kind of trouble. And no one knew of a reason anybody would want him dead.

I saved the most likely location for last: The Renaissance Gallery, in Arlington, was owned by Mary and James Colter. It had, on occasion, handled Eliot's work. James was there when I showed up.

The place looked good. Subdued lighting, satin curtains, thick carpets, just-audible classical music. Oil paintings were on display on two levels. I'm no art critic, but James smoothly assured me the artists were among the best currently working in the N.A.U. and Europe. "May I ask how your interests lie?" he asked.

James Colter didn't so much walk through the gallery as he swept through. A monarch moving among his monuments. It was easy to visualize him seated on a chair hauled about by peasants. He was fifty, with dark brown hair, and a tendency to keep his voice low as if we were in a church.

How did my interests lie?

This guy got to see my ID. "Do you have anything by K.C. Eliot?" I asked.

"Why, yes, Ms. Walker." His attitude changed slightly. The monarch was still there, but he became more distant. Consumed by pressing duties, you know. "As it happens we have." He led me into the rear. We climbed a circular staircase to the mezzanine, and he pointed to a portrait of a young man clad in hunting gear. The young man stood beside a tree, gazing serenely back at us. "This is one of his very best. He called it 'After the Hunt.'" He smiled, casting away the title. "As you can see, his balance is superb."

"Yes," I said. "Remarkable."

"This is about ten years old. Eliot hadn't planned to sell it. He used it as a demonstration piece. But, as a result of his unfortunate death, it came into our hands."

"It's quite good," I said.

"Yes." James stood back so as not to block my view.

"Do you have anything else of his?"

"No. Nothing, I'm sorry to say."

"Prints, maybe?"

He coughed politely. "We don't carry prints."

I asked how much the painting might bring. He cited a number which was considerably higher than my conversation with Judy Bergdorf suggested. "How well did you know him?" I asked.

"Eliot? Not well at all, actually." He glanced at the time. "I only knew him as a professional."

"Did he have any friends?"

"Not really. He wasn't a sociable sort."

"What about a girl friend?"

We were starting back downstairs, but he paused with his fingers lightly holding the handrail. "Yes," he said. "There was a young lady."

"Can you tell me her name?"

"Janice Something."

The name turned out to be JoBeth Androska. JoBeth had been with Eliot a couple of times when he'd visited the gallery. "Average-looking woman," according to James. She worked at the Moonlight Hotel on Wilson Boulevard.

I drove over, got lucky, and found her on duty. She looked good, certainly better than James had implied. She teared up when I told her why I was there. It took a few minutes to pry her loose from the counter. We eventually found chairs in the lobby. "It's terrible," she said. "I just don't know what to think."

"I'm sorry," I said.

"It's not knowing that drives me crazy. And the other thing is that I can't believe he'd have taken the boat out with that storm coming in. It just wasn't like him."

She started to dissolve in front of me. Then she looked around, saw that everyone in the lobby was watching, and swallowed hard. "Let's go back to the employees' lunchroom."

The lunchroom was a bare-bones place, where maybe ten people could eat. There was a long table in the center. We sat down at it, and she asked whether I thought there was any chance K.C. might be alive.

I didn't want to lie to her. I thought Eliot and Sylvia were dead. And the third person too, whoever he might turn out to be.

Her voice gave way. "I should be used to it by now," she said. "But it just doesn't seem possible. " She shook her head. "Until there's a body—"

"How was he doing as an artist?" I asked, trying to sound as if I just wanted to change the subject.

"Okay." She picked up a napkin, folded it in half, and folded it again. "He thought his work was improving. Getting better all the time."

"I mean financially."

"All right." She cleared her throat. "He was never going to make big money. He knew that."

"His studio was in Alexandria."

"Yes."

"What's happening over there now?"

"At the studio? Not much. The rent was paid through the end of the month. The executor is running an estate sale tomorrow. This weekend we're going to clear what's left."

"Who's the executor?"

"I am."

"JoBeth, I wonder if you'd mind telling me what the estate is worth?"

Big smile. "It was a surprise to me."

"How much of a surprise?"

"The accountant's going to give me the numbers within the next few days. But it looks like about six hundred thousand."

Not bad for a struggling artist. That was about nine years pay for me. "And it's going to whom?"

She looked uncomfortable. "He left everything to me."

"Nothing to the family?"

"He didn't have a family. Folks are dead. He was an only child."

"Okay."

"I didn't do it." She was sniffling.

"I know."

"Thank you."

She excused herself, went through a back door, and returned with a glass of water. Belatedly she asked if I wanted any. "Is this going to take much longer? They need me back at the desk."

"No. Just a minute or two. There was a second man with him when he took the boat out. Do you have any idea who that might have been? Big guy, black hair. About fifty, fifty-five."

"I don't know."

"Have you ever known him to do anything like this before?"

"You mean take a model out on the boat?"

"Yeah."

"Never. He was strictly professional about that."

"How about riding into a storm? Was he inclined to take chances?"

"K.C.? He's the most cautious man I know. No, he'd never do anything like that."

"But he did."

She nodded. "I don't understand it."

That didn't surprise me. In my experience women almost never know their men very well. "JoBeth, I'd like to ask a favor."

"Go ahead."

"Are you off this evening?"

"Yes. I'm done at six."

"I wonder if you'd mind letting me look around K.C.'s studio?"

She thought about it. "Why? What could it possibly have to do with the boat coming apart in a storm?"

I reached over and laid a hand on her forearm. She was trembling. "I won't know until I've looked."

The studio was located on the second floor of a stone building at the south end of Fletcher Street, over a men's clothing store. It was mostly empty when I got there, the furniture gone, personal stuff gone, just a few packing cases left in the middle of the room.

JoBeth stood inside the doorway. This is where he had his easel. Over there is where the model usually posed. Bedroom in there. Kitchen back that way.

He'd lived there. And I gathered that they'd both lived there, off and on. Never a formal arrangement. Weekends. Otherwise hit or miss. I thought about the nude models and wondered whether a girl friend can get used to that. But I couldn't see any point asking.

The place looked as if it had cost money. It was big, and if it wasn't exactly luxurious, it wasn't nickels and dimes either. "Did he do anything else besides art?" I asked. "I mean, did he have any other employment?"

"No," she said. "This was his life, right here."

"Any other means of income?"

"Not that I know of."

I took another look around the studio. Two long windows looking down on Fletcher Street. Nice curtains. Paneled walls. Brass bathroom fixtures. A tub you could swim in. "If you don't mind my asking, JoBeth, the rent here must have been fairly high."

"It is. I didn't realize how high until I got talking to the landlord a few days ago."

"How'd he manage it?"

She touched the curtains gently. Swayed, and held on. "I don't know. I guess he was doing better than I thought."

"What's in the cases?"

"Odds and ends. Brushes, canvas, paint."

"He was working on a portrait of Sylvia Ames when things went wrong."

"Yes."

"Did you know Sylvia?"

She nodded. "I knew her." She touched one of the boxes gently, with a fingertip. "I was okay with it. It's what he did. He was very professional."

"Okay."

"Nobody who came here, who modeled for him, ever had a complaint."

"You don't think anything was going on? On the boat?"

"No. I don't believe it."

"Did he complete the portrait?"

"No. Did you want to see it? I have it right here."

"Please."

It was in back, leaning against a wall, front facing in as if it were an embarrassment. She held it for me. "It's just a preliminary sketch. He was just starting."

Sylvia would have been portrayed almost in profile, clasping roses to her breast, long hair combed down over one shoulder.

She put it back, face in again. "Does he customarily do that?" I asked. "Make a preliminary sketch before starting the final work?"

"Oh, yes. He always does it. Uses charcoal."

"JoBeth," I said, "how long had he been in this studio?"

"He moved over here about three years ago. Right around the time I met him."

"Where was he before then?"

She gave an address on Warlock Avenue. One of the seedier sections of town.

"Thanks," I said. "Are there more sketches around? Or finished work?"

She shook her head no. "Maybe one or two. The last year or so, he's worked mostly on commission. Somebody wants a portrait, he does it, and the portrait goes out."

"But that wasn't the case with Sylvia."

"No. He still had hopes of making a name for himself. But it's hard. It's not simply a matter of talent. I mean, he had the talent. But a lot of it's politics."

"How do you mean?"

"Schmoozing with the gallery owners. And the distributors. And the critics. Especially the critics. K.C. never did any of that. He let his work stand for itself." She sighed, stricken by the unfairness of it all. "He has an archive. It contains everything he's ever done."

The archive was recorded in the AI's files, but the files had been transferred to her place, so that's where we went. She lived about a mile away, in a small apartment looking down on a large Italian restaurant. *Louie*'s. She broke out a bottle and we drank a round to the missing artist. Then she directed the AI to produce the archive.

There were a few landscapes, but mostly he did portraits. I guess I'd expected to see more nudes, but there were all kinds of people, kids on a wooden bridge, an elderly woman gazing across an open field, a young mother nursing her infant. There were several of the sort you find in boardrooms, an intimidating founder looking out past the rabble. His most common subjects were elderly men and women who looked boring. Stuffy. "He hated doing those," she said. "Paintings of stuck-up people who had never done anything. But it's where the money was."

One in particular caught my eye: a bearded man wearing a safari hat and a hunting jacket. He seemed a bit pompous, but there was simultaneously something heroic about the figure.

"That's Harold Clayborn," she said. When I showed no sign of recognition, she added, "Midnight."

Ah, yes. Midnight Clayborn, an adventurer who'd written books about his travels around the globe, and to a handful of other worlds.

"Does Clayborn have the painting?" I asked.

"Yes. He commissioned K.C. to do it."

"I'm impressed." Clayborn claimed to have found Sennacherib's throne. I wasn't sure what else he'd done, but his books were enormously popular. "Did you get to meet him?"

"No." She looked disappointed. "He was before my time."

"Are there any other famous people here?" I asked.

She considered it. "I don't think so."

Among the landscapes, there was a painting of a young man gazing across the Hudson. A couple of country scenes. And a moonlit beach.

"The critics said he had no imagination," she said. "But look at those."

The beach looked romantic. The moon was full, and its golden track ran to the horizon. But the fact was I'd seen a thousand like it. "Yes," I said. "Critics are not to be taken seriously."

"Absolutely right. Kristi, he had a passion for his art. Loved what he did. When he wasn't painting, we were out at the museums and the galleries. When the Retreat opened a few months ago, we were there. The first day."

I wasn't clear on what she was saying. The Retreat was a structure found in a star system that supported no life. It had been a single building on an airless moon orbiting a gas giant. It was empty when an Academy team found it, ten or eleven years ago, and it didn't look as if anybody had been there for a long time. But two *things* had lived and died there. They'd had a library and a shower and oversized furniture and apparently whatever else they needed to make themselves comfortable.

The Academy arranged to have the place disassembled and brought to Arlington and then put back together. It had taken a long time, but they'd done it and the place had opened to an excited public and outraged preservationists that past spring.

But what did it have to do with art?

"Let me show you," she said.

She signaled the AI and a portrait materialized. "This was found hanging in the main room when they first got to the Retreat." I'd seen it before. It was faded, had spent too much time in vacuum and, I guess, in pretty cold temperatures. Don't know what that does to a painting. But maybe it was just as well. The subject wasn't somebody you'd want to meet on a D.C. street at night.

They called it *The Stranger*. It had smoldering eyes and a reptilian smile and shadows in the wrong places. It wore a dark robe and a hood was pulled down over the forehead. I recalled that the experts thought it was an accurate rendering, possibly a self portrait, of one of the two creatures that had lived in the Retreat.

"K.C. wanted to see how art would look through nonhuman eyes," she said. "Did you see the mile-long lines that first day? When they first opened? We were there." She shook her head angrily. "And people accuse him of having no soul." She poured another round, and we drank to his soul.

"How'd he meet Clayborn?" I asked.

"One of the gallery owners knew him. Annie Detmer. When he mentioned getting a portrait done, she recommended K.C."

I turned back to the Clayborn painting. "He did a nice job."

"Yes, he did, didn't he? Later, Clayborn bought some of his other paintings."

"Really?"

"Yes. He was K.C.'s best customer."

"How many paintings did he buy?"

She had to think. "I believe it was five."

"Do you know how much he paid?"

"I can't imagine why it would matter. But I don't know. I have no idea."

"Did K.C. ever hint about the amount?"

"I suppose he did. He told me that Clayborn appreciated his work. And what he meant by that, I'm sure, is that he paid pretty generously." Her eyes became defensive.

"What else?" I asked.

"How do you mean?"

"There's something you're not telling me."

She took a deep breath. "I'm not sure it's anything."

"Try me."

"He was getting money from Clayborn."

"You mean other than the payments for the paintings?"

She wavered, looked like maybe yes, maybe no. "I just know payments came in."

"Regularly?"

"I don't know."

"How'd the money come?"

"What do you mean?"

"How did Clayborn make the payment? Transferral? Check? What?"

"Transferral."

"Okay," I said. "Anybody else?"

"Anybody else what?"

This kid wasn't the quickest babe on the block. "Was anybody else giving him money?"

"Not that I know of."

"Do you have access to his bank records?"

"No," she said.

"But you're his executor."

She managed a smile. "Right," she said.

It took a while, but eventually the numbers came through. Eliot had incorporated himself as Rising Wind Enterprises. And there were the purchases from Clayborn, six in all, beginning almost four years earlier. But only six. Where were the other payments?

"I don't know," she said. "K.C. told me he was sending money."

Well, there were some large deposits. Thirty thousand here, forty thousand there. Over the years they added up to almost three-quarters of a million. But this money came from a numbered account. I checked the designator. The account was listed to the International Bank, which rode serenely on the space station. "You think this is Clayborn's money?" I asked.

JoBeth didn't know. Maybe.

I looked up everything I could find about Midnight Clayborn. He became famous twenty-five years ago when Adam Hutton wrote his biography *Midnight*. The nickname had come from an incident early in his career. Arab bandits had seized some kids at an excavation site. The kids had belonged to Clayborn's workers. The incident occurred while he was digging at Ugarit. The kidnappers had demanded money, but they were a particularly bloodthirsty crew with a history of occasionally murdering hostages. Six kids were involved. And Clayborn had no inclination to rely on the honor of cutthroats.

Consequently he organized a rescue operation. A friend created a distraction by crash-landing a flyer nearby, and Clayborn with a few picked men charged into the bandit camp precisely at midnight, as the guards were being changed. There was a brief exchange of gunfire, during which he was wounded, but several of the bandits were killed, and the others fled. The hostages were rescued unharmed, and Harold Clayborn had earned the sobriquet by which the world has known him since.

He was a popular area speaker, forever talking to service organizations, graduating classes, academic groups. His next scheduled event was at the Adventurers' Club Friday evening. That was only two days away.

I was sitting in my office looking at his hologram when Jack called. (Clayborn was wearing the same safari hat as in Eliot's painting. He was a little younger, and looked quite capable of riding down a bunch of bandits.)

"Yeah, Jack," I said. "What can I do for you?"

"*You busy?*"

"What's happening?"

"*Why don't you come down to the station? I'll wait for you.*"

4.

Eliot's body had been found lying face down in the marsh grass on the western shore, a few miles north of Lexington Park.

The lab unit was there when we arrived. It was a desolate stretch of swamp, and it had been difficult to find dry ground for the emergency vehicles. We came down on a hilltop surrounded by ooze. Jack passed me a pair of boots from the locker. I took off my shoes and pulled them on. "Be careful getting out," he said. "Don't sink."

Eliot's body had come to rest against an embankment. It had been spotted by a couple of bird watchers in a boat. It now lay in the EV, where the technicians were going over it. The team leader was Catherine Sabatina. Cathie was abrasive, but she was good at her job. She turned as we approached.

"Good to see you, Jack," she said. She nodded my way. "The victim has a severe head contusion. Might have come from a collision with a spar when he went overboard," she said. "Or somebody might have used an oar handle on him."

"Okay," he said. "What else have we got?"

"He's been in the water about two weeks."

"Cause of death?"

"Let you know when we get him back to the lab."

It was getting dark. A cold wind blew off the bay. I could see a couple boats out about a mile, sailboats, drifting past. Their lights were just coming on.

Cathie and her team climbed into the EV. It lifted off and turned west.

"Blow to the head," I said.

He nodded. "That's what it sounds like." We sloshed back through the muck, got onto dry land, and pulled off the boots. "What have you got on this, Kristi? Anything?"

I told him what I'd been doing.

"So what's next?"

"Not sure yet. I'll let you know."

A few hours later I got a call from him. Eliot had drowned.

I was thinking it was time I met Midnight Clayborn. The Friday evening address at the Adventurers' Club sounded like the right venue. I got on the circuit and checked it out. Was the public welcome?

"*Sorry, but no,*" they told me. "*Members only. And guests.*"

I called around. Found somebody who knew somebody, and got an introduction to Pavel Gurov, a volcanologist. Pavel—Pasha to his friends—was a member, but hadn't been planning on attending. He would reconsider, and would be delighted to invite me as his guest if I would consent to have a drink afterward with him. He was a bit stiff, but he seemed okay. I said sure, although I suspected it would be an appointment I'd have to postpone. Then I called JoBeth and asked whether her AI was capable of imitating K.C.'s voice.

"*Sure,*" she said. She sounded suspicious. But I tried to allay her concerns. Then I told her what I wanted her to do.

The Adventurers' Club meets monthly at the Brandeis Hotel, just off Massachusetts Avenue. Pasha and I rolled in with about fifteen minutes to spare.

The Brandeis is one of these ancient places, built in the latter part of the twenty-first century. It has lots of heavy paneling and oddball lighting and what the travel agents like to call character, which means the elevators creak.

The members, as you would expect, were predominantly but not exclusively male. There were about eighty people present, milling around and nursing drinks, when a bell dinged and we filed into one of the banquet rooms. A dinner consisting mostly of inedible pork and vegetables showed up. We were seated in groups of eight, and I could see Clayborn at the head table. A few drums and spears had been placed strategically around the room, and a dark blue banner with THE ADVENTURERS' CLUB marked in silver Arabic-style letters was mounted along the front wall. A lectern stood in front of the banner.

I was, by the way, wearing an auburn wig that changed my hair from short to shoulder-length. It was the best disguise I could think of. I knew by then I'd be sitting down with Midnight at some point and asking him questions and I didn't want him remembering me from this event.

We got the food down as best we could, and eventually a small portly man, who did not look at all like an adventurer, got up from the head table, walked over to the lectern, and welcomed us. It was good to see us again. He announced that one of the members had passed away since they'd last gathered, read the minutes of the last meeting, gave way to the treasurer for a financial report, and to the membership secretary for remarks about the membership drive. I wondered, but did not ask, what the qualifications for membership were.

Finally it was time to introduce the guest of honor. "Dr. Harold C. Clayborn." Clayborn rose to considerable applause. "*Midnight* Clayborn," the moderator added.

The applause went through the roof.

He was tall, leading man handsome, though his best days were behind him. His hair was peppered with gray, but he moved with the smooth lankiness of a practiced athlete. He wore a bright red jacket, a white shirt, and gray slacks with a crease that could have cut the pork. He looked perfectly at home.

The moderator remarked how he needed no introduction, but then spent five minutes detailing his accomplishments, both on- and off-world. Finally he gave way to Clayborn, and another round of applause. Clayborn said hello in a rich baritone voice. "It's good to be with you," he said, "with people who've gone past the humdrum existence of civilized life, and reached out for something more." He was good, and I could see they loved him. "It's a pleasure to be here."

More applause.

"The past is prologue, somebody said. And if that's true, it's equally true that the experience of other civilizations, of offworld cultures, qualifies as an alternate past, as a catalog of events that might have happened here. And that is precious knowledge for the same reason that our own experience is precious because we can learn from it."

I listened for several minutes, then excused myself from the table and retreated outside into the lobby, where I sat down in a leather chair and called JoBeth.

"*Hello,*" she said.

"Ready to go," I told her.

"*You're sure I won't get into trouble?*" she asked. "*I really don't like doing this.*"

"It's okay, JoBeth," I said. "Just think of it as an experiment."

"*All right. I assume you know what you're doing.*"

Next I called Pete, at the office and told him what I needed. Then I went back to listen to the rest of Midnight Clayborn's presentation.

He had a commanding presence. I don't intimidate easily, but there was something about him that seemed almost more than human. Even when he was blowing smoke, as he did that evening. "We have no idea what's out there," he was saying in his conclusion. "The interstellar deeps still defy us. We can travel in them, but we cannot cross them. How is it that we have bluejays and philosophers and, yes, organizations like The Adventurers' Club? The answers are out there. Somewhere. We've seen just enough to be sure. But I'm sorry to say it's going to fall to another generation to find them. To leave the Big Downtown, this little island of light, and figure out what the cosmos is really up to."

He thanked them and headed for his table. They stood and applauded until he returned to the lectern. Every time he tried to sit, it started again. Finally the emcee intervened.

"Isn't he marvelous?" said Pasha.

Everyone gathered around to shake his hand. In the midst of it, he had to answer a call. I watched sudden surprise appear on his weatherbeaten face as he listened to the voice in his link. His brow creased. He held up a hand to keep his admirers at bay.

What had just happened was that he'd received a message from his AI. There'd been a call at home. Audio only. The caller had identified himself as K.C. Eliot. Eliot had left a message: "*Need to talk to you. Call you later. Don't try to reach me.*"

When he was able, he broke away from the crowd, went out into the hall, made a call, and spoke for two or three minutes. It was an animated conversation, at least on his end. I was too far away to overhear, but he was shaking his head, and he wasn't happy. Several of his admirers spilled out of the meeting room and found him, so he had to cut the conversation short.

He was engulfed again. At that point I signaled Pete. He called me and I answered in front of Pasha. I listened for a moment and then tried to look concerned. "When?" I asked. I nodded, and bit my lip. "Okay. I'll be there as quickly as I can manage it."

"What's wrong?" Pasha asked.

"My mother. She's been taken ill. I'm terribly sorry, but I have to get right over there."

Pasha was about thirty. Reasonably attractive. Blond hair, mustache, blue eyes, good smile. Not the world's best sense of humor, but it might show up, given a chance. I hated to lie to him. "I have to hustle," I said. That meant an aircab. I thanked him for the evening, delivered a chaste kiss, promised to get in touch, and hurried out of the dining room. I tossed my wig in my handbag and, when Clayborn arrived in the lobby, I assumed a safe distance and fell in behind him. He walked into the parking garage and I called for a cab. In case you're not familiar with the megalopolis rules, private flight vehicles are not permitted. You want to take to the air, you grab a bus or a taxi. Otherwise you stay on the ground. I watched him get into a black Cavallo and start down out of the garage.

The cab was waiting outside when I hit the front door. I climbed in, showed it my account, then disabled the AI, and took over manual control. You're not supposed to do that unless there's an emergency, but I figured this qualified. When the Cavallo bounced out onto Massachusetts Avenue, I was directly overhead.

He went six blocks, pulled up in front of the Memorial Hotel, turned his car over to the attendants, and strode inside.

The landing pad was half a block away. I reactivated the AI, jumped out, hustled down the street and charged into the hotel. Clayborn was standing in the restaurant queue.

I added dark glasses, and wished I'd thought to bring along a spare jacket. But I did the next best thing, checking the one I was wearing. Then I sat down in the lobby and tried to look as if I were expecting someone.

Prices at the Memorial are steep, so the help is all human. Even the entertainers. No avatars running around. Several executive-types were clustered near the front desk, wearing badges that carried their names and the label *BreezeWay*.

The restaurant was standard. Too many tables and chairs in too little space. Broad windows looked out on the traffic. It was late. The place was about a quarter full. After a minute or so the host took Clayborn to a corner table. They brought coffee, and he checked the time. He still looked unhappy.

I think I spotted the guy he was waiting for as soon as he came in the door. Tall. Taller even than Midnight. Hard features. Hair black, going gray at the temples. Well-dressed. Maybe fifty years old. He breezed through the people waiting at the host's station, located his man, and started in his direction.

The argument began before he'd even reached the table. It was low key, no shouting or anything like that, but you couldn't miss it.

I took a picture and sent it to Jack. Minutes later he was on the link. "*George Antonelli*," he said. "*He's an executive with H&B. One of their top people.*"

"What's he do?"

"*He's an engineer.*"

"Any connection with artists?"

"*Not that I know of. Haven't really had time to look. What are they talking about?*"

"I can't get close enough to tell. But Midnight's not happy."

"*Okay. Be careful.*"

Anybody who goes into my line of work needs to be able to read lips. I couldn't see anything of what Antonelli was saying; the angle was wrong. But I was able to pick up some of Midnight's comments. *Damned right!* And *Why are they something something?* He kept looking around, conscious that he was in a public place. I considered walking over and saying hello, see how they'd react, but I thought better of it. Best to be conservative until you get a good idea what's going on.

The waiter showed up, poured coffee for Antonelli, refilled

Clayborn's cup, and they ordered. When he'd gone, Clayborn didn't pick up where he'd left off, as I expected, but simply sat staring out the window.

Antonelli said something. Clayborn shook his head. No. Not possible. Somebody– He stopped and sighed. Both men checked the time, and checked it again. Coffee came. Antonelli tried it and pushed it away. He started talking again. Clayborn shook his head. No. It doesn't matter what you say.

After about ten minutes, Antonelli got up and left. He came out of the dining room like a thrown spear and went out through the front doors. A few minutes later their meals arrived.

I watched Clayborn finish eating. When he came out of the dining room, he headed directly for me and I wondered whether I'd made a mistake and he'd recognized me from the Adventurers' Club. No way he could miss me, and when he smiled in my direction, I had already begun preparing an explanation. But he went right by and into a convenience store.

I got up and headed for the exit.

5.

From a distance, the Retreat looked like a two-story turtle shell, split down the middle. The split incorporated a courtyard, which had a bench, a curving walkway, an assortment of geraniums, and a few newly-planted oak trees. There were two front doors, one in each wing. And lots of windows. The architecture was plain, without any serious effort at ornamentation, other than a few abutments and setbacks. There was a circular cupola on the roof at the rear. I saw no shielding of any kind, and it was hard to stand in front of this place and imagine it out on a moon, just sitting there. The guidebook said it had used an energy shield to seal itself off from the void, but it nevertheless looked fragile. I tried to imagine myself living there, looking out those windows at empty space, and nowhere to go. It wasn't my kind of situation.

It lies alongside the newly-built Academy museum. I paid up, one price for the whole show, and went inside.

What strikes you about the Retreat is how big the occupants were. They have avatars of the two of them outside, in the courtyard, and you stand there and look up at them. I got to slightly above the male's belt line. They were wearing robes and hoods, with eyes that scared the kids. Their foreheads were arched, and their smiles sent a chill down my back.

You walk inside and the scale of the furniture reinforces initial impressions, makes it all real, the enormous sofa and chairs, and even the massive books, all too large for human comfort. It brought back memories of being five years old.

There were books everywhere. In the western wing, there'd been a library. (I don't know whether it had been the western wing on the moon, or even whether you could have a western wing on a satellite rolling through a polar orbit. But it was on the western side in Arlington.) The original books had all been replaced by dummy volumes. You couldn't remove any of them from the bookshelves. They had been frozen when the Survey team found the site, and this of course was supposed to be an effort to reproduce the original experience. In air-conditioned comfort. But the bindings, which resembled tooled leather, were soft. I doubted that had been their condition when the Academy team first found them.

One volume lay open on a table, and another on a chair. Two printed pages in each were exposed. The lines of symbols were exactly reproduced from the originals. No one had yet succeeded in deciphering any of the alien script. But the experts were confident they could do it. Eventually.

What struck you was the portrait of the male that JoBeth had shown me. It was considerably more disquieting in person than the picture had been in JoBeth's apartment. It looked exactly like the avatar out front, but you knew that was electronic fakery. This, God help us, was real. It was mounted behind the sofa, one of those eerie pictures that made you feel you were being watched. The guidebook said that the thing was thought to be a self-portrait. And that was more disconcerting still.

It was somewhat faded. The experts put its age at several centuries, maybe as much as a thousand years. The frame was chocolate brown, decorated with intertwining curved lines.

They keep a guard near the living room portrait because it's a bottleneck. People pile up and nobody wants to leave.

There was a similar portrait of the female in one of the bedrooms. Her mood seemed lighter, and her eyes less threatening. But not so much that I'd have felt comfortable sharing a donut with her.

If you looked out the front windows, you didn't see the avatars, or the traffic on the Potomac Expressway, or the Old Pentagon Building, which should have been visible to the southeast. Instead you saw what the Survey team had seen: an enormous gas giant in the middle of the sky, its rings and moons rising high and dipping below the horizon. And, in the distance, a second ringed world. The Twins.

I'm not usually big on spectacle. I've been to the Canyon and to Yosemite and to the Alps, and I've even been to the Moon, but it just doesn't do much for me. Never did. Give me twenty seconds with a great view and I'm ready to eat. But that window! It literally made me dizzy.

The security chief was a heavyweight. Big man, lots of stomach pushing at his uniform. I showed him my ID and asked whether I could see the vid record for Friday, June 14.

"Opening day," he said.

"Yes. Please."

He led me into a viewing room and left me to it. "The AI's Hutch," he said.

"Hutch?"

"Private joke. She's a big wheel in the Academy."

So I sat down and showed K.C. Eliot to Hutch. "If he shows up somewhere I'd like to see it."

"*Eleven oh-four A.M., Kristi,*" she said. And showed me Eliot and JoBeth strolling through the Retreat living room. They stopped to look at the furniture, and through the front windows at the Twins. They glanced at a few of the books, and then wandered over and stood in front of the portrait. *The Stranger.* JoBeth said something. He nodded.

After a few minutes they moved off. Into the kitchen. Then upstairs. And finally they left.

"Thanks, Hutch," I said.

"*You're welcome. Did you want to see the rest?*"

"There's more?"

"*June 18.*"

"Run it."

Eliot was alone this time. He came in past the front security station and made directly for the living room. There, he bypassed everything else and took up a position in front of *The Stranger.* He stood studying it about fifteen minutes. It was a quiet time, and the guard didn't bother him. Then he left.

George Antonelli had no police record, and seemed never to have been in trouble. He was fifty-one, a graduate of Comstock and of West Haven Technical. He was married with two young kids.

He specialized in unique design projects, those one-of-a-kind engineering challenges where no previous experience existed, and which were not likely to be repeated. He had built the Mohan Bridge in California, and the Coronet Building in New York. But he was best known for his association with the Retreat.

He had supervised the operation to disassemble the place and bring it back to Arlington. There'd been a big fight about it because a lot of people thought it should have been left where it was. But in the end, the bureaucrats had their way, and they contracted with H&B to do the job. According to the accounts, H&B had sent their best man.

Many thought the task could not be accomplished. But Antonelli had taken the Retreat apart like a puzzle, lifted it into orbit, repackaged it, and turned it over to the cargo masters. They'd brought it to Earth orbit and delivered it to Arlington. Once there, Antonelli had taken charge again and reassembled the puzzle.

It had been, the guidebook said, a unique achievement. The actual move had required six years, although the process had taken considerably longer because of the various legal challenges and protests.

The effort had cost him his first marriage. His wife had apparently gotten tired of living without a husband and found somebody else. There had been no children.

His company, H&B, had in the meantime enjoyed a remarkable run of success. Several off-world projects had come their way, and they'd responded with energy and imagination. They'd built the black hole station at Carmalla, they'd set up a deep space transport system off Argon II, and they were in the process of designing the first serious space habitats. I couldn't help noticing that much of their business had been funneled through the Academy. Clayborn had sat on the Academy board of directors during this period. It wasn't hard to see how he and Antonelli had become acquainted.

They'd also brought back an alien starship from the same site. I wandered outside and strolled past it. It had been parked, God knew how long, on the same mountain shelf that the Retreat had occupied. I looked up at it, gray and innocuous. Kids chased each other up its ladder and peeked out through the airlock.

Inside the museum, there were artifacts from the mission, pictures of the participants, the jump suits they'd worn, schematics of their ship. You could visit the VR section and relive any of several experiences. You could watch the Academy team approach the Retreat for the first time, or Antonelli and his engineers begin the process of disassembling the building. You could visit the gift shop and buy alien dolls, or a model of the alien vessel. Also for sale were t-shirts, books, dinnerware and glasses engraved with the Academy crest. And prints of the two paintings.

The gift shop was busy on the day I was there, and the prints seemed by far the most popular items.

It struck me as odd that we didn't yet have a name for the two creatures who had inhabited that far-away rock. We still didn't know who they were, what they were doing there, or where they'd come from. They were simply strangers. In the deepest sense of the word.

I wondered what they'd have made of all the fuss, of the crowds and kids and balloons and flags and popcorn.

I wished I had a contact at the Academy. I went back in the morning, introduced myself as a representative of the William L. Albright Corporation, told them we were planning to do some off-world construction, and that I wanted to speak with someone about how they'd managed the relocation of the Retreat.

I got bounced around a bit and finally landed in the office of a deputy assistant who had actually been on the vertical moon during the operation. That's the moon where the Retreat was located. It has a polar orbit, putting it almost at ninety degrees to the rest of the system. It provides a remarkable view of the whole show, rings, moons, you name it.

His name was Al Perry, and he was more than willing to talk. Mostly, I suspect, because he thought being that far from home was pretty impressive stuff when you were dealing with a young woman. Well, reasonably young. Or maybe he thought I was a potential employer, and it looked good on his resumé.

Perry was about 45, a bit formal, prematurely receding hair, large head, short, not quite heavy, but headed in that direction.

I asked questions about the Retreat, how they'd handled the zero-gee problems, how they'd managed to take apart a structure that, as far as I could see, hadn't been designed to be taken apart. What kind of equipment they'd needed. How the pieces had been stored for the Earthbound flight. How the alien ship had been moved. Had someone figured out how to make it work and piloted it home? (It had come back in the hold of the *Sebastian Toomy*.)

Gradually I shifted the conversation around to the people involved in the move. To the Academy on-site rep. To the crew of the *Toomy*. To the H&B team. And eventually we arrived at George Antonelli.

"Good man," Perry said. "Sharp as they come."

"That must have been a tricky assignment," I said, "working out there in a hostile environment, trying to juggle equipment on a narrow shelf. Obviously he got the job done."

"Yes," he said. "He had to break a few heads to do it, but he got it done."

"Tough boss, huh?"

"Well, I don't know if I'd put it quite that way. But he doesn't have much tolerance for stupidity."

"Yeah. I worked for a guy like that once. It can be a little bit draining."

He thought about it. "He got results."

"His people resent him? The reason I ask, we'll be out in the middle of nowhere too, for a long time. I think we'll need a guy who can get along with everybody."

"Yeah. Well, I didn't mean to suggest he couldn't get along with the help. He got along fine."

"Did they work around the clock, Al?"

"No. He didn't have enough people to run that kind of operation. It costs a lot of money to maintain a crew in a place like that. He only had maybe a dozen people. And they worked regular hours. When it was their time off, he didn't want to see them anywhere around the worksite."

"I see."

"He expected them to relax, watch VR, play cards, whatever." He sat back and put his hands behind his head.

"Was that your first time off-world, Al?"

"No. I've been out to a couple of the stations. But it's the first time I've been that far."

"A lot of light-years."

"Oh, yes." He looked behind him. There was a photograph of him standing on the shelf in front of the Retreat. He was wearing an old flannel shirt and a pair of shorts. Looked absolutely summery inside the force field pressure suit that they switch on and off.

"How long were you there?"

"About six months," he said.

"A long time in a place like that. Did you ever get to be alone in the Retreat? When nobody else was there?"

"Oh, yes," he said. "Sure."

"How'd it feel?"

"You want the truth?"

"Please."

"I was spooked. The place was really creepy when you were alone. And out there, it's always night."

"Well," I said, "at least you knew that if something did happen, the others would know about it right away."

"How do you mean?"

I shrugged. "Well, if you were down working in the Retreat and there was maybe an accident, the watch officer would see it right away. Right?"

His brow wrinkled. "We didn't have a watch officer."

"What would happen if, say, your suit started to fail?"

"If I were working alone, you mean?"

"Yeah."

"I'd call for help."

"Suppose you were unconscious?"

He thought about it. "Bye-bye," he said.

6.

I spent the next couple of days watching Antonelli. I followed him to work, and followed him home. I watched him take his family to dinner at the Hong Kong Restaurant in Georgetown. He didn't do anything, or go anywhere, unusual.

While I waited for him to show me what was going on, I took to reading one of Clayborn's books, *The Life and Times of Midnight Clayborn*. It had been cowritten with somebody I'd never heard of.

The jacket featured a picture of a young Clayborn on horseback, riding down the hostage-takers under a full moon, while two children cringed against a low stone wall. There was a pyramid in the background.

I tried to remember whether the rescue had happened in Egypt. Not that it mattered. A little editorial license was understandable.

There'd been other exploits. At Umrich, where he'd recovered a set of stolen Assyrian steles, he was pursued and nearly killed by renegade Arabs. At Cislu, while he was exploring the palace of

Maraki, a wall had caved in, trapping him in the foundation for seventy-two hours. He'd dug his way out. At Safe Harbor, a world populated by voracious predators, he'd beaten off a kobala, which is apparently a kind of shark with wings. He'd been caught in the middle of two wars and countless incidents of civil unrest. He'd been arrested several times, jailed, accused of stealing treasures from Egypt, Iraq, Jordan, Israel, Mexico, Brazil, and three extraterrestrial sites. It was all true, of course, but Clayborn explains that if he hadn't taken the artifacts, they would have been left to rot in the ground, or grabbed off by a dictator who would never have appreciated their value. "These things do not belong to individual governments," he writes in his epilogue. "They belong to the human race. And I made it my business to stake that claim."

He maintains that most of what he took ended in museums. A lot of it went back to the source countries, over his protests. But he'd made the artifacts so visible, had made the public so aware of their existence, that the chances of their being stolen or abused had, he says, dwindled considerably. In 2228, he had been awarded the Legion of Merit, and the following year had won the Americus.

He'd been married twice. His first wife had been lost in a wild boat ride down the Amazon. He doesn't have much to say about it in his book, but Archibald Tetis, in *Logic of Empire*, describes the incident, and states that Clayborn blamed himself and was inconsolable for months.

His second marriage lasted four years. This was to Janet Koleeva. They'd parted amicably. In his autobiography, Clayborn has nothing but good things to say about Janet, who'd been an historian attached to the University of Pennsylvania. Their careers, he said, were just on different vectors.

In his survey of modern archeological excavations, Michael McKenna says that no one contributed more to the field than Midnight Clayborn.

I was getting nowhere with my passive approach to things. So I decided to see Antonelli.

My sense of the guy was that if I showed up at his town house, I wouldn't get past the AI. If I tried his office, they'd demand to know what I wanted to talk to him about, and again I'd be refused entry. I knew what time he generally left for home. So I took station in the lobby, but I picked a day on which he was late. More than an hour late. I went outside and sat in my car to avoid calling attention to myself. But I hung on, and eventually he showed up.

George Antonelli looked like the kind of boss that people hate. His features had a sting in them. And he was a man with better things to do than talk with strangers. I didn't get a sidewise glance until I stepped in front of him and showed my badge. "My name's Walker, Mr. Antonelli," I said. "I'm a private detective, investigating the deaths of K.C. Eliot and Sylvia Ames. May I have a moment of your time, please?"

There was a brief glimmer of surprise. But he smothered it. "Who?" he asked, in a carefully controlled voice.

"K.C. Eliot," I said. "And Sylvia Ames."

"I don't know these people. I have no idea who they are."

"I only need a moment," I said.

"You're a private detective?"

"Yes. That's correct."

"I don't have to talk to you. Get out of my way."

He tried to push past me but I didn't move. "No," I said. "You don't. I can just turn over what I have to the police, and you can talk to them instead, if you want." Now I backed away and gave him room. "Your call."

He tried to smile. He wasn't good at it. "What do you want?"

"Tell me about Eliot."

He scrunched his face up as if trying to recall. "That's the guy who was in the news, right? The one they fished out of the bay?"

"You telling me a friend of yours shows up dead and you took no notice?"

"What do you mean, a friend of mine? I told you I didn't know him."

"That's odd," I said. "Are you sure?"

"Yes. Of course I'm sure."

"Your name's in his files." Strictly speaking, that wasn't a lie. Everybody's name is listed in the registry, and the registry is, more or less, part of everyone's files. Nevertheless his eyes opened a bit more.

"I can't imagine why," he said. "I never heard of this guy."

"What about Sylvia?" I said.

His car arrived. A guy in a uniform got out and held the door for him. "Thanks, Al." Antonelli handed him a bill. "Listen, lady." He turned back to me. "I don't know Eliot, and I have no idea who Sylvia is."

"Mr. Antonelli," I said, "I know you're involved in this. Why don't you tell me what you know and make it easy on yourself? It's all going to come out eventually anyway."

He looked around to see if anyone was within earshot. Somebody, a woman, was coming out the front door. She nodded to him and started across the street. He stood with a phony smile pasted on his face until she was out of earshot. "Ms. Walker," he said, "if you have nothing but baseless accusations I think this interview's over."

"You want to tell me where you were on the afternoon of the seventeenth? The day the storm hit?"

"At home. With my wife and kids."

I made a pretense of recording it in my notebook. "You were there all day?"

He had to think about it. "Yes."

A good family guy. "You're sure."

"Of course I am."

"The police will want to verify that with your wife."

He shrugged. "They can verify to their heart's content."

"Mr. Antonelli, do you own a boat?"

"Yes. Maggie and I like to take the kids out on the Chesapeake. Is there a crime in that?"

"No," I said. "Where do you keep it docked?"

"Basil Point." He looked at the time. "Now, if you don't mind I really have to be going."

"Okay." I handed him a card. "In case you think of anything you want to tell me."

"Sure," he said.

I went back to Chesapeake Beach and showed a hologram of Antonelli to Marty. The hologram stood there, looking bored.

"George," I said, "say hello to Marty."

Antonelli rolled his eyes. Looked around the pier. "*Where are we?*"

"Walk down toward the end of the pier," I said.

He showed no sign of complying, so I directed the AI to take him over. Antonelli sighed and took a few steps. "*Satisfied?*" he asked.

I froze him in place. "Marty," I said, "is this by any chance the guy who was with Eliot and the woman when they took the sailboat out?"

He made a face. "I keep trying to tell you, I was too far away to get a good look."

"*Might* he have been?"

"Maybe. Can't be sure. It's possible."

From there I went to Basil Point. It's become a major tourist spot in the last few years. But in October it's bleak and deserted, nothing but empty streets and dead leaves.

I found Antonelli's boat at Ed's Marina. It was a twin-jet Yolanda yacht, luxurious, with wide decks and a blue and white hull. Its name, *Maggie*, was painted up front.

An elderly woman was in charge of the marina. "Ed's not here," she told me.

I showed her my ID. "Maybe you can help me."

She was gray and beefy and looked as if her feet hurt. Her name was Tina. "What do you need?"

"Tina," I said, "were you by any chance here on the seventeenth? The day of the hurricane?"

"Yeah," she said. "I was here."

I looked toward *Maggie*. "Do you happen to know whether anybody took it out that day?"

"Yeah. Nobody took it out."

"You're sure."

"Absolutely." She started to turn away.

"Do you keep track of everything that comes and goes?"

"No."

"Then how can you be so certain?"

"Because it was in maintenance that day. We were servicing the engine. Now, is there anything else?" She had other things to do.

"When did the owner make it available for service?"

"I think it was the day before. Tuesday."

"And he picked it up—?"

"A couple days after the hurricane, I think. Friday or Saturday. It was in the boathouse during the storm."

"How often," I asked, "does he get the engine serviced?"

"Every six months. Like clockwork. Antonelli's pretty serious about it. Takes good care of that boat."

"I would, too." She softened a little. "Tina, I wonder if I could have a look at the service records?"

She was reluctant. It was a nuisance. "I'm really busy," she said.

I showed her a fifty, and she took me into the boathouse and opened up. I looked back over the previous two years. Tina wandered off and I had to track her down again. She was out on the pier, talking to a customer. "Tina," I said, getting her off to one side, "you were right. He does get the service done regularly at six month intervals."

"That's what I said."

"Except this last service. It wasn't really due until November. It was performed seven weeks early."

She shrugged. "I think he said it was running rough."

"You find anything wrong? Any problems?"

She shook her head. "Clean as a whistle."

7.

Harold (Midnight) Clayborn lived in a mansion in Marquette, Virginia, on the bay shore. It was an imposing place, constructed of white stone and curving glass panels, a courtyard, and a tower in the eastern wing that served as an observatory. The house was surrounded by broad lawns, and the lawns by a high wall. There was a swimming pool in back, and a tennis court on the west side. Reluctantly, Jack took me out in a police flyer. We found the great man at home, and told him we wanted to talk to him.

"*Of course,*" he said. "*Anytime I can help the police. What's it about?*"

"It would be best," said Jack, "if we talk about it off-circuit."

"*Oh, yes. Of course. You're locked into the pad now. I'll see you in a few minutes.*" That voice was pure brandy.

The wind had shifted around to the south, brought in warm weather, and died. The result was that the area was enclosed in unseasonable fog. We dropped onto the pad and found Clayborn waiting. He came around to my side of the aircraft, and opened the door. "Hello," he said, with his customary charm. "We've got a few puddles. Watch your step."

Midnight Clayborn had come of age when we were discovering ruins on Quraqua. It was the first indication that we'd ever had company anywhere, and Midnight, as a graduate student, had wasted no time joining an expedition. Everyone who went to Quraqua during those early years eventually became famous. But in the end it was Clayborn's work at Ur and Troy, Thebes and Jerusalem, Pergamon and the Valley of the Kings, that turned him into a legend.

Jack did the introductions and explained that we wanted to talk to him about K.C. Eliot. Clayborn nodded and we started up the walkway toward the front door. "I was sorry to hear about K.C.," he said. "I don't really understand what happened. What could he have been thinking?"

"We were hoping you might be able to give us an idea, Dr. Clayborn. How well did you know him?"

"Not all that well, really." He shook his head. "Not socially at all. I bought some paintings from him. Admired his work. I thought he had great potential. But it never really developed. I think these last few years he'd plateaued."

We mounted the front steps onto a porch filled with deck chairs and potted plants. Doors opened, and we stepped into a world devoted to antiquity. The walls were covered with voodoo masks and daggers and sun disks and shields and native drums. Steles with inscriptions in Sanskrit or Egyptian or God-knows-what stood in every corner. Shelves supported vases and pieces of ironware. Display cases held books and plates and statuary. And an assortment of metal boxes. It was a museum. I stopped to look at one of the boxes.

"It's a calibrator," he said. "It's from the C-site on Quraqua."

"A calibrator," said Jack.

"Yes. It came out of an electrical generating plant."

"How old is it?" I asked.

He opened the case and invited me to touch it. The metal was pitted. "About three thousand years," he said. "If we'd gotten to Quraqua a bit sooner, we might have been able to talk with them."

"Nobody at all left?" asked Jack. He was being polite. Other worlds were too far away to care about.

"No," he said. "Nobody. You go to a place like that and you know that the inhabitants have gone extinct, it changes you. Everything they had becomes almost sacred."

"But that's true of Ur and Troy, too," I said. "Everybody's gone."

He shook his head as we passed through a set of velvet curtains into a living room. "No. The children of Troy are still with us. They wear business suits now, and hang out at the pool. But they're still around. Those unfortunates–," he looked back in the direction of the box, "–they, and everything they ever were, are gone. Except a few odd pieces." His eyes closed momentarily. "I was glad to get back to the Big Downtown."

"What's the Big Downtown?" asked Jack.

"It's the way the far travelers refer to Earth. It's us. Once you've been off-world, I mean *really* off-world, not just to Moonbase, but out there–," he jabbed an index finger at the ceiling, "–and you find out how dark and empty everything is, you acquire a distinct taste for human company. For city lights and highways and theaters and bars. For the place where life is. The common wisdom is that everybody comes home a party animal."

"Is it true?" I asked.

He smiled. "I wouldn't know. Most of what's out there, pretty much all of it, is empty. Even places where it's warm and wet–" He shook his head. "It's lonely out there, Lieutenant. Lonelier than you could ever imagine."

Chestnut-colored drapes filtered the sunlight, and a fire crackled cheerfully behind a grate. Several original oil paintings decorated the walls, and I wondered if any of them had been done by Eliot. A book, a mystery novel, lay open on a side table. He motioned us into leather chairs, opened a liquor cabinet, and asked what we would like. "I know about policemen on duty," he said with a smile. "Some of these are nonalcoholic, if you wish, and I think you'll find them quite satisfying." I went for scotch and water. Jack was a straight arrow, and got something that looked green. Clayborn, the perfect host, went with the green stuff. Then he made himself comfortable in an armchair. "Now," he said, "what can I do for you?"

Jack and I have an understanding. I get to go along on these interviews when it affects the case I'm working on, but I stay in the background. As the representative of the official authorities, he controls the interview. "I wonder if you could tell us, Dr. Clayborn," he said, "if you know whether Eliot had any enemies? Anyone who'd want to see him dead?"

He held his glass up and stared at it. "You think Eliot was murdered?"

Jack was wearing his official face, thoughtful, businesslike, nonthreatening. "At this point, we're just asking questions. We really don't know what happened."

"But you must have reason to suspect something wasn't right."

"It's only a routine inquiry." He produced a paper notebook. It was his signal to Clayborn that he was not using a voice recorder. People tend to be more forthcoming when they know that. "We don't yet understand what happened."

Clayborn shook his head. "I see. But I doubt I know anything that will help."

"Why don't you tell us about your relationship with him."

He sipped his drink and set the glass down. "As I said, there's not much to tell. I bought a few paintings from him. He seemed promising." He shook his head sadly. "Terrible waste."

It was my cue to break in. "Dr. Clayborn, you bought six of his paintings, is that correct?"

He used an index finger to count invisible acquisitions. "Yes," he said. "Six."

"It appears," said Jack, "you paid considerably more than market value for them. Can you tell us why?"

"Sure. I thought Eliot was going somewhere. The paintings were an investment. I expected the day would come when they'd be worth quite a lot."

"Nevertheless," continued Jack, "we've been given to understand the market value during the period you made the purchases was much less than you paid for them."

He finished off his drink, and asked whether anybody wanted more. We both passed, and he refilled his own glass. "I'm sure I could have bargained him down," he said. "But the truth is I liked the guy. I've been pretty fortunate in my life. It was a chance to give something back."

"How did you come to know him?" Jack asked.

"K.C.? I met him through Annie Detmer. She owns the Gaslight Gallery."

"Which is where?"

"In Wheaton. I've known her a long time. She holds periodic events. Runs a sale on a given artist, and has the artist over to talk to her customers. I was there one evening, just dropped in, didn't realize anything special was going on, and there was K.C."

"When was that?" asked Jack.

"Six or seven years ago, I guess. Give or take."

Jack made a note. Then: "Dr. Clayborn, do you maintain any numbered bank accounts?"

He looked at us and considered his answer. "Yes," he said. "You'd find out anyway, I suppose, if you really wanted to. I have a special account for business purposes."

"How do you mean?"

He made a noise deep in his throat. "You may be aware that I have something of an unsavory reputation in the academic world. If my name gets attached to a project, sometimes other sources of support dry up."

"Unsavory?" said Jack. "In what way?"

"Some of my colleagues would tell you I'm a grave robber."

Jack needed a long moment to think that one over. "Is it true?"

"Probably." He smiled. "Not that I've been unethical. The truth is that some of the most precious sites on the planet are located in areas whose governments are, um, less than reasonable. The Arab Triangle, for example." He put the glass down and leaned forward, suddenly intent. "That's where we all began. And the details are still buried in those deserts. But if you go out there and locate anything of value, you're prohibited from taking it out of the country. The local government pays what they call a compensatory amount, strictly nominal. Not that it matters."

"What does matter?"

"They sell the pieces to the highest bidder. It's strictly money. The result is that major finds disappear into the holdings of private collectors."

"I see."

"They have no more claim to the artifacts than we do."

"So," I said, "whoever finds them—"

"—Should keep them. That's exactly right, Kristi." He turned a penetrating gaze on me. "I don't want you to get the wrong idea. I've profited from my finds. I won't deny that. I mean, I have to make a living too. But most of the stuff I've brought back, almost all of it, has gone to museums or to research facilities. Some of it was donated outright."

I looked around at the furniture, the artifacts, the artwork. "You seem to have done okay."

"Most of it's inherited money. My family owns Omnicomm."

"Okay." Jack sucked on his lower lip. "Do you know George Antonelli?"

"Yes," he said. "I know George."

"May I ask your connection with him?"

"He did a lot of work for the Academy when I was on the board of directors. There's not much connection now. We have lunch once in a while. That's about all."

"You're not friends."

"Well, more or less."

"Do you have any sort of ongoing project with him?"

"Why, no. As I told you, we get together once in a while to eat. When I'm down near the capitol."

"Okay. You had a conversation with him in the Memorial Hotel Friday evening."

A surprised smile appeared at the corners of his mouth. "That's correct," he said. "Have you been watching me?"

"You want to tell us what that was about?"

He looked back at me. "You're the young lady from the Adventurers' Club."

"Yes," I said.

"Your hair was different then."

I smiled.

"Very good."

"Tell us," said Jack, "about your conversation with Antonelli."

The details seemed to escape him. "Whatever it was," he said, "there wasn't much to it. I think we were talking football."

"Football?"

"Yes. That's correct. And we talked a little bit about the presentation I'd done earlier in the evening at the Adventurers' Club. But I assume you already know all about that." Another smile for me.

"And that's all?"

"Yes. Sorry. But there was nothing very earthshaking."

"You were upset," I said.

"I'm a fan."

Jack was staring at his notebook. "Let's talk about the numbered account. Did you at any time transfer funds to Eliot?"

"No," he said. "Never."

"Just so I understand this, when you bought the paintings, Eliot was paid from a regular account?"

"Yes. That's right."

"Have you given any other money to Eliot?"

He looked as if he were having trouble remembering. So long ago. So trivial. "Why, no," he said. "I'm sure I haven't." His eyes met Jack's. "Lieutenant, am I suspected of something?"

Jack closed his notebook and put it away. "No. This is all routine, Dr. Clayborn. No need to be concerned." *Unless of course you are complicit, Midnight.* He glanced over at me. *Did I have anything else to ask?*

There were three original oil paintings in the room. One depicted a medieval crowd scene, a lot of people gathered around a fountain, wielding pitchers. Another was of a bearded man dressed in clothing from the late twenty-first century. Loaded with dignity. And the third was a rendering of a beautiful dark-eyed dancer, caught in mid-flight across a stage, coming directly out of the portrait.

"Beautiful," I said.

He looked pleased. The bearded man, he explained, was a Kahollah. The fountain was a DeRenne, and the dancer was an Olandra. Two of the names rang bells. "I wonder," I said, "if we could see the Eliot paintings?"

"Ah." He looked apologetic. "I wish I could. They're not up at the moment."

"Oh?"

"They're being reframed. If you'd like to come back in a couple of days, I'd be happy to show them to you."

"That's quite all right," I said. "I think we've taken enough of your time, Dr. Clayborn."

He walked back with us to the flyer, told us he was sure we'd discover that it was just an accident out on the bay, that sometimes rational people do irrational things, and assured us we were welcome any time we wanted to return to his home.

We lifted away, up over the tennis court. The bay sparkled in the late afternoon sunlight. Jack sighed and sat back while we swung west and headed toward Alexandria. "I'm surprised," he said, "you didn't want to come back and look at the Eliot paintings."

"Not necessary. I got what I wanted."

"Which was–?"

"He has them in the attic. Once again, we see the wisdom of not calling ahead on these things. If we had, they'd have been up all over the house."

8.

Later that afternoon I walked into the Gaslight Gallery in Wheaton. Annie Detmer was busy with customers, but she noticed me and her eyes widened enough to show me I was expected. I looked through the place while I waited. There was a nice mix of sculpture with the paintings, but I was mostly interested in whether any K.C. Eliot work would show up. I didn't see any.

Eventually, with a lot of chuckling and self-congratulation about spending what it takes, Annie's customers chose an abstract, a flurry of red and gold light cones that looked as if they were coming through an unwashed window. Annie collected her money and assured them they'd have the painting next day.

As they strolled out the front door, she approached me, and tried a smile that didn't quite fit. "Yes, miss," she said. "How may I help you?"

There wasn't much to Annie Detmer. She was old and faded and maybe after a big meal she would have made it to a hundred pounds. Her hair was washed-out and stiff. Her face sagged, and she looked tired. And there was a little of the deer-in-the-headlights in her expression.

I showed her my ID.

"I was sorry to hear about K.C.," she said. "I always thought he was going to be one of the great ones." She shrugged. "But I guess not." Another customer was coming in.

"Were you close to him?" I asked.

"No. Not really." She paused. "I liked him. I mean, he was a decent enough guy. And I think we were all rooting for him."

"Who's we?"

"Oh." She blinked. Several times. "It's just a figure of speech. But I think anyone who knew him would have wished him well."

I went through the questions. She'd known K.C. about ten years. The Gaslight had been the first gallery to sell one of his paintings. He'd been to Annie's place for dinner a couple of times. She didn't know anybody who didn't like him. Although that wasn't the same as saying he had a lot of friends. He was shy. Some people thought him stand-offish. But she couldn't imagine anyone who'd want him dead. "You're wasting your time," she said. "I don't know what he was doing out on that boat, but I'm sure it was an accident. He just wasn't paying attention. It happens to all of us."

Sure. I know lots of people who'd take a sailboat into a hurricane.

I commented that the Gallery looked prosperous, which it did. She said that she managed to make a living, excused herself, and hurried off to take care of the new arrival.

I took my time, apparently browsing among the paintings, but trying to put things together.

Still more people came in. Annie stayed busy, but periodically threw a surreptitious glance in my direction. Eventually the place emptied out again and she had no choice but to circle back to me. "Anything else I can help with?" she asked.

I'd noticed that she advertised a custom frame service. "To be honest," she said, "it's almost half the business."

"Really?"

She nodded. "Oh, yes. This is the only place in the city where you can match the frame with the artwork. You can't just put anything around a DeGrasse, you know."

"Of course not."

"When I write my memoirs, that'll be the title." She smiled tentatively. "Well." She was waiting for me to say how I had to be going.

I was looking at a sculpture of Hermes, bronze in motion. It would have looked good in my living room, but it was a trifle pricey. "Have you done any framing for Harold Clayborn?"

"Yes," she said. "Occasionally."

"Do you have anything of his now?"

"No." She looked at me suspiciously. "Why do you ask?"

"Just curious."

"Is there anything else I can show you?"

"No, thanks. I appreciate your time, Ms. Detmer."

"It's no trouble at all."

I started for the door, and paused. She stood rooted to the spot.

"There is one other thing. How well do you know George Antonelli?"

Bingo. She recognized the name, and I watched her shut down. "I don't know him," she said. "Never heard of him."

"You're sure?"

"Yes."

"Usually, a question like that, people need a minute to think."

"No," she said. "I don't know him."

I'd taken my time confirming Antonelli's story with his wife. The fact is that a wife or a mother is usually something less than a convincing witness. In these kinds of situations, you know as soon as you leave the husband's office he's going to be calling home. So I like to delay a few days. Maybe give them a chance to forget the details of any story they've cooked up.

Her name was Margaret. She was the personnel officer at Menendez Laboratories in Georgetown. She went into work usually one or two days a week. I picked a day on which she was at home, and I was able to confirm that her husband had shown up at his office.

The town house was located in a clubby section of Westwood. I didn't see any properties out there that wouldn't have come in at three-quarters of a million. There was a park across the street, and beyond that you could see the Potomac. The sky had clouded over and, when I walked up onto the porch, a light drizzle was beginning.

I identified myself, waited, and the AI asked what I wanted.

"I'd like to speak with Margaret Antonelli, please."

"*About what?*" The thing spoke with Antonelli's voice, except that all the intonations had gone out of it. The tone was impersonal, if the language wasn't.

"I'm a private investigator. I'd like a couple of minutes of Ms. Antonelli's time to verify some information."

It began to rain harder. A gust blew some of it onto the porch.

The door opened. "*Please come in,*" said the AI.

Margaret Antonelli was waiting for me just inside. She was an attractive woman. Reminded me a little of my aunt Janna. A brunette about forty. Bright, amicable eyes. A good smile. I had not been impressed by her husband and my first reaction was to wonder that she hadn't been smart enough to sidestep him.

"Hello," she said. "I hope you didn't have any trouble getting past Wally."

She meant the AI, and I said no, everything was fine.

"Sometimes he's overprotective." She led the way into a sitting room.

The interior was not what I'd expected. Once you met Antonelli, you'd have looked for gaudy. Expensive gaudy, the kind of stuff intended to display wealth and taste. But the furnishings were subdued, conservative, quiet. We sat down in a couple of armchairs. "Now, Kristi— It is all right if I call you Kristi, isn't it?"

"Yes," I said. "Of course."

"Kristi, my friends call me Maggie." She turned on a lamp to dispel the general gloom outside. "How may I help you?"

"Maggie, I'm investigating the death of K.C. Eliot."

Her brow furrowed. "Who?"

"The artist. It seems he took his sailboat out the day Walter hit."

"That was dumb," she said. Then recognition took hold. "Eliot's the one you spoke about with my husband."

"Yes. That's correct."

There was an explosion of giggles and a little blond girl charged into the room, trailing a balloon. At the same moment, I heard a child's laughter elsewhere in the house. "There are two of them," she said. "This is Jill. Say hello to Ms. Walker, Jill."

We went through a couple minutes of fun and games with Jill and her brother, Ed. He came in carrying a rubber bat. The kids were probably two and three.

"Anyway," I said when I was able to get back to the subject, "your husband says he was at home with you on the seventeenth. The day the storm hit."

"Yes?" she said. The smile had faded slightly.

"Is that so?"

"Oh, yes. He was here with me that day. We thought about leaving town, you know, with the children and all. But the house is solid. It's reinforced against hurricanes."

"So you stayed."

"Yes."

"Maggie," I asked, "were you here all day?"

"Yes, we were."

"Didn't go out at all?"

"Oh, we might have run down to the market. Nothing more than that." The kids were chasing each other around the room. Maggie shushed them and shooed them out.

"They must keep you pretty much pinned down," I said.

She brightened. "Not really. Wally takes good care of them."

The AI. Well, it made sense. Wally could tend to their needs, and you knew he wouldn't fall asleep. The perfect baby sitter. "Thanks, Maggie," I said.

She looked at me oddly. "Kristi, may I ask a question?"

"Yes. Of course."

"What is it actually you're looking for? Didn't Eliot die in an accident? I don't understand the point of your questions."

"We're not sure," I said, "there wasn't more to it than that."

"But surely you don't think George would be involved. George wouldn't hurt a fly."

He could have fooled me. George struck me as being willing to employ whatever means necessary to get what he wanted.

I was on my way back to the office when I got a call from Jack. A second body had washed up.

9.

It was the western shore again, only a few miles from the place where they'd found Eliot.

I looked at the body and remembered the hologram, the eyes, the easy smile. A beautiful young woman with her life in front of her. She didn't look so good after three weeks in the water. "No sign of violence," said Jack. He shrugged. It's a tough world.

"Are we sure it's Sylvia?"

He nodded. "It's her." We watched them lift her into the EV, close the doors, and get ready to depart.

"Where's the third body?" I asked.

He shrugged. "It'll turn up."

"You really think so?"

"I don't know. I know you think Clayborn's involved in this, but I'm an old believer in Occam's razor."

"Occam's razor?"

"The simplest, most straightforward explanation is the right one. They went out partying and they lost track of the time."

It was getting late and I was tired. "Gotta go, Jack," I said.

He put a hand on my shoulder. "There's something else, Kristi." He looked uncomfortable. "I had a call from the commissioner. He wants you to stop bothering the Antonellis."

I looked out across the bay. A pair of gulls wheeled past, chirping. "Maybe," I said, "you should have invited him down here to see Sylvia."

I went by Jules's office before heading home. As soon as he saw me, he knew. We went across the street to Mike's Bar & Grill and had a drink together and he thanked me and asked if I knew what had happened.

"I think she was murdered," I said. "I think she got unlucky. The killer was after Eliot, and she was there when he showed up."

"Why?"

"I'm not sure yet."

"Okay," he said. "I want you to finish the job. Get whoever did it."

"I intend to."

"Good."

It was dark when I got to the office. I parked around back in my private spot and climbed out of the car. I was thinking about Jules, and Sylvia, and I wasn't paying attention to anything else. That can be a mistake. I didn't realize I wasn't alone until something nailed me from behind. Lights exploded and I staggered forward and crashed against the door. There were voices. Laughter. Somebody said my name.

I tried to get up. Got to my knees. Then they hit me again. In the back. And down I went. I took a couple of kicks in the ribs.

"Hi, Kristi." I tried to twist around. See who was there.

Two of them. One short and heavy with a growth of black whiskers. One tall and lean with lots of nose. The Nose grabbed hold of my hair, dragged me to my feet, and held me. Whiskers did a quick groping search, found my weapon, jerked it and the holster free, and hit me in the stomach. But they didn't let me fall.

The fat little guy drew back as if he was going to hit me again, made me flinch, but only stroked my jaw. Then he caught my chin in the palm of his hand and squeezed. "You want to start minding your own business, Kristi." He had big ears and bad breath and a crooked smile and he needed dental work. He pushed his face into mine and crushed his lips against my mouth.

I was having trouble breathing as it was. I tried to slug him but I couldn't get a clear shot. His buddy let go of my hair and grabbed my arms.

"You taste good, Babe," said Whiskers. "Maybe I'll come back some time. Do you right."

I delivered a knee where it did some damage. He huffed and folded up while his partner got an arm around my throat and dragged my head back. "What you want to do, Kristi," he said, "is mind your own business. Forget Eliot. Let it go. Or we'll be back to talk to you again." Another punch. I couldn't really tell any more what was happening, other than that I was getting stomped. Then the lights went out.

I was still in the parking lot when I came out of it. Charlie Hazzard, who runs a bail bonding operation across the hall from my office, was bent over me, telling me not to move, asking what happened, assuring me help was on the way.

You don't pay attention, that's what you can expect.

I think I managed to say thanks. I went in and out a couple times. Lights descended and somebody was holding my wrist and the pain went away and so did everything else.

10.

"You were lucky," Jack said.

"Easy for you to say." They'd taken me to the St. Teresa Medical Center where I was sharing a room with a woman who'd just gotten enhancement therapy so she could be smarter. She was lying there watching "Uncle Tim's Family" and I didn't think it was going to work.

"Look," Jack said. "They could have killed you."

"I got careless."

"Can't do that. Not in your business." It was hard to talk over Uncle Tim. "What are you going to do?"

"What I'm being paid to. Find out who killed Sylvia."

"There was water in her lungs. She drowned. Just like Eliot."

"Yeah. I figured. But now at least I assume even *you* understand it was no accident."

"That's cruel, Kristi."

"But earned." Sunlight came through the curtains and formed a checkered pattern across two walls.

"When are they going to let you go?"

"Tomorrow morning," I said. Nothing was broken. A few parts were bent and twisted, but I'd be okay. I was still pretty high on whatever it was they'd given me. I felt no inhibitions, and nothing hurt.

"You want me to assign someone to you? Just in case they try something again?"

"I'll be fine."

"Kristi–"

"I'll be fine, Jack."

"Okay. Have it your way. Can you identify them?"

"Yes."

"You want to take a look now? Are you up to it?"

"Yeah. I think I can manage."

He produced a disk and we had to ask the high I.Q. candidate if we could shut down Uncle Tim for a bit. She objected and we compromised and waited for the show to end. Then we took over the VR system.

Jack angled the projection so she couldn't see, and began showing me holograms of various solid citizens who specialized in assault. Fat ones and tall lean ones. "*You taste good, Babe,*" said the fat ones. The lean ones all said, "*You want to start minding your own business, Kristi.*" Whiskers turned out to be Andy McCarter. Better known as 'Grapes.' His pal was Rudy Bessinger. Both had long careers as strong-arm men. "Who do they work for?" I asked.

"AlphaBeta, Inc. They're enforcers for Roman Jankiewicz."

Well, that was a surprise. Jankiewicz made popovers and other synthetic drugs. Everything was strictly legal, although various citizens' groups had been trying for years to get legislation passed to put him and his pals out of business. The problem was the usual one, though. Jankiewicz put money in the right pockets. But what was his connection with K.C. Eliot?

"Grapes and Rudy hang out at AlphaBeta," Jack said. "Officially, they're lab assistants." He glanced down at his link. "I'll send a unit right over."

"No," I said.

"What do you mean no? You're not going to let them get away with this?"

"Wouldn't think of it. But I don't want them arrested. Not just yet, anyhow."

I was still limping when I got back to the office. The first thing I did was thank Charlie Hazzard for helping out. He turned pale at the thought of what had happened. Charlie's a good guy but he doesn't like violence. He told me I needed to find a different line of work. He looked at my black eye and the bruises on my throat and wondered why on earth I'd gotten into the business.

I admitted I wasn't sure. It was what I did. Most people spend their working lives at retail counters or in offices. Same stuff happens all the time. I didn't think I could live like that. I liked to think I was a little like Midnight Clayborn. But just a little.

Charlie said he hoped I'd find something different to do before I got seriously hurt. Then he went over to his safe and fished out my weapon and holster. I put it back on my belt, thanked him, told him I owed him a drink, and went home.

I gave myself a couple more days to heal and then I went back out along the Chesapeake, visiting every boating facility I could find on the west shore. I showed Mr. and Mrs. Antonelli to the proprietors, and Clayborn, and Jankiewicz, and Grapes and Rudy. I had them walk around and say hello and ask if they could rent a power boat for the day. "*Be back well before the hurricane hits*," I had each of them say. "*And there's a bonus in it for you.*" I was looking for anybody who had sold or rented a boat to any of those people, or made pier space available to them, or done marine maintenance for them. Anybody who had so much as seen any of them. I spent three days and came away empty. So I switched over and started on the eastern shore.

On the second day, exactly six weeks after the hurricane, I pulled into Van Clay, a small fishing town, and heard there'd been a death and a fire that morning. "Hap Carlucci," the attendant told me while I was getting my fuel cells checked. "The boathouse burned to the ground and Hap was inside."

I drove over and took a look. The place was still smoldering. The pier and the boathouse had both been made of wooden planks. It was a smoking ruin. Several boats had been lost. And of course Hap, who'd been a retired police officer trying to make ends meet. The cops were not happy.

I talked to Myra Corvella, the police chief. "It was murder," she said. "Somebody walked in, took out Hap, spilled fuel all over the place, and set the fire."

"I'm sorry."

"*Somebody's* going to be sorry." Myra was a big woman, gray eyes, attractive in a masculine sort of way, husky voice. "Now then, Ms. Walker," she said, "what are you doing in town? Do you have any idea who did this?"

"I don't know. If I can pin it down, you'll be first to find out. Did they rent boats? Hap's place?"

"Yes."

"Did the records survive?"

She looked past my shoulder at the smoke, drifting slowly inland. "I doubt it."

This felt like Grapes and Rudy. I was trying to think how they'd known.

There was no point continuing my hunt along the east shore. I left the car on automatic and rode back to the office half asleep. When it pulled into my parking place, I looked around to make sure I had no company, and got out.

I wondered if somebody had been eavesdropping on me. And it occurred to me that maybe the reason for my getting jumped had been more than simply an attempt to scare me off.

They'd planted a bug.

I swept the office. And found it in my holster. At the bottom, out of sight.

Okay. I left it in place, called Jack, and told him about the fire on the east shore.

"*We've heard,*" he said. "*I didn't know it was connected with you. I'll touch base with Myra. See what she has. See whether we can help.*"

"Good."

"*What are you going to do?*"

"I think I know what's behind this. Jankiewicz lives out on Reagan Drive. I'm going to pay him a visit this evening. Late. After he goes to bed."

"*Don't do it, Kristi. Not alone. I'll go with you.*"

"We won't get anything out of him if we're both there. Let me try it my way."

"*No. It's too dangerous.*"

"Don't worry about it. The bottom-feeders will be off for the evening."

"*I'm telling you, Kristi—*"

"Don't worry, Jack. Those two nitwits are no threat."

I turned on the VR, tuned to the news, took the bug out of my holster and set it on a table where it could listen to the broadcast. Then I went into the washroom where I was well away from it, and gave Pete his instructions.

An hour after I went out the door, he was to shut off the VR, produce some background sounds that suggested I was moving around the office. Then he was to make it sound as if the office door had opened and closed. We would get footsteps down the corridor, down the staircase, and out of the building. Car doors would open and close. The engine would start, and we'd get the sounds of a vehicle pulling off the parking lot and heading out onto the expressway.

In addition, he was to monitor my commlink, and relay any transmissions through the bug. "I want whoever's listening in to get everything."

"Won't they figure out it's a plant?"

"Things'll be happening too fast, Pete. I hope."

I changed into a dark shirt and slacks and soft shoes, and had the A.I. take pictures of me slinking around in the outfit with a gun in my hand. I filtered out the office background so all I had was a Kristi Walker hologram. Pete put it on a chip, I inserted the chip into my projector, and put the projector in its accustomed place over my left breast pocket. It looked like an imitation silver clover.

When it got dark, I left as quietly as I could. The VR stayed on. Amos Wolbry was commenting somberly on the situation in the Middle East. As far as an eavesdropper would be concerned, I was still sitting there watching the news.

Roman Jankiewicz lived in Exeter, Virginia. It was one of those quiet suburban neighborhoods, well off the main thoroughfare. Lots of kids, ball fields, hedges, and churches. His house was located across the street from an American Rangers hall.

I stayed well away from it. I left the car around a corner, cut through a patch of woods, and came out a block away. From that distance I couldn't be sure which house was his. But for the moment I didn't care about that. What I did care about was the big Warrior parked in the street. There was somebody in it.

I should mention that I've worked hard on my martial arts skills, but when it comes down to it, I've always found a good stick works best. There were a few broken branches lying around. I tried several, and selected one that felt right.

The houses were separated by hedges and driveways. I'd gone as far as I could under cover of the trees. I stepped out into plain sight and began strolling casually along as if I were just going for a walk. I hid the stick as best I could.

It was unseasonably cold and I had my jacket pulled up. I tried to stay away from the streetlight. If the guy in the car took a good look, I might have a problem. But, as I got closer, I saw no sign that he was paying attention.

It was Grapes.

And it was early. They wouldn't be expecting me for another hour or so. There were no other cars on the street. A couple were parked in driveways, but they looked empty. There was no sign of Rudy. He wouldn't be standing behind a tree. It was too early, and too cold. He was probably in the living room. Watching out a front window.

I got close enough to pick up the house. It was a split-level, curtains drawn on an illuminated front room. Other windows along the front, in the east and west wings, were dark. Rudy would be at one of those.

Grapes was on the same side of the street as the house, so any observer inside did not have a good angle. Moreover, there were a couple of trees in the way.

My commlink vibrated. It was Pete. But it was too quiet out there and I knew my voice would carry. I'd talk to him later. When I could.

Grapes was parked in the darkest spot he could find, about two hundred feet from the house. He didn't want to be too obvious.

I came up behind the Warrior. Grapes must have seen me, finally, because he tried to squirm around in the seat and look over his shoulder, but he was too fat. So he settled for squinting in the side mirror. Not the world's swiftest bodyguard. I figured I just looked like one of the locals. His windows were open. That made it easier.

I walked up to him and the first thing he saw was a gun aimed at his head. "It's not set on sleep, Grapes," I told him.

"Hey." He looked scared, angry, indignant. "What do you think you're doing?"

I pointed it at his eye. "How's it going?" I asked.

"Walker!" He glanced down at his wrist. At his commlink, hidden in the darkness.

"Don't do it," I said. "Don't do anything at all unless I tell you to. Raise your voice and you're dead."

"Okay," he said. "Take it easy."

"Open the door. Slowly."

"Okay. Okay. Look, about the other night—"

"Save it, Grapes. I don't hold grudges."

"Yeah. Well, I wouldn't blame you if you were mad. I mean, I guess we were a little rougher than we had to be." He stole a glance toward the house. Probably hoping Rudy and Jankiewicz were watching what was happening. That they'd be here in a minute to rescue his sorry ass.

He opened the door.

"All right. Get out of the car."

"Okay, Kristi," he said. "I'm gettin' out. You don't have to worry about me."

"Good."

He put his left foot out onto the road.

"Take it slow," I said. "Keep your hands where I can see them."

"Yeah. No, everything's okay. Listen, if you need anything, I'll do what I can—"

"I'm sure." He got out and I motioned him onto the sidewalk. We were in front of a dark house—the reason he'd picked the spot—surrounded by a neatly manicured hedge. "That way," I said, steering him toward the front gate. It squeaked as we went through onto the lawn.

"What are you going to do?" he asked. He seemed to have just noticed the branch in my right hand. "Kristi, I'll make it up to you. Don't get excited."

"I'm not excited, Grapes."

Generally if you stand in front of someone with a stick in your hand, he expects you to bring it down on his head. But that's a dangerous maneuver. The crack on the head is de rigueur in these situations, but first you have to disable the target.

The gun was in my left hand. I could see him measuring his chances, but before he could do anything I rammed the branch into his midsection, pool cue style. He whuffed and went down on his knees. Then I banged him on the head with it and he let out a soft squeal and fell full-length on the grass.

I checked him to make sure he was still breathing. Then I gagged and cuffed him.

Meantime, the hour had expired, and I knew Pete was starting the sound effects back at the office. Anybody listening in on the bug would have thought I was just going out the door.

I moved through the hedges to the side of Jankiewicz's house, where there was a clear view of the front lawn. Then I activated the projector.

A black-clad version of myself, looking like a commando, appeared beside a tree. The hologram moved behind it, and then crossed to another tree closer to the front porch. I liked the moves. I looked pretty good. More to the point, anybody watching out the front window couldn't miss the show.

I heard movement in the house. A door opened. Then a red beam licked out and hit the tree. And found the commando. She collapsed, went through a series of spasms, and finally lay still. I couldn't help admiring my acting ability.

The front door opened. "Got the bitch," said a voice I didn't recognize.

Rudy came out, followed by a little pipsqueak of a guy in a jogging suit. I knew him from his pictures. Jankiewicz. Gray hair, pinched features. He shuffled out onto the lawn. They were both carrying guns.

"How'd she get here so fast?" Jankiewicz wanted to know. "She just left her place."

"Where's Grapes?" asked Rudy. They kept their weapons trained on the downed hologram. "If she's hurt Grapes I'm going to kill the bitch."

Jankiewicz snarled. "Worry about that later. Get her behind the hedge until we figure out what to do with her."

The angle between them was too wide. I wouldn't be able to cover both from where I stood. So I set the gun for SLEEP and took out Rudy without warning. He went down like a sack of rocks.

Simultaneously the hologram vanished, Jankiewicz jumped a foot, and I stepped out from my cover and told him to drop his weapon.

He started to turn but thought better of it and laid the gun on the grass. "Don't shoot," he said.

"Not unless you move."

"What do you want?"

I let him see I wasn't happy. "Why'd you sic your goons on me?"

"It was a mistake," he said. "We got the wrong person."

"Yeah. There's some truth to that."

"Hey, listen. I got no quarrel with you, Kristi."

"I've got one with you, *Roman*. That *is* your name, right?"

"Yes. Yes, it is. And I'm telling you the truth. It was a computer glitch."

"All right. Now, *Roman*, let me try to make something clear. I'm not going to have a lot of patience with your screwing around." I looked meaningfully at the gun and reset it. He couldn't tell how high, but I knew he'd be thinking worst case.

KILL.

He was small. Weak. Used to having other people provide muscle for him.

"Don't get excited," he said.

"Why does everybody here think I'm excited?"

"Listen." He was looking around desperately. Hoping somebody would show up. "We can cut a deal."

"Who wanted me out of the way? Was it Clayborn?"

"I don't know. This is assault. At least put the gun away."

I smiled at him, holstered the weapon, and knocked him down. Straight right to the jaw. "Sure. You'd want to take this case to court, wouldn't you?"

He sat on the grass, looking pitiful.

"Was it Antonelli?" I saw it in his eyes. "Thanks," I said.

"You didn't hear that from me."

"It doesn't matter, *Roman*. You and your boys killed the marine attendant in Van Nye. What's worse, you made me an accomplice. You listened in and you tried to get ahead of me."

"No," he said. "That wasn't me."

"Sure it was."

"It was them." He indicated Rudy and the Warrior. "I didn't have anything to do with it. I didn't know they were going to do anything like that. They weren't even working for me."

"They were working for Antonelli?"

He nodded. Yes.

"Because Antonelli rented a boat the day the storm was coming. And I'd have found out."

"You'll have to ask him."

"I'm asking *you*, Roman."

He looked at me and shook his head no. "I don't know."

"Your boys bugged me," I said.

"No. There's a mistake here somewhere."

"You were able to listen in. What about Antonelli?"

"What about him?"

"Was he able to listen, too? Was he on the circuit?"

"Yeah," he said. "It was his idea."

11.

Jack drifted down in a cruiser, followed seconds later by a medical unit. "I see you've been rousting honest citizens again."

"Those two—" Rudy and Grapes. "Search their digs and their working stations at AlphaBeta. They used hyzine to get the fire going. If you don't find traces of it somewhere, I'll be surprised."

"And when we lean on them, what are they going to tell us?"

"You're going to be issuing a warrant for Antonelli."

"Are you serious?"

"You ever know me to fool around?" They were lifting Grapes into a stretcher. He was moaning softly.

"What about *him*?" Jankiewicz.

He was cuffed. The police were walking him toward a car. I strolled over. "Roman?"

"Yeah?" He sounded angry. Tougher now, with the cops there to protect him. "What do you want, Bitch?"

"What's your connection with Clayborn?"

He responded with a string of profanity.

"Okay," I said. "Jack, you've got accessory to murder with this one. For a start."

I got more unkind words.

"Hey," Jack said. "You want to tell me what this is all about?"

"Sure." I was watching them load Jankiewicz into the car when I remembered Pete's call. "Hang on a second, Jack." I made the connection and asked him what he wanted.

"*JoBeth tried to reach you.*"

"She leave a message?"

"*She says she found a box of Eliot's journals.*"

"Okay."

"*She says there's stuff about Antonelli and Clayborn.*"

"Good. That sounds like just what we need."

"*I'm supposed to tell you it was in one of the boxes that came over from the studio.*"

"All right. Put me through to her."

JoBeth's AI answered. Then JoBeth was on the circuit. "*Hello, Kristi,*" she said. "*You ought to see what I found.*"

"What did you find?"

"*I was going through the stuff I'd stashed,*" she said, "*when I first cleared out K.C.'s place. There's a diary. And an account book. Those payments you were looking for. They're all here. In detail. Where the money came from. How much. The whole operation.*"

"Good."

"*You were right about Antonelli. He's involved in it up to his eyeballs.*"

"All right. Put it somewhere safe."

"*Clayborn, too. Kristi, those sons of bitches murdered K.C.*"

"I know."

"*You think this'll be enough to prove it?*"

"I think so. Okay, listen, JoBeth, I want you to stay there. At your apartment. I've got something to clean up here. When I'm finished I'll be over."

"*Okay. I'll wait for you.*"

"You alone?"

"*Yes. Nobody here but me. And you don't have to tell me. I'll keep the door locked.*"

The cops were doing a search while I stood off to one side. They don't like me helping. A half hour or so after I'd spoken to JoBeth, my link vibrated again.

"Walker," I said.

"*Kristi.*" It was JoBeth again. "*I think I'm getting a visitor.*"

"How do you mean?"

"*The entry blinker's on. Somebody's trying to get in downstairs.*"

"Damn." The entry blinker was a warning lamp. Somebody without a key was trying to get through the front door. "Okay, you better get out of there, JoBeth. It's probably nothing, but play it safe."

"*You're damned right I'll play it safe.*"

"Clear out. Go across the street and wait in the restaurant. In Louie's. I'll meet you there."

"*I can't do that, Kristi. I have no way to get past whoever's in the front hallway.*"

"Isn't there a back door?"

"*Not one I can reach without saying hello.*"

"Okay. I'm on my way."

I heard sounds that suggested she was running around the apartment looking for a coat or something. "*I'm scared, Kristi.*" she said.

I was pushing Jack out the door. "We need to take the flyer," I told him.

"*Kristi, I've got no place to go.*"

"How about neighbors? Can you get into somebody else's apartment?"

"*I don't know. Maybe.*"

"Try it."

"*Okay.*"

"Take the diary."

"*I've got the diary.*"

"Keep in mind they might be listening."

"*Okay.*"

"Leave the circuit open. We'll be there in a half hour."

I jumped into the flyer with Jack. "Where we going?" he asked.

I gave him the address.

"Is this an emergency? I can have a unit sent around."

"No," I said. "We should have time."

We lifted over the trees, swung in a wide arc and headed back toward Alexandria. Jack was up front with Pedro, the driver. I was in back. The eastern stars were lost in the glare coming off D.C.

"What's going on?" said Jack.

"When we get there," I told him, "I'm going to hand you at least one of the killers."

"*Kristi,*" JoBeth again. "*He's coming upstairs. How close are you?*"

"About twenty-five minutes."

"*I don't think I have that long.*" She sounded terrified.

Jack swung around in his seat, frowning. "What are you telling her? We'll be there in ten. But that's going to be too late." He punched a button on the console. "We need to send somebody."

"No," I said. "Jack, trust me. It's okay."

"Okay? Kristi, have you gone crazy?"

"JoBeth," I asked, "is there more than one person?"

"*No. I think only one.*"

The apartment house had six floors. "If you go up," I said, "can you get out onto the roof?"

"*Yes. I think so.*"

"Do it. Try to be quiet."

Jack was staring at me, his hand still on the comm unit. "Okay," I said. "Here's what's happening."

Jack talked to Alexandria alerting them to the situation. "But don't send anybody till I tell you."

JoBeth got back on the circuit. "*I'm on the sixth floor. But the goddam roof door won't open.*"

"Where's the intruder?"

"*I think he knows I'm here, Kristi. Where the hell are you?*"

"We're coming as fast as we can."

"*How fast is that?*"

"Twenty minutes. Maybe a little bit longer."

"There's Alexandria," said Pedro.

Jack was leaning forward in his seat, as if he could speed the flyer along.

I heard a bang on the circuit. "How are you coming with the door, JoBeth?"

"*It's open now. I'm on the roof.*"

"Good. Close it behind you."

"*Trying. It's warped.*"

"Can you lock it?"

"*I don't see a lock anywhere.*"

"Three minutes away," said Jack. "Time to bring in the troops."

"Go ahead." And, into the link: "JoBeth. Get away from the door. Is there anyplace you can hide?"

"*No. There's nowhere. I'm wide open up here.*" She was struggling for breath.

Jack called Alexandria. "Okay," he told them. "Send in backup."

Something in the flyer began to beep. We adjusted course slightly and started to decelerate.

"*He's here,*" she said. Her voice went up a few notches.

The carrier wave clicked off.

"JoBeth? You okay?"

She didn't answer.

"Is that the rooftop there?" asked Pedro.

"That's it," I said.

"The roof door's wide open," said Jack. "Can you see him anywhere?"

There was a parking lot on the west side of the building. But not enough clearance for the flyer.

"Land in the street, Pedro," I said. "By the front door."

He brought us down between the apartment house and Louie's Italian restaurant. Jack opened the door and scrambled out while Pedro shut off the engines. A ground unit pulled up.

"Perfect timing," Jack said. He directed one of the officers to cover the back.

In Louie's Restaurant, most of the diners had abandoned their food to crowd against the window. Among them was JoBeth.

She had, of course, not been in her apartment since the beginning of the operation.

The intruder tried to get out the rear door, but was apprehended by the officer and Pedro, who'd gone around to back him up. We could see them bringing their prisoner back through the parking lot.

"Is it Antonelli?" asked Jack.

"That'll be my guess."

"What about Eliot's diary?"

"It doesn't exist."

"So what have we proved?"

"We'll know for certain who's trying to cover things up. And if nothing else you can get the son of a bitch for breaking and entering."

More backup arrived.

JoBeth joined them. "How'd I do?" she asked.

I shook her hand. "Brilliant."

"Did they catch him?"

"Here they come now."

"Doesn't look like Antonelli to me," said Jack.

But it was. *Maggie* Antonelli. She strode forward looking angry and frustrated, and not at all like the amiable housewife I'd spoken with a few days earlier. She pulled momentarily away from the officers and confronted me. "This is your doing, Walker," she said. "I hope you're proud of yourself. What do you think's going to happen to my kids now?"

"How can they go wrong," I said, "with a mother like you?"

She tried to get free, to come at me, but the cops hustled her past.

We found a Lokker 380 in the alley behind the building. It was set at KILL.

"Did you know all along she was involved?" Jack asked.

"I'm not surprised. It took two people to kill Eliot and Sylvia."

"Antonelli was the second male."

"Sure. He had Eliot and Sylvia at gunpoint. Took them out, decked Eliot at his leisure and threw him into the bay."

"Poor Sylvia," he said.

"Yeah. He must have drowned her personally. Couldn't be sure she might not be a champion swimmer, so he would have taken her over the side and held her under. It wouldn't have been hard. He's pretty big."

"And Maggie rented a boat in Van Clay and went out to get him."

"Yes."

"You were that sure?"

"I was sure when Tina told me he'd insisted on having maintenance done that day on his yacht."

"He was establishing the fact that he hadn't used his boat."

"That's right. He was taking no chances. If he just left it at the dock unused, nobody might notice it was there."

"What about the S.O.S.? The storm had hit by the time that came in. Antonelli couldn't have still been in the boat."

"Directed transmission from shore. Relayed through the boat's radio and broadcast to the Coast Guard."

He looked happy. "Pretty good," he said.

"I get by."

"Well." He watched Maggie get into the ground unit and leave for the station.

"Inspiring woman," I said.

He nodded. "Let's go pick up Antonelli. The other one."

"Yeah." We walked back to the flyer. "You still haven't told me what the motive was. What's it about?"

"Jack, let's go make our collection. I'll tell you on the way."

To no one's surprise, George Antonelli was gone when we arrived at his town house. He'd known what had happened to Maggie so he cleared out.

I went over to see Jules and brought him up to date on everything we knew.

The hunt continued almost three weeks. He was found hiding in a mountain cabin in Bolivia. As the police closed in, he took his own life. We all felt kind of badly about that.

12.

And finally, Clayborn. I guess we wanted to go after him only after we'd wrapped Antonelli. I don't think it ever occurred to either of us that Clayborn would run. He just wasn't the type.

When we walked into his living room, he gave us the kind of big, welcoming smile you reserve for people you've been in combat with. "Good to see you, Lt. Calloway," he said. "And Kristi Walker." He looked at me, and I saw genuine warmth in his eyes. "I'm happy to say I knew from the beginning you would be a formidable pursuer. I never underestimated you the way George did." He waved us into seats. "I wish we might have met under different circumstances."

The guy was a charmer. Give him that. "Yeah," I said. "You have anything to do with sending the gorillas after me?"

He shook his head. "You should know better than to ask. I would never have countenanced anything like that. I didn't find out until after you'd arrested Jankiewicz. Had I known, I'd have taken care of him myself."

We'd remained standing.

"For the record," he continued, "I didn't know the Antonellis were going to do what they did either. I wouldn't have allowed it."

"You want to call your lawyer?" asked Jack.

"Eventually, I suppose I'll have to."

"Eliot was blackmailing you," I said.

"That's right."

"The price kept going up. And you made the mistake of telling Antonelli."

"Yes. But I should tell you that it wasn't George's fault. Left to himself he'd just have let it go. He'd've let me worry about it. It was Maggie."

"Maggie told you that?" asked Jack.

"No. George would have taken the blame on himself. But it was Maggie. They stood to lose everything if it came out about the painting. George would have been disgraced. Jailed. There would have been law suits." He shook his head sadly at the perfidy of the world. "They had two kids. Maggie came from nothing. She wasn't going back."

Jack nodded. "Where is it?"

Clayborn led the way upstairs, into the back of the house. "How long have you known?" he asked, directing the question toward me.

"Since Jankiewicz showed up. I already had an artist, a gallery operator who had a sideline making frames, and the guy who was responsible for taking the Retreat apart so it could be moved to Arlington. Then I got a chemist." It had been the last piece.

We stopped in front of a door at the end of the passageway. He unlocked it and turned on the lights. On the far wall hung *The Stranger*.

"Antonelli got the painting for you," I said. "He made the switch out at the Twins. While they were taking the Retreat apart."

"That's so. He took the painting as soon as we had the replacement ready. Years before the Retreat was shipped."

"Eliot painted the replacement."

"Sure. He was perfect for it. He was a superb technician."

"Annie Detmer supplied the frame."

He walked over and stood beside the painting. Admiring it. "Yes."

"And Jankiewicz aged it. Made it look like the original."

He nodded. Glanced at Jack. "It's the first time in my life I've wantonly broken the law, Lieutenant." He held out his wrists.

Jack produced a pair of cuffs.

I caught his eyes. "What happened to keeping treasures out of the hands of private collectors?"

"I don't know," he said. "I guess talking's easy."

After they'd left the room, I stood looking up at it. *The Stranger*. I don't know much about art, but this one had something the copy in the museum lacked. I almost thought the thing was smiling at me.

I wondered whether it would have been any more difficult to fathom than Clayborn.

PART FIVE
SHOTS IN THE DARK

Where Do You Get Those Crazy Ideas?

Conceiving kids is easy. Rearing them is hard.

In writing science fiction (and maybe fiction in general), the opposite seems to be true. Conception, the *idea*, is the key to everything. Once the idea is firmly in hand, the narrative writes itself.

A good idea is pure gold, but in my experience hard to come by. I've occasionally sat across the table from writers who claim they have more ideas than they'll ever be able to get on paper. Life is too short, they say. I envy them.

A story concept does not show up of its own accord. The writer who awaits inspiration will go hungry. A good idea, for me, is inevitably the result of a methodical effort. It is born from observation, perhaps from an item in a newspaper or a science magazine, or an experience in the street, or a few lines of poetry. Once I've seen something that intrigues me, the proper procedure is to take it a step farther. What if?

Let's try some examples. Science fiction by definition examines the consequences of technological advance. This is why, if we do anything especially well, it is surely the cautionary tale. From Mary Shelley to George Orwell to Gregory Benford, we look at where progress might eventually take us.

Supercolliders have been a boon to particle physics. One of the drawbacks, though, is the possibility that a sufficiently big one might accidentally create a particle more stable than the proton. If that were to happen, reality as we know it would theoretically disintegrate. You, me, the neighbors, and the solar system would all come apart. But the possibility is perceived as so remote that researchers have taken the chance.

I won't comment on that. Still, it's hard not to think about the situation down at the International Collider when they were getting ready to throw the switch. Surely if the risk were deemed real, there would have been a containment strategy. Just in case. A magnetic bottle, perhaps, in which to put the new particle, should it appear.

The writer will look at the situation, and he will go that extra step. Let's say the device produces the doomsday particle, but we succeed in capturing it. We imprison the thing inside that magnetic bottle. And keep it there. What happens down the road, fifty or a hundred years later, when civilization hits one of its inevitable bumps, and the power companies collapse? And the last descendant of the original scientists is now using a generator to supply the power that keeps the world from fading? That descendant is a prisoner of whatever remains of the original facility. He cannot leave. Dares not do so.

But oh yes it would be nice to get away from the bottle. To give the responsibility to someone else who, in turn, will be trapped. So a con game suggests itself. Atlas handing over the sky to Hercules. Hang onto this for a second, will you, Herk? Gotta go to the washroom. I'll be right back.

Invisible man stories have always been popular. Somebody gains the capability and invariably either causes, or gets into, a lot of trouble. So where else might we go with individual cloaking ability? What would happen if the mechanism became generally available? If the streets were filled with invisible people? Walking into one another? Plowing into invisible kids? Or invisible drunks? What might overprotective parents do with the technology? Could we ever be sure we were alone?

Or, assume we develop the ability to cure retardation. Take it a step farther: We cure someone, provide a normal mental capability. But the results of the treatment turn out to be only temporary, and the patient knows he is drifting back into the fog. Daniel Keyes, of course, used this one and gave us "Flowers for Algernon."

One evening in the early nineties, I was having dinner with a friend in a Georgetown restaurant when news came that the United States was bombing Iraq. We were at war. I knew I'd always remember that meal for that reason. It was the night the bombs fell. But then I had an idea: Imagine two friends who rarely see each other. They live on opposite coasts, perhaps. But whenever they meet, while they enjoy their salads and steaks, a disaster occurs. War breaks out. The *Challenger* goes down. An airliner disintegrates over Lockerbee. It was a natural and I wrote the story, "Auld Lang Boom," on the way home in the plane. (Okay, so I'm not good at titles.)

I once sat at a panel in a science fiction convention and heard someone comment that a person who owned a time machine could have the rare experience of attending his own funeral. Interesting idea. Most of our time travelers want to return to the past and talk to William the Conqueror, or go forward to find out whether civilization survives. But given the capability to travel through the years, who could resist returning to one's earlier life to see once again a long lost friend? Or proceeding nervously into the future to find out how long he was going to last? Or whether the guy about to marry his daughter was really the jerk he appears to be?

Again, take it a step farther: let's admit that a person with such a capability would travel frequently into the near future. To see his grandkids, maybe. To see who'd win the next presidential election. Maybe even to see his widow, and tell her one more time he loved her. In that way, he'd achieve a kind of immortality. Even after he'd been buried, he'd persist in showing up at family events. The relatives would never be sure whether long-dead Uncle Mort might not arrive for the wedding. Maybe he'd even attend his own funeral.

The introduction to "In the Tower" credits Matthew Arnold's sonnet, "A Picture at Newstead" as the source of that story. Arnold describes the tragedy that befell Lord Arundel, who "struck, in heat, his child he loved so well." The blow caused brain damage, and the child was thereafter retarded. Arundel, driven by guilt and a determination to punish himself, hired an artist to paint a mural in his gallery, capturing the moment of the crime, the father with the staff, the child falling forward, his gaze already vacant. An exquisite punishment for the perpetrator, Arnold suggests. But there was a second story: What would the experience of painting such a mural do to a sensitive artist?

So it becomes possible to construct a story in which an eminent and successful artist has disintegrated emotionally after some terrible experience, the nature of which is unknown to the reader, and to the artist's lover. His work has darkened, his life has fallen apart, and ultimately he crashes his flyer. The lover, the obvious viewpoint character, sets out to uncover the truth. She eventually realizes that the solution to her quest is in a submerged house, whose owner (the Arundel character) has also committed suicide. With the basic idea in hand, it is now possible to construct the story. One need only avoid making things too easy for his protagonist.

A. E. Housman's exquisite Poem XXII in *A Shropshire Lad* provided an ideal scenario: Soldiers are marching by on their way to war. The poet establishes a passing eye contact with one, recognizes they are likely to meet no more, and concludes:

"... Dead or living, drunk or dry,
Soldier, I wish you well."

It's perfect. All we need do is keep the part that sings, the momentary meeting between strangers who recognize a common humanity/heritage/struggle. And take it a bit farther. One way to do that is to arrange a meeting that will take place across time rather than space, and between separate species. So, in "Melville on Iapetus," a young woman comes face to face on one of Saturn's moons with a figure carved out of the rock ten thousand years earlier. It is a self-portrait, created by an alien. The image is clearly female, and it forever watches the ringed planet, which hangs permanently over the same range of hills.

Saturn is of course achingly beautiful from that site. And the creature had apparently been alone. (Its footprints are still preserved.) The young woman's imagination takes over, and she sees the challenge that intelligence faces in a cold and sometimes frightening universe.

What had brought her so far from home? she wonders. *Long since gone to dust, no doubt. Nevertheless, I wish you well.*

Another approach is the Father Brown technique. G. K. Chesterton's classic detective at one point explains his method for ferreting out criminals, as opposed to the science of deduction as espoused by Sherlock Holmes: Father Brown is not interested in the various brands of tobacco the suspects use, or in the arrangement of locks on a door. Rather, he says, "I look for someone who behaves out of character."

A prime example appears in "The Sign of the Broken Sword." Father Brown and his aide, Flambeau, visit the churchyard monument of Arthur St. Clare, a military hero killed years earlier in Brazil. He was, Brown says, "a decidedly prudent commander," careful of the lives of his troops. But in his final engagement, he charged a substantially larger Brazilian force in a move everyone agreed was silly, and was thoroughly beaten. Why would he have done that?

When Flambeau admits he has no idea, Father Brown asks where would be the best place to hide a leaf? "In a forest."

Where, Father Brown continues, would be the best place to hide a body?

As a method for developing stories, it's hard to beat. It's ideally applicable in science fiction. I used it in "Cryptic," an early story written largely between freight trains at the depot at Noyes, Minnesota. A man devotes his life to directing SETI. He works thirty years on the project, while his colleagues urge him not to throw his career away. No positive result is ever announced, and eventually funding is cut off, the project is terminated, and he retires. Shortly thereafter, he dies of a heart attack while shoveling snow for a neighbor. But when his replacement arrives at the observatory to pursue other objectives, he begins clearing out the former director's safe and discovers that the search apparently had *succeeded*. That an artificial signal had been intercepted. But why were the facts kept quiet? I knew if I could come up with a good reason, something other than the weary notion that the truth was too terrible for the world to know, I'd have a decent story. "Cryptic" made it to the final Nebula ballot, and a large slug of the credit belonged to Chesterton.

I hope I'm not suggesting any of this is mechanical. Methodical, yes. But never mechanical. We are looking for situations that grow out of the passions, that take on a life of their own. Ideas that the writer really cares about.

Some years ago, at a graduate school luncheon, I discovered (or hatched) a passion that has never gone away.

The luncheon was held at a faculty member's house during early summer. The day was pleasant, and we were wandering between the patio and a book-lined study. The host, whose name was Chad Dunham, was standing with one or two other instructors in a crowd of students near a glass door that led out onto the patio. We were munching sandwiches and sipping Cokes, talking about Renaissance Italy, and how exhilarating the search for the classical world must have been. Monasteries were yielding up dusty copies of Cicero's letters, old libraries were finding Lucretius and Seneca in their stacks. Xenophon reappeared from Constantinople; Plato came from Athens to engage and eventually defeat Aristotle. And the brilliance and color of pagan civilization, repressed by an aggressive religious faith until it had been almost forgotten, re-emerged at the doors of St. Peter's.

Dunham had a passion for Homer and Aeschylus and the rest of the Aegean crowd. But what was significant, as it always is with good teachers, was his ability to transmit not only his knowledge, but his enthusiasm. What a marvelous experience it must have been, he was saying, to have been part of the great search. To have spread sail and headed to sea looking for Odysseus.

Well, I'm getting a little overwrought here. But there we were, a small group of middle American types, wanting desperately to be outward bound for Hellas. In Alexandrian fashion, we mourned the cold twentieth-century reality where there were no more classical scrolls to find.

Somebody had a story: a scholar of the period was returning from extensive travels around the Mediterranean with a trunk full of works previously believed lost. This scholar would have fit nicely with my luncheon companions. He was of course ecstatic with his success and anxious to get home to show his colleagues what he'd recovered. But as they neared the coast of Italy a storm blew up and the ship went down. With the trunk.

What, we wondered, had it contained? Lost epics of Homer? Tacitus volumes V-XII? One of Sophocles' missing plays? Pericles' *Commentaries on the Peloponnesian War*?

But let's apply our basic rule and ask what else comes into play? For example, what happened to the scholar? (Nobody knew.) How could one begin to imagine the agony that must have overwhelmed him?

I couldn't get him out of my mind. I thought about him in class next day while we talked about the flow of the *Iliad*. Eventually I brought him home to Pennsylvania. He became a distraction, not unlike a tune you can't stop humming.

Years later I started writing science fiction. And the scholar began showing up in various guises in my work. I discovered an inclination to write about things that have become lost. And about the people who lost them.

One of my earlier stories, "Last Contact," was set on a world explored and settled during the human age of expansion. But eventually the starships went away. They and Earth have been forgotten. The last records of the great days, of the explorers who mapped and charted the Orion Arm, exist in a few crystals. But only one or two people understand the significance of the crystals, and they are eventually pushed aside so the crystals can be distributed as jewelry to young brides. (This actually happened with Schliemann's Trojan artifacts, which were hidden during the second world war, their true nature forgotten, and given away as above.)

A Talent for War recounts an expedition by an interstellar vessel that discovers new information about a legendary hero, a truth long lost to history. In The *Engines of God*, an entire race of advanced ET's has managed to get lost.

I tried to exorcise the tendency. "The Fort Moxie Branch," a 1988 story, describes a library run by a superhuman agency whose sole purpose was to retrieve valuable works that might otherwise be dropped overboard, so to speak. They had, for example, Shakespeare's *Nisus and Euryalus*, eliminated from the canon because of its homosexual content; Thomas Wolfe's *God and Country*; and Conan Doyle's "Adventure of the Jazail Bullet," which explained why Watson's wound seemed to migrate from his shoulder to his knee.

But the tendency has never gone away. A story written for Shawna McCarthy's *Realms of Fantasy* describes three burglars stumbling onto a cache of items that appear to be relics from, among other places, Olympus. I always feel at home in places like that museum.

The most potent demonstration of the technique I can think of is Robert Heinlein's "The Green Hills of Earth," which has been among my favorite stories since I first read it waiting in a dentist's office a half century ago. A poet, whose health will not allow him to return to Earth's gravity field, wanders the spaceways and dreams of his lost world.

The Martian Chronicles owes much of its atmospheric power to the lost Martian civilization which forms the back story for the book. Combine it with the description of the illusory town in "Mars Is Heaven," a town that feels as if it came directly out of Ohio, circa 1925, and the reader can't miss Bradbury's sense of a better age.

Another track a writer can follow is to arrange for a character to confront long-held beliefs when the evidence suggests he may be dead wrong. Arthur Clarke does this brilliantly in "The Star," in which a Jesuit navigator on an interstellar flight discovers the soul-searing truth about the star of Bethlehem.

Or we can create a problem, like a life-threatening leak in a spaceship, and devise a method to deal with it that is both ingenious and practical. (No supertechnology allowed.) Robert A. Heinlein again comes immediately to mind with "Gentlemen, Be Seated."

Science fiction also allows the writer to violate the laws of physics. (I know what you're thinking, but it's perfectly okay to do this provided one of the characters notices, and says something along the lines of, "We're going to have to go back and look at everything we thought we knew about gravity theory.")

This type story is usually light, in the best sense. Good examples are Walter S. Tevis's "The Big Bounce," in which scientists devise a basketball of sorts that *gains* energy from friction, rather than losing it; and "The Holes Around Mars," Jerome Bixby's brilliant tale of a superdense golf-ball sized moon orbiting the red planet, just a few feet off the ground.

During my Navy days there were several popular myths—urban legends in today's parlance—going strong. One was the Philadelphia Experiment, which eventually became a movie. Another was the notion that the Cold War was trumped up. After all, it made no sense for two World War II allies to threaten one another with total destruction, especially when neither side could realistically hope to survive the conflict. Ergo, the US-Soviet standoff was a hoax.

If so, what was it about?

The truth, we were hearing, was that there really was something to the UFO accounts, then widespread, and that the nations were jointly arming against the possibility of invasion. The Cold War was a cover story. So as not to alarm anybody.

I can confess they alarmed me.

Several science fiction writers have used hoaxes to power stories. The effect can be explosive, and no one did it more effectively than James Gunn, with "The Cave of Night."

These are only a few of the techniques that can be used to come up with story lines. There are of course many more. The point is that waiting for inspiration never works. Well, maybe not never. But I've not yet known it to stick its head in my door.

Infinity Beach

Note: This was written for Water's Edge, *a publication of* The Florida Times-Union. *It started the train of thought that eventually ended in the novel of the same name. And of course I kept the title.*

Melville had it right. There's something deep down in our wiring that calls us to the sea. It might be a dimly-remembered sense of going home. Or maybe it's all that water (eighty-five percent of the human anatomy by one count) sloshing around inside us. Or it might even be that we're incurable romantics, and where else does the moon ever look so bright, or the sky so near, as when we watch from a lonely stretch of beach?

When I was growing up in South Philadelphia, we took a week each summer to go to Wildwood or Atlantic City, where the waves were far bigger than I was. It was love at first sight between me and the surf. Or, as I later discovered, me and that great beast of an ocean that lay out beyond the piers, rumbling and roaring through the night. It called to me then as it does now, and I can remember lying awake listening to it. I promised myself that when I grew up, I'd live in Wildwood, or some place very much like it. Later, when teachers began talking about the Garden of Eden, I became immediately suspicious of the story. There was no mention anywhere of the sea, and I knew there could have been no paradise without that long, curved horizon to look at in the cool moonlight.

World War II broke out when I was four years old. The magnitude of the disaster was immediately apparent because we canceled our 1940 trip to the shore. My father explained there was no point going. The boardwalk would be closed at night, and the lights would be off all along the coast. That was a necessary precaution against German U-boat commanders, who could use them to silhouette targets. I wasn't sure about the details of naval tactics, but I conceived an undying animosity toward German U-boat commanders. And I concluded that the war was being fought to allow little kids to return to the ocean.

But it occurred to me that the opportunity to travel to a Wildwood whose lights were out had possibilities. I pictured myself playing in the sand at twilight (when we were usually eating dinner), watching the darkness settle over the boardwalk and the beaches, and staying out there until I could see the track of the moon on the water. Unfortunately I had some difficulty explaining the advantages to my father. He listened and nodded in the way of grown-ups everywhere. And suggested we had a duty to stay home. We did not go back for seven years.

When I thought it out, I began to suspect that, if I objected to the subs, I also objected to the lights. The reason for this seemed slippery and I couldn't quite lay hold of it. But it was so, all the same. At night, you stood on the boardwalk and the ocean receded behind the incandescence of Laughing Sally and the Caterpillar and Molly's French Fries. It got *lost*.

The experience left me with a sense of what I liked best about the sea. Not the fluorescents and not the roller coasters and certainly not the crowds. Give me a deserted beach, send everybody home, and turn off the power.

Most of us don't understand about lights. They're good for advertising and security and finding your way around. They work well for cities and shopping malls and expressway exits. But a seacoast is a special kind of place. It's like the edge of a forest, or the foothills of the Rockies, where we're standing at the rim of our daily existence, and looking out at something quite different.

Some years ago, I did a story for the anthology *Full Spectrum* (Bantam, 1988), predicating a branch library which specialized in collecting classic works which had disappeared for one reason or another. They had, for example, the lost histories of Tacitus; several of Sophocles' missing dramas; even Shakespeare's *Zenobia*, a wicked attack on Elizabeth, and consequently not published during his lifetime, and subsequently mislaid. They also had several unknown Conan Doyle stories.

I needed an appropriate setting, a place where such a thing might somehow be perceived as possible. Inevitably, that meant a location where the unknown rolls up against the outer driveways.

To serve the purpose, I created Fort Moxie, a mythical North Dakota town on the edge of the Great Plains. It was a place where you could stand in your second floor bedroom window and look out into a night unbroken by any artificial light all the way to the horizon. And you knew instinctively that this was a sacred place, one of those areas where the infinite touches down.

The Jacksonville coast and the Georgia islands are like that, but I suspect it's hard for natives to notice. People on Cumberland Island, in Fernandina and Atlantic Beach, on St. Simons and Jekyll, take their ocean pretty much for granted. It's there, and you can swim in it, or sail on it, but once you've said that, what's left?

Despite growing up in Philadelphia, I passed my thirtieth birthday before I thought it worthwhile to stop by Independence Hall. We tend not to notice the extraordinary if it happens to be at our doorstep.

In the early spring of 1986, I drove over to one of the beaches on St. Simons Island with my wife Maureen, and Sheila Williams, now the editor of *Asimov's*, to get a look at Halley's comet. It was, as I recall, a cool, damp evening. The comet was a bust. If it was up there, I never saw it. Or if I saw it, I didn't recognize it. Take your pick.

But none of that mattered. What mattered was that the sky reached down to touch the sea, and we three city-types could feel it. We were in the presence of two oceans, one of water and one of infinite space, and they both somehow got all mixed up that night. If you pick the right spot, where the only real sound is the murmur of the surf, it's possible to go out to the water's edge and feel your blood run in sync with the tides.

Stroll along the damp sand after dark and you discover a tendency to lower your voice, in the way people do in an empty church. I can recall looking east over the ocean from a beach on Jekyll Island and seeing the belt of Orion, the three brilliant stars Mintaka, Alnilam, and Alnitak. The dimmest of them in absolute terms is Mintaka, which is twenty thousand times as luminous as the Sun. These are *bright* stars. All three are about 1500 light years away, which is a considerable stroll. We are looking at them as they appeared when the Roman legionaries were running out of gas in Gaul. Think about that for a minute. Think about how quickly the light runs across the bedroom when you turn on a lamp, and try to imagine a place so far that light needs one a half millennia to get here from there.

Somehow, on the beach, you can *embrace* that immensity. It sweeps you up and makes you a part of itself. And not in the sense that you come to feel inconsequential. In fact, quite the reverse is true:

you are the part of the universe that *thinks*. That whole show is up there for you and me.

You have to let go a little bit at such times, forget the mortgage, get away from the job, and let the mind just open up. Then sea, sky, land, and night all meet, and that meeting inevitably sets us thinking about who we are, *what* we are. It's why coastlines attract mystical legends: every seaport has its stories of abandoned ships putting into harbor, of haunted lighthouses, of the voices of drowned sailors in the murmur of the tide.

People who lived on St. Simons before the causeway was built, when the only connection with the mainland was by boat, still tell of a pair of doomed adolescent lovers. The girl's father wanted to end the romance, so he moved to the island. But young love, as any parent knows, is not easy to discourage. The boy attempted to swim the channel. When he did not arrive at the appointed time, the girl began prowling the beaches, looking for him. Today, people driving through the area at night have reported seeing her specter on the highways, near the coast, still seeking her lost lover. One never hears such a story on the south side, say, of Chicago.

What's particularly interesting about this legend is that identical versions can be found in Japan and Scotland. And I suspect three or four dozen other places open to large tracts of water.

By daylight we laugh at apparitions. We believe in a mechanical universe, run in a straightforward manner by the laws of physics and mathematics, rather like a well-oiled machine. Astronomers can predict eclipses into the seventh or eighth millennium. We know how old the sun is because we can measure the relative abundance of hydrogen and helium and contrast it with its heavier elements. No ghosts need apply.

Still, when we stand on a Jekyll beach, we can feel the world turn beneath us. And we suspect that if there is a place anywhere on Earth where the mystical might show up, it is here.

An ocean's edge is by definition a meeting place between the magnificent and the mundane. We listen to seashells and hear our own heartbeat.

Why We Should All Be Reading Science Fiction

Recently I was invited to address a library fundraiser not far from home. It was a quiet event. I talked about where some current trends might lead, how we may soon have the opportunity to watch *Casablanca*, but dispose of Bogart and Bergman and cast ourselves in the leads. I've always pictured myself leaning over the piano, delivering one of the film's many big lines, "Sam, I told you never to play that in here." Or standing at the airport telling Bergman how we'll always have Paris.

When it was over, one of the guests approached and, in the kind of voice he might have used talking to a ne'er-do-well brother-in-law, informed me that "I don't read science fiction myself. But I have a nephew who does." His tone suggested that the nephew had a wide range of curious traits.

The lady in the lobby and the gentleman with the nephew, in one form or another, show up everywhere, at Kiwanis meetings, at benefit luncheons, at school events. They always say the same thing, with minor variations. They have no taste for science fiction. Consider it strange. A curiosity. And I feel sorry for them. They've missed something that's very special, and for them the train has probably left the station.

They think science fiction is an interstellar shoot-out, good-looking guys and beautiful women in snug uniforms doing battle with giant bugs that ride sleek space ships and talk funny. They associate it with "sci-fi," that relatively mindless form of entertainment which allows special effects people to have field days. They think of it as berserk robots, as aliens both cuddly and voracious, as starships pouring on the coal to escape the vanguard of someone's armada.

But that's not what it is, at all.

When I was twelve, I picked up a copy of Ray Bradbury's magnificent *The Martian Chronicles*, a collection of loosely-connected tales about the first voyages to a Mars that unfortunately does not exist.

This was Percival Lowell's Mars, a world with canals and vast deserts and strange music and long-dead cities.

And even a few Martians.

I still remember riding Bradbury's survey ship down to the surface (they didn't use landers then), looking out through a porthole while we descended through wisps of cloud and came to rest finally on the cool flat sands. Less than a half-mile away lay a small Martian town. But it had picket fences and white clapboard houses. A church steeple rose through a cluster of trees. The captain opened the hatch and a wind that smelled of early autumn blew against the hull. From the town we could hear a piano. Incredibly, someone was playing "Beautiful Dreamer."

We've all had some memorable moments with books. I got drenched when Ahab lashed himself to the whale, and I was chilled when Milton's God, tired of listening to Adam's complaints about being alone, asked "Who is more alone than I?" Walt Whitman's tribute to Lincoln left me in tears, as did Hector's farewell to Andromache. I loved charging after the hound with Holmes and riding with the Light Brigade. But I don't recall ever experiencing a jolt quite like the one induced on that still Martian afternoon by that piano.

The glory of science fiction has little to do with battles between space armadas or attacks by monsters. That is the stuff of the 1930's and, in its written incarnation, was left behind a long time ago. More or less. A monster, one must concede, can still provide a fair amount of good times for everyone.

But the joy that comes from a well-constructed science fiction tale results from watching people struggle with the implications of discovery. Or technological advance. The characters may be learning that extended youth for everyone is a dangerous and deadly business; or that communication with another intelligent species, however benign that species may be, has a distinct downside. They may be trying to recover human knowledge in a post-apocalyptic world, or striving to figure out what really happened among the rings of Beta Pictoris IV. But whatever else it is, it's a *search*, a rousing, exhilarating, sometimes terrifying, leap into the dark.

"*I don't read science fiction myself.*"

What a pity. I can't imagine any reasonable life without it.

I grew up in a South Philadelphia rowhouse. Streets were narrow, and the various ethnic groups disapproved of each other and pretty much kept to themselves. We all lived in our own enclaves. And my sense of the others was that they were somehow not fully human in the same sense I was. It was a belief encouraged, indirectly and otherwise, by the institutions and people among whom I lived.

But one cannot survive an encounter with A. E. Van Vogt's terrifying Couerl, or engage in conversation with Fred Hoyle's Black Cloud, and still think that skin color or religious opinion constitutes true difference. One learns quickly that, poised against the infinite that extends around us in all directions, we are a single species. And ultimately should be one family. If there is any constant philosophical stance that should be taught in schools round the globe, that's it. We are one family.

There are other cautionary lessons: that change is constant and flexibility essential; that there is inevitably a price to be paid for technology; that we cannot predict the future with any degree of probability; and that ingenuity, applied with persistence, can overcome most problems.

What other advantages can we gain?

Scientific tales tend to promote an interest in the way the universe works. I have no figures to support this, but numerous men and women in the sciences, and particularly in physics, astronomy, and space technology, have reported the early influence of Heinlein, Clarke, Asimov, and their peers on their career decisions. You want your kid to help build shuttles? Or keep an eye open for errant comets? Get him a book by Greg Bear.

We live in an age of decreasing literacy. I was an English teacher for ten years back in the sixties and seventies, before the problem became endemic. But even then, students were far too busy with the TV and the exhilarating business of growing up to want to read very much. Yet if they do not form the habit by the end of their high school years, it isn't going to happen. And their lives will be far grayer for it. I concluded during my first few days in the classroom that my responsibility to my students was not to insist that they read *David Copperfield* or *The Mill on the Floss*, which happened to be in the textbook and was therefore encouraged by the authorities. Rather, what I wanted to do was to show them the sheer joy that books can bestow. If I could create in them a love for reading, I knew they'd find Dickens on their own.

Nothing worked better than science fiction. Together, my students and I confronted Arthur Clarke's eerie "Sentinel," and considered the implications of subscribing to belief systems as demonstrated in Isaac Asimov's unforgettable "Nightfall." We debated Robert Heinlein's solution to traffic problems in "The Roads Must Roll," and laughed at C. M. Kornbluth's methods for keeping a moronic society going in "The Little Black Bag." And we searched for a solution to the impossible dilemma posed in Murray Leinster's "First Contact."

I like to believe that at least some of them went away with an appreciation of the rewards to be found in a good book. In all kinds of books. In history and science, in the classics, in Mark Twain's essays. If I'm right, for some of them at least, the launching pad was manned by people like Ray Bradbury and Gregory Benford.

My father died thirty years ago, and would not have recognized the world we live in. Typewriters and milk wagons and dial phones and 45 rpm records are gone. He would have been astounded by the internet, by the capability to watch movies in his home, by a hundred fifty channels, by satellite communications, by our knowledge of the human genome.

Recently, when a researcher announced he'd cloned a sheep, large sections of the American public went into near-shock to learn that such a capability existed. President Clinton informed us of his dismay that someone might try to clone humans next. And suddenly cloning was a major moral issue, as if it had arrived without warning from a distant star.

As I write this, the government has all but shut off funding for stem cell research, a procedure that promises to provide cures for some of the most devastating diseases and injuries.

Science fiction readers have known for decades that cloning was coming. They've been aware of the potential in genetic manipulation. They've had time to consider the implications, to read about these technologies, to talk them over, and to reach some firm conclusions. No surprise for them.

When breakthroughs come, say, in slowing (or even halting) ageing, the voters will be shocked again. Whatever will we do about social security? What about population problems? Will funeral directors go out of business? Will my boss be around forever?

Some of us will already have a reasonable grasp of the implications. But most people, including the majority of our politicians, will behave as if a tidal wave had just rolled in.

• • •

So we can argue that science fiction teaches some exceedingly worthwhile lessons about life, that it promotes science and technology by igniting the enthusiasm of the next generation of researchers, that it promotes literacy by capturing the interest of readers in their formative stage, and that it accustoms us to thinking about tomorrow, so that we are not caught by surprise when the world changes abruptly.

It also accustoms us, certainly more than any other type of fiction, to thinking about change, to learning the value of flexibility.

There's at least one other reason to sit down with Kathleen Ann Goonan or Catherine Asaro or Walter Jon Williams: They consistently give us an intriguing ride.

Blundering Through

Occasional Thoughts on Where Writers Go Wrong

I occasionally participate in seminars for persons who want to write and publish novels. There's never any doubting the determination of the attendees. They're going to see their names on the spine of a book from Ace or HarperCollins, and they don't much care what it takes. Many have been pursuing the effort, through all the usual adversity, for years. One woman claimed to have seventeen unpublished novels at home.

Like other professions and crafts, writing requires a combination of talent and technique. And undoubtedly some luck. We can't do much about the luck except to be persistent. Talent is supplied by a higher power, but it's aided and abetted by reading widely. And not just in one area. Read science and history, read the classics, read Mark Twain.

And take the time to acquire proper technique. And there is where we can help ourselves.

We might start by recognizing that the editor's only real obligation to us is to look at the first page of the story we've submitted. (It's a rule.) Maybe a few pages if it's a novel. The editor (with his team of screeners) sees countless manuscripts that are going nowhere, and when he picks up our submission, he is looking for a reason to put it back down and move on. Our task is to make it impossible for him to do that.

The editor knows, if he's bored on page two, or has seen a red light on page one, there's no point going farther. The readers won't do it, so it doesn't matter how magnificent the writing becomes on page five, or how breathless the action gets as we race toward the climax, because only masochists will get that far. So back it goes to the writer, with the usual form letter. Thank you very much, but it doesn't meet our editorial needs at the moment.

And it never will.

We won't be talking here about mechanical fundamentals. Everyone knows not to single-space, or to write a pompous cover letter, or to warn the editor that the material is copyrighted and she'd be advised not to try to make off with it. That information is available in any of a number of writers' publications. If you're not sure about the details, do some research and take the advice seriously.

Instead, we'll move directly to the text and ask the basic question: Where might things go wrong?

The ideas included here are those which have worked for me, or those which I've violated and sworn an oath to do no more. They will not necessarily match the opinions of all working professionals. (Hardly anything does, other than that we all want to stay out of plane crashes.) By and large, we'll be talking about the tendencies of aspiring writers that editors often complain about, either in private or in forums, and which they routinely cite as reasons to reject manuscripts.

If we want to sell our novel or our story to one of the major publishing houses, that publisher in turn will want innocent readers to pony up three bucks for the magazine, or maybe twenty-five if we get what we really want and the thing goes between hard covers. So the reader's question to us would be, as the perpetrator of this chain of events, What am I getting for my money?

And what is our answer?

Are we going to take her to places she's never been before? Allow her a seat behind the eyes of one or more of our characters, to experience an emotional ride? Is she going to be sometimes terrified and sometimes delighted? Will she recall what it was like to fall in love the first time? To gaze across a mysterious sea on a world light-years away? To encounter a new kind of intelligence in a dark forest on Aggad II?

For that kind of flight, the reader will put down her cash and consider it a fair bargain. But we must deliver. And we have to keep in mind the nature of the deal: We aren't simply going to tell her what emotions she should be feeling; we're going to create the world and the experience and put her down on the ground, and make her feel them. When it rains in our book, she's going to get wet.

So what are those red lights that trigger the form letter?

1. OVERWRITE. *"She was a wondrous creature, lovely and scintillating beyond belief."*

I used to be an English teacher, and I'm convinced that if there is a judgment, I'll be called to account for (among other things) the way

I assigned essays. It's the way almost everyone assigns essays. Book report is due Wednesday, minimum five hundred words.

Five hundred words? That means we write as much as possible. Quantity counts. Hit five hundred and quit.

The same thing happens in college. Remember the blue books? The more you write, the better the grade. What that teaches people is to stretch sentences, to shovel in everything that can possibly be gotten through the hatch, and to add every conceivable kind of qualifier.

Editors in general maintain that the single most common reason they can't get past page one is that the manuscript is overwritten. Padded. Redundant. Verbose. Like this paragraph.

Early in my career, Frank Elley at *Chess Life* offered to buy a story from me, but stipulated that, at eight thousand words, it was too long. Subscribers didn't really like fiction that much, he said. He liked it, but he only had room for three thousand words. So he gave me a choice: cut to the desired length, or agree to let *Chess Life* do it for me. Or, he added, they could regretfully return the story.

I protested. Cutting it in half would take the heart out of it, I said. It's all muscle and sinew *now*. There was no fat to trim.

But Elley was adamant and when at last I agreed to "see what I could do," I started by eliminating two scenes. They were, I thought, good scenes, with some tension and some sharp dialogue. But they didn't really advance the narrative. So out they went.

Next I went through the language. I looked for ways to shorten sentences. I tossed out adverbs by the carload. Most of the adjectives went, too. By the time I'd finished, the story was down to 3800 words. Elley said okay.

Later, when I had occasion to look at both versions, I realized that the shorter one was better.

The story was "The Jersey Rifle." Charles Sheffield has said in print that it's the best chess story ever written. I liked Charles. He always knew good stuff when he saw it. And Frank Elley deserved a substantial piece of the credit. In fact, this is probably a good time to recognize the efforts of a host of editors (and my wife Maureen) over the last twenty years who have consistently given me good advice, usually in the form of things that needed to be cut.

The *Chess Life* experience got me thinking about the compact between writer and reader. The writer's obligation is to create an illusion so *real* that the reader *lives* the experience. The reader should be drawn into the narrative, forgetting that he's simply reading words on a page. Anything that reminds him of that, any factual error, any gratuitous authorial remark, any misused word, any redundancy, any piece of bad research, threatens to shatter the illusion.

Robert Heinlein's celebrated three rules for success are that the writer should write, should send what has been written to the editor, and should rewrite only at the editor's demand.

Heinlein may have been stretching things a bit. The first two admonitions are essential. The third is another matter. Maybe the system worked for him, but it doesn't work for anybody I know.

Everybody's first draft is weak. Most of us won't show a first draft to the family cat. The only hope we have to get to a professional level of writing is to rewrite until the work becomes effective. (If that's a task that will take us forever, we might want to consider a career at Walmart or in law enforcement.)

I need a minimum of three drafts to get things right. I've gone considerably higher. *Deepsix* went through at least eight. *Omega* came in at about twelve. Give or take.

What do we do in subsequent drafts? Make sure the narrative makes sense. Tighten the sentences. Look for repetitive phrases. Ensure that the dialogue sounds natural. Keep an eye open for any scene that does not move the action forward. And if we find one of these, no matter how subtle, how clever, or how much we like it, out it goes.

Hemingway says somewhere that we should let nouns and verbs carry the freight. Treat everything else with suspicion. And note how much weaker the preceding line is if we make it "considerable suspicion." Or "lots of suspicion."

2. FORGET TO TELL THE STORY. *"But this is a novel of scientific extrapolation. The real issue here is what the aliens look like and why they do those strange ceremonies. The narrative is secondary."*

The narrative is never secondary. And science fiction isn't really about science. Never has been. Science is only the bus that gets us to the action. The issue is not, for example, how the human race will respond to the discovery that there really are little green men out there. It is how the specific characters the writer has created are going to react to first contact. Why? Because the reader identifies with them, or at least she does if we've done our job.

We watch the action through the eyes of our viewpoint character. We feel her elation and her uncertainty as the *Surveyor* draws near the alien craft and everyone on board falls silent. Nobody in our reading audience is wondering at that point how this event is going to affect the human race. Or what the sociological consequences will be. This is white knuckle time.

We need to be sure the reader is on the bridge with the captain. She needs to *see* the alien ship, the glint of burnished metal in the baleful light of Alnilam. She has to be aware of the curious geometry of its design, and of the sensor pods forward that swing quietly to track her approach. But she does not need a full schematic, nor a lengthy discussion of someone's assessment of its thrust mechanism.

The story is about the characters. It is our job to carry the reader along on an adventure, and not to provide an engineering treatise or an astrophysical extrapolation. Let us suppose an alien civilization lives on a world orbiting a gas giant, and that giant has a permanent storm, like the one on Jupiter, which seems to stare down from the skies like a divine eye that never blinks and never sets. It would be a mistake to go into detail about how the eye has affected the development of that civilization. Nobody really cares about alien sociology. The only thing that matters is the effect all this will have on our characters. It is why we no longer spend a great deal of time explaining how our antigravity devices work. Push the button and the weight goes away. Fine. Now let's get on with the action.

3. INSUFFICIENT MOTIVATION. *"Well, Professor, there's not much chance we'll come back alive. But it would be nice to know for certain whether this really was a Carthaginian colony."*

The acquisition of scientific knowledge is sufficient to justify someone's risking his life, provided we've prepared the reader first by showing the character as being driven to know the truth about the Carthaginians. Or the Martians. Or whomever. But simply allowing the reader to make the assumption that a given character can be motivated by a thirst for esoteric information, however, will not work.

Motivation is the engine that drives the narrative. If it is lacking, if the reader begins to wonder why on earth Professor Becker is going to so much trouble, we are lost.

Motivation is most effective when it springs from a universal emotion or ambition with which we can all identify. Thus, it usually works best if a character wants to know the truth about the first expedition not because of what it may or may not have uncovered, but because his son (lover, wife, lifelong friend) was lost during the original mission. Preferably under mysterious circumstances. And she needs to know the truth. Cliché? Sure. It became a cliché because it works.

What motivates us to take chances? Love. Vengeance. Money. Curiosity. Determination to prove oneself. All clichés. All universals. In *A Talent for War*, Alex Benedict was motivated largely by his fear that, if he didn't press on, a young woman in whom he was interested would conclude he was cowardly.

This brings us to the question of villains. How do we make a villain credible?

The answer is probably that you don't. A villain, pretty much by definition, is there for the sole purpose of raising obstacles and giving the protagonist something to do. And the reader knows it.

I don't think anyone, in real life, twirls his mustache and thinks of himself as a villain. Even Hitler seems to have believed he was on the side of the angels. So if Clyde the Merciless is essential to our storyline, we need to make sure that he justifies himself, at least in his own eyes. Ideally, he has a point of view equally defensible to that of the protagonist. That gives us an antagonist rather than a villain, someone to whom the audience can relate. Moreover, it pitches the drama to a higher level. One thinks of Captain Nemo attacking warships to prevent combat.

Villainous characters seem to be rarely necessary in science fiction. We'd be pressed to find one abroad in most of the great novels. There is none in *The Time Machine* or in *Frankenstein*. There is none in the Foundation novels, or in any of the tales of *The Martian Chronicles*. One probably looks in vain through Heinlein's short fiction. I can recall few in recent novels. And I doubt that the average issue of the major SF magazines publishing today would present us with one. This is primarily a result of the nature of the field, which at its best is a literature of discovery, usually pitting the protagonist against some aspect of the natural or social world, as in Greg Bear's *Darwin's Radio*, where the protagonists confront evolutionary forces and the social reactions they unleash.

Villains seem most at home in westerns and in Sam Spade.

4. UNBELIEVABLE CHARACTERS: *"He was the best skier ever to set foot on Olympus Mons."*

Unless this line is followed by a comment that he was also the only skier to show up on Olympus Mons, this story is probably dead already. Maybe he *was* the best ever. But assuming Mons is now a resort, it makes the character a little harder to sell to the reader. Why?

Because the reader has probably never been the best skier anywhere. Or the best anything else.

It doesn't matter how exciting the story line is if the reader doesn't care whether the characters live or die. When Conan Doyle killed off Sherlock Holmes, an angry mob showed up outside his house. It might have been a dangerous moment, but I suspect Doyle, despite his complaints, was overjoyed.

Editors and readers often complain about weak characterization. It doesn't seem, on the surface, that it should be that hard to create people with whom the reader can engage. Why then do we so easily go wrong?

Most of us, when we're reading, identify readily with people like ourselves: The person who *would like* to be the best skier in town but who is more likely to break a leg falling over the bathtub. There's a universal law, an equation, that stipulates no matter what the competition, someone else wins. The money. The cheerleader. The glory. Whatever. And if there is an occasional and happy exception to that general principle, it is the rarity of the event that provides its exquisite thrill. We don't win routinely, as the top gun does.

It's human nature to empathize readily with the underdog. This is the character for whom we root. Recognizing this simple fact is helpful if we are to fulfill our side of the compact, to give the reader an emotional ride.

So we create people like ourselves, who get scared when the hurricane blows ashore and begin to wish they'd left town, who perform heroic deeds only when they are driven to the wall. Am I suggesting we create characters who are failures? Not at all. Rather we should opt for characters who reflect the way most of us think, who have been successful in their everyday occupations, but only routinely so. Middle management, rather than the CEO. People who win just often enough to delight in the taste of victory. Kim Brandywine, in *Infinity Beach*, is a barely competent astrophysicist who makes her contribution to the cause of science as a fundraiser. Priscilla Hutchins, the heroine of several novels, is a run-of-the-mill star pilot who can't fix things on the ship when they break down. If duct tape won't handle it, she has a problem.

But surely there's a place for heroic characters? For those who are naturally fearless and supremely competent? What about James Bond?

It can be made to work. Although the literary version is not quite the superman of the films. But he is the exception, rather than the rule. And it's possible to argue that even Bond only succeeded because John Kennedy let it be known he was an avid fan.

A hero of the Olympian mode can nevertheless be useful. Let's give him a dangerous quest and a slightly reluctant companion who is persuaded to feel confident and safe in his companion's presence. Let's show him using both brain and skill to get them past their first danger. And then let's kill him off. In chapter two. Leave the sidekick to save the bacon.

I was reluctant to use Vice President Charlie Haskell as the viewpoint character in *Moonfall* because people find it hard to identify with vice presidents. My original intention was that his political flack, Richard Haley Daley, would be the protagonist, but events wouldn't permit it. Charlie took over despite everything I could do, and Daley pretty much disappeared from the narrative.

That suggests another area in which we can go wrong. Most people who attempt to write a novel start with an outline. Once it's put together, should we stick with it? If the characters want to go somewhere else, should we allow it?

Sure. Give them their head. If you're writing a plot-driven novel, which seems to be what I tend to do, you need to know where to start, and where you're going to finish. Other than that, it's probably a good idea to keep the outline as a guide, but not as a restriction. If we force characters to act against their inclinations, the readers will pick it up. That is not what this person would do under these circumstances, they will say. The writer is pulling strings.

Fallible characters are believable characters. They can be wrong sometimes. They can be stubborn. They get scared. They have lives outside the novel. The reader need not know the details, but the writer should.

They should speak the way real people speak. One good way to check that we've accomplished this is to go back and read the dialogue aloud. Does it sound natural? Is this the way people really talk?

Usually we need to give the reader a glimpse of what the character looks like. Just two or three details are usually enough, and the reader can fill in the rest. Dickens is a master of the brief detail that tells us everything we need to know. "There never existed in his station a more respectable looking man," he says of Steerforth's servant, a minor character. "He was taciturn, soft-footed, very quiet in his manner, deferential, observant, always at hand when wanted, and never near when not wanted—" Raymond Chandler delivers a boozy, willing blonde or a hard-eyed mobster with his own brand of precision.

Incidentally, we want to be careful about stereotypes. It's too easy to portray the funeral director as cool, efficient, and cynically sympathetic. Or the lawyer as an ambulance chaser. Or the used car salesman as dishonest. These are all stock characters wheeled out of central casting. Even a character of whom we actively disapprove, a bigot or a bully for example, works better if the reader can see him as a real human being, with his own hopes and fears. I was very careful, in The *Hercules Text*, to treat my televangelist as a man who honestly believed what he was preaching. He caused a lot of trouble, but he presented his own viewpoint honestly. And therefore he worked far better than a standard Elmer Gantry model would have.

5. UNSYMPATHETIC CHARACTERS: *I know they might grate a little at first, but by the end of the book you'll love them.*

Some years ago, a proof copy of a forthcoming novel arrived with a request for a blurb, one of those comments designed to help the book sell. It was a quest novel, half a dozen people setting out to discover a missing scientific treasure. The plot was clever, the mystery intriguing, and the narrative rattled along at a good pace.

But there was a problem. The characters were, without exception, mean-spirited, sullen, querulous, vindictive, argumentative, and narrow-minded. They didn't like each other, they were spiteful, and they whined constantly. (Okay, they didn't really whine, but they had so much else going against them it didn't matter.)

I called the editor. Look, I said, I'd like to help, but I can't stand these people. If they all died in chapter two, I wouldn't care.

They improve as time goes by, the editor explained helpfully.

But I didn't think I wanted to spend any more time with them.

Well, continued the editor, don't give up too soon. The whole point of the mission is that they learn to get along, and eventually they become fast friends. It's how they succeed and it's what the book's about.

When do they become fast friends?

Well, it builds gradually.

Oh.

It takes a while. It happens at the climax.

I won't make it that far, I said.

It is possible to create serious drama with characters we don't like. But it's not a technique to be tried in our first fiction efforts.

It's much smarter to arrange things so the protagonist is likable. That *somebody* is likable. Give the reader someone to root for. After all, we want the reader to experience an emotional ride based on the experiences of this character. As opposed to simply feeling gratified when he gets his.

6. WRITE ANOTHER XENA STORY. *This'll work fine. I saw it on TV last night. Just change the names, throw in a dragon, and nobody'll notice.*

At least one major editor has commented on the number of people submitting stories that could have come right out of a Xena episode. She would like, as would every other serious editor in the business, to see a little originality. Everybody recognizes that originality is hard to come by. Maybe it's the most difficult task imposed on a writer. It is after all possible to argue that there are no original plots left in the world. Haven't been since Homer, someone said once.

That's an exaggeration, of course. One has only to look at Charles Sheffield's mysterious goings-on at Alpha Centauri in *Aftermath*, or the complex black hole intelligence that Gregory Benford created for *Eater* to know that it's still possible. But it's the ultimate test of a writer's ingenuity.

If our imagination doesn't seem to work, if no fresh perspective shows up, if we can't find new ground that hasn't been trod over many times before, it may be that we were designed for another profession. That's okay. As they say in the westerns, we play the cards we're dealt.

7. DESTROY THE ILLUSION: *I tell you, Hodgkins, we're all doomed.*

What illusion? you ask. The illusion of reality. The illusion that what's going on is actually happening. That the reader is there. That he's part of it.

During the course of a recent writers' seminar, I was reading a student story in which the first-person narrator encounters an old acquaintance on a clifftop overlooking the sea. The sky is ominous, rain coming, somewhere in the distance a dog barking. So far so good. I was there. I could feel the storm building, could hear the ocean rumbling against the rocks below.

Then, safely within the perspective of the viewpoint character, I turned my attention to the acquaintance, whose name was Michael.

Michael was short, mildly overweight, with thick black hair. He delivered pizzas for a living. And the narrator mentioned almost casually that once, years ago, *Michael had touched the stars.*

I was drawn in. While the darkness gathered and the rain began to fall, I waited to hear how this magic had occurred.

Michael was, the writer added, pococurantic.

Pococurantic?

The storm vanished, as did the clifftop, the ocean, and the magic. I was back in my living room, consulting my dictionary.

The writer was showing off his Random House, and in doing so he'd blown away the illusion that the storm and the meeting were really happening.

Wooden dialog does the same thing. Our characters have to sound like real people when they talk.

Another pitfall is to make a mess of the viewpoint. If you're describing the action through the eyes of one character, stay there. Don't jump around. If you're doing the omniscient author, stay that way. Don't narrow your view periodically from inside someone's head.

Another is using coincidence to move things along. A character should not glance out a window and happen to see the assassin who's been following him all day. The antagonist should not be delayed at a critical moment by an automobile accident. (There's an interesting exception to all this: Coincidence can be used to start off the initial action. For example, the viewpoint character sees someone who's supposed to be dead coming out of a hardware store. Or it can work *against* the protagonist. Accidents are fine if they slow down his escape from the murderous aliens on his track. But they may not inconvenience the aliens.)

Even sharp lines are suspect. If a reader stops to admire a particularly witty remark by the author, he's reminded there is an author, and that he's reading a book. If we've written a line that we especially admire, Hemingway suggests we get rid of it.

8. IGNORE ARISTOTLE: *The Million-Year Novel and Look Out.*

You remember Aristotle. He argued for the unities. Arrange things so the action happens in a limited space, over a limited time. Some gifted writers have given us superb novels that roam across the light-years and down the ages. Usually they employ superluminals or relativistic effects or cryogenics, so that it's possible to collapse the action within a relatively short period during the lifetime of the protagonist.

I once heard an editor suggest that beginning novelists confine themselves to a single world, and try to arrange things so that the action happens across no more than a few weeks. Better yet, a day or two. This is Aristotle again, a recognition that readers cannot digest time in large chunks. (None of this applies, of course, if the characters have a time machine.)

I'd add that it often helps to set a clock running early on. If we don't get the marvelosium back to Earth by next Wednesday—Well, I need not remind you of the consequences.

9. NEGLECT RESEARCH. *The Golden Isles are so in Nebraska!*

I once called an observatory to ask for information. What might a spectranalysis show that would lead an observer to suspect that a star was artificial? A construct, something put together by an intelligence? I had no idea, and didn't for that matter have a clue whether that kind of deduction might even be possible, no matter what anyone saw. I called the National Optical Observatory and connected with one of the astronomers. I introduced myself and put the question to him.

He thought about it a minute. "Lithium," he said.

"Lithium," I repeated.

"Right. It wouldn't have any lithium."

"Do stars normally have lithium?"

"They all have it."

"Why would you leave it out?"

"Because you don't need it. If somebody were making a star, there'd be no reason to include lithium. It doesn't do anything. The star would work just as well without it."

In case you're wondering whether experts will respond to people whose names they don't recognize, be assured they love to field off-the-wall questions on their specialty, and they don't much seem to care who asks them. "I want to blow up a star," I told an astrophysicist on another occasion. "Is there a way to do it?"

"Give me a few minutes, kid," he said, optimistically. "I'll get back to you."

He was as good as his word. "Do you have a way to inject antimatter into it?" he asked.

Sure. I had all sorts of advanced technology. "Would that do it?" I asked.

"Absolutely." His voice rang with excitement. I could almost see him rocking back and forth at his desk. "It'd blow hell out of it!"

A word of warning. It's hard, in a novel, not to get something wrong. Some aspect of the science, a geographical detail, a piece of history. It usually happens because there's something we've always known, are absolutely certain about, that turns out to be incorrect. Since the beginning of the Cold War, I thought that Offutt Air Force Base was located in Colorado. Get that sort of thing wrong, and the illusion we've been talking about fizzles.

Speaking of verisimilitude and illusion, we also need to be certain we are internally consistent. If we establish that a character has gray eyes, or displays patterned speech of one kind or another, that must remain constant throughout. Use index cards or whatever works to keep track of details. I was horrified to discover, after publication of the original *Hercules Text*, that a Soviet ambassador is described at one point as the son of peasants, and several chapters later as a distant cousin of the Romanovs.

It's difficult to keep track of everything, especially when we're plunged into the white heat of creation. But we have to do it.

10. PUT A PISTOL ON THE WALL AND FAIL TO USE IT: *A red herring in the eye.*

Our plot calls for the protagonist to be involved in an automobile accident. But accidents are weak plot elements. They are coincidences, allowed in life but in fiction only under carefully arranged circumstances. Therefore, if we're determined to go ahead with the collision, we will want to set it up properly.

How to do it? The usual method is to establish early that somebody's car has a problem. Defective brakes, perhaps. As soon as the reader hears that, he knows an accident's coming. It's like the general's pistols in Hedda Gabler. As soon as she hauls them out on stage and begins admiring them, everybody in the house knows somebody's going to take a bullet.

If the characters in a novel, or a film, hear a report on CNN that three hardened convicts have escaped, we should begin setting out the extra sandwiches, because we know that the convicts will shortly arrive at the front door.

Keep in mind, by the way, that setting up the reader's expectations implies an obligation. The writer is required to play fair. To deliver. If Uncle Edgar is mixing a batch of lubricants in the basement, and we are told the mixture is highly combustible, we will expect a blast at some point. We will in fact *demand* a blast.

We cannot fail to blow up the basement and claim the lubricant was a red herring, designed to give the reader something to worry about.

The symbolic kind of set-up, the brake failure, the appearance of the general's pistols, and so on, constitutes a direct signal to the reader, bypassing the viewpoint character, who would NOT in the normal course of events draw the inference.

11. KEEP SECRETS FROM THE READER. *"But Albert, you see, has access to a time machine!"*

On a related subject, critical information available to the viewpoint character must be made available to the reader. I once conceived a story idea in which a surprise ending would reveal the locale to be Soviet Georgia, rather than the American state. Shawna McCarthy, then editor at *Asimov's*, patiently explained why I couldn't do it. Why people would show up at the editorial offices and throw rocks.

In his classic story, "To Serve Man," Damon Knight presents us with a group of aliens who arrive on Earth, say nice things, wave a document imprinted with the story title (but with the contents of the document in their own language), and offer to take lots of folks on cruises around the galaxy.

The protagonist, who is skeptical of all this good feeling, struggles to understand the alien language so he can read the rest of the document. It is of course a menu, and the reader finds out when the protagonist does, at the climax. The effect is explosive.

Suppose Knight had allowed his protagonist to learn the truth early, but had kept it from the reader. "My God," says the protagonist on page three, "so *that's* what they're up to." The reader concludes correctly that he's being subjected to blatant manipulation. The illusion fails, the reader gets annoyed at the machinations, and today no one would ever have heard of 'To Serve Man.'

It's okay to fool the characters, and the reader along with them. But it's NOT okay to fool only the reader.

One exception to the general rule: Information may be withheld if the reader is informed of the fact. Thus, before setting off to confront the killer, Holmes tells Watson, "Here's what you must do."

12. TELL THE READER WHICH EMOTIONS SHE'S SUPPOSED TO FEEL. *"Terror gripped his heart with icy fingers."*

Okay, if we can't tell the reader point blank that our hero is scared/overwhelmed with passion/gloriously happy, what *can* we do?

Actually, there's nothing wrong with saying, flat out, that Kabbala is delighted. That information is probably important. Just don't expect the reader to feel that same charge of ecstasy. Tears will not automatically run down anyone's cheek simply because we reveal the fact that Mona has filled up. We have to do better than that. So how do we manage it?

We are now, perhaps, into the real magic of story-telling. The illusion. When it rains, we agreed, the reader will get wet.

In *Moonfall*, a giant comet is on a direct course for Luna. A mass evacuation is underway. But there won't be time to get everyone away from Moonbase. The facility's chaplain is young, single, devoted to his faith. And his whole life lies before him. He's scheduled to leave on an early flight.

This is a glorious opportunity to go for the most compelling kind of conflict by forcing him to confront what he says he believes. Would Jesus, he asks himself, run away and leave someone else to die in his place?

He stares at his phone, realizing that he could call the operations office, tell them to give his seat to someone else. I wanted the reader to feel his dismay and his fear. But how to arrange it?

I asked myself what most of us would do, confronted with that situation. While we struggled with that kind of decision. Do we call Operations and tell them we'll stay behind? I suspect almost all of us would sit a long time and stare at that phone. And probably make a few grabs for it.

So we're back to the symbol.

Here's another glorious opportunity to overwrite. The phone sits there like a coiled cobra. It would fill his vision, crowding everything else out.

Maybe it's best to just have it rest on the table, cold and black and polished. And let the chaplain think about everything he stands to lose. His fingers brush the handset. If we've taken care earlier to develop the character, if the reader feels the imminence of the chaplain's quarters, nothing more will be necessary.

In Dickens' *Christmas Carol*, there is an overwhelming moment when Scrooge and his accompanying Spirit stand watching the Cratchets at dinner. They have just witnessed the generosity of the father, who insists on toasting his penurious boss. And Scrooge has been watching Tim.

"Spirit," he asks, "tell me if Tiny Tim will live."

The Spirit could have answered, "No, he's going to die if he doesn't get some medication, if you don't ease up and give them a break." But Dickens went symbolic. "I see a vacant seat by the fire," replied the Ghost. ". . . And a crutch without an owner–"

It's hard to believe tears were not running down Dickens' own cheeks when he wrote those lines.

The empty chair and the crutch. Dickens is now into the reader's psyche, and it hurts.

Suppose no universal symbol is handy? Is that a problem? In fact, they're always handy. We can use anything to suggest loss, or any other emotion. A hat, worn by a lover now gone, can be effectively employed if the writer takes time to set the stage. A set of electric trains, a cache of old letters, a reading lamp, an antique clock. It is in fact difficult to imagine anything that cannot be given emotional content and trotted out when we need it.

13. USE TOO MANY CHARACTERS: *No, now that you mention it, the professor doesn't really do anything. But he's so interesting. Has a lot of good lines. Lends color to the plot. Absolutely fascinating character.*

One of the problems we have is that we tend to fall in love with our own work. Maybe it's the recollection of the time spent writing lines and scenes that, in retrospect, do not advance the plot. Maybe it's a notion that anything we've written should be preserved for posterity. Whatever it is, it's a perspective that inhibits us from treating our written work the way we should treat any other product of our hands or minds. If there's something wrong with it, get rid of it.

Excess characters clog the pace. They get in the way, force the reader to remember extra names, create confusion with dialogue, and periodically fall into the works.

Frequently, a whole passel of minor characters can be combined into one. Onboard a starship, for example, do we really need half a dozen separate officers if they have no function other than to make it appear that the captain has authority over a lot of people? A single AI–or an exec, if you prefer humans–can take the place of the entire crew. Remember that the reader has been exposed by generations of English teachers (who don't know any better) that any character whose name appears twice is *significant* and must be remembered. Let's give them all a break.

While we're on the subject of characters by the numbers, dialogue flows much more easily when only two characters are present. If there are three or more, the writer feels constrained to identify the speaker with each line. We don't necessarily have to do that, but the reader DOES like to know who's talking, and it isn't always obvious.

14. TAKE TOO LONG TO GET THE ACTION GOING: *I know, but first I have to introduce the characters. And there's some stuff about Mytopia that the reader has to know.*

Lewis Shiner has observed that one should begin a narrative as close as possible to the climax. He was talking about short fiction, but the rule can be generally applied. There's a widespread suspicion that editors reject stories and novels without reading the entire manuscript. And that is a correct interpretation of what happens.

The story goes that Isaac Asimov was once confronted by an indignant person who complained that she'd submitted a story to the editor at *Asimov's*, that she'd stapled pages two through sixteen together, and that the manuscript had been returned with the staples still in place! "Madame," the good doctor is reported to have said, "one does not have to eat the whole egg to know that it is rotten."

Editors see an enormous number of manuscripts. They haven't time to be patient. And, they will argue, neither have their readers.

That is why we should start with a bang. A hook, as they say in the writing classes. Use that first line to fire the shot in the dark, or produce the eerie laughter in the shed, or run that dark shadow through the moonlit clouds.

A novel grants somewhat more leeway. We might be allowed a chapter or two to get things going. If we need some space to get things set up, then we might look at using a prologue to capture the reader's imagination. One of the beauties of the prologue is that it need not conform to Aristotle's notions of unity. It can portray action that happened twenty or thirty years earlier. The only requirement seems to be that it get the action moving.

A few other principals we might want to follow: We should make sure that critical events happen onstage, where the reader can see them, rather than having a messenger arrive from somewhere with the news the aliens have just invaded. The protagonist should solve his own problems. It's not a good idea to set him against impossible odds, and then have the Marines show up to bail him out. (If we're going to send in the Marines, they should arrive moments after the good guys have triumphed.)

Name as few characters as possible, and use names that are easily differentiated. We don't want fifty characters all named T'Pallah, Ch'Tanga, and P'Landra.

Finally, before we submit to a publication, we should run the finished product past a local editor. This might be a spouse, a girl friend, somebody down at the writers' group, or the pizza delivery guy. Doesn't matter, as long as it's somebody with reasonable judgment, and whom we trust to tell us what he really thinks. When he does, and it isn't what we want to hear—it usually won't be—we should consider carefully what we've learned. If there's merit to the observations, make the changes.

And do not get surly about it. Once we do that, the person becomes useless to us. He will, in the future, either refuse to look at a manuscript, or take it and tell us what he thinks we want to hear. There is no one more valuable in a writer's life than his personal editor. When that individual points out the problem, pacing's too slow, protagonist is unbelievable, the dialog's flat, whatever, we should say thanks and take the person to lunch.

A Golden Dozen
Twelve Stories To Demonstrate to Reluctant Seniors What They're Missing

Most English teachers figure out pretty quickly that their primary duty to their students has little to do with letting them in on the fine points of Hiawatha and "Sinners in the Hands of an Angry God." During the sixties, when I took my stand in the trenches, I wasted no time trading *The Mill on the Floss* for something that would start a fire under my students. After a number of trials over a period of years, I found that nothing succeeded like science fiction. In particular, Ray Bradbury's *The Martian Chronicles* grabbed kids by the throat and refused to let go. The stories listed below had much the same effect. A lot of years have passed, but I suspect they still exercise their magic.

English teachers may want to take note.

The following tales worked well with my students. That was thirty years ago, and tastes can change. But I suspect they'd still hold their own.

On the other hand, they are only twelve out of a treasury of brilliant fiction. There's plenty of exquisite material out there.

1. Asimov, Isaac, "Nightfall,"
2. Bixby, Jerome, "It's a Good Life"
3. Clarke, Arthur, "The Star"
4. del Rey, Lester, "Helen O'Loy"
5. Deutsch, A.J., "A Subway Named Möbius"
6. Godwin, Tom, "The Cold Equations"
7. Gunn, James E., "The Cave of Night"
8. Heinlein, Robert, "The Green Hills of Earth"
9. Knight, Damon, "To Serve Man"
10. Leinster, Murray, "First Contact"
11. Miller, P. Schuyler, "As Never Was"
12. Tevis, Walter S., "The Big Bounce"

Unfortunately, these stories don't exist in a single volume.

The method that worked best for me was to establish a classroom library with several anthologies, get the kids interested by literally reading a couple of them to them, in the classroom, suggesting others, and inviting the students to keep journals of what they'd read on their own, and their reactions. This exposed them to considerably more than simply the stories listed above.

The method wasn't one hundred percent successful. (None ever is.) But we had a lot of breakthroughs.

Science Fiction: An Eye On Tomorrow

At non-science fiction social gatherings, I am sometimes referred to as the "Buck Rogers guy."

Actually I remember Buck fondly, charging around the solar system squaring off with Venusian pirates, interplanetary dictators, and smugglers operating inside the rings of Saturn. He used a ray gun with proficiency, employed a rocket belt for short flights, and spent much of his time rescuing a young woman named Wilma Deering from the designs of villainous characters straight out of central casting. It was heady stuff. For a ten-year-old.

Unfortunately, most people outside the genre still see it cast in that mode. For the most part, it is only Buck and the monsters that make it to the multiplex or the TV screen. Cowboys in space.

Rocket-powered cavalry to the rescue. Someone trying to take over the world.

The non-SF world views us with suspicion. Newspapers that will review graphic novels about ax-wielding serial killers won't go near SF novels. Authors who want to climb high on the best seller lists insist that their time-travel books not be labeled science fiction.

I can't imagine my own life without the magnificent tales of Burroughs and Williamson and Heinlein, which lifted me above the south Philadelphia rooftops of my boyhood and gave me the stars.

I have no statistics to support this, but it appears the vast majority of our readers got started early. The effect only seems to happen if one is exposed while young to the elegance and mystery of good SF. If that doesn't happen before, say, the age of fourteen, it might be that we pick up a kind of inoculation against the magic, possibly induced by Hollywood, with its incessant parade of interstellar wars and monsters lumbering toward New York. Or possibly by the adults who, with the best of intentions, indoctrinate us in other forms of silliness as well.

Science fiction is not so much about science as it is about characters facing the unknown. Dealing with the consequences of new knowledge. Trying to cope after the experiment inevitably goes wrong. Or perhaps worse, goes right. Distant Alnitak is interesting, not because it may harbor a hostile civilization, but because we don't know what it harbors.

Maybe, in some unexpected way, it will reveal to us our own place in the universe.

More than thirty years after having read Clifford D. Simak's "Construction Shack," I can still recall my reaction to discovering, on Pluto, the plans for the construction of the solar system. What earthbound tale can match that kind of revelation?

What narrative anchored in, say, the Baltimore suburbs, can take us so far?

Is anybody out there?

Does another civilization exist somewhere? Does someone else watch the stars and wonder? And of course the related question: What impact would that news have? Or, on the other hand, what would happen if, after a long examination, we began to suspect we were in fact alone? The only thinking creatures anywhere?

This is the kind of question science fiction asks. And attempts to answer. Not whether something actually showed up at Roswell, but what the consequences of such an event might be.

A friend who is an historical novelist recently wondered in all innocence why I don't write something more serious. Some civil war books, maybe. The truth is, I'm not a big fan of the nineteenth century. People lived relatively short lives. (The average age for males in the U. S. at the turn of the twentieth century was only in the mid-forties.) There wasn't much in the way of a decent painkiller. They didn't know dentists from barbers. And nobody could cure anything. Worse, they had all that bloodletting and slavery and imperialism and religious fanaticism. It's just not a place I wanted to visit. And in general preceding centuries were worse. In some cases, a lot worse.

And no, I'm not saying the problems went away. Hardly. I suspect that's why I tend to write about the future. The light's better up there. People have learned to make sense. (That might be wishful thinking, but as long as *I'm* writing the book, I control the setup.)

Then how about, my friend suggested, a good mainstream novel? About lawyers, maybe. Or something charting the gradual decline of a family over several generations? I suppose it just comes down to a matter of taste, but I have a hard time getting excited about yet another teenager growing up under difficult conditions in Tempe, Arizona.

Or about who administered the poison to Aunt Sarah.

Come stand with me on the northern plains at midnight, where we can watch the aurora borealis flickering overhead, and track a meteor down the curve of the sky. Remind me as it erupts in a shower of sparks that it was around before the Grand Canyon showed up, and that I'm out there watching its demise.

Look past it to the stars, once thought to be the lights of heaven, somehow fastened to the interior of a dome. Imagine how mystical the movement of the heavens must have seemed to the Romans. What was the sun, and how did you explain that it set in those western hills and showed up again rising over the Mediterranean each morning? Surely there was a tunnel under the ground.

We've come a long way.

Now we know what the stars are. We understand their composition; we even know what has powered them through the ages.

We can chart their life cycles. But we still don't have the answer to the big question. Who's out there?

Pick a star. Canopus, perhaps. (We'll have to head south to see it.) It's approximately fifteen thousand times brighter than the sun, a class F yellow-white supergiant. It's completed its hydrogen burning cycle and is in the process of dying. If we could travel out there, would we find anyone? Probably not. But who knows? I'd like to look.

Perhaps there would be some ruins. Maybe some footprints on one of the moons.

Maybe.

It's those footprints that jog the imagination.

Science fiction is about *maybe* and *what if.* What happens when the biotech breakthroughs that researchers are now predicting for the first quarter of the new century begin seriously to deter aging and we discover that death and decay can be held off perhaps indefinitely? Or when we find ourselves living in a house that's as smart as we are, and maybe has feelings as well? Or when the climate heats up and the oceans begin to take back Tokyo and Los Angeles? When it becomes possible to *design* a child?

Science fiction, aside from its entertainment value, which is quite high, serves a particularly useful social purpose. We live in a time of constant and accelerating evolution. *Change.* No one in the developed countries today experiences life anything like his grandparents did. My father was born before the Wright Brothers flew, before radio messages were transmitted, before we had cars. He lived to see the moon landings. One lifetime.

We've always resisted change. We're wired that way, probably because, until recently, change has inevitably meant bad news.

The barbarians were at the gates, the river was spilling over its banks, plague had broken out again. Today, technological and social evolution is an intrinsic part of the way we live. Who can keep up with the gadgets anymore? Or the shifting lifestyles?

Some of us like to write about the accelerating pace of discovery. About whether we'll be able to create artificial intelligences that will be able to perceive things we ordinary humans can't. I'll admit up front those possibilities scare me.

I'm not sure what we'll do if we reach a point when we've figured everything out and there are no mysteries left. Think about that.

We know that if we get the right amount of sunlight, the right amount of carbon, mix in a little water, and arrange for some stability, pretty soon you have a world full of automobile dealers, talk show hosts, and religious fanatics.

What would we do if we ran out of worlds to conquer? It's a scary possibility. It would certainly be the end of science fiction. And of one of the core drives that makes us human. And makes us worthwhile.

Literature is designed to allow us to live through imagined experiences. So the question becomes, Why on earth would I want to live through one more coming-of-age narrative, or yet another account of how a woman's jealousy wrecked her family, when somebody like Arthur Clarke or Greg Benford is offering me a ride on the Centauri Express? Why would I want to read one more cautionary tale set in south Jersey about the damage that lying or selfishness can do, when I can watch the same action evolve while looking out the windows of a ship orbiting a gas giant at Gratification IV?

The truth is, for those of us alive today, and probably for as many generations as will follow, there'll be no physical escape from the solar system. Everything's too far away. If Socrates had been able to launch a ship to Alpha Centauri, the nearest star, and that ship had traveled at the speed of the Apollo flights to the moon, he would not yet have arrived. In fact, he'd need roughly another 50,000 years to get there. So maybe we'll go, but I have my doubts. And I know for damned sure I won't be making the flight.

That means we are left, at least for now, with only the dream. With the images that Nancy Kress and Ben Bova and David Brin can produce. But that's not really a bad deal. If I'm going to have to tangle at some point with aliens who feature filet McDevitt on their menu, I'd just as soon do it in a script written by Fred Hoyle.

If science fiction is about anything, it is about change. Its implications. How we should react. What the risks might be. That is why the narratives so often take the form of cautionary tales. "If this goes on—," we say, "here's what might happen."

Here are the potential consequences if we fail to develop a defense system against asteroid impact, or negotiate an international agreement to stop and reverse the spread of nuclear weapons, or provide adequate safeguards against the escape of engineered life forms. Here's what happens if we allow children to be indoctrinated in exclusive religious beliefs, if we fail to accept people for who they are instead of what their ethnic background is, if we do not find a way to stabilize long-term population growth, if some of the more populous nations continue reproductive policies that give us two or three times as many males as females.

On the positive side, we can demonstrate the benefits to be gained from taking time to ensure the health of the environment and from developing a global society in which everyone has a fair opportunity to live a reasonable life. Even in its Buck Rogers mode, science fiction has much to say about the human family. No one who's ever looked an intelligent (but hungry) spider in the eye will ever again worry about the color of someone's skin.

It's no coincidence that the first interracial kiss on American TV occurred on a science fiction show.

Interview
Conducted by Thomas Harbach for Phantastisch, *2004.*

PHANT: What was Jack as a boy? Nose in the book or head in the stars?

MCDEVITT: Baseball player, Boy Scout, comic book aficionado.

Developed an interest in astronomy fairly early, and I always enjoyed reading. I've had a lifelong passion for science fiction. And there were things I wanted to see up close. I wanted to cruise past a white dwarf, to follow the action while a binary system encounters a third star, to ride along while archaeologists unearth an alien civilization, maybe to be present when we actually encounter a set of neighbors. We live in a remarkable place. I wanted to have a hand in looking around. Even if it was a fictitious hand.

PHANT: Looking back at the beginning of your career: What impressed you as a reader and later as a writer? Did you look at special kinds of books and writers—especially in SF—? What changed over the years?

MCDEVITT: The beginning of my writing career came fairly late. In my mid-forties. I always liked Mark Twain, Dickens, Dostoevsky, Damon Runyon, Ring Lardner, John DosPassos. Among SF writers: Ray Bradbury, Robert Heinlein, John Wyndham, Arthur Clarke. And a lot of others. I didn't read much SF between my teen years and the time I started writing, a quarter century later. I like science, history, political books. Like the American Library's collection of Thomas Jefferson.

My personal Favorite SF book is Bradbury's *Martian Chronicles*. I don't see how anyone can sit with the crew of the third mission and look out at that small Martian town with its picket fences and its church and frame houses, open the hatch and hear someone playing "Beautiful Dreamer," and ever be the same. The book is dynamite, the guy left behind on Mars who can never get to the phone before it stops ringing, the sentient dying house in "There Will Come Soft

Rains," the kids whose father takes them to the canal where they can see the Martians.

On the other hand I never had any interest in Cyberpunk or the New Wave.

PHANT: Any recommendations for young aspiring writers? What is your opinion of workshops?

MCDEVITT: Learn to believe in yourself. Most people are far more talented than they realize. They're held back by self-doubt. Too many years listening to people tell them they shouldn't do this and shouldn't do that. Workshopping has its place. What everybody needs, beginning and established pro alike, is an inhouse editor. We need somebody close by, a spouse, a friend, a cousin, someone with decent taste, who will look at our work and tell us what he really thinks. Not what we want to hear, but the truth.

PHANT: In your opinion: concerning internet magazines, is it easier for a new writer to start today in comparison to ten or twenty years ago?

MCDEVITT: There are more markets, so it stands to reason the answer would be yes. And once you see that first story in print, you realize it's there for the taking. I once listened to a radio interview of Harlan Ellison in which he said precisely that: Once he'd sold his first story, he knew there was no limit to what he might do.

PHANT: In your career, was there any time you wanted to give up? You had quite a lot of jobs during your lifetime. Did these experiences help you for example in giving your characters a life of their own?

MCDEVITT: If you mean, trying to get published, the answer is no. I was fortunate. I sold the first story I ever wrote. So I didn't have reason to get discouraged. And yes, I did go through a series of careers. All have contributed.

I gave up once. LaSalle College conducted a short story contest for each incoming class. I won it in 1954 with a story called "A Pound of Cure," and they published it in *Four Quarters*, the school's literary magazine. I thought I was on my way. Then I read *David Copperfield*, realized how extraordinarily good Dickens was, understood I'd never be able to write at that level, and decided I'd better find another way to make a living. Next best, I thought, would be to become a prize-winning journalist. During my senior year I offered my services to *The Philadelphia Inquirer*, but they pointed out the draft had first dibs. So I joined the Navy.

I served four and a half years, much of it in the Far East. When my obligation ended, I applied to *The Washington Post*. They offered a position as copy boy, which sounded like a step back. I returned to Philadelphia, drove a cab briefly, became an English teacher, and eventually took a customs inspector's job on the northern border.

After "A Pound of Cure," I didn't write another word of fiction for a quarter-century. Generally, when people give up, I think it's because they lose confidence in themselves. The good news is that most of us seem to be more talented than we realize. But we spend our early years with all sorts of authority figures telling us don't do this, don't do that, look out you'll break it. Even teachers generally show us what we are doing wrong and ignore what we do that's right. What shines. After a while we begin to believe it.

PHANT: Coming back to your books: I always get the impression deep space is still one of the most fantastic adventure playgrounds for your heroes and yourself. Are you missing the chance or challenge to be with them out there?

MCDEVITT: I would have been when I was twenty-five. But now, I'm quite content to let other people go out and take their chances with unforgiving environments.

PHANT: You are wrapping up the Priscilla Hutchins plotlines started with *The Engines of God*. Are you satisfied with the way the books turned out?

MCDEVITT: Sure. If given the chance, I don't think I'd change anything major. Certainly not the perspective.

Not the sense of the cosmic, not the rescues, not the tribute to valuable things that get lost (as in *Chindi*), not the guest appearance of H. L. Mencken as Gregory MacAllister in *Deepsix* and *Chindi*. I've had a few letters from guys wanting to know if I can arrange an introduction to Hutch.

PHANT: Priscilla is a three-dimensional character, able to love, to hate, to work, and to be sure of herself. What is her appeal in the eyes of her creator?

MCDEVITT: She operates largely surrounded by males, recognizes that a lot of problems are caused by testosterone, and doesn't mind it at all. Except when it gets someone killed.

I used to do management training for the US Customs Service. (They have a different name now, but I forget what it is.) We frequently broke students into five-person teams, put them in a plane, took the plane out into the desert, and crashed it. (Virtually, of course.) Their problem was to survive. They would be forced to make a series of life-and-death decisions. We wanted them to communicate. To come up with the smart choices.

The make-up of the teams didn't seem to matter much. They lived and died at the same rates whether the teams were composed of airport and seaport people, or border types. Or whether they were groups of inspectors, import specialists, or agents. The only substantive difference we saw came when we analyzed the teams by gender.

The mixed groups, males and females, usually died.

When women were involved, the men started making decisions based on demonstrating their courage, and the women tended to become relatively passive. Don't ask me why. The all-male groups survived about half the time.

The all-female groups almost always got through. They seem to communicate better than men. Maybe they listen better. In any case, I liked to think of Hutch as a woman who doesn't allow herself to be influenced by the emotions raging around her.

PHANT: Anything you'd like to add to this series? Any artifact you'd like to unearth?

MCDEVITT: I wouldn't be averse to doing more with it. If the right storyline showed up.

PHANT: . . . *Polaris* (is) a sequel of sorts to *A Talent for War*. Going back to *Talent*: the setup, the destruction of a war hero legend, was kind of fascinating (and) old-fashioned. Sometimes I got the feeling I was reading a future account of "The Man Who Shot Liberty Valance." Was this your intention?

MCDEVITT: *Talent* was originally begun as a straightforward combat-in-space tale. I was playing off "Dutchman," a story I'd written for *Asimov's* a couple of years earlier. But somewhere around chapter eight I began to realize I had a much better narrative if somebody a century or two down the line had to try to unravel what had happened. So I tossed everything over the side and started over. I really never felt, despite what the cover said, that the Christopher Sim legend was destroyed, that he was a "fraud." Sim was in my mind still heroic. But the nature of his heroism took on a different caste.

PHANT: In more than one novel you combine the past—legends, myths, artifacts, incorrect historical conclusions—with the uncertain future. Do you believe it is essential to know the past to make the right decision for the future? Is it easier to keep the legend? Or should we get at the truth regardless of the cost?

MCDEVITT: I'm not sure, Thomas. It's probably not essential to know our past to make the right decisions, but it sure increases the odds of getting things right. As to truth and myth, sometimes our mythologies make it easier to get through some of the assorted losses we take along the way. How would we handle funerals without someone to assure us that Harry has gone to a better world?

PHANT: In your novels, I like the special Jack McDevitt feeling, the special sense of wonder in a modern setting. Your works are working in the opposite direction of, for example, the baroque new space operas coming out of Great Britain. Is it a conscious decision to offer a modern form of Golden Age space opera to your reader?

MCDEVITT: The simple, and accurate, answer is that I do what, probably, we all do: I write what I'd like to read. I like to visualize people—real ones like you and me, as opposed to superhumans loaded with biochips, or princes of the realm, or whatever—encountering, and having to deal with, the kinds of problems we can expect to see if we ever really get clear of the solar system.

PHANT: Starting with a new novel: What is your approach and can you describe your way of working on the text?

MCDEVITT: The most difficult part of the process, for me, is to come up with an idea that will sustain a novel.

Researchers go out to watch a planetary collision and discover at the last minute that one of the worlds had been home to a civilization. So they send a mission down to take a look. But a quake destroys the landers. You have three or four starships in orbit, but no vehicle capable of going down and mounting a rescue. And nobody close enough to get there in time (*Deepsix*).

Come up with a solution, and the novel becomes easy to write.

Or, we're on an Earth that's been destroyed by a virus a thousand years ago (*Eternity Road*). Everything's lost, the history, the science, everything. There's a legend that a library exists, a storehouse of information. A team goes in search. Two years later, the leader returns—alone—and says they found nothing. Shortly afterward, he walks into the Mississippi and drowns himself. His son finds a copy of *A Connecticut Yankee* in his bedroom. It's evidence that they did indeed find the library. But why would he have lied? Devise a reasonable solution, send out a second mission, and enjoy the ride.

Polaris is a good example of the method. Seven people vanish from the interior of a starship. The pressure suits are still there. The lander's still on board. There's no habitable world in the system, especially after the destruction of the sun by a brown dwarf. (That's why they're there.) There are no aliens.

PHANT: Although especially known for your novels, you are a prolific short story writer. Do you believe the modern SF short story still appeals to contemporary readers?

MCDEVITT: SF works best at the shorter lengths. In my view.

But people like novels. They want to spend time with the characters and the situation. I don't know why. I guess it's the wiring. The short story is probably the more natural form for SF. We are present at a discovery or, more frequently, we witness the results of a technological breakthrough. Usually, of course, things go wrong. SF works best as a cautionary tale. We learn that immortality may not be all it's cracked up to be, that contact even with congenial aliens may have a downside, that designing babies may create serious problems. The idea is presented, we watch the action, and the narrative moves to its natural conclusion. SF works most effectively when only one thing has been changed, allowing us to see the result clearly. In a novel, a lot of things change, or the impact of the technology gets lost in four hundred pages of charging around. This is not to say the novel doesn't work in the genre, but simply that the short story is the purer form.

PHANT: You've won almost every award for your books and stories. Anything very special to your heart? Any award you'd like to win again or for the first time? What is the meaning of an award?

MCDEVITT: I'd be delighted to win the John W. Campbell again. *Omega* received that one and we celebrated for a month. I've never won the Nebula or the Hugo. Either of those would be nice. It's always a pleasure to have readers or colleagues express their admiration by granting an award. Ideally, I'd like to be above needing the approbation of others. But in truth it's a glorious feeling.

PHANT: Concluding with the person Jack McDevitt: Could you give us a little insight into the man behind the writer, and into his interests and passions?

MCDEVITT: I think the human race is worth saving. Despite all the arrogance and stupidity, we still help at the Special Olympics and push stranded whales back into the ocean. I think we need more than anything else to open our minds, to take a long critical look at the unproven things we accept as Truth. Uncompromising religion, for example, is at the heart of Middle Eastern problems.

And in fact it never helps anybody.

I'm a member of the US Chess Federation, although I haven't played competitively for years. I'm a Phillies and Eagles fan. Fell in love with the Sherlock Holmes stories, read them all during the summer of 1955, and have since been annoyed at Doyle for not writing more. Gilbert Chesterton's Father Brown was another delicious character.

I enjoy chess and bridge, classical music, fire places, snow storms, lunch with friends, theater, rainy afternoons, and train rides.

PHANT: What are your plans for the future? Your wishes, your hopes?

MCDEVITT: Thomas, I'm at that happy age where I will settle to have a future. I'm happily married, with good kids now grown, and I'm writing science fiction for a living. When I was seven, I had two ambitions: to play shortstop for the Phillies, and to do what I'm doing now. One out of two ain't bad.

PHANT: Thanks a lot for the time.

Celebrating Jack McDevitt
by Michael Bishop

All the way back in 1989, introducing Jack McDevitt's lovely story "The Fort Moxie Branch" in *Nebula Awards 24,* I wrote, "McDevitt has a natural, self-effacing prose style that never raises any barriers between the reader and the tale being told.

And ever since hearing him read at an SF convention in Atlanta, I can no longer read his work without hearing his distinctive voice caressing each word—an eerie, but also a strangely comforting, experience."

I have begun this tribute to Jack by quoting myself because, even after almost fifteen years, this phenomenon—hearing Jack's voice as I read his work—persists. Oddly, I do *not* experience this phenomenon reading the works of other writers whom I admire, even when I've heard and presumably registered their distinctive voices. As a result, I've come to believe that it occurs because a couple of laudable attributes of Jack's character must resonate with a couple of desiderata of my own, namely, self-knowledge and authenticity. (Jack, by the way, would bounce the Latinate *desiderata* in favor of the Anglo-Saxon *needs*, and, nowadays, so would I.) Anyone reading Jack's fiction or his essays encounters a writer who values rationalism, clarity, integrity, exploration, and a sense of forward-moving purpose. His voice gives breath to these values, whether that voice is the one with which he speaks, or the one(s) embodying his literary method(s).

Jack and I first met in person, I believe, in the summer of 1987 at a Sycamore Hill Workshop in Raleigh, North Carolina. He and Carol Emshwiller were probably the two oldest attendees, but Jack still considered himself (even after several fine stories and a stunning first novel, *The Hercules Text*), something of a novice. I recall, though, that his workshop story, the aforementioned "The Fort Moxie Branch," pleased just about everyone, and that I envied Jack because Lew Shiner, an astute and stringent critic as well as an accomplished fiction writer, cited its opening paragraphs as virtually pitch perfect. Lew praised the directness of the language, the ease with which it evoked small-town life in North Dakota and a sense of impending mystery, and the fact that its rhythms echoed those of unaffected American speech. And, of course, the story spoke to all of us at Sycamore Hill. It did so by focusing on the preservation of worthy literary work, even work little noted or totally unknown in its own time, by an interstellar "cultural salvage group," and also on the integrity of one human writer who rejects this kind of immortality on sheer cussed principle. I could not help identifying Jack's first-person narrator—even though this is a justly well-established critical no-no—with the author of the story, Jack himself.

Talking to Jack at Sycamore Hill, I realized that the evident virtues of his prose sprang in large part from the clear but unobtrusive virtues of the man. He smiled easily, made light of himself, showed daunting knowledge and love of the field in which he had chosen to work, and encouraged all us other attendees without pretending to like everything equally well. He had then, as he still has, an adult's full experience of life behind him, but he also evinced an alert child's readiness to learn and a taste for natural wonder. "The Fort Moxie Branch" shows this taste for wonder in an earthly, almost a domestic, setting, whereas Jack's gripping novel *Chindi* (2002), which restored my faith in the flexibility and the intellectual legitimacy of space opera, reveals it against a thrilling intergalactic backdrop.

As Jack writes in a brief essay about *Chindi* on his web site, "*It seems to us that, in a well-run universe, things that matter would somehow stay on the record. That they should survive beyond the memory of those who knew them. That we could be assured that, somewhere out there, the Hanging Gardens are alive and well.*" What Jack does not say, but strongly intimates, is that too often we lose things that matter, that knowledge of many significant human events and constructs *passes away*, and that not only have the Hanging Gardens perished but so have astonishments of which we remain totally, but by no means blissfully, ignorant.

In short, Jack points an accusing finger at the universe for its demonstrated indifference to the noteworthy achievements of our species, and by implication at whatever creative force manifested the universe. Clearly, Jack more than hints, the universe *ain't* well run, and how can any sort of justice, much less conservation of creativity, inhere in that disturbing fact?

Unlike me (and sometimes I can't help regarding Jack's articulations of his philosophical stance as more defensible and self-consistent than my own) he does not buy into the notion of a personal god who marks the fall of every sparrow and counts the hairs of our heads. We have talked about this matter—how can genuine friends avoid talking about it?—and we have each written about it. What I want to stress here, however, is that even during rigorous disputation Jack behaves with disarming civility. (I could write a song: "*It's alarming/How disarming/Civility has become today,*" etc.) Jack may not see how you can logically hold your position, but he listens, he honors your sense of your own conviction, and, in a wistful, maybe even quasi-envious way, he regrets that life's hard-knock lessons, the accidents of fate, and the horrific panoramas of human history do not permit him to embrace the solace of professing believers.

Nonetheless, his regret does not prompt him to back away from a position painfully arrived at.

More than I can say, I admire both the integrity of Jack's position and the unassuming courage necessary to sustain it, for if Jack does not believe in a monotheistic overbuddy, he does believe in a number of praiseworthy phenomena, all of which show up in his work. Jack believes in the necessity of scientific enterprise, in the likely efficacy of human cooperation in bringing about a better world, in the importance of decency in interpersonal relations, and in the goad to human transcendence implicit in the vastness and the mystery of the universe. He believes that a single, small, human gesture in the direction of either justice or love *counts* (even when the universe does not appear to register it), and that any notion sabotaging this belief diminishes us as sentient creatures suspended between the demons of our ids and the angels of our aspiring selves. I might add here that Jack obviously does *not* believe in irrationalism, fanaticism, cruelty, opportunism, pretension, or shirking one's responsibility. In short, Jack is a far-seeing humanist, checking optimism with a keen eye and pessimism with hope. He may not believe, as Faulkner early in the Cold War pretended to, that humanity will "prevail," but he does believe—judging by his work—that we will make a damned fine account of ourselves. Or, at least, that we *can* do so if we tilt toward the angels already inherent in our humanity.

Whoa, I can hear some readers of this appreciation murmuring. Why so all-fired serious and metaphysical, Bishop?

Jack McDevitt writes entertaining science fiction. Why do you want to go and get all apeshit profound and pseudo-theological on us? Actually, I don't. I just can't think about either Jack or his work without confronting the *joy* that I take in *his* hard-won joy in both life and the profession of writing science fiction.

Over the past twenty-plus years, by dint of loving commitment and a work ethic to shame the most constipated Calvinist, he has produced a remarkable body of work, including short fiction masterpieces ("The Fort Moxie Branch," "The Jersey Rifle," "Cryptic," "Time Travelers Never Die," "Ships in the Night," etc.) and novels of such staggering scope (*A Talent for War, The Engines of God, Ancient Shores, Infinity Beach, Chindi*, etc.) that I must invoke the names of Stapleton, Heinlein, Haldeman, Benford, and Bear to find suitable comparisons. This past summer, deep in the final revisions of *Polaris*, his latest novel, Jack wrote offhandedly in an e-mail, "God, I love what I do," and his work captures the exhilarating truth of this assertion. Joy suffuses even his darkest work, and sometimes he writes stories of heart-stopping *grimness*, with final lines hinting of cataclysmic changes, if not imminent doom, for our entire species. But Jack laughs in the face of such darkness, taking joy from the little godhood that all writers presumptuously assume when they sit down to tell a story.

Jack also takes joy in passing along to others what he has learned about writing. Two of his essays, "The Fine Art of Collecting Rejections," and "Twelve Blunders: How Aspiring Writers Get It Wrong," catalogue two dozen mistakes, a dozen per essay, to which nearly every writer, novice or established pro, has fallen oblivious or forgetful prey. I don't plan to list them all here, but will say that although Jack has expressed gratitude to me for encouraging him, I have never given him such helpful practical advice as he gave me in "Twelve Blunders." A note, almost an afterthought, to his second designated blunder, "Go for That Smooth First Draft," cautions writers against designating a set time every day to write, urging instead a more achievement-centered approach: "*Better to set a goal of writing a specific scene. Today we will write this section, we'll do the conversation with the AI, and when we're finished, we'll reward ourselves by taking the rest of the day off. We'll get more done that way, in less time.*" Recently, working on my first solo novel in three or four years, I put Jack's advice to the test. Guess what. His method works so much better than roping off squares of time that it feels like liberation. In short, Jack has bequeathed to me a measure of his own joy in the creative process by passing along, as if it were spare change, a simple but effective writing tip.

After Sycamore Hill, by the way, Jack and I linked up for other events, including in the early to mid 1990s a celebration of science fiction at the main library in Brunswick, Georgia, where the McDevitts live. (The tenacious director of this library secured not only Jack and me for readings, talks, and panels, but also Ursula K. LeGuin, John Kessel, and F. Brett Cox, who served as both participant and moderator.) We've attended each other's book signings, and in 1996 we mounted a kind of barnstorming sf-nal Martin & Lewis show down coastal Georgia on behalf of new story collections—*Standard Candles* in Jack's case, *At the City Limits of Fate* in mine. I recall sitting side by side on stools with Jack in a meeting room in the library at Kingston, the two of us fielding questions about space travel, Ray Bradbury, and literary imagery and relishing both our interaction with enthusiastic readers and each other's company. By contrast, once during the 1990s, when Jack could not make a signing of mine at the SF & Mystery Book Shop in Atlanta, owner Mark Stevens handed me a telegram that Jack had sent apologizing for his absence and wishing me well. A *telegram*! That gesture, so redolent of an earlier day, so downright classy, contains encyclopedias about Jack and specifically the joy that he strews about simply by being, well, Jack.

After Sycamore Hill, Jack and I usually had our lovely and supportive wives, Maureen and Jeri, in tow or assiduously towing.

Maureen functions moment by moment as the mojo in Jack's joy, encouraging, protecting, feeding, critiquing, cheerleading, and partnering. She warrants an appreciation of her own. You would find your own joy in Jack's presence signally augmented if you had the chance to say hello and talk to Maureen, meanwhile privately acknowledging her as half of a dauntingly smooth-running team. With the McDevitts, Jeri and I once took an elegant meal in the restaurant of a ritzy hotel on St. Simons Island, over the causeway from Brunswick, and one evening Maureen fed me in her kitchen, along with Jack and Jack's late mother, when Jeri could not come, too. Indeed, the McDevitts' hospitality went further than they could know in helping me cope with professional doubts and worries about a transient health problem. Although Jeri and I have often urged the McDevitts to visit us here in Pine Mountain (once, incredibly, the site of a World Fantasy Convention), family responsibilities made that an untenable option. Only when a hurricane threatened Brunswick and the local authorities told residents to evacuate did Jack telephone asking if he, Maureen, and his mother could lodge with us during the danger period, a request to which we excitedly agreed.

Ultimately, the McDevitts found a place nearer their home in which to weather the storm, and I rued—a little, only a little—their good fortune. Now, however, we renew our invitation and encourage Jack and Maureen, once the finished manuscript of *Polaris* reaches its publisher, to take a break.

Although fellow Georgians, we live too far away from one another.

A reader of this collection can visit any number of Jack's worlds through these stories and commentaries. Or also by sampling one or more of his novels. (Believe me, any McDevitt title will serve.) I promise you the taste of joy, both as bracing storytelling and as a gustatory metaphysical revelation of the man himself, my friend, colleague, role model, and esteemed elder, Jack McDevitt.

—Michael Bishop, Oct 13-14, 2003

PART SIX
BIBLIOGRAPHY

Jack McDevitt Bibliography

NOVELS

The Hercules Text. Ace Books (Ace Special) mass market original, November 1986. Locus Award winner, Best First Novel.

Ancient Shores. HarperCollins (HarperPrism) hardcover, April 1996. Signed First Edition, Easton Press. Science Fiction Book Club selection. Mass market edition, December 1996. Nebula finalist.

Eternity Road. HarperCollins (HarperPrism) hardcover, May 1997. Signed First Edition, Easton Press. Science Fiction Book Club selection. Mass Market edition, April 1998. Darrell Award.

Moonfall. HarperCollins (HarperPrism) hardcover, April 1998. Science Fiction Book Club. Mass market edition, January 1999. Nebula Finalist.

Infinity Beach, HarperCollins (HarperPrism) hardcover, 2000. Signed First Edition, Easton Press. Science Fiction Book Club. Mass market edition, Eos, February 2001. Nebula finalist.

Chase & Alex

A Talent for War. Ace Books mass market original, February, 1989. Mass market reissue, June 2004.

Polaris. Ace Books hardcover, November, 2004. Signed First Edition, Easton Press. Science Fiction Book Club selection. Mass market edition, November 2005. Nebula Finalist.

Seeker. Ace Books hardcover, November, 2005. Signed First Edition, Easton Press. Science Fiction Book Club selection. Mass market edition, November 2006. SESFA Award.

Hutch and the Academy

The Engines of God. Ace Books hardcover, October 1994. Signed First Edition, Easton Press. Science Fiction Book Club selection. Mass market edition December 1995.

Deepsix. HarperCollins (Eos) hardcover, March 2001. Science Fiction Book Club selection. Mass market edition January 2002. SESFA Award.
Chindi. Ace Books hardcover, July 2002. Science Fiction Book Club selection. Mass market editon October 2003. Nebula finalist.
Omega. Ace Books hardcover, November 2003. Signed First Edition, Easton Press. Science Fiction Book Club selection. Mass market edition, November 2004. Nebula finalist. Winner, John W. Campbell Memorial Award, best novel.
Odyssey. Ace Books hardcover, November 2006.
Cauldron. Ace Books hardcover, November 2007.

COLLECTIONS

Standard Candles (Introduction by Charles Sheffield). Tachyon Publications hardcover, August 1996.
Ships in the Night (Introduction by Mike Resnick). Altair Australia trade paper, 2005.
Outbound (Introduction by Barry Malzberg). Hardcover from ISFiC Press, Deerfield, Illinois. November 2006.

SHORT FICTION

*Included in *Standard Candles* #Included in *Ships in the Night*

"Act of God," *Microcosms.* Gregory Benford, ed. (DAW), 2004. Also: *Year's Best SF 10.* David G. Hartwell and Kathryn Cramer, eds., Eos, 2005.
"Auld Lang Boom." *Asimov's.* Oct, 1992*.
"The Big Downtown," *Down These Dark Spaceways.* Mike Resnick, ed. (SFBC), 2005.
"Black To Move," *Asimov's* September, 1982*.
"Blinker," *Analog.* March, 1994#.
"Combinations," *Chess Life.* December, 1986.
"Crossing Over," *Twilight Zone.* January-February, 1983.
"Cruising Through Deuteronomy," *F&SF.* June, 1995*.
"Cryptic," *Asimov's* Apr 1983, Nebula Finalist*. Also: *Year's Best SF.* Gardner Dozois, ed. , 1985; *Gedanken Fictions.* Thomas Easton, ed. (Wildside), 2000.

"Date with Destiny," *When the Music's Over.* Lewis Shiner, ed. (Bantam Spectra), 1991.
"Dead in the Water," *Not of Woman Born.* Constance Ash, ed. (Roc), 1999#.
"Deus Tex," *Realms of Fantasy.* Feb, 1996#. Also, *This is My Funniest,* Mike Resnick, ed. (BenBella Books, 2006).
"Dutchman," *Asimov's,* February, 1987*.
"Ellie," *Asimov's.* May, 1995*.
"The Emerson Effect," *Twilight Zone.* December 1981. Also: *Wondrous Beginnings.* Steven H. Silver and Martin H. Greenberg, eds. (DAW), 2003.
"The Far Shore," *Asimov's,* June, 1982#.
"The Fort Moxie Branch," *Full Spectrum.* Lou Aronica and Shawna McCarthy, eds. (Bantam), 1988*. Nebula, Hugo finalist Also: *Nebula Awards 24.* Michael Bishop, ed. (Harcourt, Brace, Jovanovich) 1988.
"Glory Days," *F&SF.* August, 1984.
"Good Intentions," (with Stanley Schmidt), F&SF. June 1998#; Nebula Finalist.
"Gus," *Sacred Visions.* Andrew M. Greeley and Michael Cassutt, eds. (Tor), 1991*.
"Happy Birthday," *The Further Adventures of the Joker.* Martin H. Greenberg, ed. (Bantam), 1990. Also: *Legends of the Batman.* Martin H. Greenberg, ed. (MJF Books), 1997.
"Henry James, This One's for You," *Subterranean* #2, Spring, 2005.
"Holding Pattern," *Realms of Fantasy.* December 1996.
"Ignition," *Future Washington.* Ernest Lilley, ed. (WSFA Press), 2005.
"In the Tower," *Universe 17.* Terry Carr, ed. (Doubleday), 1987.
"It's a Long Way to Alpha Centauri," *Pulphouse.* Summer, 1990.
"The Jersey Rifle," *Chess Life.* January, 1983*.
"Kaminsky At War," *Forbidden Planets.* Marvin Kaye, ed. (SFBC), 2006.
"Lake Agassiz," *Full Spectrum 3.* Lou Aronica, Amy Stout, and Betsy Mitchell, eds. (Doubleday), 1991.
"Last Contact," *Asimov's,* June, 1988#.
"The Law of Gravity Isn't Working on Rainbow Bridge," Limited edition by W. Paul Ganley, Apr, 2003.
"Leap of Faith," *Asimov's.* May, 1989.
"Melville on Iapetus," *Asimov's.* November, 1983.
"Midnight Clear," *Christmas Forever,* David G. Hartwell, ed. (Tor), 1993#.
"The Mission," *Crossroads.* F. Brett Cox and Andy Duncan, eds. (Tor), 2004.
"Never Despair," *Asimov's.* April, 1997.
"Nothing Ever Happens in Rock City," *Artemis,* Summer, 2001. Nebula Finalist#. Also: *Nebula Awards Showcase.* Vonda N. McIntyre, ed. Roc), 2004.

"Oculus," *Analog,* Jul/Aug, 2002#.

"Promises To Keep," *Asimov's.* December, 1984*. Also: *Year's Best SF.* Gardner Dozois, ed. (Bluejay), 1985; *Christmas Stars.* David Hartwell, ed. (Tor), 1992; *Isaac Asimov's Christmas.* Gardner Dozois and Sheila Williams, eds. (Ace) 1997; *Explorers.* Gardner Dozois, ed. (St. Martin's Griffin), 2000.

"Report from the Rear," *Aboriginal.* Spring, 1998#.

"Ships in the Night," *Amazing Stories.* Oct, 1993, winner UPC Award#.

"Standard Candles," *F&SF.* January, 1994*

"Sunrise," *Asimov's.* March, 1988.

"Talk Radio," *Betcha Can't Read Just One.* Alan Dean Foster, ed. , (Ace), 1993.

"Tidal Effects," *Universe 15.* Terry Carr, ed. (Doubleday), 1985*.

"Time's Arrow," *Critical Mass.* Autumn, 1989#. Also: *The Fantastic Civil War,* Frank McSherry, Jr., ed. (Baen), 1991; *Timegates,* Jack Dann and Gardner Dozois, eds. (Ace), 1997.

"Time Travelers Never Die," *Asimov's.* Apr, 1996. Hugo, Nebula finalist*. Also: *The Best Time Travel Stories of All Time.* Barry Malzberg, ed. (ibooks), 2002; *Time Machines.* Bill Adler, Jr., ed. (Carroll & Graf), 1998.

"To Hell with the Stars," *Asimov's.* December, 1987*. Also: *The Loch Moose Monster.* Sheila Williams, ed. (Delacorte Press) 1993.

"The Tomb," *What Might Have Been.* Vol III, Gregory Benford and Martin H. Greenberg, eds. (Bantam Spectra), 1991#.

"Tracks," *Asimov's.* December 1989.

"Translations from the Colosian," *Asimov's.* September, 1984*.

"Tyger," *Asimov's.* May, 1991*.

"Valkyrie," *There Won't Be War.* Harry Harrison and Bruce McAllister, eds. (Tor), 1991.

"Variables," *F&SF.* July, 1997.

"Voice in the Dark," *Asimov's.* November, 1986.

"Whistle," *Full Spectrum 2,* Lou Aronica, Shawna McCarthy, Amy Stout, and Patrick LoBrutto, eds. (Doubleday), 1989.

"Windows," *Adventures in Sol System.* T.K.E. Weisskopf, ed, (Baen), 2004.

"Windrider," *Asimov's.* July, 1994#.

OUTBOUND

November 2006

Outbound by Jack McDevitt was published by ISFiC Press, 707 Sapling Lane, Deerfield, Illinois 60015. One thousand copies have been printed by Thomson-Shore, Inc. The typeset is Berthold Baskerville, Condensed Helvetica Light, and Zapf Dingbats printed on 60# Nature's Natural. The binding cloth is Arrestox B Black. Design and typesetting by Garcia Publishing Services, Woodstock, Illinois.